# Alien Bonds

ISBN: 978-0-9979898-2-3 (paperback)
ISBN: 978-0-9979898-3-0 (Kindle format)
ISBN: 978-0-9979898-4-7 (ePub format)

# Alien Bonds

**by Carmen Webster Buxton**

Cracked Mirror Press

Rockville, MD

**Other Cracked Mirror Press Books**

**by Carmen Webster Buxton**

*The Sixth Discipline*

*No Safe Haven*

*Tribes*

*Shades of Empire*

*Where Magic Rules*

*The Nostalgia Gambit*

*King of Trees*

*Saronna's Gift*

*Turnabout*

As this story was inspired by my parents' divorce,

it seems only fair to dedicate this book to their marriage.

**Note to readers:**
There is a glossary of Wakanrean terms on page 377.

# Chapter One

Dina ran one hand down the smooth red fabric of her fanciest party dress. The loose folds of the long skirt hid the tiny bulge of her pocket com. She put on her jacket, and the gray gloves she had worn to work that day. She would need to buy gloves in more colors now that she had to wear them whenever she left the apartment.

Her desk com beeped and spoke. "Call from the Third Confederation Liaison Office." Instead of answering on her pocket com, Dina sat down at the desk. Hopefully, there was nothing wrong with her residency status.

A black-haired man in a blue and brown ThreeCon uniform smiled engagingly at her as soon as she acknowledged the call. "Hello, Citizen Bellaire. Remember me?"

Dina had met so few humans on Wakanreo that placing him was easy. "Of course. Your name is Jared Harlingen, and you were the ThreeCon representative at my orientation. Is there anything wrong with my residency permit?"

"No, no." His blue eyes lit with amusement. "Believe me, this call is entirely personal."

Dina was suddenly shy. "I see."

He grinned again. "Actually, I'm hoping you're free this evening. I just got two tickets to the wrestling matches."

It was the last invitation Dina would have expected. "Wrestling matches?"

He nodded. "Believe it or not, Wakanrean wrestling is great entertainment. And it's a wonderful way to learn about Wakanrean culture."

1

It sounded a lot more appealing than a blind date arranged by an old school friend. Dina was tempted to accept, but her Fantaran upbringing had been very strict. "I'm sorry, but a friend of mine invited me to a party at the Terran Embassy tonight, and I said I'd go."

His face betrayed no overt sign of disapproval, and yet Dina suspected he wasn't pleased. "The Anniversary bash? Bah! It'll be deadly dull—a whole herd of Terrans congratulating themselves on their achievements, with just a few Wakanrean celebrities invited so the Terrans can show they're not too proud to rub shoulders with the locals—figuratively speaking, of course. Nothing so exciting as actual shoulder-rubbing will occur. You won't enjoy yourself at all."

"You think so?"

"I know so. Believe me, watching Wakanreans try to throw each other to the floor will be infinitely more interesting."

Dina suspected he was right, but she shook her head. "It sounds like fun, but I promised my friend I'd go to the party."

He grimaced with exaggerated fatalism. "Ah, well! My loss is Ambassador Inoue's gain. Perhaps another time, then?"

"I'd like that. And thanks for the invitation."

His eyebrows lifted. "How's it going in general? Is Wakanrean standoffishness wearing you down?"

So it wasn't just her perception. "It's just that everything is so different here," she equivocated.

Jared smiled at her attempt at diplomacy. "They're not naturally unpleasant people. We Terrans created a bad situation."

Dina was puzzled enough to be blunt. "What does that mean?"

He lifted his hands in a persuasive gesture, "Wakanreo asked ThreeCon to keep us out. The Terran government balked, and finally they hammered out the 'no-touching/wear-gloves-at-all-times' rule. It may have prevented the original problem, but it's caused its own set of headaches."

Dina wrinkled her nose. "I can see that. I feel like I have a contagious disease."

"You do, in a way. So far as we know, all of us Terrans have the potential to destroy a Wakanrean's life."

"But," she protested, "I don't understand why the no-touching rule is so inclusive. You said in the orientation that some humans—Terrans, I mean—have set off the Wakanrean mating process—"

"*Shahgunrah*," he interrupted.

"Yes, *shahgunrah*. You said some Terrans caused it to start in Wakanreans, and because it's a once-in-a-lifetime event, it meant they could never mate with anyone else."

"Precisely." He smiled his approval.

"Yes, but what about the ones who've already mated? Aren't they safe?"

His benign smile slipped a little. "You have me there. It's true. Any Wakanrean who is already *shahgunrahai*—mated—is immune to *glashunrah*—false *shahgunrah*."

"So why does everyone at work treat me like I have the plague? They can't all be single."

He shook his head. "Sorry, I don't have time for a history lecture on what's happened on Wakanreo in the last seventy years."

"Oops, me, too. I mean I have to go. Thanks for calling."

"Sure thing." His easy smile returned. "I'll call you in a few days. Meanwhile, give my regards to the Ambassador."

"Do you know the Terran Ambassador?"

He reached for something on the bottom of his screen. "I'm ThreeCon's liaison officer for the entire Wisutan region. Ambassador Inoue knows me well enough to hate my guts. See you soon, I hope."


DINA exited the autocab, carefully extracting the skirt of her gown, and looked around for the entrance to the embassy.

What had appeared to be a tower at one corner hid an alcove with an arched entrance-way. Relieved, Dina stepped up to the door monitor and took out her pocket com. She pressed her thumb onto the device and then held it up to the scanner; the door opened.

She stepped inside. The space was shadowy, almost somber. Soft music filled the gloom, but she saw no sign of Arliana.

Dina left her jacket at the coat check and turned toward the curving central staircase that wound up to a huge wall-to-wall mezzanine. Under the mezzanine, Dina could see illuminated instruments moving in the darkness, the musicians mere shadows behind them.

She had started toward the steps, but before she could do more than grasp the banister, a voice called her name.

"Dina Bellaire! There you are!"

Dina looked up. Arliana Cheng stood at the top of the stairs. Her iridescent blue gown—as long as Dina's and more elaborate—revealed her considerable cleavage. Arliana had muted the effect by draping her bare shoulders with a long trailing scarf of the same blue fabric.

"Dina!" Arliana cried again, running down the stairs in a swift, gliding descent. Her scarf billowed out behind her like the wings of some exotic insect. Between that and the silver glitter liberally dusted over her short black hair, she definitely drew the eye.

Dina smiled to herself. Had Arliana been waiting to make that maneuver? "Hello, Arliana."

"I was afraid you were going to be late." Arliana slipped one hand through Dina's arm.

"It took me a while to decide what to wear," Dina said. She glanced around. "This place is huge."

"It was built as a mansion by a wealthy Wakanrean." Arliana bent her head close to whisper. "Our companions are at the top of the stairs. Mine is the black-haired one. I saved the redhead for you."

Dina glanced up and saw two Terran men in tight-fitting formal trousers and belted jackets standing at the top of the stairs. Both were smiling, although the black-haired man looked truly amused while the other man seemed merely polite. Her date was the shorter of the two, Dina noted with a mental sigh.

Arliana pulled her up the steps at a rapid pace, giving her little time to size up her companion for the evening. Dina wouldn't have called him a redhead, except, of course, that true redheads were very rare. This man's hair was so dark an auburn that the dim lighting made it brown with reddish highlights. His eyes were brown, and his complexion the usual golden tan common on Terran colony worlds.

He had a pleasant face at any rate. Dina held out her hand at Arliana's urging. "Hello. I'm Dina Bellaire."

"Erik Kordes." He shook her hand.

He wasn't wearing gloves. In fact, of the four of them, only Dina's hands were covered. Both the men had gloves tucked under their belts, but if Arliana had any on her person, she had concealed them well.

"And this is Ben," Arliana concluded the introductions. "Let's all get something to drink, shall we?"

"If you like." Ben led the way through the crowd. "But all I've seen so far is amber wine."

Arliana made a face as she let go of Dina's arm to take Ben's. "Pooh! Practically kiddie wine. Too bad the Ambassador is so intent on pleasing the natives."

Dina glanced around at the assembled company. At first she saw only a sea of human forms and faces. Then she noted a considerable number of Milorans scattered through the crowd, their massive size making them resemble boulders on a shoreline. There seemed to be fewer Shuratanians, but then their small bodies made them inconspicuous.

"There don't seem to be any Wakanreans here," she said, as Ben accosted a servoid whose tray held an array of tall wine glasses.

"There are at least a dozen for sure." Arliana accepted a glass from her date. "I know because I got the authorization for the invitations to go out. The Ambassador has asked some local celebrities—a few dance actors and wrestlers, the Prefect of Wisuta, a couple of singers, and the rest poets and writers."

"I heard the Prefect declined." Erik sipped his amber wine. "Probably doesn't want to risk contamination."

Arliana laughed. "No, I'm sure she's safe enough. She has a mate, remember?"

"So where are these celebrities, then?" Dina asked. It made her uncomfortable to hear the three of them disparage Wakanreans without any regard for their own status as guests on the planet.

"There are two of the dance actors," Ben said with a sideways nod of his head toward a clump of people in one corner. "The two tallest ones in that bunch are big names in the Wakanrean dance theater."

Dina glanced toward the group and saw that there were indeed five Wakanreans mixed in with a larger group of Terrans. Taller than the Terrans, they also seemed intent on keeping their distance from them. "Oh, you mean the woman in the blue trousers and the man in the striped cape?"

Erik smiled in appreciation. "I'm impressed, Dina. It took me weeks to be able to tell Wakanrean men from Wakanrean women."

Arliana tittered. "Naturally. The women are all flat-chested."

Dina tisked at her friend. "Don't be silly. You can usually tell whether humans—Terrans— are male or female from their faces."

"Yes," Erik answered her comment without waiting for Arliana to speak, "but I know Terran faces very well. I'm not very good at any part of Wakanrean anatomy."

"It's not that different without the fur," Ben said. "If you were to skin a large Terran and a small Wakanrean, it would be difficult to tell them apart—except for the claws. And if you peeled back the musculature and left only the skeleton and organs, it would be even harder."

"You're a doctor, aren't you?" Dina asked, sipping her own wine.

He took a long drink from his glass before he answered. "Of a sort. I'm an endocrinologist, but I don't practice."

"Then what do you do?" Dina said.

"Research."

Dina was curious. "How did you two meet, Arliana?"

Her friend waved one hand in an airy arc. "Oh, all the Terrans in Wisuta know each other."

Ben looked amused. "There are between thirty and thirty-five thousand Terrans on this planet, and most of us live in Wisuta."

"Well, they know *about* each other, at any rate," Arliana said.

"Besides, we all work at the Embassy," Erik added. "I'm in Accounting, Arliana is in Systems, and Ben here is in Monitoring."

"I thought you said you did research," Dina said.

Ben put his empty wine glass down on a passing servoid and grabbed a full one. "I do, in a way. I monitor and evaluate Wakanrean biomedical research."

"Oh," Dina said, unenlightened.

"I refuse to talk about work," Arliana said. "This is supposed to be a party. Let's get something to eat."

She pulled Ben behind her and made her way through the crowd. Dina followed. It was a relief not to have to worry about touching anyone. Previously it had bothered her to brush up against total strangers, but after three days working at Quafray, physical contact felt comfortable and reassuring.

They came to a buffet table lavishly covered with food, but Arliana didn't seem happy. "Umph! More local stuff. I'm not that hungry."

"What's that?" Dina pointed at a tray of what appeared to be delicate blue flowers drizzled with green frosting.

"*Ishgua*," Erik said. "Broiled undersea creatures served with a garnish of edible mold."

Arliana shuddered, and Dina had to smile. Moving from Fantar to Croyzan had made her friend more adventurous about sex, but not about food. For Dina it had worked the other way around. "Sounds interesting." She took an *ishgua* from the tray and sniffed it.

It had a delicate but pungent odor, almost like the smell of seagrass back on Fantar. She popped the *ishgua* into her mouth. "Tasty."

Ben took one also, but both Erik and Arliana left them alone. They moved farther down the table and found a platter of grilled meat on sticks.

"Oh, *juija*, that's okay," Arliana said with relief.

"*Juija* are small herd animals raised for food," Ben said. "They taste almost like chicken. Try some."

Dina took a stick and nibbled the meat off of it. The *juija* was chewy and mild, a little sweet and salty at the same time.

As they walked, Dina noticed that Arliana and Ben were drifting away. Erik, on the other hand, had moved much closer.

"So," he said, holding her arm to steer her away from a cluster of people, "Arliana says you're a chemist at Quafray."

"A very junior chemist. And I'm only an employee, not a member. I've only worked there for a few days."

"You must be pretty damn good to get your foot in the door with Quafray. They're one of the biggest companies on Wakanreo, and Wakanreo is a real leader in chemical technology."

"I know that," Dina said, a little irritated, in spite of the compliment, to think he felt a need to explain this. "Why else would I move all this way just for a job?"

And why else would she have agreed to live on such an alien world? If she had known she would have to work surrounded by beings who regarded her with suspicion, she might have said no. The Wakanrean who had interviewed her on Croyzan had seemed overly formal at first, but he had warmed up after a few minutes.

"Most of us come for the money." Erik sounded almost bitter. "It's not like Wakanreo is a draw in the accounting universe, I can tell you."

"Arliana told me she got a big bonus for signing a two-year contract."

He nodded. "Me, too, of course. I expect pretty much everyone on the Embassy staff got a bonus and a raise, except the Ambassador."

"Why not her, too?"

His smile was just a tad supercilious. "You don't follow politics on Terra, do you?"

"No. I've never even been there."

"Neither have I, but I know what's going on. Before she came here, Ambassador Inoue was the head of a huge Terran conglomerate—Mitsubishi-McNeil-Volkstag, I think it was. I'm sure her salary now is a fraction of what it was then."

"Then why would she take the job?" Dina glanced around the room at the shifting crowd. A few more Wakanreans had joined a cluster of people near the center of the room.

"For the glory." Erik snatched a pair of wine glasses off a servoid's tray. "More wine?"

All at once a wave of vertigo struck Dina. "No, thanks. I don't think I should drink any more for a bit. I can feel that first glass all of a sudden."

"You can't get a decent buzz from one glass of amber wine." Erik tossed off half a glass in a single gulp.

This flat dismissal annoyed Dina, but she let it pass. "What glory is Ambassador Inoue gaining on Wakanreo?"

"Ah!" Erik stopped to survey the room. "She hasn't gained it yet, but if she can persuade Wakanrean companies to license their chem tech, she'll go home with one hell of a trophy feather."

"But what does a trophy buy her?" Dina took a deep breath. What was wrong with her? She felt like she had run up several flights of stairs.

Erik raised one eyebrow, as if he were trying to look sage. "Well, since Terra is pretty much run by corporations these days, I expect she thinks she could write her own ticket." He nodded at the cluster of people in the middle of the room. "That's her, you know—the woman talking to that blonde Wakanrean guy."

Dina stared; seen from the back, the man in front of Ambassador Inoue looked deceptively human. The way the column of his neck met the curve of his skull seemed familiar. Even the sheaf of silver-white hair that made up his headcrest could have been a fashionable haircut. The dark cape draped over his shoulders was a little out of fashion, but a few Terran men were wearing them.

"That's one of her local stars she's sucking up to," Erik went on. "That one is a singer, I think. God, I hope she doesn't ask him to sing. Wakanrean music sounds like someone torturing small animals."

"Really?" Was it just her, or was Erik rather wearing?

"I think the two in blue are wrestlers. That's one thing I'll give the Wakanreans. Their wrestling is superb entertainment."

"That's what Jared said."

Dina had the satisfaction of seeing her date look dumbfounded. "Jared Harlingen? You know Jared?"

"Only slightly. Actually, I was wondering if he was invited tonight."

Erik let out a breath of explosive displeasure. "Not bloody likely. The Ambassador can't stand him."

"He said that," Dina said, wondering if she was being indiscreet.

"You seem pretty chummy with Jared."

It wasn't said as a question, but Dina detected a speculative note in Erik's voice. "Is that bad? Is there something wrong with Jared Harlingen?"

"Nothing except he's always beating my time." He put down his glass and turned to face her. "Arliana said I should wait until later to ask you, but what the heck—Do you want to go to my place for a more intimate get together? I've got better food and booze than the Ambassador is providing, and I'm sure the two of us could have more fun alone."

Dina felt her face flush red. She hated that she couldn't control her tendency to blush. Ever since she had left the comfortable familiarity of her native world, she had found herself in such situations. No longer shocked, she still couldn't stop herself from reacting as a Fantaran.

"I'm sorry." She fought to keep disapproval out of her voice. "I have to be at work very early tomorrow morning."

Erik's eyes opened wide. "Oh, come on! You can't possibly be offended. Arliana said you were married on Croyzan."

Her mortification faded, and annoyance replaced it. "I fail to see that my life or my reactions are any business of yours."

Erik's jaw went slack. "What?"

Dina put her glass down on a nearby table. "It seems Arliana miscalculated in thinking we would hit it off. I think I'd better go."

He blinked. "What century do you all live in back on Fantar? Arliana isn't a prude about sex. How was I to know you are?"

Annoyance morphed into anger. She was trying not to judge him, but he had no qualms about judging her. "Well, it looks like Arliana's miscalculation is now a certainty. Will you say good night to her for me?"

"You're really leaving?"

"Certainly." She nodded instead of offering her hand. "Have a pleasant evening. Although if that takes finding a woman who's liberal-minded enough to go home with you after two minutes of conversation, I have my doubts. Good night."

She turned on her heel and stalked off, not looking back until she was almost to the stairs.

By then all she could see of Erik was his retreating back. Dina felt a qualm of remorse. Obviously, his idea of polite behavior would never be acceptable on Fantar, but did she have any right to apply Fantaran standards here on Wakanreo? In any event, she had to explain her premature departure to Arliana.

She turned to survey the crowd again, looking for any sign of iridescent blue and silver. She didn't see Arliana, but she noticed the silver-headed Wakanrean had left the Ambassador's circle and was standing by himself in the middle of the room.

Dina wasn't sure, but she thought he was staring at her. She took a few steps toward the stairs, and his eyes followed her so closely there was no doubt that she was the object of his scrutiny.

No, his animosity. He looked angry—furious, in fact. She had never seen a Wakanrean show so much emotion. His eyes gleamed with rage, and his nostrils flared wide. She took another step toward the stairs, and the Wakanrean began to walk rapidly toward her.

Dina fought panic. What could she have done to make him so angry? She hadn't come close enough to any Wakanreans to offend anyone. She clasped her hands together to reassure herself that her gloves were on.

The silver-haired Wakanrean came closer still. Under his cape he wore a long, blue robe instead of the trousers and loose, tunic-style shirt favored by Wakanreans of both sexes. He was very close now. His golden facial and body fur combined with the creamy white of his crest reminded her of some Terran animal, but she couldn't remember which one. Other than the dark blue trim on his robe and the diamond-shaped pattern that decorated his sandals, his only adornment was a piece of silver jewelry fastened at the base of his throat; she couldn't tell if it was pinned to his robe or his chest fur.

Dina could feel herself breathing faster, her heart pounding hard. She should walk away. Why couldn't she move her feet? She stood waiting by the mezzanine railing, as still as if she had taken root in the floor.

The Wakanrean stood in front of her. He glared down at her, his face contorted into a scowl, his amber eyes glowing with contempt.

"I beg your pardon." Dina tried to keep the quaver out of her voice. "Do I know you?"

He was so close, she could feel the heat from his body. Either that, or the room had gotten suddenly warmer. Dina felt herself flush from head to foot.

He didn't answer, but all at once it was as if his anger was a physical thing, an invisible mass, pushing against her. She stepped backward, stumbled, and almost fell.

She reached for the mezzanine railing behind her, and in the same instant, the Wakanrean grabbed her arm.

Dina froze, utterly baffled. The orientation had said clearly that Wakanreans would always avoid touching a Terran, and yet here was one not only touching her, but holding her firmly by the arm and helping her to stand.

The orientation had also failed to warn her that a Wakanrean's touch was so warm it almost burned. Dina could feel a flush of heat on her arm where his hand still gripped it. She stood straighter and looked into his face. He had typical Wakanrean features—an arched nose, large round eyes, a wide mouth.

His expression changed as she watched. His anger faded to confusion. He looked almost stunned. His nostrils still flared, but from the way his eyes had opened wide, Dina knew he was surprised rather than angry.

Neither of them had taken a step since he took hold of her arm. Dina swallowed once, conscious of discreet glances and overt stares from those around them.

"I'm all right," she said finally, wondering if she was speaking the truth. The dizziness had passed, but she still felt lightheaded. "Thank you, but you can let go now."

He loosened his grip but didn't release her for a few seconds. When he did, he brushed her bare arm with the back of his hand. Dina was amazed when it sent shivers of anticipation up her spine.

"This is unexpected." His wonderfully resonant voice had a rich, warm timbre to it that made Dina's shivers change from anticipation to yearning.

"Yes," she said, unsure of what he meant, but afraid to give offense.

"Where do you live?"

"I have an apartment in the off-world sector," she said, wondering why she was answering him. She fought the urge to close her eyes and just listen to that wonderful voice.

"My house is in the cliffs outside the city. Let's go there instead."

"All right."

It took Dina a moment to realize that she had agreed to go home with him.

He smiled; she had never seen a Wakanrean smile such a warm smile. It made him seem very human, and she knew that he was pleased at her answer. When he turned for the stairs, she followed him, moving as if they were linked with an invisible wire. They walked down the steps without touching or speaking. Dina was aware of many eyes following them.

She didn't bother to collect her jacket, and it was cold when they stepped outside.

Dina shivered, and the Wakanrean immediately put his arm around her. It felt warm and comforting, and she pressed against him gratefully, ignoring the shocked stares of Wakanrean passersby. They walked part way down the block, and then he stopped and pulled a valet fob from his pocket. He activated it, then wrapped her in an embrace. Dina clutched him back.

A tiny part of her brain told her that she was acting irrationally, but the rest of it didn't seem to be paying attention. It was like watching someone else—a character in a play. She had no sense of being in control of her actions.

After a minute, a dark shape hovered in the air above them, and a private flyter dipped down to street level. The door opened, and the Wakanrean helped Dina to enter, then climbed into the pilot's seat.

The craft rose slowly. Once they were above the city skyline, the Wakanrean entered a destination on the control panel, and pressed a switch.

The windows opaqued as he reached for Dina. She was as eager to touch him as he was to touch her. She ripped off her gloves so that she could feel his fur, soft and silky under her fingers. The tiny voice in her head that urged her to move away grew very faint indeed.

Instead Dina closed her eyes to enjoy the pleasant sensations of being so close to a Wakanrean. The heat of his body provided warm reassurance, and he had a pleasing musky scent, just a little like freshly-spun wool.

Dina leaned her head against him. She could feel his fur, soft against her cheek, his mouth warm on her neck, his hands tenderly caressing her body. She knew she should ask him to turn the flyter around and take her back to the party. She formed the words in her mind—an apology for misleading him, a plea not to be annoyed—but she didn't say even one word aloud.

Dina was afraid to open her eyes for fear she would awake from a dream. The Wakanrean, on the other hand, betrayed no hesitation in the way he nuzzled her neck.

After a few more minutes, a claxon sounded. Dina opened her eyes and jerked in alarm. It wasn't a dream.

The Wakanrean pulled away from her with a small sigh. "We're here." He hit the same switch and the windows became transparent again.

They were hovering near the sheer face of a cliff. A circle of lights illuminated a landing port door. When the door slid open, the Wakanrean deftly piloted his flyter to a smooth landing.

"Welcome to my home," he said.

Dina didn't know what to say, so she said nothing.

He opened the flyter door and helped her out, then led her by the hand down a long, winding corridor. Lights came on as they walked. After they passed the entrance to a lift tube, the corridor took a turn and ended in a wide doorway. On one side a standard ID panel glowed softly, and on the other a carved wooden stick hung from the wall.

The Wakanrean grasped the stick and twisted it until the cord that held it snapped. He grinned at Dina as he put a hand on the ID panel to open the door. "I've waited a long time to do that."

He seemed very satisfied, almost triumphant.

After the door opened, he tossed the stick inside, took Dina's hand, and stepped into the doorway. "Come, little one. Our destiny awaits us."

Sudden terror overwhelmed Dina. She was alone with a stranger—a member of another species—in a place that seemed completely isolated. Her own inability to control her actions frightened her more than anything the stranger had done. Her heart thumped with fear against her ribs.

The Wakanrean still held her hand. Dina knew instantly that he was worried.

"You don't need to be afraid of me." His voice was gentle, almost as if he were speaking to a child. "I could never hurt you. And I won't do anything you don't want me to do."

Dina could only nod in response. She knew it was the truth, and it reassured her, even though she realized with a shock that there wasn't much she didn't want him to do. He stood waiting, and she understood that he was reluctant to act in a way that might frighten her. She stepped through the doorway until she stood beside him, then reached up to put her arms around his neck and pull him into an embrace. His arms encircled her in response, and Dina lost all fear of him.

The door shut behind them with a snap.

# *Chapter Two*

Dina woke in utter confusion. She sat up abruptly, aware that she wasn't in a familiar place. For just one second she told herself that she was in her new apartment, but not used to it yet, and then she realized that she was somewhere else entirely.

Huge windows covered most of the far wall, their ledges wide enough to provide a comfortable seat. The view told Dina that she was quite high up, and that it was very early in the morning. Framed by the pale yellow walls, the red Wakanrean sun shone low in a vast expanse of blue-green sky.

Three bright, abstract murals covered most of the walls. Dina herself was naked, and in an enormous box-like bed. There were no pillows or sheets, only a pile of thick shaggy, fur-like bed coverings. She wasn't at all cold, however, because the warm, furred body beside her radiated heat.

A long, sinewy arm, also furred, curved around her in an embrace, pulling her remorselessly closer. A silver-white headcrest lifted from the bed and two golden eyes stared at her sleepily, the pupils almost invisible in the bright morning light.

"Good morning," the Wakanrean said.

"Good morning," Dina said faintly.

He smiled and pulled her down next to him so that he could nuzzle her neck, then kissed her mouth.

Dina felt her face flush as she remembered at exactly what point the night before he had learned how to kiss. He hadn't needed to learn much else.

15

The Wakanrean laughed at her, a warm comfortable laugh, and stroked her shoulder as if to reassure her. "I can't tell if you're regretful or merely embarrassed."

She was surprised at his perceptiveness. "A little of both."

He released her and sat up, then climbed over the edge of the bed to get to his feet. He walked to where a red, green, and purple tapestry hung on the wall and took it down from its hooks. When he draped it around his waist like a skirt, Dina realized it was a garment, not a wall hanging. Or perhaps it was both.

"I'll get us some *quascha*," he said, "and then we can talk."

"All right." She fought the impulse to clutch the bed covers around her as he started for the door. From what she remembered of the night before, there wasn't much point in hiding her body now.

On the other hand, he was at least partly clothed, so why should she be naked? She hunted through the room and finally found her undergarments slung under a chair. She pulled them on, but couldn't find any more of her clothes. She turned hastily, aware that the Wakanrean was coming back.

A moment later he came through the doorway. "Looking for something?" He was holding a mug of dark, steaming liquid in each hand.

"Yes." Dina accepted a mug when he held it out to her. "I can't seem to find my clothes."

"Ah!" He had a gleam in his eye as he sat down on the window ledge. "I think you'll find them in the main room. If I remember correctly, I took off your dress, and you threw it across the room. There were also stockings—that's the word, yes? If I recall, you left them on the floor."

Dina could remember now, too. She tried not to blush again as she sat cross-legged on the edge of the bed and sipped the hot drink. She found it sweet and fragrant.

"I thought you'd like it." He stretched out his legs. "Most Terrans do."

Dina tried not to stare at him, but he looked very alien in the bright sunlight. His fur and headcrest were so utterly non-human that she felt a kind of fascination with them. His eyes held hers. Flecks of orange and brown dotted the golden irises that were larger than those of any human eye. The silver pin was indeed pinned to his chest fur, as there was nothing else to which he could fasten it.

Dina forced herself to stop staring and tried to make polite conversation. "I'm not used to thinking of myself as a Terran. I know it's culturally responsive to use home world names for species, but I've never been to Terra, so I have trouble identifying with the word Terran."

He nodded. "I can see where you would. Still, if you try to translate the word 'human' into our language, it just comes out as *qatorai*, which is our word for ourselves. Using planet names is more clear-cut."

"I suppose so."

"We didn't introduce ourselves last night. My name is Kuaron Du."

"Dina Bellaire."

He smiled and sipped his *quascha*. "We find ourselves in a somewhat awkward situation, no?"

"Very awkward," Dina said, relieved to hear him describe it so. She took a deep breath and plunged in to what she needed to say. "Look here, I don't want you to get the wrong idea. I never did that before."

He looked confused. "Never did what before?"

"I never went home with someone I'd just met." Her explanation came out in a rush as it dawned on her that she had turned Erik down, and three minutes later gone home with this alien, who had made exactly the same proposition with even less conversation. "I mean, I wasn't a virgin or anything, but still—I mean I usually get to know a man—I mean before I—oh, hell!"

Kuaron put his cup down on the ledge, then stood up and took hers from her, setting it down beside his own. He climbed onto the bed next to her and took her hand. "I know this must be difficult for you. I was astounded at first. For someone who never expected *shahgunrah* at all, it must have been frightening."

Even with the comfort of him sitting so close, the word disturbed her. "What? What are you talking about?"

"I'm talking about our *shahgunrah*." His facial muscles stiffened into a frown.

She stared at him. "Our what?"

"Our *shahgunrah*," he repeated. "Surely you must have realized that's what happened? Why else would you have come here with me?"

Dina stared at him and tried to make sense of the words. "Are you saying you think we—we mated or bonded or whatever?"

"We found *shahgunrah*. Or it found us."

"But that's not possible!" Dina blurted out. "That's simply not possible!"

His expression grew enigmatic. "How can something be impossible if it's already happened?"

"Bosh!"

He blinked, bewildered. "Bosh?"

"Look, I'm a scientist." She pulled back from him so she could study his face. "My field is industrial chemistry, not galactobiology, but I know enough about other worlds to know that Wakanreans are the only sentient species who actually, um, mate. I mean, they—you—don't *choose* a mate—"

"You don't have to explain *shahgunrah* to me," he interrupted. "I know very well how it works. I've seen it many times."

"Yes, well," she said, mortified, "I suppose you have."

"I know it's unique to my people. But I also know it started between us last night. And it's growing stronger every minute."

"Look, Kauron—"

"Kuaron," he corrected.

"Oh, sorry." First she lectured him on his own biology, and then she got his name wrong—all while half naked in his bedroom. "But surely I'm right that *shahgunrah* is something that happens only between Wakanreans?"

He nodded. "That has always been true in the past."

She felt a rush of vindication. "So what makes you think we started *shahgunrah* instead of just suddenly getting attracted to each other?"

Kuaron's smile was sardonic. "Wakanreans never feel that kind of attraction without *shahgunrah*."

The concept staggered Dina. Did that mean there was no such thing as thinking someone was sexy? "Really? You mean you never felt *any* attraction to a Wakanrean woman before this?"

"My best friend is a woman. I liked her the first time I met her, but I don't think that's what you mean."

"Not if you never felt the urge to do anything more intimate."

He looked down into her face. "I never felt that until last night—when I came near you."

It seemed to Dina that she could feel a wave of warm emotion cascading from him, almost like steam rising when water hit the hot stones in a sauna. She made herself ignore it. "Anyway, even assuming you've started *shahgunrah*, what makes you think I have? I guess I should have paid more attention at the orientation, but I know they said Terrans could set it off in Wakanreans without it being reciprocated."

"They can. That's why I was so angry last night. Until I touched you, I thought it was *glashunrah*."

"*Glashunrah* is one-sided mating?"

"Yes." His expression showed his amusement. "You must have paid some attention at your orientation."

"I paid enough to know I'm in trouble," she said grimly. "The best I can hope for is they'll deport me."

Kuaron shook his head again, once, emphatically. "No! They can hardly deport you for this. It's not your fault."

"And that's another thing—I thought it was safe for Terrans to be around Wakanreans so long as they don't touch any of them?"

"That's true of *glashunrah*. It doesn't start without physical contact—several seconds at the very least."

"Really?" Dina's indignation grew as she thought about it. "Then why are we treated like lepers?"

"What are lepers?"

"People with a contagious disease."

Kuaron looked uncomfortable, and Dina knew it wasn't a pose. "Well, it angered people when we found out about *glashunrah* and then the Terrans refused to go away."

"I can see that. I'm sure the Wakanreans at my office would love for me to ring a bell when I walk around, just like lepers used to do."

"Where do you work?"

"Quafray," Dina said, not even trying to keep the pride out of her voice.

Kuaron looked suitably impressed. "What do you do at Quafray?"

"I'm a Most Junior Quality Assurance Chemist," Dina said. "And you're a singer, aren't you?"

That surprised him. "How did you know that?"

"Someone at the embassy party pointed you out." She held back a smile as she remembered Erik's comment about Wakanrean music.

"What's funny about that?"

"What? Nothing."

"Then why are you amused?"

She stared at him. "How did you know that?"

"*Klunar*," he said, as if that one word explained everything. When Dina said nothing, he added, "It's one aspect of *shahgunrah*."

Another new word. "I thought *shahgunrah* was—well, what we did last night."

"That was *taal*—or rather, *taal* was what we felt—what made us act as we did."

"But—"

"Let me explain," Kuaron said, picking up his mug and resuming his place on the window seat. "*Shahgunrah* has three aspects: *klunar*, *taal*, and *haictor*."

"*Klunar*, *taal*, and *haictor*," Dina repeated, feeling as if she were back in school.

"Good." Kuaron sounded very like a teacher. "*Klunar* translates as 'mirroring,' but most Terrans call it empathy."

"I'd heard that Wakanreans were empathic with their mates," Dina interrupted.

"*Shahgunrahai*," Kuaron said, "not mates. Mating isn't specific to *shahgunrah*."

"I see. And what about the other two aspects?"

"*Taal* is passion—overwhelming passion that you feel for your *shahgunrahai* from the moment *shahgunrah* starts."

"What? All the time?" It sounded scary and a little impractical. How did they get anything done?

"No, not all the time." Kuaron sipped his *quascha*. "It's strongest now, during *shahkuun*, it's true, but even though it wanes, it lasts a lifetime."

The industrial chemist in her was intrigued. "Too bad you can't bottle it."

Kuaron looked lost at the reference, so Dina made a fluttering motion with the fingers of one hand. "I'm sorry. Go on, please."

"The third aspect is *haictor*. I have a Terran friend who insists it's merely part of *klunar*, but Wakanreans have always considered them as separate things."

"What is *haictor*, then?" Dina asked, postponing for the moment further investigation of his friendship with a Terran.

"It's the sense of being connected, of always knowing where your *shahgunrahai* is when he or she is close. It's also the last aspect to manifest itself. We say that *taal* and *klunar* struggle for first place, and *haictor* always comes in third."

"So, if we've both gone through *shahgunrah*—"

"Started *shahgunrah*," Kuaron corrected, "and we did."

"If we've started *shahgunrah*," Dina amended, "why don't I feel these things?"

"You do. I know because of *klunar*. Since I feel what you feel, I know when you're reacting to me."

"Bosh!"

"What is this bosh?" Kuaron said, a complaining note creeping into his voice.

"Look here, Kuaron." She pronounced the name carefully. "I'll admit I got very turned on last night, but you're talking as if I had changed into another person entirely."

His eyes glowed with enthusiasm. "You have, in a way. You just met me, and yet you can tell whether I'm angry or sad, happy or aroused. I'm not only a stranger, I'm an alien to you, and yet, in some ways, you know me better than you know anyone else."

There was, Dina realized with a shock, a profound sense of satisfaction coming from him. "Good lord, Kuaron! You're glad about this! You not only believe we're *shah- shah*-whats-its, you're overjoyed that it happened."

"Yes."

"Why?"

He put his mug down on the window ledge and crossed the room to stand in front of her and take her hands. "Because I had given up hope. I thought I would never find *shahgunrah*—never know *taal*, never feel *klunar*. I feared I would live out my life alone."

Dina felt a cold chill grip her at these words. This stranger saw her as the culmination of a dream. He had spent his life waiting, and now he thought the waiting was over—because he had met her. The irony of it struck her; for once it was the man who welcomed commitment, and the woman who was terrified by the idea of being trapped in a relationship.

"What's wrong?" Kuaron demanded. "What did I say that made you so afraid?"

He knew! He knew at once that she was afraid. She remembered how his emotions had seemed like a physical presence in the room the night before, and how he had known when she was amused. For the first time, the thought that he could be right about what had happened took root in her mind.

Kuaron sat down next to her and held her close. "Don't be afraid, *acubai*. We have each other now. Whatever happens, we don't have to face it alone."

There was a warm glow of reassurance radiating from him, but even then, Dina pulled away, terrified. "I have to go." She jumped to her feet.

It was Kuaron's turn for consternation. "What?" He looked up at her, anxiety emanating from every hair on his body. "Go? You mean go *now*?"

"Yes, now. If I don't leave now, there's no way I won't be late for work."

"Work?" He stood up and towered over her. "You can't possibly go to work!"

"Why not?"

He spread his hands in a helpless gesture. "It's *shahkuun*. You won't last the day away from me."

"Hah!" Any sympathy Dina had felt at his distress evaporated at the seeming conceit in his words. "Where's my dress?"

She didn't wait for an answer but started for the doorway. She plunged through it and was surprised into an exclamation as she entered the main room. She had seen it only briefly the night before, and in dim lighting. Now she looked around, surprised at how different it was from the bedroom.

The rough back wall that ran the length of the room looked as if it had been carved from living rock. The room was very long, with almost floor-to-ceiling windows that looked out on the entire valley of the twin rivers, with the city of Wisuta in the center where the rivers met. Dina could see the sparsely-populated suburbs, giving her a good idea how far they were from the city's center.

At the far end of the room stood an enormous table with benches and chairs around it. On the stone wall opposite the windows, leafy plants climbed to the ceiling from planters carved into the rock. In a niche toward the middle of the wall, a large globe of Wakanreo revolved slowly; it hung in the air, unsupported, over a cylindrical base; three tiny orbs representing Wakanreo's three moons circled it slowly.

Dina took in the globe, the spacious, open room filled with oversized sofas and hassocks, and the huge wooden table. She remembered the private flyter Kuaron had summoned.

"Good gracious, Kuaron! You must be rich. Being a singer must pay very well on Wakanreo."

He moved closer to her. "I'm not rich, only comfortably well off. And I'm not an ordinary singer, I'm a *qatraharai*."

She should leave. Really, she had to go. Her already-stern boss would be livid if she came in late on her fourth day of work "What's a *qatraharai*?"

"Someone who sings the *qatrahs*," Kuaron said reasonably. "You would have heard me sing if I hadn't come close enough to you to start *shahgunrah*. The Ambassador had asked me, and I had agreed to sing one *qatrah*."

"Maybe some other time. Where's my dress?"

Kuaron pointed, and Dina noticed a small red triangle on the back of a sofa. As she moved closer, she saw that it was part of the hem of her gown. The remainder of the garment hung from the back of the sofa onto the floor behind it.

"Red." Dina picked up the dress and shook it out. "I would wear red. Now I have to go home in a red evening gown."

"You're going home?" Kuaron had followed her. "I could go with you."

She looked up at his anxious face and felt a surge of passion. "No," she said firmly, as much to herself as to him. "I'm only going home to change clothes. I have to go to work."

Kuaron said nothing, but he stepped closer. Dina felt her heart begin to pound, faster and faster.

"No," she said again. She meant the word to be loud and firm, but instead it came out as a breathy whisper. It didn't sound convincing, even to her.

"There's no fighting *taal*." Kuaron slipped his arms around her.

Dina dropped the dress and embraced him back. "Oh," she moaned, as his hands tugged off her undergarments.

As soon as she was naked, Kuaron lifted her up and laid her gently on her back on the sofa behind her. When he put one knee beside her and leaned over her, Dina reached for the fastenings on his skirt-like garment.

"How do you take this off?" she demanded.

Kuaron pulled on the clasp, and the thing fell to the floor.

"Oh, my," Dina said faintly. She now knew a lot more about Wakanrean anatomy than she had ever dreamed of knowing. It was indeed very similar to human anatomy, especially since there was one place where male Wakanreans had no fur. And Wakanreans, were, of course, bigger than Terrans.

For his part, Kuaron seemed to have learned a good deal about Terran anatomy; he ran one hand down her torso, letting just the tips of his claws brush her skin.

Dina sighed in anticipation, and caressed his neck and chest in return. Kuaron's hand reached her leg, and he stroked the inside of her thigh in the same way. Dina's sigh changed to a moan.

This time Dina was unable to ignore the feelings she sensed from Kuaron. When she touched him, she felt not only her own rising excitement, she felt his, and she knew it was the same for him.

The next several minutes proceeded at a dizzying pace. Dina felt as if she were drowning in a flood of sensation. It swept over her rapidly, blotting out conscious thought and obliterating any consideration but enjoyment of the moment. When her climax came, the intensity of sensation was so profound, it was almost painful. Her ecstasy finally waned, but was resuscitated into a final burst a few seconds later as she sensed Kuaron's passion peak.

For almost a minute, Dina couldn't bring herself to move. She lay there in a haze of languid satiety and wished for nothing to change. After a bit, she became aware of Kuaron's weight, and when she opened her eyes, she could see that he was supporting himself mostly with his knees and hands.

She shifted position reluctantly, moving toward the edge of the wide sofa. Kuaron responded by doing a push-up and then coming down on one side of her body, so that he lay next to her, against the back of the sofa.

Dina let out another sigh, this one a mix of reluctant admiration and apprehension. "You do that awfully well for someone who was a virgin until last night."

"I was *toshugai*. And that was our fourth time."

"You must be a damn quick learner, then."

Kuaron's smile was bland. "No. It's easy to learn what to do when you always know whether the other person is pleased or not. I don't see how Terrans manage without *klunar*."

"There's something in that. No one can fake an orgasm with *shahgunrah*."

Kuaron looked totally perplexed. "Why would anyone want to fake an orgasm?"

She shook her head. "I can't explain a few thousand years of Terran relationships all at once. Let's just say that the capacity for deception isn't always a good thing."

"Very few things are always good."

"I won't argue with that." Dina looked up at his face and saw that the pupils in his eyes had again narrowed to tiny dots. It made his irises look even more like the golden stones in her great-grandmother's amber bracelet. "And I won't deny that that was the best sex I ever had in my life. But I still have to go."

Waves of distress emanated from him.

"Please!" Dina said, without waiting for him to speak. "Please don't be upset! I'll come to see you in a few days. I just need to sort this out."

He propped himself up on one arm so that he looked down at her face. "You don't understand. This is *shahkuun*. *Shahgunrah* has just taken root in us, and we have a tremendous need to be together during this time. If you leave now, we'll both be very ill."

Dina lifted her head to kiss his cheek. She had never kissed him with just affection before, and she sensed that he was a little confused by the gesture.

She pulled away, and sat up. "I'm going to get dressed. Where's the bathroom?"

He sat up behind her, then waved a hand toward the bedroom door. "If you need a toilet, there's one in its own closet, in the bedroom. If you want to wash, the bathing room is on the corridor. You can go in through the bedroom or through the entrance hall."

Dina got up and collected her clothes, finding her stockings under a small table that held carved animal figurines. She stopped to feel in the pockets of the dress and was relieved to find her pocket com. The message counter showed 12 messages, but Dina clicked the com off. She would listen to them later. "Where are my gloves?" she said, suddenly remembering that she would need them.

"They must be in the flyter." Kuaron reached for his robe-skirt. "I'll get them."

Dina clutched her bundle of clothing and headed for the bedroom. She used the toilet first, and then went through the other bedroom door to the corridor and found the bathing room.

Her first sight of it was almost as arresting as the main room had been. A huge mosaic made of tiny tiles covered most of the back wall. The abstract design consisted mostly of a large gray-green iridescent blob with small red and orange splotches decorating it. An enormous pool—almost big enough to swim in—occupied one end of the large room, while the other held a row of open showers. Three slanted shafts cut into the ceiling let in a raft of morning sunlight, and when Dina looked up, she saw three patches of a beautifully clear blue-green sky. The shafts must angle out to the cliff face.

Dina deferred a more thorough investigation of the room in favor of a brief shower, and dressed quickly once she was dry.

Kuaron had dressed also, in a loose-fitting shirt and trousers. He was waiting for her in the main room when she walked into it, her long dress swishing around her ankles as she moved.

He stood, stiff and disapproving, not saying a word, and it occurred to Dina that he might not want to fly her back to Wisuta.

"Oh!" she said. "Can you get an autocab to come all the way out here?"

"Yes," he said, his distress clear. "I'll call one if you insist, but I wish you'd listen to reason."

"I do insist," Dina said, relieved. "And you need to understand that you're offering me Wakanrean reason, and I'm a Terran. The idea of staying with someone I just met doesn't sound like reason at all."

Kuaron said nothing but brushed past her toward another open doorway. Dina followed, and found herself in the kitchen. One corner was taken up with a complicated-looking com center. While Kuaron put through a call, Dina inspected the appliances. She noted that while the kitchen servoid parked in another corner looked sophisticated, there was no sign of a food synthesizer. Instead, there was a strange metal cabinet partly covered with a steel rack.

"What's that?" Dina asked, her back to Kuaron as she heard him complete his call.

"That's the stove," Kuaron said from behind her.

Dina knew suddenly that he was moving closer even though he hadn't made a sound. Wordlessly, she stepped out of his way as he reached around her to press a control on the front of the cabinet. Instantly, flame whooshed from under the rack, lighting a corner of the surface.

"Whoa!" Dina jumped backwards. "You mean you actually *cook*?"

"Of course." He pressed the control again, and the flame disappeared. "The ovens are over there," he added, with a wave at two panels set into the far wall.

"But why? I mean, obviously, you can afford a food synthesizer."

"Because food is important to me. A lot of us don't like to trust such a significant part of our culture to a machine."

Dina stared at the stove. She realized she was very hungry. "Interesting."

"If you'll stay for a while, I'll cook you some breakfast."

Dina was tempted, but she shook her head. "Can I have my gloves, please?"

He led the way back to the main room with her trailing behind him. He picked her gloves up from the low table and handed them to her without even looking back to see where she was.

Dina took them almost reluctantly. "I—I feel like I should tell you I had a nice time."

He turned to face her at this, his mouth twisted in a bitter approximation of a smile. "It wasn't a party."

"No, I suppose not."

He said nothing in reply. It was, Dina realized, the most awkward silence she had ever had to fill. "So, how long does this phase last?" she said at last.

"Ten or twelve days, usually."

"I see."

"No!" he said explosively. "You don't understand at all. *Haictor* has started, and still you insist this isn't *shahgunrah*. You're going to make us ill if you do this."

"We'll see," Dina said, trying to make her tone placating. "Try to look at it from my point of view, Kuaron. I worked hard to get this job, and I don't want to lose it now."

"Bah! No one is ever fired for finding *shahgunrah*. You can even be excused from standing trial until *shahkuun* is over."

The temptation to stay almost overwhelmed Dina. She took a deep breath. "Maybe every Wakanrean can be excused from work, but in my case, Quafray hired a Terran. In fact, they went to a lot of trouble to hire a Terran."

Kuaron still looked agitated. "I understand that. But we found *shahgunrah* in a very public place. You left the party with me after only a few seconds of conversation, and I'm a very well known *qatraharai*. Someone must have noticed."

"Someone?" Dina smiled at his naiveté. "They were *all* staring at us."

"Were they? I wasn't paying attention to anyone but you."

Dina's amusement dissipated. "You sound just a little bit like a guy on the make."

Kuaron was bewildered. "A what?"

"Nothing. It's just that up to now the most refreshing thing about this experience has been the lack of piffle."

"What's piffle?"

"That's a nice word for the things a man will say to a woman when he wants sex."

"All I had to say was 'let's go my house'."

"I know." It hadn't worked for Erik, or anyone else until now.

Another awkward silence.

This time Kuaron spoke first. He bent down and picked up a small electronic note pad which he then held out to Dina. "I put my com code and the location of this house in here for you. Don't lose it; I'm not listed anywhere, and the summit port will warn off any vehicle that doesn't have the code."

She hesitated just a second, but decided to accept it. After all, if she had the code, she could call or not as she pleased. "Thanks," she said, taking it from him, and slipping it into her pocket. She glanced out the window hoping to see a glimpse of the autocab, but there was nothing but empty sky and a great view. "Oh, heck! Can't we sit down and talk nicely?"

Kuaron took two steps to the nearest sofa and sat down on it. "What do you want to talk about?"

Dina sat across from him. "Tell me about yourself. You said I knew you, but it's not true. All I know is you're a singer."

"A *qatraharai*."

"A *qatraharai*. Tell me more."

He gave a quick convulsive gesture with his shoulders and for a moment she thought he was having a spasm of some kind, and then she realized it was only a Wakanrean shrug. "What do you want to know?"

"I don't know," Dina said, trying to imagine herself in the same situation with a human male and failing. "How old are you?"

"Forty-seven."

Dina blinked in surprise; it seemed an advanced age to have remained a virgin. "Forty-seven in Standard years?"

"No. ThreeCon imposes the Terran language on us, but not Terran time measurements."

"Oh." Dina did the math in her head. "Then you must be about forty-one in Standard years." She waited, but Kuaron said nothing. "I'm twenty-eight," she added.

"You may be twenty-eight on your world, but here you're thirty-one or thirty-two, depending on when your birthday falls."

He might be a singer, but he was quick at arithmetic. She was intrigued by the way his tone of voice exuded disapproval. She wondered if it would be as apparent to other people or if it was a result of *shahgunrah*. "Are you from Wisuta?"

"Yes."

"Then you have family here?"

"My father, several aunts and uncles, and many cousins."

"Where's your mother?"

"She died some years ago."

This wasn't helping. But she kept trying. "I'm sorry to hear it. You don't have siblings or grandparents, then?"

He shook his head once, very emphatically. "Not siblings, no. I'm an only child. My mother's parents are dead, and my father's parents moved to Jitsin some years ago. My father needs to live in Wisuta because of his career."

At last! He had volunteered a piece of information. "What does your father do?"

"He's a highly-placed bureaucrat."

"And where is Jitsin?"

"Not that far away—about a hundred and sixty kilometers south of here."

"Well, at least your grandparents are reasonably close then."

"Yes."

Dina gave up. "All right. Let's just sit here in silence until the autocab comes."

"No. Now you tell me about your family."

She was pleased that he wanted to know, but she shook her head. "No fair. If you want to know, you have to ask *me* questions."

He didn't smile, but she could sense that he was amused. "All right. Are both your parents alive?"

"No, my father died when I was eleven."

She could feel the warmth of his sympathy, even across the space between them. "That must have been painful for you."

"Yes."

He smiled openly now, clearly amused at her turning the tables on him. "And your mother?"

"She's still alive. She remarried some years ago, but she still lives on Fantar, where I was born."

"What is Fantar?"

"It's a Terran colony world—a recent colony, not a sleeper world."

"Is it a large colony?"

"The world is large, but the population is still small. There's not a whole lot there except an enormous archipelago of islands."

Kuaron looked surprised. "Islands?"

"Yes, islands. I miss the sea, sometimes, and going to the beach. I was never far from it growing up."

He nodded at the globe in its niche. "We rarely visit the beach. Too risky with three moons all influencing the tides."

"Tides are one aspect of the sea that I don't know much about. Fantar has no moon, so the tides were always negligible."

He opened his mouth to comment, but the com panel emitted a beeping sound.

"The autocab is here," he said, getting to his feet, "if you're sure you have to go."

Dina stood up. "I'm sure."

Kuaron crossed to the kitchen. "You'll have to take the lift tube to the summit," he said over his shoulder. "There's a landing port up there. My security system won't allow a vehicle in the landing bay unless I authorize it."

"No problem." Dina watched him operate a part of the console that she realized must be a security panel. "I don't mind."

He came back into the main room and waited.

Dina walked to him and kissed his cheek. "Goodbye, Kuaron."

"No. You'll be back soon."

"Maybe," she said. "But I have to find out just what's happened to me. Maybe I'll go to a doctor tomorrow, if I can get off work."

"You're not ill."

"I don't know whether to hope I am or not." She turned to go and her long skirt rustled as she moved.

"I'll go up the lift tube with you," Kuaron said, moving toward her.

Panic set in. She could never leave if he was standing right next to her, exuding equal amounts of concern and sex appeal. "No, please don't. I can manage a lift tube just fine by myself."

She walked to the door and opened it, then walked through without looking back. She didn't dare look back.

KUARON stood at the window and watched the autocab grow smaller and smaller until he could no longer distinguish it against the bright morning sky. He sighed as he turned from the window and sat down on a sofa. As he put his feet on a hassock, he closed his eyes and took a deep breath. Dina's scent lingered in the air, that strange, tantalizing scent, so familiar and yet so alien. It provided reassurance even now, when he could no longer feel her presence with *haictor*.

Kuaron opened his eyes and stared up at the ceiling, trying to sort out what he was feeling. His life had taken an incredible turn, in the literal sense of the word. It was inconceivable that he should have found his *shahgunrahai* at last, but that she should be a Terran woman.

He thought back to that moment at the embassy, when he first realized that *shahgunrah* was starting. He had been overjoyed to think that he had found his *shahgunrahai*. His eagerness had withered instantly once he realized whom it was he had scented. He had never been so angry in his life as he was at that moment when all his senses coalesced to tell him that the only *shahgunrahai* he would ever have was a Terran woman.

It was only after he had touched her that he had understood that it was true *shahgunrah*. Impossible as it seemed, it had to be real. She felt *klunar* as well as *taal*, and Kuaron was sure *haictor* had started for her before she left him. He had never heard of a Terran experiencing any aspect of *shahgunrah*, let alone all three.

Kuaron leaned his head farther back. He had a good idea what his father would say when he heard the news. He hadn't cared for Kuaron's forming a friendship with a Terran man; finding *shahgunrah* with a Terran woman would make his father blazingly angry—if he could be brought to believe it at all.

Who would believe it? It was only because he could feel it so inescapably that Kuaron himself could accept his *shahgunrah* with Dina. If he had seen another Wakanrean leave the party with her, he didn't think he would have believed it was anything more than an unfortunate case of *glashunrah*.

This reminded him that his father wasn't the only one he would have to persuade. Triascou wouldn't take the news well. Even though she and her *shahgunrahai* had been at the party with him, she would never believe that Dina had gone home with him because of *shahgunrah*. Triascou had made her opinion of Terrans known when Kuaron had brought Jared to one of her concerts. She was even worse than his father in her prejudices, and unlike him, she didn't have a government position that prohibited her from publically voicing her intolerance. Her behavior at the embassy party had proved that. Her willingness to insult her hosts had mortified him.

Kuaron hadn't thought himself prejudiced, but he could still recall his shock on looking into those alien eyes, the irises so small, and a deeper brown than was normal. The feel of her naked skin was stranger still, it smoothness oddly satisfying.

There was no denying Dina's exotic nature, and yet, he had known as soon as his hand closed on her arm that she was his *shahgunrahai*. Truly, it seemed that the poets who spoke of what was meant to be were in the right of it. In his forty-seven years, he had met so many people without ever feeling the tide of *taal* rising in him that he had given up hope. And then when he least expected it, *shahgunrah* had overtaken him.

Kuaron spent a brief moment wondering how *shahgunrah* with a Terran was possible, and then gave it up. He wasn't well versed in any of the basic sciences, let alone complicated ones like genetics or biochemistry.

A twinge of pain assailed him, a cramping in his stomach that almost mimicked hunger. Kuaron knew better. He could feel the discomfort of Dina's absence growing in his mind. It would only get worse.

She would return, eventually. Fear had driven her away. Fear of him, in a sense. Fear of being tied to him forever in a way she didn't yet comprehend. No matter how much she trusted him not to hurt her, she couldn't bring herself to *want* to be with him as he wanted to be with her.

But still, *shahgunrah* would bring her back. He knew it. He only hoped it wouldn't take her too long to accept that she no longer had a choice.

And then the pain hit him again, and began to grow. She must be quite far away now. Kuaron gasped as his back muscles spasmed; his shoulders ached already, and the muscles of his stomach tensed in anticipation. He groaned and clenched his teeth as his intestinal tract twisted and convulsed. The pounding in his head intensified. He lay back on the sofa and prayed that Dina would return soon.

# *Chapter Three*

Dina stepped down from the cab with an effort. The cold hit her at once. The cab had been heated, but now the air of the roofport held a bracing chill, almost as cold as it had been on the summit of Kuaron's cliff. Dina shivered in her thin dress, but it wasn't the frigid air that troubled her. If anything, the cold provided a welcome distraction from the pain that resonated deep inside her, echoing in her muscles with every step she took. Kuaron had been right.

She managed to stagger to the lift tube entrance, but it was all she could do to stay on her feet. Once on her own floor, she walked as fast as she could, one hand on the wall the whole way. As soon as her front door closed behind her, she collapsed onto the floor.

"Good morning," the desk com said. "You have sixteen messages."

"Shut up!" Dina said, lifting her head from the floor.

The com was silent, but its message light continued to blink remorselessly.

Dina got up on her hands and knees and crawled to the bedroom, heedless of whatever damage she might be doing to her party dress. She dragged herself onto the bed, and then propped herself up on a pillow so she could see the com on the bedside table.

"Attention, com unit," she ordered. "Play my messages one at a time, oldest first. Don't bother with the date and time unless I ask."

"Dina, darling!" Arliana's voice cried as her face appeared on the screen. "Are you still out with your new friend? My God, have you caused a gale! I know I told you to be more adventurous, but you jumped off the wrong end of the boat. Call me as soon as you get home, and I'll tell you why."

There was a click and then her face appeared again, looking anxious.

"Dina!" Arliana said again. "Where are you? I tried your office and they said you haven't come in yet. What's going on? Are you okay?"

There was another click. Arliana's next plea was briefer, and was tagged for acknowledgement, so Arliana would know that Dina had heard it. After that one came three messages from neighbors Dina barely knew, asking her to call if she knew anything about what had happened at the embassy party.

Interspersed with these were four messages from the Terran embassy, including one inquiring if she had left her jacket. The others merely asked her to call; the last one was tagged.

When the machine stopped, Dina counted in her head.

"Attention, com unit. That's only ten messages. What happened to the other six?"

"The remaining messages are blank," the mechanical voice said.

"Who are they from, then?"

"I cannot report that information. The code was blocked."

Dina lay back on the bed and then looked at the time displayed on the com. A spasm of pain hit her, and she rolled on her side and clenched her teeth until it abated. When she felt strong enough, she staggered to her feet and began to unfasten her dress.

She had the long gown off when the com beeped again for an incoming call.

"Com unit, who is that call from?" Dina said as she emptied the pockets of her dress and then threw it in the corner. She pulled some trousers and a shirt from a drawer, and then sank down onto the bed to put them on.

"I don't know," said the console.

"Then take a message, but don't put through the call."

There was a brief pause before it answered. "Your new message is blank."

Dina finished struggling into her shirt and trousers, then took a small clothes case from the closet and began to stuff clothing into it, mostly undergarments, with assorted other items thrown in as she came across them.

"Not much time," she muttered to herself as she moved to the com panel to make a call. It didn't take her long, as there was a menu option just for what she wanted. Once that was done, she sat down on the bed to rest for a moment, and try to determine if she was forgetting anything. She had just slipped on a pair of comfortable shoes when the front door panel beeped.

"Dina Bellaire!" a familiar voice shouted as someone pounded on the door. "Dina, are you in there?"

Dina snapped her case shut and carried it into the living room. When she opened the door, Arliana Cheng stood there, her hand raised to pound on the door again. She stared open-mouthed at Dina.

"Hello, Arliana," Dina said. "How are you?"

"How am I?" Arliana gasped, as if this were an insult. "Is that all you have to say? The *police* came to my house this morning!"

"I'm sorry they bothered you." Dina gritted her teeth as she felt a wave of pain overtake her.

Arliana's gaze raked Dina up and down and then darted to the clothes case in her hand. "Where the hell do you think you're going? You look like death warmed over."

"I know." In spite of the pain, Dina couldn't hold back a chuckle. "One of the nicer things about what's happened is that it no longer matters what I look like."

"What?"

Dina stepped into the hallway and shut the door behind her. "Can you help me get to the roof port? I called a cab, and it should be here any minute."

"Dina!" Arliana sounded genuinely distressed. "Do you know what you're doing?"

It was a darned good question. "Not really. But I expect I'll figure it out as I go along."


WHEN the door at the bottom of the lift tube opened, Dina saw Kuaron lying on the floor in the corridor. He had apparently set the lift to admit her, as she hadn't had any difficulty in entering the tube.

"Kuaron!" She knelt beside him. "Kuaron, are you all right?"

He lifted his head and managed a weak smile. "I will be soon, now that you're back."

"Let's get you inside," Dina said. "Can you walk?"

"I think so." He pulled himself up with her help.

He was very heavy, but he wasn't helpless, and once he got to his feet, he staggered along with Dina steering him more than holding him up.

When they got to the main room, Dina put down her case and helped him to lie down on the huge, wide sofa. She started for the kitchen, but he grabbed her hand.

"Don't leave me."

"I'm just going to get you some water."

"I don't need water. Stay with me."

"All right."

When he closed his eyes, she lay down beside him. His arm curved around her, and she rested her head on his chest and lay still for a long time, listening to the sound of his heart.

Just when she was certain he was going to sleep, Kuaron gave a sigh and pulled himself to an upright position. "I think I'll cook us something to eat now."

Dina sat up next to him. "Are you sure you're up to it so soon?"

He slipped an arm around her and squeezed her gently. "I'm fine now. You weren't gone that long."

She wrinkled her forehead. "You knew I'd have to come back. You knew what it would be like."

"Everyone knows. That's why *shahkuun* is a legal excuse for missing so many things."

"I can see why." Dina pulled away and tucked one knee up under her chin. "So what happens now? Do we just stay here and screw each other silly for days on end?"

He frowned. "*Shahgunrah* is not a bad thing, Dina. It's not evil or base."

"I suppose not," she said, relenting. If this situation was distressing for her, he wasn't to blame. "I'm sorry. It's just that it's still difficult for me to accept what's happened. I went out expecting to spend one evening at a party, and now I can't go home."

He moved closer and put his arm around her again.

They sat still for a moment, and then Dina sighed and patted his arm. "Come on; you promised me food."

Kuaron smiled with relief. "What would you like?"

She shook her head. "I don't know Wakanrean food well enough to ask for anything. Wakanreans don't seem to have different food for different meals, do you?"

Kuaron looked confused. "Different from what?"

"From other meals. On Fantar, there were certain foods we generally ate only at breakfast, and others we ate only for dinner."

Kuaron's confused expression grew more pronounced. "Why? Was there something peculiar in the food that made it nourishing only at a certain time of day?"

"No, not really. We just *like* certain food for certain meals—like cereal grains only at breakfast."

"Do they taste different at breakfast than at dinner?"

Dina had to laugh. "No. I give up. I guess it doesn't make that much sense when you really think about it."

"I don't suppose most customs do," Kuaron said, getting to his feet. He held out his hand. When Dina took it, he pulled her to her feet so fast she almost flew off the sofa. "Time to cook. You can help."

Dina wasn't much help, but she did hand him things when he asked for them. Under Kuaron's direction, she cut slices from a loaf of dense bread and laid them out on plates, while he neatly quartered several small, round, pulpy fruits and sautéed them in a pan. The fruit gave off a tantalizing sweet but oily fragrance as it cooked, and Dina realized she was very hungry.

Kuaron smiled at her eagerness. He took a covered bowl from the larder and set it on the stove.

"What's that?" Dina asked.

"Leftover *shuishfa*," he said, lifting the cover to stir something that looked like a gray-brown pudding.

Dina was skeptical. "It doesn't look especially appetizing."

"It tastes better than it looks. It's made with different meats and vegetables, so it's good for you, and very filling."

Dina didn't see this as much of a recommendation, but a short while later, when Kuaron scooped two generous helpings of *shuishfa* onto their plates, she had to admit, it smelled wonderfully hearty—almost like beef stew.

Kuaron spooned the cooked fruit onto the bread and handed Dina her plate. "Here. Be careful, the plate is warm."

"Oooh, it's a thermaplate," Dina said in surprise. "I thought you liked to do things the old fashioned way?"

"I said we like to fix the food the old fashioned way," Kuaron corrected her as he picked up his own plate. "I never said we were fanatics."

They sat at the large table and ate without talking for a few minutes. Dina was too hungry to feel a need to make conversation.

Kuaron watched her while he ate, smiling when she wolfed down the *shuishfa*. "You liked it?"

"Yes. Very much. Should I ask what's in it?"

He smiled even wider at this. "Nothing terrible. Mostly it's root vegetables and chunks of meat pureed together and cooked with wine and spices."

"That doesn't sound so bad," Dina said, licking her fingers. There were no napkins on the table. "You seem completely well now."

"So are you."

"Yes."

"But you're still apprehensive?"

Dina blinked, still not used to the jolt of disorientation that came from someone else knowing what she was feeling. "I suppose I am. You were expecting this—hoping for this. Even if I wasn't what you had in mind, you were still prepared for the idea of having a *shah-gunrahai*. It was a real shock for me."

"I know that. And I know I must have frightened you. You were terrified last night."

She shook her head, not willing to let him think she was afraid of him. "That was just because I couldn't control myself. I know you won't hurt me; I knew it last night."

"You'll get used to it—to me—in time."

Dina wasn't prepared to think about the future, so she changed the subject. "I think we might have caused something of a diplomatic incident, though. There were some blank messages on my com when I got home. I didn't think anyone could blank out their identity on a call, but someone did."

Kuaron's eyes widened, and Dina felt a surge of alarm from him. "Do you think it was ThreeCon?"

Dina shook her head. "My friend Arliana said the police had been to her house. I assumed she meant the Wakanrean police."

"Wisutan," Kuaron corrected. "Unless—"

"Unless what?" Dina asked, when he didn't complete the sentence.

"I'm not sure. If someone had complained because I touched you, it would have been a matter for the municipal authorities. However, in controversial criminal cases, the Prefect of Wisuta has been known to pass the matter on to the regional authorities."

"So there are regional police?" Dina asked. It seemed to her that he was very uneasy about something.

"There's an investigative force that deals with serious crimes, and those that cross local boundaries."

"And you think that our finding *shahgunrah* will be a matter for these regional police?"

Kuaron pushed his chair back from the table. "They won't know we found *shahgunrah*. They'll think it's *glashunrah*."

Dina considered this, and smiled a sour smile. "With you playing the part of the poor unfortunate Wakanrean and me as the randy Terran?"

"Yes. They won't know any better."

"I suppose not." She picked up her plate. "Where do I put this?"

Kuaron leaned over and put his own plate onto the oval design in the middle of the table. He pushed down firmly, and the oval sank into the table surface, revealing a service hatch. "The servoid will put them away once they're clean."

Dina followed his example with her cup and utensils while Kuaron collected the other dishes. Once the table was clear, he went into the kitchen and returned with a small bowl of liquid and a cloth. As Dina watched, he washed his hands in the bowl, dried them on the cloth, and then passed them both toward her.

"What is this?" she asked.

"It's a cleansing solution. It cleans your hands."

Dina dipped her hands in the solution and sniffed. The scent was pleasant, almost woodsy. She rubbed vigorously, then dried her hands as Kuaron had done.

When she looked up, Kuaron had wandered out to the main room and stood looking out at the view.

"What are you thinking?" Dina said, coming up behind him.

He reached behind him and grabbed her by the waist, pulling her close against his side. "I'm wondering what's going to happen. I was so concerned about how you felt, I hadn't spared a thought for the legal aspects. This could be—rather strange."

"Why?"

He looked down at her, his expression an odd mix of bemused surprise and apprehension. "Because *shahgunrah* isn't usually a matter for the courts or the legal system. It's not a legal thing at all, although there are many laws governing what happens to people after it occurs."

"So there's never a ceremony or a license or anything?"

He shrugged that same convulsive shrug that had disconcerted her before. It was even more startling when she was so close to him. "Most places require people to register their *shahgunrah* within a certain amount of time after it occurs, for tax purposes if nothing else. And in this region, *shahgunrahai* usually hold a gift-giving after *shahkuun* is over."

"A gift-giving?"

"Yes. New *shahgunrahai* are often very young. Their friends and relations come and give them useful household items so they're prepared to keep house."

"That's not that different from what we do. I suppose it makes sense in any culture."

"Yes."

She slid her arm around him to return his embrace. The increased closeness made his apprehension even more inescapable. "So why are you so worried?"

He touched the small silver ornament he wore. "I'm afraid people may be upset because of this."

She peered at the design engraved in the silver. It looked like a lopsided pentagon with a series of elaborate loops and whorls beside it. "It's pretty, but what is it?"

"It's called a *heicha*. Lots of people wear them, but it's the design that's significant. It's the mark of Paruian. Do you know about her?"

"I think so," Dina said, struggling to remember. "I read up on your history as much as I could on the way here. Wasn't she a sort of combination prophet and saint?"

"In a way. In her lifetime, her doctrine stressed the need to achieve peace rather than any religious tenet. Although she never claimed divinity, after her death, a group of her disciples founded a religion that venerated her. Over the centuries, that group split into many sects, each with its own view of Paruian's life and work. And even the people who don't see her as divine, revere her as the Prophet of Peace."

"So, do you belong to one of these religious groups?"

"No," Kuaron said, smiling. "It's ironic, but I'm not particularly religious."

"Why is it ironic?"

"Because I'm descended from Paruian, through my mother. My mother was rather skeptical of all religions herself. She never allowed my father to instill any of his own religious tenets in me, but he's quite devout."

"So you think your father and other religious people will be upset about me?"

"Possibly. The thing is, I'm well known as a *qatraharai*, so every-one knows I'm a *parundai*."

Dina sighed. Yet another word that didn't occur in Standard. "A which?"

"A descendent of Paruian. No one else ever wears her mark."

"Oh," Dina said, studying the silver *heicha*. "So that tells every-one you're a *parundai*?"

"Yes."

"But if you don't believe in Paruian, why do you wear it?"

"I don't believe she was divine," he said, "but I do hold her in tre-mendous respect for what she accomplished. We were very warlike, and she changed that. Some people say she advanced our civiliza-tion many centuries."

"Okay, so she was a major prophet," Dina began, when she was interrupted by a loud insistent beeping noise from the com.

"What's that?" Dina asked.

Kuaron moved toward the com. "It's the summit alarm, but that's odd. I've programmed a warn-off code into the transponder. The knocker is off the door digitally as much as it is literally. No one would be so rude as to intrude at such a time as this." He checked the panel and frowned. "It is someone on the summit."

"Shouldn't we answer it?"

He didn't reply but instead punched a button on the panel. Immediately, the com screen lit up, and the image resolved itself into a Wakanrean man's face.

He wore a gray uniform trimmed with red, and an expression that registered extreme discomfort. "Good morning, *parundai*."

"Who are you?" Kuaron demanded, wasting no time in pleasant-ries. "And what are you doing on my roof?"

"I'm truly sorry to disturb you, *parundai*," the man said. "My name is Under-captain Hulac Oim, of the Global Army of Wakanreo. I'm attempting to locate a Terran woman named Dina Bellaire."

"So?"

"I'm very much afraid, *parundai*, that I must ask you if she's in your company."

"It seems to me that it's no business of yours who is in my company."

The under-captain ducked his head in an embarrassed gesture. "Ordinarily I would agree, but as it happens, I have a warrant to bring Dina Bellaire before the Planetary Administrator."

"What?" Kuaron said. "There's no way that she can go with you now."

"So she is there, *parundai?*"

"Yes, she's here. Now go away. Come back in ten days or so."

"I'm sorry, but I must insist that you admit us now. You should know that I'm empowered to force an entrance to this house should it prove necessary."

The under-captain seemed in great distress as he delivered this demand. Kuaron frowned and stared at the image on the screen. Dina stood some distance away, out of range of the com, and watched Kuaron anxiously.

He looked at her, a question in his eyes. Dina couldn't see any point in putting up a fight they were sure to lose. She nodded.

"Very well," Kuaron said. "I'll open the lift tube. You may come in."

He entered a code on the security control panel next to the com, and then came over to where Dina waited.

"What happens now?" she said, looking up at him. "I can't very well hide under the bed."

"We'll see. If they truly have a warrant, it may not be possible to ignore it."

She clutched his arm. "I won't ask if I'm in trouble. I think the proper question is—how much trouble am I in?"

"Don't worry. If they try to deport you, I'll go with you."

"You will?"

"Of course."

She gave him a measuring look. "I'd be touched if I didn't know how intolerable the alternative is."

He smiled, but shook his head in reproof. "The overwhelming need to be together lasts only during *shahkuun.* Once that's over, we'll still feel *klunar,* and *haictor,* but *taal* will be more manageable, and parting won't be physically painful."

"Oh."

Before Kuaron could say more, there was an authoritative knock on the door.

"Come!" Kuaron called.

His voice must have unlocked the door because four Wakanreans in gray and red uniforms entered, advancing through the entrance hall into the main room.

Kuaron let go of Dina's arm, and the two of them stood waiting side by side but not touching.

The under-captain walked at the head of the group. He seemed not to know where to rest his eyes. "Good morning, *parundai*," he said, standing stiffly in front of Kuaron and bowing from the waist, hands behind him.

Kuaron ignored the greeting. "By what right do you intrude on my house when the knocker is off the door?"

The under-captain stood up perfectly straight and handed Kuaron a data slate that glowed as soon as he touched it. Kuaron read it carefully, and passed it to Dina.

"As you see," the under-captain said, his eyes sliding off of Dina's face and coming to rest at a point somewhere above her right shoulder, "the warrant is signed by Administrator Sadoc himself. It directs that Dina Bellaire, a citizen of the Third Confederation of Planets and legal resident of Wakanreo, be brought before him at once."

"On what grounds?" Kuaron asked, handing the warrant back after Dina passed it to him.

The under-captain made a strangled noise in his throat before he spoke. "Violation of the Wakanrean interdiction on physical contact between Wakanrean citizens and those of Terran descent."

"I see," Kuaron said dryly. "And the Planetary Administrator is handling those complaints personally?"

"In this instance, yes, *parundai*," the under-captain said, in a voice devoid of sarcasm or insinuation.

"As it happens," Kuaron said, "Dina Bellaire has recently become my *shahgunrahai*. I believe the law still forbids a warrant to be served during *shahkuun*?"

The under-captain shuffled his feet. Dina had a fanciful idea that under his fur he was turning a bright red. "As to that, *parundai*, I've been instructed that a valid *shahkuun* can exist only between two or more Wakanreans."

Kuaron was stone-faced as he considered this, but Dina knew he was apprehensive. After a moment, he nodded. "Very well. We will both go with you."

The under-captain practically quivered with concern. "But, *parundai*, my orders are to bring *Kantai* Bellaire only—no one else."

"And are you prepared to commit violence against my person to stop me from going with her?" Kuaron asked.

The under-captain hesitated. He glanced behind him at the other three uniformed Wakanreans, and then back at Kuaron. "No, *parundai*."

"Then we both go."

The under-captain capitulated with good grace, waiting while Dina fetched her jacket. He stood back to allow Kuaron and Dina to precede him through the doorway, and followed them down the corridor. They all took the lift tube to the summit, where the squat gray shape of a military transport waited for them. The under-captain held open the door to a small cabin, and then shut it firmly behind them from the other side.

Dina heard a click as if the door had been locked, and then she took a seat wearily. Kuaron sat next to her. He looked at the cabin windows and gave a harsh laugh.

"What's wrong?" Dina asked, a little worried at the anger she sensed from him.

Kuaron indicated the nearest window that, like all the others, had been set to opaque. Dina could see out of it, but just barely. "It's as if he's afraid someone might see us together."

"Who's afraid?"

"My father."

The comment struck Dina as a complete non sequitur. "What's your father got to do with this?"

"My father's name is Juzao Sadoc."

It took Dina a moment to connect the name. "Your father is the Planetary Administrator?"

Kuaron nodded.

"Why didn't you tell me?" she said indignantly.

He shrugged. "I told you he was a highly placed bureaucrat."

"But—the Planetary Administrator!"

Kuaron was unrepentant. "It's not as if he's the head of state; the Arbiter of the Legislature has that status."

"He doesn't need the title. He just runs everything."

Kuaron's answering smile was more grim than amused. "He does it very well, too. He's quite popular, you know? Aside from the fact that he makes the transports fly on time, people admire him because he cares so little for what's said of him."

Dina could feel the mix of anger and regret he exuded. She laid a hand on his arm. "You love him, don't you?"

"I did." Kuaron leaned back in his seat. "But I may never forgive him for this."

"Is it so terrible?"

Kuaron closed his eyes and then covered them with his arm. "What do you think will happen if *taal* strikes us when we're in his office?"

Dina felt a tremor of anxiety at the thought, but she couldn't repress a smile. "I think your father had better be prepared to vacate his office, that's what I think."

Kuaron moved his arm, opened his eyes, and let out a sigh. "He won't believe it, *acubai*. Think how difficult it was for you to believe it, and you could feel what was happening to you."

"Then we'll just have to find a way to persuade him of the truth."

Kuaron leaned over and very gently kissed her mouth. "I shall have to investigate this kissing business," he said as he nuzzled her neck. "There's more to it than I thought at first."

"You do seem a quick study," Dina said as she opened her eyes.

The trip to Central Administration took some time, as the complex was located on the other side of the valley. The transport traveled at a reasonable speed, but it flew a wide circle around the city itself, and finally began to descend as they neared the cliffs on the far side of the valley.

Kuaron explained their route to Dina as they passed landmarks. No one disturbed them during the journey. A few minutes after the vehicle set down the cabin door clicked open.

"We're here, *parundai*," the under-captain said. He waited politely for Kuaron and Dina to exit the cabin and then climb down the ramp to the ground.

A ground car stood ready, and at the under-captain's direction they boarded it, and found themselves shut inside a closed compartment, unable to see out at all.

"This seems excessive." Kuaron's grumble was almost a growl.

Dina patted his arm. "Don't let yourself get so angry, Kuaron. No one's hurt us so far."

He didn't answer, but she could feel that he was still upset.

The car moved forward, but stopped within a few minutes. When the door opened, they stepped out of the vehicle, and were quickly ushered into a large, blocky, gray stone building that reminded Dina of the medieval fortresses in her Terran history text. The nervous-looking young Wakanrean woman who greeted them directed them to an anteroom. Dina took off her jacket and prepared for a long wait, but it was only a matter of seconds before the wide double doors on the far side of the room opened to admit them.

Very deliberately, Kuaron took Dina's hand and stepped through the doorway, walking with his head high, oblivious to the uniformed escort who still accompanied them. Dina was suddenly conscious of the fact that she had left her gloves back at Kuaron's house. She walked beside him in trepidation.

Everything in the Administrator's large and well furnished office seemed slightly oversized. The windows were very tall, the desk massive, and the chairs large even by Wakanrean standards. Thick draperies masked the sunlight, and the dark reds and browns of the upholstery did nothing to dispel the gloom.

The man behind the desk looked nothing like Kuaron to Dina's inexperienced eye. He was about the same height when he stood up, but his body fur was dark brown, and his headcrest jet black. Only his golden eyes, the line of his shoulders, and the set of his jaw were at all familiar to her.

He stared at her—no, he glared at her—and then he barked something in Wakanrean.

Kuaron answered him in Standard. "I will not wait outside. Nor will I allow you to dictate my actions."

The Administrator replied sharply, still in Wakanrean.

Kuaron continued to speak in Standard. "I will speak as I please. And if I show no respect for your age or our relationship, it's because you've shown no respect for me."

"Respect!" Juzao Sadoc said, changing to Standard. "It's pity I feel for you! That a *parundai* should fall victim to the Terran aberration is something that shames us all."

"There is no shame in *shahgunrah*," Kuaron said, "as you've told me many times. If we're to talk of shame, what about my shame in being dragged here—at such a time—by armed soldiers?"

"The law has been broken," Juzao said, "brazenly and wantonly broken! There must be an accounting for this."

Kuaron's mouth curled in a saturnine smile, almost a sneer. "And now you're acting as a magistrate? It's amazing you have time for such a trivial matter considering your other responsibilities."

"Trivial!" Juzao almost shouted.

"Yes, trivial!" Kuaron shot back at him. "The law against Terrans touching Wakanreans is enforced by the municipal authorities. Why are we not in the municipal hall instead of here?"

Juzao Sadoc looked every bit as angry as he sounded. "The law is a global law. In this case, the Prefect deferred enforcement to the regional authorities, and the Regional Administrator also opted to defer jurisdiction to me."

"Bah! Name me one other time when you've dealt with such a situation personally! You've abused your position to bring us here, and you know it."

"I didn't request *your* presence at all," Juzao said, with a darkling glare at the under-captain still hovering silently in the background. "You chose to come here."

"Of course I did. How could I not, when you dragged my *shahgun-rahai* here?"

Juzao's anger seemed to break, and he stared at his son with a mixture of compassion and sadness. "She's not your *shahgunra-hai*, Kuaron. You know it as well as I do. Even if she's infatuated enough with you to risk deportation, she's still only a Terran."

Dina felt compelled to speak at this disparaging judgment. "*Only* a Terran? Does being a Terran put me on the level of pond scum or something?"

Juzao seemed to really see her for the first time. He frowned as he studied her. "You may consider yourself as good as exiled, woman. I've checked your records. You were told the law less than a week ago, and yet you chose to break it. You'll have to take the consequences."

Dina sucked in her breath in dismay.

Kuaron pulled her closer. "If you force Dina to leave Wakanreo, then I'll go with her."

Juzao stared at his son in consternation. "Kuaron, have you truly run mad? Do you know what you're saying?"

"Of course I know it. I'm quite serious, *Ayzanai*. If you deport her, then I'll leave Wakanreo forever."

Juzao's eyes opened wider in an unfocused stare. "*Shahgunrah* is fully developed, then? There is no going back?"

"There was never any going back. It wasn't like it was with the *huishfanai*. I scented her across a crowded room."

"That's impossible," Juzao said flatly, coming closer to stare at Dina from less than a meter away. "It didn't happen until she touched you."

"She didn't touch me," Kuaron said. "Not until later, at any rate. At the embassy, it was I who touched her. I had no choice. I was already feeling it before I even got close. I tell you I scented her."

Juzao looked at Dina and shook his head once, in the same emphatic way Kuaron had. "It's impossible," he said again.

Instead of answering, Kuaron lifted Dina's hand so that her wrist was right under his father's chin. Juzao's eyes widened in surprise.

"What?" he said, and he took Dina's hand.

She thought for a second he was going to kiss her wrist, but instead he merely sniffed it delicately.

"She smells almost Wakanrean!"

"Yes," Kuaron said. "I'm trying to tell you, *Ayzanai*—it's not *glashunrah*. Dina feels it also—not only *taal*, but *klunar* and *haictor*."

"But," Juzao said, dropping Dina's wrist, "that's not possible. She's a Terran!"

"I don't know *how* it's possible, I only know it has happened."

Juzao stared first at Dina and then at Kuaron and then back at Dina again. He took a deep breath and let it out, and then addressed Dina.

"Is this true, woman?"

"Yes," Dina said. "And stop calling me 'woman.' I have a name."

His gaze was stern. "You allege that you—a Terran—have experienced the most intimate and ancient aspects of Wakanrean life?"

"Look," Dina said, her anger rising as she felt the injustice of his blaming her for *shahgunrah*, "I didn't ask for this to happen. I went to a party, dammit, and the next thing I knew I couldn't stop myself from going home with a man who walked up to me and said 'let's go to my house.' I can assure you that's not typical behavior, not for me."

Juzao waved a hand. "Everyone knows Terrans feel lust—"

"Lust!" Dina said angrily.

"There's a difference between *taal* and lust," Kuaron said. "You've told me that often enough. If you won't believe us, then give us a chance to prove it."

Juzao's expression registered surprise at this request. "How?"

Kuaron said something in Wakanrean that Dina couldn't understand except for the single word *haictor*. Juzao looked thoughtful,
and then he nodded and spoke in Wakanrean to one of their escorts.
The man answered him and left the room.

"What's going on?" Dina demanded. "What's happening?"

"My father is arranging a little test for us," Kuaron said. "Don't
worry. It won't hurt."

"What won't hurt?"

"You'll see soon enough."

A moment later, the soldier returned carrying a square of red
cloth. He handed it to Juzao who folded it into a triangle and then
folded it again twice. As he moved toward Dina, she realized it was
intended as a blindfold.

Kuaron reached for the cloth. "I'll do it, *Ayzanai*."

"No," Juzao said. "I'll do it. It's not much of a test otherwise."

Kuaron looked reluctant, but he allowed his father to step up
to Dina and bind the cloth around her head so that it completely
covered her eyes.

Dina wasn't only blinded, she was mystified. "What's going on?"

"Don't worry, *acubai*," Kuaron's voice said. "I won't let anything
happen to you. Everything will be fine. Just do as my father directs."

Dina stood nervously while someone—she thought it was Juzao—
patted the blindfold. She could feel that whoever it was stood very
close to her, and she assumed he must be making sure she couldn't
see. After a moment, hands took her by the shoulders and spun her
around in circles.

"Wait!" Juzao's voice said.

Dina waited. There were shuffling noises and whispers in
Wakanrean as people moved about the room.

"Now," Juzao's voice said confidently. "Point toward Kuaron."

Without hesitation, Dina turned around and then pointed
straight ahead.

There was silence for a moment, and then Juzao's voice spoke
again, a good deal less confidently this time. "It could be just a
coincidence. We'll try again."

They performed the same maneuver three more times, with
Kuaron in a different place every time. Each time, Dina pointed
without hesitation, certain that she knew where he was.

"Well?" she said after the fourth time. "Can I take this thing off
now? This game is getting old."

"Not yet," Juzao said in Standard. This was followed by what sounded like a question in Wakanrean.

Kuaron's voice answered after a moment's hesitation. Whatever he had said was quite brief and totally unintelligible to Dina.

"What's going on?" she said.

"A moment," Juzao said, reverting to Standard. "Wait there."

After a few seconds, hands took hold of Dina's shoulders again, turning her rapidly in a circle.

"Do I point now?" Dina asked, certain that Kuaron was behind her.

"No, not yet," Juzao said. "Just wait."

Dina stood still, a sense of unease growing in her. All of a sudden, she felt a sharp pain. She knew quite well no one was touching her, and yet she felt pain.

"What is it?" she demanded. "What are you doing?"

The pain grew until Dina could hardly bear it. She realized suddenly that it wasn't her own pain she felt but Kuaron's.

"Stop it!" she shouted. "Stop it! You're hurting him! Stop it!"

She ripped off the blindfold and spun around. Kuaron sat in a chair, his face contorted in pain. One of the soldiers was bending his arm behind him so severely that it looked in danger of breaking.

Dina flew to Kuaron just as the soldier released him. "Are you all right, Kuaron?"

"Yes," Kuaron said with a gasp. He stroked her hair briefly, and then looked up at his father.

Dina couldn't understand what he said to the elder Wakanrean except that it contained the words *haictor* and *klunar* and ended in the word *taal*.

Juzao didn't answer right away. He moved to his desk and sank into his chair as if he felt a need to sit down.

"Well, *Ayzanai?*" Kuaron said. "Are we free to go?"

Juzao looked up at him as if he were a great distance away. The elder Wakanrean shuddered suddenly, and then held up his hands in a gesture of helplessness. "A formal complaint was filed. There is a law."

"I've made no complaint," Kuaron said.

"If it comes to that," Dina said, "you've touched me several times tonight, Administrator. You didn't worry about that law when it got in your way."

Juzao stared at her, but Dina had the impression he didn't really see her. His gaze moved to his son's face. "Thank Paruian your mother isn't alive to see this."

Kuaron spoke sharply in Wakanrean, a dozen curtly uttered words of which one was *shahgunrahai*. Juzao reacted as if he had been struck in the face.

"Are we free to go?" Kuaron said. "If not, then charge us formally. It should make an interesting trial, no?"

Juzao looked shocked. "Trial?"

"Certainly," Kuaron said. "Even Terrans are entitled to a trial— if you recall the terms in the Articles of Confederation that our people signed when we joined the Third Confederation of Planets."

Juzao shook his head, not once emphatically in denial, but back and forth, as if he were trying to clear it. "There can be no trial."

"Then we're going," Kuaron said. "If you remember, you intruded on our *shahkuun*. You may thank my feelings for my mother that I don't bring charges against you for that."

Juzao lifted his chin and glared at his son, but when he answered in Wakanrean, it seemed to Dina that he was addressing the under-captain and not Kuaron.

Apparently, she was right, because the under-captain bowed to Kuaron and waited by the door.

Kuaron took Dina by the hand and led her from the room, without a word spoken or even a backward glance.

# *Chapter Four*

The under-captain escorted Kuaron and Dina back to the same transport, and again showed them to the same small, closed cabin.

Clutching her jacket against the cold, Dina sat down with relief. "Thank God! I thought for a moment your father was going to throw the book at me."

"What book?" Kuaron sat down beside her.

"It's just an expression. It means to punish someone as completely as is allowed."

"Oh."

"And anyway," Dina said, her indignation rising, "you deserve not to understand me. I hate not knowing what people are saying. What was all that about?"

"All what?"

"All of it. I don't recall every instance, but you kept using words I didn't understand, even when you weren't actually speaking Wakanrean. What's *huish- huishfa-* something?"

"*Huishfanai?*"

"Yeah, that."

"It's not a that, it's a they. *Huishfanai* means the maimed ones. That's what we call Wakanreans who start *shahgunrah* with Terrans."

"Oh. Well, why couldn't you say that instead of saying *huishfanai?*" Dina said in exasperation.

"Some things don't translate well." Kuaron didn't sound at all apologetic.

"Well you didn't translate at all," she said. "I thought you were going to be nice about it—you refused to argue in Wakanrean with your father—and then you deliberately switched to Wakanrean so I couldn't understand you."

Kuaron's smile was sympathetic, but he stopped short of apology. "It was a test to see how much you could tell with *haictor*. It was more convincing if it was obvious you didn't know what was going on."

"Okay. Then what was that little gibe at the end of it—the one where you mentioned *klunar*, and *haictor*, and then *taal*?"

"Oh, that," Kuaron said, his smile widening. "I just asked my father if he had a test for *taal* as well as the other two."

"And what about your answer to his crack about your mother not being alive?"

Kuaron's smile disappeared. "I told him you were my *shahgunrahai*, and if he couldn't treat you with respect, then he'd never see my face again."

Dina felt a pang of distress. Her very existence was causing a family feud. "Kuaron! I don't want to come between you and your father."

"Don't worry, *acubai*. He's stubborn, but he'll come around in the end."

"And what does *acubai* mean?" Dina said, giving in to her annoyance. "You keep calling me that."

Kuaron looked abashed. "It just means 'little one.' I won't call you that if you don't like it."

Surprised, Dina shook her head. She was taller than most of the men she met. No one had called her little in a long time. "No, it's okay. I just wanted to know."

Kuaron clasped her hand. "I'm sorry. I didn't learn Standard until I started school."

"You speak it very well. And anyway, let's get back to your father. Are you so sure he'll accept what's happened? He seemed very angry at me."

"He'll have to accept it. The nature of *shahgunrah* is you don't get to choose. Everyone knows that. We even have a saying for it. '*Taihona yai taihona.*' You get whoever you get. No matter what they hope for, everyone learns acceptance."

The arbitrariness of *shahgunrah* struck her like a thunderbolt. Kuaron had grown up knowing that if he found someone to spend his life with, their age, gender, and personality would be totally beyond his control. The realization that every single Wakanrean lived life under the same circumstance aroused her compassion. It was her first real insight into Wakanrean character. "And what do Wakanreans hope for when *shahgunrah* strikes?"

"I don't know that everyone hopes for the same thing," Kuaron said. "But certainly anyone who wants children hopes for someone of the opposite sex. Men hope for a woman young enough to have babies."

It was a dizzying thought. An entire species found this method of mating perfectly natural. "But if they don't get that—if they get someone of the same sex, or someone too old to have children—then it's just too bad and no one tries to change it?"

"They can't change it. No one can change it."

Not only arbitrary but absolute. "Well," Dina said, "I suppose I knew that intellectually, but it never sank in before. So basically, your father would have accepted anyone—any Wakanrean—as your *shahgunrahai*."

"Eventually, yes. But he would have been disappointed if it had been a man or an elderly woman. He wanted grandchildren very much."

Dina sniffed. "I'm not sure I'm willing to feel sorry for him. The man had you tortured just to test us."

"It wasn't torture. I agreed to it. I wanted to go home."

"It sure looked like torture to me," Dina said with a shiver.

Kuaron put his arm around her, and Dina leaned against him for comfort. After a few seconds, she was dismayed to realize she felt more than soothing support coming from him.

"Kuaron, not here!"

"I'm sorry, *acubai*."

Dina flushed as she felt her own passion rising, her breath coming faster in spite of her efforts to stay composed.

Kuaron wrapped her in an embrace and held her tightly. "Don't fight it! Don't fight it! You'll only make it take longer."

"But, Kuaron! Someone could come in—"

"No one will come in, not while we're in flight. It's all right. We have time."

Dina sighed and realized that he was right. Arguing was point-less, and would only delay the inevitable. She made no protest when he took off her jacket, then laid her on the floor and began to unfasten her trousers. Very soon after that she found herself unfastening his.

Only when they had finished was she moved to complain. "Damn!" she said, propping herself up on her elbows. "This is embarrassing."

Wordlessly, Kuaron handed her her underclothes. Dina sighed and put them on, grateful that the door had stayed closed the entire time. Just as she was straightening her shirt, the transport set down with a gentle thud.

"Whew!" Dina said, reaching for her jacket. "That was too close for comfort."

Kuaron looked puzzled but asked no questions, and a moment later the door opened.

THE remainder of that day, a restless energy consumed Dina. In an effort to take her mind off their confined status, Kuaron took her up to the summit, where a small garden occupied a fairly level space between the flyter park and the stone wall on the edge of the cliff.

Dina admired a bed of knee-high bushes whose amber leaves grew in fanciful spirals. Behind them a row of taller plants, some-thing between a bush and a tree, screened the flyter park from view. Two benches placed at right angles to each other offered a place to enjoy both the view and the delicate, flowery scent of the bushes. "It's lovely up here."

"I'm glad you like it. I'd like to have a real *zagathuan* someday, but I didn't want to put one up here, so far from the house itself.

"What's a *zagathuan?*"

"Well, I suppose you would say it's just a room that's outdoors. Wakanreans like fresh air."

Dina had to smile at this, even while she clutched her jacket around her and shivered from the cold. "Kuaron, you spend all day inside the house."

Kuaron immediately sat down wrapped one arm around her. "Yes, but the force field windows let in the fresh air. Are you cold?"

"A little," Dina said. "But I'm warmer now. Thanks." She snug-gled against him and studied the nearby cliffs, empty of signs of life except for vegetation and a distant small animal that clambered over the rocks of another crag.

"Why did you build your house way up here?" she asked. "Isn't it rather lonely?"

"Sometimes. But I wanted solitude."

"Trying to get away from eager fans?"

"Maybe a little. But also, I wanted to get away from *shahgunrah*."

Dina was surprised. "I thought you wanted *shahgunrah* to find you?"

"I did. In fact, I was so desperate I went to a *gaichufa*."

"What's a *gaichufa* and why is it so terrible to go to one?" Dina asked, snuggling closer in an effort to take every advantage of his body heat.

"Basically, it's a giant gathering of *toshugai*," he said, giving her an affectionate squeeze and rubbing her arm vigorously. "The meet-ings are held in huge chambers with proctors to keep order. The proctors lead everyone in a sort of dance that's choreographed so that everyone is close to everyone else for at least a minute or so."

"Sounds just a little like Saturday night at the Young People's Social Club back on Fantar," Dina said with a smile, "except we didn't have formal proctors."

"You need proctors at a *gaichufa*. With so many people who might be compatible in one place, there's always the danger that you'll go from being *toshugai* to being *shahgunrahai* with more than one person. That's a complicated existence, and not many people want to risk it."

"I can believe it," Dina said, breathing on her hands to warm them. "So, does this dance work?"

"For some people, it does. They arrive alone but go home with their *shahgunrahai*."

"So it's just like what happened to us?"

"Yes, of course. Except they're all hoping for it to happen. In fact, they have to fill out a form with the name of a contact to notify, and they must wear a badge so the proctors can tell who has found *shahgunrah* with whom."

Dina grinned. "That's even more like the Young People's Social Club. They're big on name tags."

"So you went to these social events on your world?" Kuaron asked, looking down at her with interest. "You wanted to meet someone?"

"Sure I did. But I wasn't really looking for someone to settle down with. I just wanted a nice guy to date every now and then." She gave him back the same appraising look he had given her. "Don't Wakanreans ever date?"

He grinned. "Not in the same sense that Terrans do. I have friends of both sexes and we occasionally go places together, but if you reach a certain age and you can be with them and not start *shahgunrah*, then you know they're not the one. I can remember being disappointed I didn't meet anyone in *qatraharai* school because I would have had a *shahgunrahai* who shared my passion for the *qatrahs*."

"Meeting someone is certainly more absolute for Wakanreans than for Terrans." The light breeze that had been blowing gusted to a real wind; Dina shivered again. Even with Kuaron holding her she was getting colder. "Did you go to another *gaichufa*?"

He shook his head. "It was too humiliating. And I couldn't bear the thought of further disappointment."

Dina glanced back out at the view of Wisuta. "Moving up here seems an extreme reaction to a bad first date—even if it was with a few hundred women."

"It was more than my disappointment from the *gaichufa* that drove me to build my house here. You see *shahgunrah* happen sometimes in Wisuta, in the street or in a shop. Once it happened at one of my concerts. It pained me to have to see other people find what I was seeking, so when I became successful enough, I built my house out here."

Dina let out a sigh. "Well, it finally found you—just where you least expected it."

"Yes, it did."

Dina pulled free of him and jumped to her feet. "Okay, I'm ready to go inside."

Kuaron smiled. "I'm sorry you're so cold," he said as they started for the lift tube. "Would you like to see the rest of the house?"

Dina couldn't resist walking faster. "Why not?" she said over her shoulder. "It looks like I'm going to be here for a while."

They went down the lift tube and through the entrance hall to start their tour with the study, which had a door from the main room and another to the interior corridor that ran the length of the house. The study was a small room, with a desk and a few chairs, and shelves filled with small objects in varying shapes.

"What are all those figurines and things, Kuaron?" Dina asked. "I saw some in the other room, too. Do you collect them or something?"

"In a way." Kuaron moved a carved animal shape to display it better. "It's rude for a private patron to pay a *qatraharai* openly, so they always hide the fee inside something that has intrinsic value, as if the money is just part of the gift. *Guidros* are objects made just for this purpose." He picked up a beautifully sculpted abstract shape that looked to Dina like an elongated teardrop made of cast gold. When Kuaron pressed a small notch on the side, the top half of the teardrop popped open to reveal a brightly enameled hollow interior. "See?"

"It's very pretty," Dina said, looking over the collection. "And you have so many. Do you keep all of them?"

Kuaron shook his head. "I did at first, but not anymore. Now I only keep the ones that are either beautiful or valuable—or those that have special meaning for me." He picked up a tiny carved wooden figure that looked like a miniature child's doll to Dina. "This was from my first private performance."

Dina held the wooden figure between her thumb and forefinger. "The detail is amazing, considering it's so small."

"Yes. You can look at them anytime you like. I go through them now and again, to winnow them out, so be sure to tell me if there are any you want to keep."

Dina didn't comment on this offer or its implication that she would be around long enough to become attached to his belongings. "What's next?" she said instead.

"The rehearsal room," Kuaron said, leading the way through the door to the corridor. "It's down this way."

"This house seems awfully big for one person," Dina said as they walked. "How many bedrooms are there?"

"Six."

"Six!" she repeated. "Why do you need six bedrooms?"

"When I built it, I still had hopes that one day I'd have a family of my own. And I have a large number of relations, as you'll discover once *shahkuun* is over. Wakanreans expect their relatives to house them when they visit in the area."

"What does that mean, I'll discover you have a large family once *shahkuun* is over?"

He exuded a mild anxiety. "I told you about the gift-giving. Friends and relations come to visit and bring a gift."

So she would be obliged to meet a horde of Wakanreans, all of whom could be as angry at her as his father had been. "Oh, that."

Kuaron opened a door. "Here's my rehearsal room. It's where I practice before a performance."

Dina looked around with interest. The large, utilitarian chamber had no windows and no skylights to provide natural light, no visual distractions at all, not even a picture on the wall. Except for two chairs and a table, a foam-like coating covered all the horizontal surfaces.

"Is that for the acoustics?" Dina asked, indicating the foam surfaces.

Kuaron nodded. "The sound in here is as perfectly balanced as our technology can make it."

Dina studied the far wall where several expensive-looking pieces of electronic equipment for recording and playback were built-in. "So, do you sell your recordings?"

Kuaron looked shocked, and Dina could sense he was genuinely horrified at the suggestion. "The *qatrahs* are never recorded."

"Well, then why do you need all this equipment?"

"I should have said they're never recorded except for study. I need to hear myself."

"Oh." Dina noted a small, bright, silver sphere hanging from the ceiling in one corner of the room, right at Kuaron's eye level. "What's that?"

"It's just to help me focus. I always meditate before I sing. In fact, there are times when singing is almost like meditating. I use a focus point to concentrate my energy."

"Interesting." She felt a little lost, never having had any exposure to a professional performer of any kind, let alone a musician.

"So," Kuaron said, and Dina could sense a contained apprehension, "do you think you'll stay with me?"

She looked up at him, a little surprised at the question. "Are you asking me to stay with you?"

"I didn't know I had to ask," he said in surprise.

"I suppose you don't. But you're saying it's voluntary? I mean, I'll be able to leave if I want to leave?"

"Eventually. After *shahkuun* peaks in a few days, and we feel *taal* begin to lessen its grip, we'll still feel a need to be together. It just won't be as strong or as constant."

"Peaks!" Dina said, horrified. "You mean it hasn't peaked yet? It's going to get worse?"

"You could say worse." She could feel his distress. "Or you could say it's going to get better."

"I don't mean to complain, Kuaron," she said, "but I'm already so sore I can barely sit down."

"I'm sorry."

"It's not your fault."

Kuaron smiled at this, and drew her close. "It's not likely to be anyone else's."

She enjoyed the feel of his fur against her cheek, and she let him nuzzle her for a few moments before she pushed him away.

"Let's go," she said. "I want to see all six bedrooms."

The first three bedrooms were comfortably but uniformly furnished. Dina suspected they had been decorated by a commercial service. After they saw the three guest bedrooms at one end of the corridor, they walked to the other end of the house and saw the two that were nearest Kuaron's bedroom.

"These rooms are a little larger," Dina said as they left the second one.

"I'd hoped to make them into children's rooms."

Dina was surprised. "They don't look at all childlike. The furniture is exactly the same as in the other rooms."

Kuaron radiated embarrassment. "Well, no. If I were to actually furnish them like children's rooms, it could bring bad luck."

It was, Dina realized, an admission that he was superstitious. "But it wasn't asking for trouble to go ahead and build such a big house?"

"No," he said, a trifle defensive. "I do have a lot of relatives."

She gave him a covert glance. "So you really wanted children?"

He lifted one hand in a casual gesture as he opened the door to the bathing room. "Most Wakanreans do."

She looked around the room, which like the study, was lit by skylights. "Now this room I've already seen." She pointed to the abstract mosaic. "I like that design. It's nice."

"It's an undersea scene," Kuaron said. "That gray-green iridescent shape is a large sea creature that acts as a host for all those
little red and orange things that eat the scum off of its skin."

Dina studied the mosaic more carefully. "I think I liked it better
when I didn't know what it was. So, is this all of the house?"

"Except for the game room. That's off the main room."

"Okay, let's go see it then. Maybe I'll find a game to keep me
busy?"

"We can look, at any rate," he said, opening the door to the corridor, "but I don't promise you'll like any of the games. I bought most
of them to keep my younger cousins entertained when they visit."

Dina was surprised when he walked the length of the main room
and, just past the dining table, opened what had looked like a floor-
to-ceiling mural. It was a door, she realized, well camouflaged and
quite sound proofed. When he turned on the first game, she understood why. It was electronic and very noisy.

After a brief demonstration, she decided Kuaron was right about
the games. The electronics were elaborate, but there was no real
point to the games themselves; completing one successfully accomplished nothing. They varied as to how much skill was required,
and some were educational—a sop, Kuaron admitted, for one of his
aunts who was a teacher and deplored time-wasting entertainment.

The only games that appealed to Dina at all were the old fashioned Wakanrean variety like the one that involved a small ball,
pebbles for counters, and a wide playing board marked with
squares.

"I'll show you how to play it if you like," Kuaron offered.

"Not now," Dina said, moving back to the main room. "I'll save it
for when I'm dying of boredom."

She looked out at the view that, like the summit, was spectacular, then turned back to study the main room. This, then, was
home—for a few weeks, at any rate. "Well, now that I know my way
around, I know what I want to do. I want to try out that pool!"

"The soaking pool?" Kuaron asked. "You want to soak?"

"Why not? It's not like we have plans to go out."

"But it's almost time for dinner."

"We can eat later."

"All right," Kuaron said, pleased. "I'll join you, then."

DINA was surprised to find that Wakanreans showered before they bathed. Kuaron insisted on taking a shower while the water in the pool heated to a comfortable temperature.

"This seems a little redundant," Dina said, stepping in beside him. "I mean, we're washing twice."

Kuaron looked surprised as he soaped his body fur vigorously. "Not really. We use the pool only to soak and relax. My mother used to soak for an hour every evening, when I was growing up. We had some of our best talks then."

Dina felt the shock deep in her Fantaran soul. "You mean you got in the water with her—naked?"

"Certainly. Why not?" Kuaron rinsed the lather off his face.

"I don't know," Dina said, trying to articulate why the idea seemed so questionable. "It's just not something Fantarans would do with a parent of the opposite sex—certainly not after puberty."

"My father never had the patience to soak for long. He'd come in for a bit, but he always wanted to be doing something else very soon."

"Doesn't it dry out your fur to soak for long periods of time?" Dina asked, soaping herself in turn.

"Oh, no." Kuaron stepped out of the shower. "We add a compound to the water that's good for our fur." He shook himself all over, then headed for the pool. "Come on. The water should be warm enough now."

Dina thought for a moment that he was going to jump in, but instead he merely sat on the edge and slid in feet first. He let himself sink under the surface and then pushed himself up enough that his head was out of the water. He shook his head back and forth, spraying water everywhere.

Dina turned off the shower and went into the pool more slowly. The water was comfortably warm and had a slippery feel to it. She moved her arms experimentally, and then leaned back so that she was resting on one of the ledge-like seats that lined the edges of the pool. The light from the skylights made the air look almost solid, the water was soothing, and beside her Kuaron gave off a wonderfully familiar musty scent.

"Ummm," she said, closing her eyes and feeling the warm water lap against her neck. It came almost to her chin. "I could get used to this."

Kuaron pulled her closer. "Do you think you could get used to me, Dina?"

She opened her eyes and looked at him. "I am getting used to you."

"You don't find me repulsive or alien?"

She stroked his wet chest fur with one hand. His scent was even more noticeable when he was wet. He had finally removed the silver *heicha*.

"I don't find you repulsive in the least, Kuaron."

"Because of *shahgunrah*?"

"I suppose so," she said slowly. "It's difficult to sort out what I feel from what *shahgunrah* imposes on me." She looked up at him. His eyes looked solemn, almost worried. "What about you?" she asked. "Do you find me repulsive or alien?"

"No. It surprised me, in a way. When I knew I was starting *shahgunrah* with you, I was angry at you because I thought it wasn't reciprocated. But even then, I remember thinking that you were the most beautiful Terran I had ever seen."

Dina was touched. "Thank you, Kuaron. I know that was probably *shahgunrah* at work, but still that's very sweet of you to say that—especially because Wakanrean women have a different body shape from Terran women. I know if Wakanrean women look flat-chested to us Terrans, then I must look pretty strange to you."

"That part of you doesn't look that alien," Kuaron said. "Wakanrean women's breasts become more noticeable when they're pregnant or nursing."

Dina was amused. "So we all look like new mothers to you? I've heard it said that's why humans—Terrans—evolved as we did. A Terran female who looked fertile was more likely to attract a mate."

"We used other criteria."

"I'll say," Dina said with feeling. "You must have a really keen sense of smell to be able to smell the difference between Terrans and Wakanreans from a distance. To me, neither one has any smell at all unless I'm really close, or the Terran is very sweaty."

"Wakanreans don't sweat in the same way," Kuaron said, "and we do have a good sense of smell."

"And you are very sweet," Dina said, returning to her earlier comment.

He smiled, but shook his head. "You were afraid of me. I could tell that. I must have frightened you considerably."

"Only because you were so angry at first. Of course I was scared. And I didn't know what was going on."

"We still don't know why it happened."

"I realize that. It's worrying."

"But you're not afraid of me anymore?"

"Of course not. I know you now."

He sat down on the ledge beside her, then picked her up and held her on his lap for a while, almost as if she were a small child. Dina leaned back against his chest, closed her eyes, and enjoyed the feeling of security she felt with his arms around her. After a while, Kuaron stood up, still holding her.

He nuzzled her neck, and then sighed. "I'm sorry, *acubai*."

Dina clutched him, knowing very well what was coming. Kuaron laid her down on the crimson floor tiles and then pulled himself out of the pool beside her.

Dina let out a small sound of distress, almost a whimper.

Kuaron stroked her shoulder. "I'll be as gentle as I can be."

"I know. It's not your fault."

He was gentle, but Dina still pulled away as soon as it was over. "Ach!" she said. "How much longer will this go on?"

"It's only the third day. In a day or two, *taal* will peak. From then on, we'll notice our desire begin to wane. In five or six days, we'll be able to control ourselves again."

"Five or six more days!" Dina tried to imagine it and couldn't. "I don't know if I can last that long, Kuaron."

"It won't be that bad."

She sighed, aware of his distress. "I'm sure it's wonderful for a Wakanrean." She laid her arm on his torso. "And I do enjoy it—you know quite well I do. It's just that humans—Terrans—aren't built for this kind of marathon orgy—at least I'm not."

She could feel his concern for her like a warm glow under her hand. "Should I call a doctor for you?"

Dina shook her head emphatically. "No, thanks. There's no way I could go to see a doctor now."

"Of course not," Kuaron said in surprise. "The doctor would come here."

Dina broke out in a laugh. "Who ever heard of doctors visiting sick people? Maybe on Wakanreo they do, but Terran doctors expect you to go to them."

"That's ridiculous."

"On reflection, you might be right." Dina lay down on the floor on her stomach and rested her chin on her hands. "In any event, there's no way I'd see a doctor for this, anyway. The story might get out, and I'd never live it down."

"Live what down? What do you mean?"

"I mean I'd be mortified if people found out I needed a doctor because I spent days doing nothing but make love over and over."

"Why should that be embarrassing?" Kuaron asked, lying down on his side next to her.

"It just would," Dina said, pushing herself up from the tiles. "Take my word for it."

"But, Dina—" Kuaron said, scrambling to his feet.

"No, Kuaron. My mind is made up. Let's go fix dinner and stop talking about this."

Dina continued to maintain this attitude for the next two days, even when *taal* peaked so strongly that they made love five times in one afternoon. They didn't even bother to get out of bed that day, spending all their time curled up together trying to rest and talk between fits of overwhelming passion.

"Why are you unhappy?" Kuaron asked as Dina stared out the window.

"I'm not unhappy."

Kuaron made a tisking noise with his tongue. "Don't be so foolish, *acubai*. You know I can tell when you lie."

"Oh, all right! I guess I am a little unhappy."

"Why?"

Dina pondered before she answered him, trying to put her feeling into words. "I suppose I feel a sense of loss," she said finally. "I had my life all planned out, you see, and now it's all gone. I was going to meet a nice man—a nice Terran man—get married again, and have children this time. We were going to—"

"Get married *again*?"

Dina could feel his rising sense of unease, and knew he would feel her own guilt for not having told him her history sooner. "Yes. I guess I never told you I was married for a while."

"When was this?"

"It was before I got my advanced degree. His name is Lior Bergman, and I met him at the university on Croyzan. We fell in love and decided to get married." She debated whether she should explain that being married had sheltered her from requests for casual sex but concluded that he wouldn't understand why she had felt a need for such shelter.

"So you have a husband?" Kuaron asked, clearly more concerned with the present than the past.

Dina could tell he was troubled; she could feel it almost as palpably as the heat from his body. She patted his arm and snuggled up against him in the bed. "No, not anymore. It's all right, Kuaron. We didn't stay married long. We didn't renew the contract when it came up."

"Contract?"

She nodded. "On most Terran worlds, when two people get married, they specify a term limit for the contract—usually one or two years to start with—and then when that's reached, they both have to renew it or they're not married anymore."

Kuaron made a nose of disgust. "It sounds more like a lease than an intimate relationship between two people."

He had a point. "I suppose it does. In any event, when my fellowship was up, Lior and I decided not to let the relationship drag out any further. We just let the contract expire."

"How could you do that? How could you make an agreement to be together knowing it might not last forever?"

"But for us, that's what makes it easy. It's when you think it's forever that it's really difficult."

"It all sounds ephemeral and capricious," Kuaron said, his tone disapproving.

"Maybe it was, but at least it was my choice."

Kuaron's pupils were tiny dots in the bright afternoon sunlight, making his eyes jewel-like again. Somehow this made his expression difficult to fathom. He almost managed to look inscrutable, even though she could easily sense his displeasure.

"Is choice so important to you?" he said.

"Yes," Dina said at once. "At least it was," she added. "Quite frankly, Kuaron, I'm so confused these days, I don't know anymore."

Kuaron wrapped her in a snug embrace. "You know that I care about you, and want you to be happy?"

"Yes."

"And you know I'd never harm you?"

"Yes."

"But that's not enough?"

"I don't know!"

Kuaron sighed and rocked her slightly in his arms. "Go to sleep now, *acubai. Taal* is only sleeping, and you need your strength."

Dina let her head drop on his shoulder, and after a while she drifted into sleep.

BY the ninth day, Dina had become so accustomed to Kuaron's presence that she felt as if he were truly half of her. She always had a sense of where he was, anywhere in the house, and she found that it was useless to go to bed before he did, because she couldn't sleep unless he was beside her.

At the same time, *taal* lessened enough so that they didn't make love during the day at all, and only once each night. Dina was still sore, but she found it much more bearable. Kuaron still urged her to call a doctor, and she still declined.

On the tenth day, Kuaron came out of the corridor and sat down next to Dina as she sat reading in the main room.

"Did you want something, Kuaron?"

He blinked as the light hit his eyes. "It can wait if you're busy."

She put down her book reader. "I don't mind stopping." She could feel his anxiety. "What's wrong?"

"Nothing is wrong, but this is the last day of our *shahkuun*, Dina, and we need to talk,"

She sat up straighter. "Are you sure it's the last day?"

He made a chopping gesture with one hand. "Yes, I'm sure it's ending. It's time for you to decide. Do we go ahead and host a gift-giving, or will you go back to the off-world quarter and live without me?"

It was almost like a marriage proposal, except that it came at the end of the honeymoon. Even though it was a question and not a demand, Dina felt pressured. "Is it that permanent? I mean, if we have the gift-giving, is it legally binding?"

Kuaron took her hand. "*Shahgunrah* isn't a legal thing, *acubai.* There are no vows, no contracts, no legal ties at all. No one enforces it or validates it. It's simply a bond between two people. If you choose to leave me, nothing will stop you but *shahgunrah* itself."

She stared at him and thought about her apartment in the off-world quarter. She imagined going back, fixing meals alone, eating alone, sleeping by herself in her bed. The thought left her cold and empty. And after all, it wasn't as if she had to stay forever.

"No," she said. "I mean, no, I won't leave. I'll stay—for now at least."

His face broke into a broad smile. Dina could easily sense his elation at her answer. "We need to order food, then. We'll put the knocker back on the door tonight, and our company will come tomorrow afternoon."

"Kuaron," Dina said, "are you sure anyone will come?"

"No," he said. "But we have to be ready if they do."

"Can I invite Arliana?"

"You don't invite people." He patted her hand. "If someone is a relative or a friend, then they come."

"Arliana might not know that. I want to call her,"

Kuaron nodded. "All right. Tell her to come any time in the afternoon. It's bad manners for anyone but close family to stay more than an hour, if you can let her know that without being rude."

"I'll try." Dina reached up to touch his cheek, and then kissed him right where she had touched.

Kuaron took her hand and held it under his chin, rubbing it against the edge of his jawbone as if he found the sensation pleasant. Dina slipped her hand free and stroked his fur. She remembered studying him from the back at the embassy, and she decided that no one could ever mistake a Wakanrean for a Terran from the front.

Kuaron's face was distinctly triangular—wide cheekbones, and a narrow, prominent chin. A fine, downy fur covered his face, the same pale gold color as his body fur, in contrast with the longer, creamy white hair of his headcrest.

"You're very sweet, Kuaron," she said.

"You've said that before. Is that a good thing?"

"Yes."

She could feel a sudden rush of passion from him, and she was surprised when he suddenly stood up and started for the door.

"Where are you going?" she asked.

"I'm going to soak in cold water."

"But why?"

"Because you still hurt. And we can control ourselves now."

Dina was grateful but conflicted as she stared at his back as he went through the door to the corridor. She knew him pretty well now, but she still didn't know whether she should be sorry she had gone to the party at the embassy or glad.

# *Chapter Five*

Kuaron placed the knocker back on its hook by the front door that evening.

"So what happens now?" Dina asked when he came back inside.

"Now I take the warn-off code off the com, and we listen to our messages."

Most of the messages were for Kuaron, including an invitation to sing at a concert in ten days time. There were two messages for Dina, one at her own code from Arliana, and one on Kuaron's code from her supervisor at Quafray.

"How did Quafray ever know I was here?" Dina said in surprise.

"My father must have told them. It came in on my personal line, and that's not listed anywhere."

The message was from Dina's supervisor and had been sent a few days before. It said simply that she could take as much time as she needed to be away from work.

"Wow," Dina said, surprised. "That's a relief. I still have a job."

Arliana's message was a request for Dina to call her, which she did, inviting her friend to visit the next day for the gift giving. Arliana seemed quite curious, but she didn't press Dina to confide in her.

Dina was happy Arliana hadn't asked her how she felt about what had happened, as she was still unsure herself. She put that thought out of her mind the next morning as she busied herself with the preparations.

Kuaron turned the cleaning servoid loose on the house with orders to clean everything, and it promptly began moving through the main room, its wheeled base sucking up dust and dirt from the floor and carpets while its three extensible arms dusted and polished furniture. Kuaron and Dina laid out the food the caterers had delivered, turned the security system off completely, and sat back to await their guests.

Dina was a little nervous, and she was happy when their first visitor turned out to be a lone Wakanrean, a shy young man whom Kuaron introduced as his father's sister's son. The cousin bowed to Dina with visible apprehension and presented her with a small statuette, unwrapped, made of dark blue stone cleverly carved to resemble a *chundin*, a Wakanrean predator that reminded Dina of a much larger version of the cats she had seen on Terran starships.

Dina thanked him suitably and pressed him to partake of food and drink. He moved away from her gratefully, as if he found it stressful to be near her, and wandered over to the table where the food was laid out.

Dina had no time to ponder his reaction, as their next visitors, a family of four, were arriving. Kuaron introduced his aunt, her *shahgunrahai*, and their two children to Dina.

As soon as these callers were suitably greeted, their gift accepted and food proffered, more people arrived. Very soon Dina decided that Kuaron hadn't exaggerated; he did indeed have a host of relations. Most of them treated her with politeness tinged with a faint distaste, as if they would prefer to be elsewhere. Dina wore her gloves the whole time, trying not to offend anyone by appearing to scoff at Wakanrean law, even though, she realized there was a profound irony in observing the law only for the moment.

After half an hour, Kuaron introduced her to a tall woman in a brightly painted robe. She was, he said, another cousin, his father's eldest brother's daughter. She was accompanied by her *shahgunrahai*, a severely dressed man who looked to Dina's inexperienced eye to be several years older than his mate.

Kuaron accepted their proffered gift of a set of ten ornately carved spoons, and took them off to the table where he had placed the other gifts.

Left momentarily with his relations, Dina bowed and offered her gloved hands, but the cousin disdained them in favor of a brief hug.

"We're family now, after all," she said cheerfully as she released a very startled Dina. "I hope you'll call me Oiganna." She flicked a hand in a careless gesture at her *shahgunrahai*. "And this is Heingeon."

No word of censure was uttered, but Dina got a strong impression of disapproval from the older Wakanrean. She saw an answering spasm of irritation cross Oiganna's face and knew that the woman must have felt her *shahgunrahai's* disapproval.

"It's good to meet Kuaron's *shahgunrahai* at last," Heingeon said, bowing.

Unsure of whether his censure was directed at herself or Oiganna, Dina bowed back, but didn't offer her hands. "Won't you have something to eat and drink?" she said, waving a gloved hand at the laden table.

"Not just now, thank you," Heingeon said.

"I'd love some wine," Oiganna said, smiling at Dina. "And it *is* a pleasure to meet you. We were so afraid Kuaron would be *toshugai* forever."

"Thank you," Dina said, a little unsure of what else it would be proper to say.

Kuaron relieved her of the need. He came up beside her, handed his cousin a glass of wine, and nodded at her *shahgunrahai*. "My Aunt Liegi is here, Heingeon, if you want someone to talk about the economic situation with you."

Heingeon brightened visibly, made a brief excuse, and moved away at once.

"You shouldn't encourage him, Kuaron," Oiganna said. "He's dull enough as he is."

"I would call him conservative rather than dull," Kuaron said.

Oiganna made a disapproving noise with her tongue, and drained her wine glass in a long swallow. "You're too kind. Just look at him!"

In a dramatic gesture, she pointed with her chin at where her *shahgunrahai* stood with three of Kuaron's other relations. Dina had to agree that both the dark color of his suit and its plain lines, unbroken by ornamentation of any kind, made Heingeon look stern.

"He doesn't like to call attention to himself," Kuaron said. "Many people don't."

"Ah, but I'm not one of them." Oiganna lifted her arms so that her long, full sleeves flapped like wings and displayed the swirling lines of bright blues, purples, and reds that decorated her robe.

"That's a beautiful outfit," Dina said. "I love the colors."

"Thank you," Oiganna said, looking pleased. "Did you tell her, Kuaron?"

"No," Kuaron said, and Dina could sense his amusement. "It was a genuine compliment, Oiganna."

"What?" Dina asked, perplexed.

"Oiganna is a clothes painter," Kuaron explained. "She always wears her own creations as a form of advertising."

"Oh." Dina looked at the robe with new respect. Something about it was vaguely familiar. "Did you make Kuaron's *xuschi*, too?"

"I painted it, yes," Oiganna corrected. "Kuaron wouldn't let me paint anything for him that he wears in public."

"I like your designs," Kuaron said. "I just don't feel comfortable being the brightest thing in the room."

Oiganna didn't seem upset with this excuse. Indeed, she smiled complacently. "My creations *are* very bright. I like color."

"Do you always do abstract designs?" Dina asked.

"Mostly," Oiganna said. "Generally, I deal in color and form as it relates to the body, without regard to representational art. But occasionally I throw in an animal or plant design just for fun." She waggled one finger at Kuaron. "And I want you to know it wasn't my idea to give you spoons! Spoons! The very idea!"

"It's a traditional gift," Kuaron said soothingly.

"Bah! Tradition!" Oiganna waved her arms dramatically.

"Well, you can never have too many spoons," Dina said. "And they're very pretty."

Oiganna looked mollified. "I picked them out. Heingeon wanted plain ones."

Before Kuaron could answer, another group of people walked in the door.

"Will you excuse us, Oiganna?" he said.

She waved her empty wineglass in an airy gesture. "Of course."

Dina watched over her shoulder as Kuaron led her over to the next set of relations. Oiganna didn't join her *shahgunrahai*, but instead poured herself more wine and started a conversation with the shy young cousin who had brought the statuette.

"What an interesting couple," Dina murmured to Kuaron.

"Yes," he said, and Dina could sense some underlying anxiety. "Let's hope they don't make a scene."

Dina turned back to face their new guests and paid no more attention to the clothes painter or her stern *shahgunrahai*. When the main room filled up, people spilled out into the kitchen, the game room, and even Kuaron's study.

Arliana came midway through the afternoon, shortly after Oiganna and Heingeon left. The Terran woman looked very conspicuous among so many tall Wakanreans, and Dina went to her at once, as soon as she saw her friend walk in the open doorway.

"Arliana! Thanks for coming!"

"Oh, hello, Dina," Arliana said, relief evident in her voice. "You look much better."

"Thank you. Come and have something to eat."

"I'm not hungry, thanks," Arliana said. "But I brought you this." She handed Dina a small package wrapped in lacy white Wakanrean writing paper.

"Thank you so much," Dina said, taking the gift and concluding that whoever had taught her friend about Wisutan customs had neglected to tell her they considered it wasteful to wrap gifts—something she herself had just learned. "Will you have something to drink, at least?"

Arliana accepted a glass of wine. She sipped it cautiously, and looked around the room at all of Kuaron's friends and relations. "So, it's true you've bonded with this Wakanrean guy?"

"Yes, it's true."

Arliana shook her head in frank amazement. "How?"

Dina smiled; she could identify with her friend's bewilderment. "I don't know. It just happened."

"Wow!" Arliana said, awe evident in her tone. "You should have seen the fuss when you left the party with him, Dina. I mean some of those Wakanreans were steaming mad! And I thought the Ambassador was going to rip someone's head off, she was so angry. For a while I was afraid it would be me."

"No one stopped us from leaving," Dina said.

"No one quite believed it at first," Arliana retorted. "It got really quiet in the room after you went out. And then the whispering started. So many people were whispering, it was like a sort of muffled roar in the room. It took me a few minutes to sort out what had happened, what everyone was whispering about, and then I couldn't believe they were talking about *you*. I mean, I thought you were still with Erik. First he came and told me you'd gone home by yourself, and then the diplomatic staff all descended on me and demanded to know who you were."

"I'm glad I didn't know that at the time. And I'm sorry if they bothered you."

"Well, the embassy staff weren't too bad—it was the Wakanrean police the next day. They were sure it was some kind of plot—a put-up job in some way. I told them over and over that you would never do that, but they didn't seem to want to believe me."

"No, I suppose not."

"Anyway, things seem calmer now. It's funny there was never anything in the news bulletins, though. I thought for sure there would be."

"Kuaron says they won't mention it because he's a *parundai*."

Arliana didn't look as if she saw this as a reasonable excuse, but she didn't argue. Instead, she sipped her wine and studied the crowd. A moment later, a tall shape loomed up behind them.

Dina knew it was Kuaron before she turned. She smiled up at him and introduced him to Arliana, who looked slightly cowed in Kuaron's presence.

"Hello," Arliana said. "Nice to meet you. I've heard a lot about you, of course. I'm sorry we never got to hear you sing at the party."

"Do you like the *qatrahs*?" Kuaron asked.

Arliana's expression was noncommittal. "They're very interesting."

Kuaron's answering smile didn't seem forced or artificial. "That's what most Terrans say when they hear a *qatrah* for the first time."

"Most Terrans have no ear for real music," a voice said.

Dina turned to find a Terran man almost at her elbow. He was about her own height, or just slightly shorter, with dark brown hair and blue eyes that twinkled from under straight brows. His skin was a shade darker than her own, and he wore a blue uniform with brown trim and the emblem of the Third Confederation of Planets on his sleeve. Even without the uniform, Dina would have known him at once.

"Jared Harlingen!" she blurted out. "What are you doing here?"

"Congratulating Kuaron," Jared said with a bow in Kuaron's direction. "And wishing you both the best of luck."

"Jared!" Kuaron said, returning the bow. "I didn't think you'd make it. Do you know Dina?"

"I didn't think I'd make it either, but here I am," the Terran said. "And I met Dina at her arrival orientation, which I helped to present."

For some reason, Dina found herself fighting a blush. She recovered enough to introduce Arliana. Jared offered his hand to both women, and Dina noted that Arliana gave Jared a warm glance and seemed almost reluctant to release his hand after she shook it.

"Nice to meet you," Jared said. "Sorry I had to come in uniform, Kuaron. I was afraid I'd be too late if I went home to change."

"We don't mind," Dina said. "We're glad you came."

"We sure are," Arliana said. "We Terrans are in pretty short supply around here."

Dina was annoyed at this remark, as the people with whom Arliana seemed so uncomfortable were mostly Kuaron's family, but she said nothing. Kuaron caught her eye and gave her an affectionate glance. Dina could feel his sympathy.

"Why don't you show Arliana the view from the windows, Jared?" Kuaron suggested. "I'll bet she's never seen Wisuta from this high up."

"I'd be happy to," Jared said promptly. "Shall we go, Citizen Cheng?"

The two of them went off, and Dina leaned closer to Kuaron. "I'm sorry. Arliana never had a grain of tact in her life."

"I don't mind," Kuaron said. "If it weren't for her, I might never have found you."

Dina felt herself flush with delight at this compliment. Kuaron put his hand on her arm as if he wanted to feel her pleasure more strongly.

"And anyway," Kuaron went on, "Jared will keep her occupied. He's quite successful at attracting Terran women."

Dina looked up in surprise. "How do you know that?"

"We talk about it sometimes. I was curious about how Terrans mate."

"And he told you?"

Kuaron stroked her arm. "Why are you so disapproving? Is this related to how Terrans feel shame about sex?"

How odd that even after the last few weeks, she was still a Fantaran at heart. "I suppose so. Certainly it's considered tacky to reveal intimate details about what one does with one's bedmates."

"Oh, we never talked about that. I wanted to know what makes Terrans attractive to one another."

"And what did he say?"

"He said Terran women care more about whether a man is interesting than whether he's handsome. They want him to respect them, but they also want him to stand up for himself."

"Hmmm."

"What does that mean?" Kuaron asked. "Was Jared right or wrong?"

"I suppose," Dina said meditatively, "that he's right about some women. But I think to some extent that's what many Terran men like to think Terran women want. They like to think women are less shallow than men because it lets them off the hook as far as their own looks. Did your knowledgeable friend comment on what Terran men want from women?"

"He said, in general, Terran men are swayed most by appearance. He said a truly beautiful woman can almost choose her mate at will."

Dina laughed at this. "Well, at least he's honest about that."

"It seems strange to me. I didn't believe him when he said it. What do looks matter in the long run?"

"Probably not that much."

"*Shahgunrah* is a better way."

"Come along," Dina said, linking her arm through his without even thinking about it. "We have other guests to worry about."

Arliana and Jared left together half an hour later. Before they went out the door, Dina managed to get Arliana alone for a few seconds and asked for the name of her doctor. Arliana gave her a peculiar look, but she divulged the name readily enough, and even offered to call for an appointment for Dina.

"Thanks, anyway," Dina said, "but I think I'd rather do it myself."

Arliana made no comment, and Dina saw her to the door.

The crowd thinned considerably after that. There were only about a dozen people in the main room when Dina looked up and saw someone she recognized standing in the doorway.

She went to Kuaron immediately and touched his sleeve. He was speaking to one of his many cousins, but he turned at her approach, and followed her glance. As soon as he saw who stood waiting, he walked across the room with his hands held out in a gesture of greeting.

"Welcome, *Ayzanai*," he said, touching hands with his father and then bowing.

Juzao Sadoc had put down two parcels to return his son's greeting. He picked them up now, and his eyes scanned the room as if he were looking for someone.

"Dina," Kuaron said. "Come and greet my father."

Dina stepped up beside him, and Juzao bowed to her. From the tall, narrow bundle, he pulled a crystal decanter filled with amber wine, which he then presented to her with some ceremony.

Kuaron seemed inordinately pleased at this gift. He took it from Dina and placed it on a table against the wall. "Thank you, *Ayzanai*."

"That was for tradition," Juzao said, handing Kuaron the second parcel. "This is from your mother. She wanted you to have it on this occasion. I'm only sorry she's not here to give it to you herself."

Dina could tell that Kuaron was moved by this sentiment. She could feel the warmth of his love for his father as well as his sense of loss, presumably from thinking about his mother.

Kuaron pulled the cloth wrappings loose from the bundle he held and revealed a *quascha* kettle. It looked very old; a mosaic of tiny pieces of tile that decorated the handle was missing a few tiles, and the bottom looked as if it had been scorched on a real fire.

"It's been in the family a long time," Juzao said.

"Yes," Kuaron said. "Thank you."

His father sighed and turned as if he meant to leave.

"Wait!" Kuaron said. "Can't you stay for a while, *Ayzanai*?"

Juzao looked happy at the invitation. He turned back to Kuaron, smiling, and accepted an offer of food and drink. Dina watched him as he talked to several of Kuaron's many cousins. He seemed a different man from the Wakanrean who had been so angry when he had first met her, and then so utterly defeated when his son had forced him to accept what had happened. At ease in the midst of family, Juzao smiled and laughed as he ate and drank.

Dina stepped next to Kuaron and then pulled him a little ways apart from the others.

"Is something wrong?" Kuaron asked.

"No," she said. "I just wondered—you seemed happy to see your father. I didn't know if you would be when I saw him standing there."

"I know," Kuaron said. "I had wondered if he'd come today. But my aunt told me my father called everyone and virtually ordered them to come. If anyone tried to *schubao* out of it, he bullied them until they changed their minds."

"*Schubao*?"

"Oh, sorry." He made a wriggling gesture with one hand. "A *schubao* is a small animal that lives in the roots of trees. It can fit into the tiniest crevice because its bones aren't all connected, so it can squash itself into whatever shape is needed. To *schubao* is to wriggle away from something—either physical danger or just a commitment to do something."

"So, since your father went to the trouble of making sure we had a real gift-giving, you forgave him for dragging us out during *shahkuun*?"

"I suppose I did," Kuaron said, sounding a little surprised. "I realized it when I saw him looking so tentative. That's not his usual style at all."

"I know. I remember."

Kuaron looked down at her, and Dina felt a twinge of concern from him.

"You're not still angry at him, are you, *acubai*?"

"*I* was never angry at him—except when he had his soldiers literally twist your arm."

Kuaron chuckled. "That was more typical of my father—do whatever it takes to get the job done."

Dina glanced around the room. "He did a good job this time. No one really wanted to come, but they all did."

There was a sudden stab of regret from Kuaron.

"What's wrong?" Dina asked.

"Nothing."

Dina tisked her disapproval. "Don't be silly. I know something made you sad. What was it?"

Kuaron was silent a moment, and then he looked around the room as he spoke. "My father has a lot of influence with my family, but neither his position nor the force of his will can convince everyone that our *shahgunrah* is real—or that it's a good thing."

"What does that mean?" And then the answer came to her. "Oh! There was someone else you wanted to come, and they didn't!"

"Yes. My friend Triascou. My father called her, but she refused to come."

"Because she doesn't think it's *shahgunrah,* or because she doesn't think it's a good thing?"

There was an even longer pause before Kuaron answered. "Triascou doesn't like Terrans," he said at last. "Jared loves the *qatrahs,* but when I took him to one of her concerts, she was rude to him."

"So she's a bigot?"

Kuaron seemed unwilling to agree. "Her uncle is one of the original *huishfanai*. His whole family feels that the man was wronged by the Terrans. There are those who agree with them."

"I see."

Kuaron frowned. "Don't be so disapproving. Have you told your mother about what happened between us?"

"No," Dina said. "I'm still trying to find a way to tell her in a way that she'd understand."

"Perhaps there isn't one. My father is trying, but it's hard for him, too."

Whatever reply Dina was going to make, she forgot it as more of Kuaron's relations came up to say goodbye. They all began to drift out in twos and threes, and in a little while only Juzao remained.

He prepared to take his leave also, embracing Kuaron heartily in a bear hug that Dina had learned was a customary farewell among close kin. He surprised her by embracing her, too. The hug was so brief as to be transitory, and so indefinite that she wasn't sure he actually made contact, but still it was a gesture of reconciliation.

Dina smiled up at him. "Thank you for coming."

Juzao disclaimed, slapped Kuaron on the back and went through the doorway without looking back. When the door shut behind him, Dina and Kuaron were alone.

Dina sighed. "So that's it for visitors? I mean, no one will come tomorrow or the next day, will they?"

"Not in droves, certainly," Kuaron said, taking her hand and leading her back to the main room where they both sank onto a sofa. "If a relative wanted to come today but couldn't, they might stop by in the next week or so to bring a gift, but not without calling first."

"Thank God!" Dina said, leaning against him.

Kuaron put an arm around her and held her tightly. He bent his head down to nuzzle her neck, and Dina felt a warm glow of contentment from him.

"I'm very happy I found you, Dina," he said, his voice muffled by her hair. "I hope you decide to stay with me always."

Dina clung to him and let out a small sigh of surprise. "Do you know what, Kuaron? I hope I do, too."

# *Chapter Six*

The next day, Dina felt a little adrift. *Shahkuun* was over, but because she was reluctant to go into the city by herself, she still felt restless and confined.

Kuaron gave her an anxious look as she sat down to breakfast. "What's wrong, *acubai*?"

"Nothing," Dina said. "Nothing specific, anyway. I just don't know what to do with myself. I don't quite feel up to starting back to work—"

"It's too soon," Kuaron interrupted. "You should wait another day or two."

"I don't mind putting off work, but I'm going a little crazy shut up here with just you and me."

"Well, if it helps, we're due for company—small scale company. Jared is coming in less than an hour. He called while you were in the shower."

Dina was surprised. "Why? I thought you said yesterday was it as far as uninvited guests?"

"It usually is, except for family, of course. Jared said he had something he needed to talk to us about. That's why he called so early—to be sure we were both still here."

His casual acceptance of an early morning visit struck Dina as odd. But then, his friendship with Jared was odd.

Kuaron smiled. "What's so fascinating?"

"You are—you and Jared both. I haven't been here long, of course, but it seems to me that not that many Wakanreans have friends from among the off-world population—certainly not among the

85

resident Terrans—and not that many Terrans bother to cultivate any Wakanrean acquaintances."

"I suppose that's true," Kuaron said. "It's true Jared is my only Terran friend. I don't think he has many Wakanrean friends—not friends in the sense that he spends time with them when he's not working."

"How did you meet him?" she asked, sipping her *quascha*.

Kuaron smiled reminiscently. "He came up to talk to me after a performance I gave. I'd never met a Terran who liked the *qatrahs* before. At first I thought he was just making up to me for some other reason—maybe to meet my father. You Terrans seem a lot more impressed with *Ayzanai's* position than most Wakanreans. But Jared was so enthusiastic about the *qatrahs*, it was impossible to dismiss him as a mere *nyesh*. He'd only recently started studying the *qatrahs*, so he didn't know much, but he made up for it with enthusiasm."

"So, do you talk mostly about the *qatrahs*?" Dina said, deciding to wait until later to ask what a *nyesh* was.

"We did at first. Later I would ask Jared questions about Terrans, and sometimes he would ask me questions about my people."

"You mean about *shahgunrah*?"

"Not generally, no," Kuaron said, with a wry smile. "Not so much because it's a personal topic, but because I had never experienced it."

"Oh."

"Why is this so interesting to you? Didn't you ever have friends who weren't Terran?"

"Not really," Dina confessed. "I didn't know any growing up— remember Fantar's insular to the point of being backward—and when I went to graduate school, I was rather shy—not because there were non-Terrans in my classes, but because Croyzan is a much more advanced world. I felt like a hick."

"Pardon?"

"An unsophisticated person from a rural setting," Dina explained the idiom.

"Ah! We would say a *weichard*."

"What's a *weichard*?"

"A rather slow-witted animal that lives in vast herds on the plains. If you take one away from the rest of the herd, it wanders in circles, hopelessly bemused."

"Most of your idiomatic expressions seem to come from animals."

"Don't Terran analogies also use animals? I know I've heard Jared use many of them. He once described a Terran trader as being as slippery as an eel."

"What's an eel?" Dina asked, mystified.

"I believe he said it's a marine animal with a long, sinuous body and no limbs."

"Oh," Dina said. "Jared must be a native Terran, then. I knew a few in graduate school and they used to refer to Terran animals like that, as if we should all know what they meant. I generally know only about the Terran animals we had on Fantar—cats, dogs, horses, and the like."

"Jared is a native Terran. He told me so. He lived on Terra until he enlisted in ThreeCon."

"So what does he want to talk to us about today?" Dina asked, turning the conversation back to where it had started.

Kuaron shook his head. "He wouldn't say over the com. We'll have to wait and ask him when he comes."

Dina had to be satisfied with that answer. A short time later, she and Kuaron were both watching the news bulletins when an alarm sounded.

"What's that?" she asked, confused because it didn't sound like the summit alarm.

"It's the landing port door opening," Kuaron explained, switching off the set. "Jared asked if he could use it, so I gave him the code to open the port doors."

He went to the front door and opened it, and in a matter of seconds, Jared Harlingen walked through the doorway.

"Hello, midget," Kuaron said with a slight bow.

Jared bowed back. "Hello, furball. Thanks for letting me use the landing port. I'm pretty sure the roof port on the summit is under observation."

"Whatever for?" Kuaron asked, closing the door.

"That's what we need to talk about," Jared said, following him back to the main room. "You two have really put a cat among the pigeons."

"A what?" Kuaron asked.

"A *chundin* in a herd of *juija*," Jared translated.

Kuaron looked enlightened, but Dina was annoyed, as the Wakanrean idiom was as meaningless to her as the Terran one.

"What does that mean?" she demanded.

"It means to put a predator among its prey," Kuaron said. "How did we do that, Jared?"

"Good question," Jared said cheerfully. "I wish we knew."

"Do you always talk in riddles?" Dina said, even more annoyed.

"Yes, he always does," Kuaron said, showing neither surprise nor irritation at his friend's obfuscation. "Sit down, Jared, and tell us what you mean."

They all took seats, Dina and Kuaron sitting together, and Jared across from them.

"Okay," Jared said, stripping off his gloves, "here goes. I hate to be the one to break it to you, Kuaron, but you and Dina are now *the* hottest topic for conversation anywhere on Wakanreo. There's not a bar or a *quascha* parlor anywhere in Wisuta where they aren't discussing the *parundai* who found *shahgunrah* with a *fijazhai*."

Kuaron frowned heavily, and Jared waved a hand to forestall him. "It's not my choice of words, remember, Kuaron."

"What?" Dina said. "What's a *fijazhai*?"

"Technically," Jared said, "it just means any off-worlder—any non-Wakanrean. But the word comes from an ancient term for strangers—alien invaders, in a way—and it's come to be a pejorative."

"So they're talking about me and Kuaron," Dina said. "So what?"

"For one thing," Jared said, "I know for a fact that even without any official announcement, the news has spread throughout all three continents. And for another, it's not just that they're talking, it's what they're saying."

"And what is that?" Kuaron asked.

"Well, it varies," Jared said. "In most of the bars, there's still a lot of skepticism that it's true *shahgunrah*. I think your father put most of that to rest, Kuaron, but it may take a while for the information to sift down to the Wakanrean in the street. Then there's the religious angle."

"What religious angle?" Kuaron said apprehensively.

"Well," Jared said, his tone grim, "among some sects that revere Paruian, this event is seen as being miraculous in nature—Paruian intervening to help her descendent. In other sects, it's seen as sacrilege."

Dina could feel a sudden cold fear come from Kuaron, and she slipped her hand in his.

"But they can't hurt us can they?" she asked Jared.

"I don't think so," Jared said. "But anyway, it's not the religious fanatics I'm worried about—not in the short term, anyway."

"Who then?" Kuaron said. "Who worries you, Jared? Why are you here?"

"Because you're my friend," Jared said. "I wanted to warn you about what's going on at the Terran embassy."

"What's going on at the Terran embassy?" Dina demanded.

"All sorts of things," Jared said, reaching into his pocket. He pulled out a pocket com and consulted it, flipping screens rapidly. "It's been eleven days since the two of you met at the party at the embassy. It took about four days for it to sink in that this wasn't just another case of *glashunrah*; this was the real thing. Then, five days ago, the Terran embassy applied for an entry permit for a scientific team of eight Terrans—except three of them aren't scientists at all."

"What are they?" Dina asked.

"They're lawyers. One of them is an expert on ThreeCon citizenship as it applies to Terran colony worlds."

"I don't understand," Dina said. "What do these Terran lawyers and scientists have to do with us—with Kuaron and me?"

"I think it has everything to do with you. What you have to understand is that the Terran government really pushed for Wakanreo to join the Third Confederation." Jared leaned back in his chair and waved his hands as if he were clearing the air. "Let's back up a bit. Do you mind if I give you both a short history lesson?"

"He's only asking because you're here," Kuaron said to Dina. "When it's just me, he never asks, he just does it."

Jared grinned but didn't refute the accusation.

"I don't mind," Dina said, "so long as you promise to come to the point sometime today."

"I will," Jared said. "Okay, let's go back in time about seventy years. The Third Confederation discovers Wakanreo. Why do you suppose we made contact so soon after we found you?"

Kuaron blinked in surprise. "We met all the requirements for membership: we had a unified system for governing the planet, we'd had no war in almost a century, and we were technologically advanced enough that we had some form of space flight."

"Ah, but your space flight was very primitive," Jared said, an argumentative gleam in his eye. "Certainly you had no idea ThreeCon was watching you. And your global government was only loosely in control. In terms of time, you weren't that far removed from the bad old days of going to war over every little thing. The Shurata- nians were all for giving you another century or two to advance on your own, but Terra pushed for contact as soon as possible."

Dina made an exasperated noise. "Okay, we get the point. Now tell us why ThreeCon made contact!"

Jared grinned at her. "Two reasons. One was because the Wakan- reans had made tremendous strides in certain areas—mostly because of their chemical skills. They had found clean-burning fuels, balanced their ecological and technological needs, and pro- duced a booming global economy that fostered innovation. The Terrans wanted in on that innovation.

"Secondly, except for Terra, Wakanreo is the only world where the genetic code of life is built on deoxyribonucleic acid—DNA. Wakanreans are so much like Terrans, physically, biochemically, and genetically, that we couldn't wait to study them."

"So you're saying the Terrans rushed things?" Kuaron said.

Jared held out his hands. "You bet. Not that Wakanreo seemed at all upset at first. In their past history, Wakanrean cultures were rarely xenophobic. *Shahgunrah* made it difficult to fear outsiders. No, at first the Wakanreans were as eager as the Terrans were to do business. However, once the *glashunrah* problem became appar- ent, it was a different story. Wakanreo wanted as little to do with Terrans as possible. So Terra began to do research on *shahgunrah*."

"What?" Kuaron demanded. "That's illegal!"

"It is here," Jared said. "It's not on Terra or any of her space sta- tions or colony worlds."

"But there are no Wakanreans in those places," Dina said.

"Maybe not, but there are genetic labs that can tell you a lot just from DNA samples, and with Wakanreans, those are easy enough to get. Just follow Kuaron around with a vacuum nozzle and you'd have all the samples you could want—especially in the spring when he starts to shed his winter coat."

Dina looked at Kuaron suspiciously. "Is that true, or is he being facetious again?"

"It's true," Kuaron said. "But if the Terrans are really doing research on *shahgunrah*, this could be serious. Most Wakanreans are fanatical on that subject. They're very against it."

"Why?" Dina said.

"Because," Jared said, without waiting for Kuaron to answer, "*shahgunrah* is what makes Wakanreo what it is—not just the people but the world itself. All their cultures have been shaped and defined by *shahgunrah*. All you have to do is compare them to Terra, and it's obvious."

"Maybe it's obvious to you, but I don't see it," Dina said.

"Think about it," Jared said, leaning forward in his chair. "Terrans and Wakanreans are incredibly similar. But unlike Terra, Wakanrean cultures have never had real caste systems. They had inherited wealth and feudal systems, but they never stratified people because *shahgunrah* couldn't be controlled as marriages were. It's a lot harder to look down on the domestic staff if they're your children's *shahgunrahai*.

"On Wakanreo, the only thing a plastic surgeon does is make people with deformities or injuries look normal. No one worries if he puts on a few kilos or develops a wrinkle or two. A Wakanrean doesn't attract a mate by being young or beautiful or thin or tall or anything other than what he or she is."

"Maybe," Dina said, "but we had times in our history when the attraction between two people affected the course of events. Wasn't there a war started when a prince from one city abducted a queen from another city or something like that?"

"That's only one event," Jared said. "Besides, your example illustrates my point. On Terra, that event caused a war. On Wakanreo, no one ever went to war because people from two different political entities started *shahgunrah* together. They always knew the parties involved had no choice in the matter. Short of killing one or both of them, there was no way to stop it."

"Okay, okay!" Dina said. "I believe you. *Shahgunrah* has made Wakanreo what it is today. But why don't Wakanreans want to know how it works?"

"Because," Jared said, "everything I've just said could change if *shahgunrah* could be controlled. If you could manipulate how and when people find *shahgunrah*—and with whom—you could permanently alter Wakanrean society."

Kuaron nodded. "It's true. Every now and then some scientist would propose studying the mechanics of *shahgunrah*, but the idea was always so unpopular that it was never permitted."

"So no one can tell me why this happened to me?" Dina said.

"Not at the moment," Jared said.

"Well," Dina said, a touch of hostility in her tone, "one side effect of that is, no one can tell me whether it'll last forever, either."

Kuaron gave her a concerned stare, but it was Jared who answered.

"I don't see why it shouldn't—unless someone tries to end it artificially."

"What?" Kuaron's question was almost a roar. "What are you talking about, Jared?"

"Those Terran lawyers," Jared said. "I think they're coming here to help the Terran government take Dina into custody."

"Take me into custody?" Dina said. "I haven't broken any laws."

"Well, technically, you have," Jared said, with a nod of his head at their two intertwined hands. "You're breaking it right now."

"The no-touching rule is a Wakanrean law," Kuaron said. "And the government of Wakanreo has chosen not to prosecute us."

"A wise choice," Jared said. "A trial in these circumstances could start riots. However, what we've got here is a war of competing interests. The Wakanrean planetary government has been pushing ThreeCon for more restrictions on Terran visitors, and the giant Terran corporations are looking for a way to assure their Wakanrean hosts that the *glashunrah* problem will go away." Jared looked at Dina.

"Into this mix," he went on, "we throw a ThreeCon citizen of Terran descent who suddenly and inexplicably experiences the biological phenomenon thought to have been unique to Wakanreans. I think the Terrans see Dina as their shot at solving this puzzle. They may even use the near-hysteria in some of the more fanatic Paruianite cults to justify seizing Dina and attempting to find out exactly what made it possible for her go through *shahgunrah*."

Abruptly, Dina felt a hot, angry blast of emotion from Kuaron.

"No!" he shouted. "No one will take Dina!" He let go of her and grasped the edges of the table in front of him with both hands, as if he were trying to control his rage.

Dina saw that his claws were out and was afraid.

"Don't *jiewa* on me, Kuaron," Jared said, his voice mild. "It won't help anything, and it'll scare the hell out of Dina."

Kuaron glanced at Dina, and she felt his fury ebb.

"What is it?" she asked. "What's happening to you, Kuaron? What's *jiewa*?"

Kuaron took a deep breath and let it out slowly. "You tell her," he said to Jared, and then he got up and paced around the room.

Jared stared at the edge of the table where Kuaron's claws had left deep grooves in the surface. "Well," he said, "you know how sometimes a Terran will get really scared and do something amazing—something they couldn't ordinarily do, like lifting a skimmer?"

"I think I know what you mean," Dina said. "I once saw a woman lift a heavy steel grate to get her child out of a drainage ditch. She pulled him up by one hand, too, as easily as if he'd been a toddler, and he wasn't."

"Exactly," Jared said. "When we Terrans get all worked up, adrenalin floods our bloodstream and we can do more in the way of physical exertion than we could otherwise. Wakanreans have something similar, but it doesn't just make them stronger and faster, it makes them mad as hell. If you threaten a Wakanrean, he or his parent or his *shahgunrahai* may well come after you on the spot—claws out and crest high. Wakanreans call this reaction *jiewa*."

Dina shivered and looked at Kuaron. "What does *jiewa* mean literally?"

Jared looked surprised at the question, but he answered it. "It comes from the root word *jie*, which means to protect."

Dina found this fact strangely reassuring.

Kuaron stopped pacing and came back to sit beside her. "It's all right, *acubai*. I'm fine now. I was just frightened."

Instinctively, Dina stroked the back of his arm. "You scared me a little."

"I know. I'm sorry."

"Anyway," Jared said in a determined voice, "I have to go to work soon. But in the meantime, I wanted you two to know the situation. I'd be real careful going anywhere alone, Dina. I doubt very much they'll try anything when Kuaron's around—partly because of *jiewa* and partly because he's a *parundai*. And the fact that his father is Juzao Sadoc doesn't hurt either."

Jared smiled as he spoke, Dina and Kuaron were both startled when he began to laugh.

"What's so funny?" Kuaron asked.

"I was just thinking—if Dina had sat down and tried to think of the most conspicuous Wakanrean she could find *shahgunrah* with, she would have come up with your name, Kuaron. You're very well known as a *qatraharai*, you're a *parundai*, and to top it off, your father is the Planetary Administrator."

Kuaron smiled, but Dina was anxious. "So is that bad or good?" she asked.

"On the whole," Jared said, "I think it's good. The *parundai* part is the Terrans' excuse for interfering, but it also makes it more difficult for them to push you two around. And fortunately, Dina's marriage expired, so she has no husband to protest about *shahgunrah*, even long distance from Croyzan."

"How did you know that Dina had been married?" Kuaron asked.

"Arliana told me," Jared said.

Dina made no comment, but she was suddenly consumed by intense curiosity about Arliana and Jared. She knew her friend was almost as casual about sex as any native-born Terran, and Arliana's reactions to Jared had as good as announced that she found him attractive. What the two of them had done when they left the gift-giving was none of Dina's business, and yet she couldn't stop herself from wanting to know.

Still, good manners made it rude to ask, so Dina said nothing.

"And also," Jared added, almost as an afterthought, "I've been prying."

There was a brief silence at this announcement. Dina looked from Kuaron's guarded expression to Jared's frank countenance. She knew Kuaron wasn't actually angry, but she sensed a certain wariness.

"Prying?" Kuaron said.

"Yeah," Jared said, leaning back in his chair. "I think it's time I clued you in on something, Kuaron. I'm not your average liaison officer. The Terran government aren't the only ones worried about the situation here on Wakanreo. ThreeCon would like to see a little less hostility in Wakanrean relations with outsiders, especially Terrans. My orders are not just to do the usual checking up on off-world visitors to be sure they follow local laws and customs. I'm also supposed to look for opportunities to warm things up a little."

"Like befriending the Planetary Administrator's son?" Kuaron asked.

"That's why I spoke to you the first time," Jared said. "I wasn't lying about being impressed with your performance, but I did hope you'd get me close to your father."

"You must have been disappointed when you found out we were barely speaking at the time."

"I was. Your father isn't known for having a fondness for Terrans, and I rather thought I'd hit on the ideal way to approach him."

"Tough break," Kuaron said.

"I didn't mind," Jared said. "For one thing, I came to like you. For another, once I had met your father, I knew it would never have worked. He dislikes Terrans too much."

"He hugged me yesterday," Dina said.

Jared lifted his brows. "You're part of the family now."

"So why are you telling me this, Jared?" Kuaron asked.

"Because I feel like a slime ball for not having told you before," Jared said. "I consider you a real friend, and I wouldn't want anything as rampantly dishonest as the true reason I met you to get in the way of that friendship."

"It's all right," Kuaron said, and he held out his hand.

Jared started to return the gesture automatically, but before his hand grasped Kuaron's, he stopped and stared at the Wakanrean.

Kuaron smiled and continued to hold out his hand. "Touching you is no longer a threat to me. I assure you I won't file a complaint if you don't."

Jared grinned back in delight and shook Kuaron's hand firmly. "I never thought I'd get to do this."

Dina was gratified to have a chance to ask her own question. "That's something I asked Jared about before and he wouldn't tell me. If it can't hurt a Wakanrean who's already found *shahgunrah* to touch a Terran, then why do they make the law so absolute?"

"Sheer bloody-mindedness," Jared said cheerfully, letting go of Kuaron's hand.

"I prefer to call it an excess of caution," Kuaron said. "But from what my father has said to me, Jared is right. Our world wanted the benefits that ThreeCon membership would bring, but we didn't want to have to accept the Terrans with it. The no-touching rule was our revenge."

"Sort of like your friend Triascou?" Dina asked. "She's rude to Terrans for revenge."

Jared looked astonished. "Have you met Triascou lu Huaic, Dina?"

"No, but Kuaron told me she refused to come yesterday."

"That's what I figured," Jared said. "In fact, I rather counted on it when I came myself."

Kuaron laughed. "You're a fraud, Jared. I know very well you're not afraid of her."

"The woman is a *guarga*," Jared said with conviction. "She's a head taller than me, and she scares me to death."

"What is a *guarga*?" Dina demanded.

"A sort of dragon creature from ancient Wakanrean myths," Jared said.

"She's not so bad," Kuaron said. "And she's a very good *qatraharai*."

"You're better," Jared said at once. "At least, your technique is better."

"Thank you," Kuaron said, obviously gratified.

"Well, anyway," Dina said, "it seems to me that the best thing would be to find out how to stop this whole *glashunrah* phenomenon so everyone could relax."

"That may be rather difficult," Jared said, getting to his feet, "without knowing what causes *shahgunrah* in the first place."

Kuaron frowned as he rose to his feet, and Jared moved toward the door.

"I'd better get going," he said, "before Kuaron *jiewas* again. I've got to get to work, and I don't have time to stop at the infirmary."

"You're incorrigible," Dina said severely, rising to walk him to the door.

"I know," Jared said with a grin. "I work at it. See you later, Kuaron."

"Goodbye, naked, clawless weakling," Kuaron said. "Thank you for warning us."

Jared laughed and called over his shoulder, "You're welcome, hairy, towering hulk. Be careful!"

Dina shut the door behind him and turned to Kuaron.

"Well," she said, "what do we do now?"

# *Chapter Seven*

"First," Kuaron said, "we take you to the doctor."

Dina grimaced. "What if I'm not ready to see a doctor?"

"Why would you ask your friend for his name if you weren't ready to go see him?"

"Oh, all right! I'll go. But I'm going alone."

She could sense Kuaron's distress.

"*Acubai*, you just heard Jared tell us how dangerous that could be."

"That was his theory. I didn't hear much hard evidence to support it."

"Jared knows what he's talking about. He's no fool—even if he talks like one, sometimes."

"Look," Dina said, "this is embarrassing enough as it is. It'll be a lot worse if you come with me."

"Embarrassing?" Kuaron thundered. "What's embarrassment compared to your safety?"

Dina opened her mouth to argue, but she realized there was little she could say. "Very well, then, I'll let you come with me so long as you—so long as you—"

Kuaron stared as she broke into uncontrollable laughter. "What's so funny?"

"Nothing," Dina said, wiping her eyes as she regained control of herself. "It's just I was about to make you promise not to do anything to make yourself conspicuous. And then it occurred to me that there's no way you could help being conspicuous sitting in a Terran doctor's office."

Kuaron's eyes gleamed at the thought. "I'll stand out a trifle, no?"

"You'll stand out one hell of a lot," Dina said. "And I don't suppose I can do a thing about it—except maybe get used to it."

"So we'll go today?"

"Yes," Dina said, "if I can get an appointment. I hope Dr. Mehtar is available."

He was, and Dina succeeded in securing an appointment that afternoon. The automated program that answered her com call confirmed the date and time and gave her the address. "Where's the Megato Complex?" she asked Kuaron.

"It's in the off-world sector," he said. "It's a cluster of offices, stores, and restaurants that are all scaled for Terrans. Jared often takes women there for dinner."

Dina gave him an appraising look. "It seems to me that all your experience with Terrans comes from being friends with this one man. He's something of a smooth operator, too."

"Is that bad?"

"I don't know yet," Dina said. "I'll let you know when I find out."

IT took less time to reach the Megato Complex than Dina had expected, as it proved to be in the nearby suburbs of Wisuta. When Kuaron pointed out the huge roof port to her, Dina hastily checked the complex's directory to be sure the place where he was setting the flyter down was convenient to Dr. Mehtar's office.

"You could just wait here for me?" Dina suggested as he turned off the engines.

Kuaron gave her a look, and then pushed the contro to to open the flyter doors. Dina climbed out with a sigh.

"Well, here goes," she said as they approached the lift tube entrance. "I hope you're satisfied."

Kuaron gave a deep chuckle. "I will be when you're better."

Dina chose to ignore the double meaning of this comment, and stepped into the tube. It hummed as her foot touched the floor, and hummed again a moment later when Kuaron got on beside her.

"Dr. Mehtar's office, please," Dina said.

Sensing that no one else was approaching, the tube shimmered as the force field door was established, and then smoothly slid downward at a rapid rate. A second later, the force field vanished.

"Go left out of the tube," a disembodied voice said. "Dr. Mehtar's office is the third door on the left."

"Thanks," Dina said.

"Why do you always thank machines?" Kuaron said as they walked. "You thank the com at home."

"I don't want to get in the habit of having bad manners," Dina said. "If you always say thank you when you've ask for something, then you'll never be rude to a person."

Kuaron smiled, and stroked her cheek. A Terran woman who was coming out of an office stared at them, and then looked away hastily.

Kuaron let his hand drop to his side. "I'm sorry."

"It's not your fault," Dina said. Deliberately, she put her arm around his waist and leaned against him as they walked. "Let's go see the doctor so we can go back to screwing like crazy every night."

The woman hurried away, and Kuaron grinned at Dina—a wolfish grin that gave his face a predatory look. "Do you always enjoy shocking people or only when they do things that annoy you?"

"Actually," Dina said, releasing him, "I'm rather prim by Terran standards, but I don't like it when people judge me without even knowing me."

"She merely looked chagrined."

"She looked disapproving. Now let's go."

She pulled him through a door that had Dr. Mehtar's name listed, along with two other doctors, and found herself in the middle of a comfortable room where two Terran women waited, one reading, and one sitting glumly. Both of them looked up, and then stared in surprise when they saw Kuaron.

Dina smiled politely and took a seat, with Kuaron following suit beside her.

A window in the wall slid open, and a brisk-looking woman in a blue medtech's coverall gave them a professional smile that slipped when she saw Kuaron sitting next to Dina in a chair that looked too small for him.

"You must be Dina Bellaire?" the woman said.

"Yes," Dina said. "I'm a little early."

"No problem. If you'll give me your records now, then you can step into an examining room and get ready for Dr. Mehtar to see you."

Dina rose and was annoyed when Kuaron stood up next to her. She gave him a darkling look, but his answering stare was bland, and she knew it would be hopeless to argue with him.

Deciding that discretion was the order of the day, Dina walked through the arched doorway into the corridor where the medtech waited. She handed the woman the medical history card she had brought from Croyzan.

"Oh," the woman said in surprise as she looked past Dina at Kuaron. "I thought—I mean, you did want the doctor to examine you?"

"Yes," Dina said.

The medtech looked even more flustered, but she indicated an open door, and Dina walked through it. Kuaron followed her silently, almost close enough to touch her.

"If you'll remove your clothes, please," the medtech said, resolutely ignoring Kuaron, "and put on the amplification robe, Dr. Mehtar will be right with you."

"Thank you."

As soon as the door shut behind the medtech, Dina kicked off her shoes and started to undress. "You do realize even Terran husbands don't subject their wives to this, don't you?"

"You say that as if being a Terran husband is the worst possible thing a person could be," Kuaron said. "And most Terran husbands don't worry about their wives being kidnapped."

Dina smiled as she slipped off her trousers. "Do you think Dr. Mehtar would kidnap me?"

"I've never met him, so I couldn't say. I'm only following Jared's advice not to let you out of my sight."

Dina shrugged off her underclothes and stood stark naked. She picked up the amplification robe draped over one end of the table and slipped it on. "What will you do if Dr. Mehtar refuses to examine me while you're here?"

"Why would he do that?"

"I don't know," she said, sliding onto the examining table. "Medical ethics, maybe?"

Before Kuaron could answer, the door chimed and then opened abruptly. A middle aged Terran man of average height and build stood in the doorway. He wore a doctor's tunic and a diffident expression.

"Hello," he said, hesitating, and then stepping into the room as if he was unsure he really wanted to enter it. "I suppose your—that is, this gentleman needs to be here?"

"He thinks so, certainly," Dina said.

"How do you do," Dr. Mehtar said, with a slight bow to Kuaron.

Kuaron bowed back but said nothing.

"Well," Dr. Mehtar said resolutely, "I've run your record card through my medi-scanner, so I know your history. But I was wondering why you needed an exam now? You had a complete medi-scan a little over month ago and nothing was wrong."

"Yes, well, I have a little problem."

The doctor looked at Kuaron and then back to Dina. "Yes?"

Well aware that she was blushing scarlet, Dina related her symptoms. Dr. Mehtar didn't so much as blink. He directed her to lie back on the table, which promptly reshaped itself to accommodate her, and then he twitched her robe into place where the hem had fallen outside the medi-scanner's perimeter.

Very soon after the exam started, Dr. Mehtar informed Dina that she had an infection, but he surprised her by telling her that although her vaginal tissue showed signs of inflammation it was her urinary tract that was infected.

"It happens sometimes with new Terran immigrants," he said. "But don't worry. It's easy enough to treat. I can take care of it right now."

"Great," Dina said.

"You can put your clothes on now," the doctor said a minute later, putting down his hypnospray. "I've given you a treatment that will cure the infection and another one for the inflammation. However, if you want to heal quickly, you should consider showing some, er, restraint."

"Yes, well," Dina said, refusing to meet Kuaron's gaze, "sometimes restraint is difficult to achieve."

"If nothing else," the doctor said, "you can be more creative about what you do to satisfy your, um, appetites."

Kuaron broke into a low chuckle and spoke for the first time since the doctor had come into the room. "*Taal* doesn't urge you toward creativity. *Taal* has only one appetite, and when it's hungry, there's no satisfaction until it's fed."

The doctor looked nonplused at this interjection. He picked up a blood sample cube from a tray and changed the subject. "Would you mind if I took a blood sample before you leave, Citizen Bellaire? I'd like to check something out."

"What is it?" Dina asked, pulling on her underpants.

"It may be nothing," the doctor said. "It's just that your cervix looks a little blue."

Dina sat up. "What does that mean?"

The doctor made a noncommittal gesture with one hand. "The most common cause is a first pregnancy, but it's not definitive."

"That's out," Dina said. "I had a birth control inoculation only a year ago."

"I know. That's another thing I want to check."

"Go ahead, then," Dina said.

The doctor pressed the sample cube against her inner arm for a few seconds until the cube beeped once. Dina watched as he dropped the cube into his pocket.

"I'll be back in a moment," he said. "Why don't you finish dressing, and then come see me in my office?"

"All right."

As soon as the doctor was gone, Dina began to pull on her clothes, frantically.

Kuaron came across the room and stood very close to her. "What did that mean?"

"What?"

"Why did the doctor take a blood sample? And what is a cervix?"

"A woman's cervix is the opening to her uterus—her womb. Apparently, mine has turned a funny color."

Kuaron stared at her gravely. "Could you be pregnant?"

Dina flushed red. "No! This is ridiculous, Kuaron. Not only did I have a birth control inoculation only a year ago, I haven't had sex with anyone except you in six months—no, eight months."

Kuaron looked even more grave. "Could you be ill, then?"

"I don't know!" Dina said, fastening her shirt.

Suddenly, Kuaron pulled her close. "It'll be all right," he breathed into her ear. "You'll be fine. You're not ill. I know it."

Dina clung to him and tried to fight her rising sense of panic. The door chimed again, and they pulled apart just as it opened.

Dr. Mehtar stood there looking very ill at ease.

"I'm sorry," he said. "I'm really sorry. I didn't know when I agreed to this—if I had known, I would never—I mean, I can see that this will be difficult—"

He broke off abruptly as someone pushed him aside. Two Terran men stood in the doorway; one was tall and looked about twenty-five; the other was shorter and was old enough that his hair was going gray.

"Dina Bellaire," the older man said, "on behalf of the governments of Fantar and Terra, I hereby take you into protective custody. Come with me, please."

Kuaron gave a fierce roar and stepped in front of Dina. He shouted something in Wakanrean, but Dina didn't understand him, and the other two Terrans didn't seem to, either.

"Step out of the way, please, sir," the younger man said. "Citizen Bellaire is coming with us."

Dina was terrified because she could feel an intense rage coming from Kuaron. She laid a hand on his shoulder in an effort to calm him. "Kuaron, please! Cool down!"

He reached back and pushed her gently but firmly into the corner, and then turned to face the two strangers. Dina could see that his claws were out, and every hair in his headcrest stood erect. He gave what was almost a growl of warning and uttered a guttural expletive in Standard.

"Get out!" he said with an effort. "Get out, now!"

In response, one of the two raised a weapon and fired. There was a faint hum, and Kuaron's whole body twitched convulsively but he stayed on his feet and lunged toward them. The man who had fired cursed, stepped back a pace, lifted his weapon and fired again. Kuaron gave a groan and sank to the floor.

Dina rushed to him and bent over his inert body. She was relieved when she saw his chest rising and falling, and felt a pulse in his throat.

"You bastard!" she shouted at the stranger with the stun gun.

"He'll be fine in a few hours," the man said. "You'd better come with us now, Citizen Bellaire."

"Go to hell!" Dina looked around for a weapon and found the doctor's tray of instruments. She picked up the heaviest-looking implement and threw it at the stranger. The man ducked in time to avoid having it hit him in the head, and at the same time there was an anguished cry from Dr. Mehtar in the hallway.

"My instruments!" he cried, peeking around the door. "Those are very expensive."

"You can go to hell, too!" Dina screamed at him. She picked up the tray, dumped it over, and raised it into the air as she rushed at the shorter man. She had almost made contact with his head when the taller man wrenched the tray out of her hands.

In a matter of seconds, Dina was subdued. Once the strangers had fastened her wrists behind her with a loop of flexible alloy, she was reduced to cursing at them.

Dr. Mehtar slipped through the door as soon as it was clear Dina was no threat, and began to hunt around on the floor for his instruments.

"Listen, you damned son of a bitch!" Dina shouted at him as she was led away. "You call Jared Harlingen at ThreeCon Headquarters in Wisuta and tell him what happened. Maybe he'll be able to keep Kuaron from taking you apart once he wakes up."

The doctor didn't answer. Dina's last view of him was as he knelt on the floor looking down at the large but still form of Kuaron Du.

# Chapter Eight

Jared Harlingen surveyed the still sleeping Wakanrean lying stretched out on Dr. Mehtar's examining table. Kuaron's chest rose and fell with reassuring regularity, and Jared knew he was in no danger.

A small being in a blue and brown uniform stepped through the doorway. His skin was a pearly gray, his head round and hairless. His facial features were only vaguely humanoid, as his nose was a small bump in the middle of his face, and his eyes were tiny, round, and a solid emerald-green in color, with no hint of iris or pupil. His mouth was his most human attribute, with both his lips and teeth having a more familiar appearance. His long flexible ears, on the other hand, sprouted from near the top of his head, and looked prehensile. His small stature and general air of vague indecision made him seem childlike—naïve and unsophisticated—but Jared knew him well enough to know better.

The new arrival wore gold epaulets on his small shoulders and a Planetary Commander's stars on his collar. Jared jumped to his feet and saluted.

Planetary Commander Marochh shu Sstad returned the salute absently. "Well, well, Jared. What have we here?"

"A problem, I'm afraid, sir. I didn't want to say too much on the com. I wasn't sure if this area of the complex is being monitored."

The Shuratanian glanced at his wrist com. "It's not," he said definitively.

"Very good, sir. Let me explain. This is Kuaron Du. I'm sure you've heard about what happened to him several days ago at the Terran Embassy?"

105

"I read your report on it. You seemed quite certain the incident was genuine."

"Kuaron is a friend of mine, sir. I know him well. There's no way he'd be involved in a fraud."

"And the young woman?"

"I had met her briefly, at her orientation, and I met her again at Kuaron's house. I don't think she's capable of faking something like this."

Commander Marochh's eyes gave nothing away. "You seemed just as certain she wasn't being coerced."

"Yes, sir. She was comfortable with Kuaron. In fact, they seemed to be rather fond of each other already."

"Haruuumm," Marochh said, clearing his throat in the Shuratanian manner as he looked down at the sleeping Wakanrean. "It looks as if someone is less fond of your tall friend."

"Indeed, sir. I warned the two of them just this morning that the Terrans were showing an inordinate amount of interest in what had happened to them. I never thought the Embassy staff would be so ignorant of Wakanrean culture as to attack a *parundai*, though."

Marochh's bright, jewel-like eyes gleamed at this information. Jared wished he knew what that meant. "You warned them, did you?"

"Yes, sir."

The smaller man surveyed the room, which still showed signs of Kuaron's abortive attack and Dina's frustrated defense. "It doesn't seem to have done much good."

"No, sir. As I said, I misjudged the Terrans."

"So now they have the young woman in question?"

"Yes, sir, they do. And according to what that miserable excuse for a doctor says, there's an even bigger complication. Dina Bellaire is pregnant."

The Shuratanian blinked once, and then his left ear twitched. "Pregnant?"

"Yes, sir."

The Commander sucked in his cheeks as if he were thinking, and then his right ear twitched. "Do you know who the father is?"

"Well," Jared said slowly, "the thing is, from what I know of her, I very much suspect it's Kuaron Du."

"What?"

"I know it sounds incredible, sir," Jared said, "but a little over a month ago, Dina Bellaire left Croyzan. She had to have exhaustive medical tests run for the Wakanrean screening program, as all Terrans do, and she was *not* pregnant at that time. The doctor says she's barely pregnant now—not more than two weeks at the outside, he says. From what her friend told me, I don't think Dina Bellaire would go to bed with a man she met her first day on Wakanreo—not without *shahgunrah,* anyway."

Marochh's eyes sparkled even more. "You're talking about spontaneous cross-species interbreeding—from two species that evolved on different worlds! Do you know how astronomically unlikely that is?"

"Yes, sir," Jared said. "I also know that something about Dina Bellaire made her able to undergo *shahgunrah.*"

"Haruuummmmm." Marochh drew the noise out into a long drawn-out hum that told Jared how shocked he was at the suggestion.

"I got this away from the doctor," Jared added, handing his superior officer a blood sample cube. "It's half gone but we should be able to do a DNA analysis, plus evaluate the pregnancy."

"A good suggestion," Marochh said, slipping the cube into his pocket. "Now what do we do with him?" He nodded at Kuaron.

"That's a problem, sir. I'm not sure I want to be here when he wakes up. It was a hell of a lot of work getting him on the table while he was unconscious. I don't think I'm up to keeping him on it once he's awake."

"How long has he been out?"

"Almost an hour. When they took Dina away, she told the idiot doctor to call me, and he did. Once I saw what had happened, I called you right away."

Marochh looked almost amused. "Why do you keep disparaging the doctor?"

"He was in on it, sir. Apparently, the Terran embassy knew from Dina's friend Arliana Cheng that Dina was going to be here, and they set the whole thing up with the doctor. For some reason, he feels remorseful now that he knows she's pregnant. Apparently it was okay to sell her out when he thought it was just some Terran out for a good time, but now he thinks he's put her pregnancy at risk."

The Shuratanian blinked again, and both ears twitched simultaneously and twisted together momentarily. "It had better not come to that." His tone was mild enough, but Jared was profoundly grateful he wasn't employed at the Terran embassy.

"No, sir."

Marochh straightened to his full height of four feet, ten and a half inches, not counting his ears. "Very well. Call Administrator Sadoc now. Tell him what's happened to his son, but don't mention that I was here. For now, you can let him think you're involved on a purely personal level."

"Yes, sir."

"As soon as the Wakanrean authorities arrive, leave here and come to my office at headquarters. I'll make sure the base commander knows you're at my disposal for the time being."

"Yes, sir," Jared said, giving a hurried salute as the smaller man left the room.

DINA paced back and forth in the tiny room where she was confined and then threw herself down on the cot against the wall, the only piece of furniture in the room. She had no idea how long she had been there, as they had taken her pocket com, and there was no window in the room.

The door clicked, and Dina sat up abruptly. Unlike the two men who had snatched her so easily from the Megato Complex, this woman wore the uniform of the Terran diplomatic corps, a gold tunic over black trousers.

"Step this way, please, Citizen Bellaire," she said, holding the door open."

Dina rose and followed the woman into the hallway. If she had had any thoughts of attempting to escape, they evaporated at the sight of two well armed guards who waited by the door. They fell in step behind her as they wound their way through several corridors.

When they finally stopped, they were outside a wide door. The uniformed woman opened it, and then stepped back to allow Dina to enter the room.

Dina walked through the doorway with her head held high; she was apprehensive but determined not to let it show.

The woman waiting behind the big desk in the center of the room didn't look at all intimidating. Her dark hair was streaked with gray, and she was petite, much shorter than Dina. In fact, she reminded Dina of her grandmother.

"Come in, Citizen Bellaire," the woman said, rising to her feet. "Come in and sit down, and we'll have a nice chat."

Dina remembered where she had seen the woman's face; it was Ambassador Inoue.

"A nice chat?" Dina said. "Maybe you're in the habit of chatting with people who kidnap you, but I'm not."

"Now, now," the Ambassador said. "That's not a constructive attitude at all. Sit down and I'll explain what's happened."

"I know damn well what's happened." Dina stayed resolutely on her feet. "You had me forcibly removed from my doctor's office, that's what happened."

"Yes, dear, but you don't know the reason."

"Oh, don't I? You want to use me to find out what causes *shahgunrah*—maybe even to learn to control it."

Ambassador Inoue pressed her lips together in a grimace of annoyance. "I see a certain ThreeCon liaison officer has been busy meddling in what doesn't concern him. Has Jared Harlingen filled your head with scary stories about nasty Terrans?"

"No. In fact, he misled me into thinking you were too sensitive to Wakanrean traditions to commit assault on a *parundai*."

The ambassador frowned and sat down. "We never expected *Parundai* Du to be there. And it was self defense, not assault. He threatened our officers. They were only protecting themselves."

"They threatened me first. They pushed Kuaron into *jiewa,* and then stunned him once he'd made it clear he wouldn't let them take me away. If he's hurt in any way, you're in big trouble."

"I'm quite sure he's fine," the ambassador said. "Wakanreans and Terrans are quite similar, and a standard stun gun has no lasting ill effects on either species."

"They shot him twice," Dina said, still aggrieved.

Ambassador Inoue waved a hand. "Even then, I'm sure he'll be fine. It'll just take a little longer for him to come out of it."

Dina crossed her arms over her chest. "So what happens now?"

"Why, we see what we can do to help you, my dear. After all, you've had quite a nasty shock, haven't you?"

Dina stared at the older woman suspiciously. "What the hell are you talking about?"

"I'm talking about the peculiar behavior that you exhibited when you got close to a certain Wakanrean man," the ambassador said, giving her a warm, maternal smile. "We know you tried to fight it—your friend explained how you were unable to stay away from him—and now we're prepared to help you resist these abnormal feelings."

"I don't want to resist them!" Dina shouted. "And what's more, you have no right to take me into custody at all."

"Now, dear," the ambassador said. "Think about it. You've been here less than twenty days. You've only known this man for twelve of them. How can you say a rational human being would want to give in to inexplicable, overwhelming lust for a total stranger?"

"It's not lust, it's *taal*," Dina said, as fierce as Inoue was gentle. "And don't you mean a rational Terran?"

The ambassador's smile was almost regretful. "Let's not descend to sarcasm, my dear."

"Stop calling me your dear. As it happens, I hate your guts. And what's more, I'm not even a Terran citizen, so you had no right to snatch me like you did."

"That's right, you're not a native Terran, are you? You're from Fantar."

"I am," Dina said with satisfaction. "I hold Fantaran citizenship, and thus ThreeCon citizenship, and I'm a legal resident of Wakanreo. Terra has no rights over me."

"Not originally, no. But when we notified Fantar of what had occurred here on Wakanreo, the government of the colony asked us to intercede on your behalf."

"What?" Dina could feel her face flush with anger. "Why, you sanctimonious, interfering bitch! What the hell did you tell them?"

The Ambassador looked almost hurt at the question. "The truth, of course. I understand your mother was very upset. But then, they're not very used to non-Terrans on Fantar, are they?"

Dina stared at the other woman with her mouth open for a moment, and then she clenched her teeth as she glared at her. "You're truly foul. You don't care whom you hurt, do you?"

For the first time, Ambassador Inoue looked seriously annoyed. "Oh, come now, Citizen Bellaire! Surely even you can see that there's more at stake here than one person's comfort?"

"Of course there is!" Dina said, letting her disgust show. "There's one hell of a lot of money riding on this, isn't there?"

Inoue leaned across her desk. "So you scorn money, do you? Did you think the colony on Fantar was built on good feelings? It costs a lot of credits to establish a colony, and even more credits to maintain it until it can support itself. And whom do you think paid for it?"

"I'm sure Terra did. But if it was done from the goodness of their hearts, I'd be very surprised."

The ambassador threw up her hands. "This is getting us nowhere. We acted within our rights as representatives of the government of Fantar, and we're still within our rights when we demand that you cooperate with our investigation."

"Cooperate?" Dina said incredulously. "You really think I'm going to cooperate with you?"

"After all, my dear," the ambassador said, "you really have no choice. Resistance could be hazardous—in your condition."

Dina stared at her, trying to control the sense of panic these words engendered. Finally, she sat down in a chair.

"That's better," Ambassador Inoue said brightly. "And in time, you'll see that you're much better off this way. No matter how delightful it was to be shut up in your little love nest in the cliffs, your overly aggressive mate is bound to get upset once he finds out you're pregnant. Wakanreans are completely monogamous, you know. They don't understand about these things at all."

Dina's eyes widened in surprise. She swallowed, but said nothing. If she truly was pregnant, then everyone was in for a tremendous shock. It would be best to hide the true state of affairs until she had had a chance to sort all the possibilities out in her head. With any luck, they would keep her locked up alone for a few hours, and she would have time to think of a convincing lie.

The ambassador appeared to take her silence for acquiescence. Her hand reached for the com. "Now, I'll just call in a few of our medtechs, and we'll get started."

KUARON awoke with a splitting headache. He groaned and put one hand to his head, and at the same time, he opened his eyes.

He was very surprised to find his father bending over him. When he sat up abruptly, his father stepped back a pace.

"How do you feel?" Juzao said.

"I have a headache," Kuaron said. "What happened?"

"Don't you remember?"

Kuaron shook his head a few times, to clear it, and sat up straighter. He looked around the room, surprised to find himself and his father alone in a doctor's office clearly scaled for Terrans. "Dina!"

Juzao nodded. "They took her away."

Kuaron surged to his feet and then stood there in confusion. "Where? Where did they take her?"

"We don't know yet. Calm down, Kuaron. You won't help anything by starting *jiewa*."

Kuaron made himself take a deep breath and sat down. "I already did. When the two men pushed the doctor out of the way and said they were here to take Dina, I *jiewed*. I remember now. I never felt it that thoroughly before. I would have killed them if I could have reached them."

"In the long run, it may turn out to be just as well that you couldn't reach them."

"What?" Kuaron said, his head snapping up.

"We'll get her back. They had no right to take her. But one thing we don't need is for you to make things worse by killing someone."

Kuaron took another deep breath and tried to think. "How did you know about this?" he said abruptly. "Why are you here?"

"Your brains are waking up at last. Your *shahgunrahai* is as smart as she is dainty. She told the doctor to call your Terran friend. He came here and found you, and then called me."

"Jared? Dina told the doctor to call Jared? Why didn't she tell him to call you?"

"Think about it," Juzao scolded. "Would a Terran doctor have called me? No, she did right. The doctor felt comfortable calling ThreeCon for help, and since that *nyesh* is a friend of yours, he called me himself."

Kuaron put his head in his hands and rocked back and forth a few times. "What do we do now, *Ayzanai*?"

"We file a protest with the Planetary Commander," Juzao said. "I've already called him. We have an appointment in an hour."

Kuaron let out a profound and unhappy sigh. "I had just found her, and now they've taken her away."

"We'll get her back."

Kuaron let his shoulders droop. "I hope we can do so very soon, *Ayzanai*. It may well be that Dina is pregnant."

"What?" Juzao said, his tone a mixture of anger and astonishment. "Who is the father?"

"It's difficult to believe," Kuaron said, "but I think I am."

# Chapter Nine

Jared tugged at the snug-fitting collar of his dress uniform and hoped the day would go well. He studied the hearing room covertly, noting all the participants and their positions in relation to each other.

Juzao Sadoc sat at a table with the Wakanrean delegation, which included his deputy and two representatives of the Planetary Legislature. Juzao had opted to present Wakanreo's arguments personally, and Jared was wondering whether this was a good idea or not. Certainly he was a better choice than Kuaron, who sat beside his father looking almost ill with apprehension.

At a second table, placed at an angle to the first, sat the Terran delegation. Ambassador Inoue had decided to let her legal experts speak for her. The team lined up beside her included three Terrans, two men and a woman. Behind both tables, two rows of chairs had been set up for witnesses, and for those ThreeCon and Wakanrean officials who had elected to be present.

Facing the participants' tables, the dais where Planetary Commander Marochh shu Sstad sat at a third table was slightly raised to indicate ThreeCon's position as the arbiter of the dispute. Jared's chair was on his right, quite close, but one step down, as befitting his subordinate role as Marochh's adviser on local customs. He held a terminal on his lap, in case Marochh asked him any questions he couldn't answer on his own.

"Now," Marochh said, raising his voice but not bothering to use the microphone in front of him, "I believe we're ready to begin."

The room grew quiet, and Marochh read through a statement of Wakanreo's complaint against Terra.

"As outlined in the Articles of Confederation," Marochh said at the end, "all disputes between member worlds are to be decided by the Third Confederation. Do both parties concede the truth of this statement, and consent to obey my findings?"

Juzao Sadoc allowed his deputy to rise and give Wakanreo's consent. The Terran reply was delivered by the leader of their legal team, a burly middle-aged man, fair-haired and ruddy-faced, who spoke curtly but affirmatively.

"Very well," Marochh said. "We will proceed. Administrator Sadoc, please present your grounds for complaint."

Juzao rose to his feet. "Thank you, Commander Marochh," he said, with a graceful bow in the Shuratanian's direction. "I'd like to begin by outlining the events that preceded the actions that caused me to file this complaint. I want to enter into the record an account of that period of time when Dina Bellaire, a citizen of Fantar and recent immigrant to Wakanreo, met Kuaron Du, a citizen of Wakanreo." Juzao turned toward Kuaron and gestured toward him. "*Parundai* Du is a well known *qatraharai*, a singer of ancient songs. As noted by my use of the honorific '*parundai*,' he's descended from Paruian, the Prophet of Peace. He also happens to be my son, but that, unlike the other facts, is not relevant to this case.

"I ask that *Parundai* Du relate to us what happened when he and *Kantai* Bellaire were both in the same room for the first time, thirteen days ago."

When Marochh assented, Kuaron stood up and moved to the witness chair. He gave his name and his oath to tell the truth, and then sat down looking a little apprehensive.

"Tell us, please, *parundai*, what happened thirteen days ago," Juzao prompted.

Kuaron related the events of the embassy party, what he had said and done, and how he had felt when *shahgunrah* started, what he and Dina had said to each other.

"Very well," Juzao said with a benign smile. "We'll skip over the next few hours. Suffice it to say that you both indulged in the intimacies that are perfectly normal for two people who have just begun their *shahkuun*."

"If I might ask, Administrator," Marochh said. "Please define any Wakanrean terms you use. We all know what *shahgunrah* is, but we may not know many of these other Wakanrean words."

"Certainly, Commander," Juzao said. "*Shahkuun* is a period of several days—usually at least nine or ten—in which a newly mated couple are allowed complete privacy to begin their *shahgunrah*. During this time they experience intense levels of *taal*—overwhelming passion for each other—that is another aspect of *shahgunrah*."

Marochh looked at Kuaron. "And did this happen to you and Citizen Bellaire, *parundai*?"

"Yes," Kuaron said. "Of course. It was some days before we could control ourselves."

Marochh's expression was inscrutable as he waved his hand. "Proceed, Administrator."

"Now," Juzao said, "on the second day of your *shahkuun*, what happened that surprised you?"

Kuaron shifted in his seat again. "We were disturbed. Four soldiers of the Global Army arrived in a military vehicle."

Juzao nodded. "At this time, Commander, I should like to defer the remainder of *Parundai* Du's testimony. I wish to call Under-Captain Hulac Oim, of the uniformed branch of the Wakanrean Administrative Corps, to present his evidence."

Marochh agreed, and Kuaron returned to his seat while his place was taken by the officer called.

Juzao had the man relate, in great detail, the trip to the Administrator's office and all the steps he had witnessed in the tests of Dina's ability to feel *haictor* and *klunar*. The Terrans leaned forward in their chairs at this description.

"And when *Kantai* Bellaire demonstrated clearly that she knew *Parundai* Du was in pain—even though he hadn't made a sound— what did you conclude?"

"I decided they must truly be *shahgunrahai*, Administrator. I didn't know if it was a miracle or merely some kind of bizarre coincidence, but there was no other explanation. You knew it yourself. You let them go."

"Yes, I did. Thank you, Under-captain."

The man resumed his seat in the back of the room, and Kuaron returned to the witness' chair.

"Now, *parundai*," Juzao said, "what happened after *shahkuun* ended?"

"We held a gift giving," Kuaron said. "Most of my relatives came, and a few friends. Dina's friend Arliana Cheng came also."

Juzao approached Marochh's chair with his hands held wide. "For the record, Commander, *shahgunrah* is not defined by any kind of legal contract. It simply is or it isn't. But once it has happened, in Wisuta it's recognized by the family and friends of the new *shahgunrahai* with a day in which everyone visits and brings a gift. This event happened for *Parundai* Du and *Kantai* Bellaire. According to Wakanrean custom, they have standing as *shahgunrahai*."

The Terran woman sitting next to Ambassador Inoue jumped to her feet. "We wish to enter an objection, Commander. In fact, no Wakanrean court has handed down any ruling on this particular gift giving."

"No court has received a formal dispute about it," Juzao said. "But the Planetary Administrator's office informed the Wisutan magistrate's office of what had passed, and *Kantai* Bellaire has not been charged with violating the law against contact between Terrans and Wakanreans. By not charging her, the magistrate's office has, in effect, recognized the validity of their *shahgunrah*."

Marochh glanced at Jared. "Liaison Officer Harlingen, can you tell me if this is true?"

Jared cleared his throat and looked at Kuaron. His friend was staring at him. "It's difficult to say, sir," he said, turning to Marochh. "No such situation has ever arisen, so there's no precedent to follow. Certainly, a Terran who was known to have violated the law could be deported. That's what happens when it's a blatant, willful violation, and I'd say this instance is as blatant as you can get."

Ambassador Inoue appeared unable to contain herself as she rose to her feet to speak. "Commander, I object to this man giving evidence as if he were an impartial adviser. He's a close friend of *Parundai* Du."

"Do you dispute the truthfulness of Liaison Officer Harlingen's statement, Ambassador?" Marochh asked.

"No."

"When he says something you feel to be biased or untrue," Marochh said, "you may complain. Until then, I see no reason why I should be deprived of advice from someone who's been on this planet for several years and whose job it is to be familiar with local laws and customs. Please resume your seat."

The Ambassador sat down with ill grace.

Juzao moved on to asking about the next day's events, and Kuaron described the trip to the Megato complex.

"What happened at the doctor's office?" Juzao said.

"We were attacked," Kuaron said. "Two men were waiting outside the examining room. They shot me with a stun gun."

"If I may speak, Commander?" the Terran team leader said. "*Parundai* Du wasn't fired upon until he acted aggressively toward our officers."

Kuaron set his jaw and gripped the sides of his chair as if he felt a need to control himself. "They said they were going to take Dina into custody—to take her away from me."

"And did you threaten the officers at that time?" Marochh asked.

"I told them to get out," Kuaron said. "And they shot me. I started towards them, and they shot me again."

"He actually shouted at them in anger," the Terran team leader interjected. "And they fired at him with a stun gun that left no lasting ill effects."

"If I might point out, Commander," Juzao said, "the only embassy staff who are legally empowered to carry weapons—even nonlethal weapons—outside of the embassy grounds are Ambassador Inoue's personal guards."

"These gentlemen were part of the same staff," the Terran lawyer said.

"But the Ambassador was nowhere near the Megato Complex at the time," Juzao said.

"That fact doesn't change their status," the team leader said.

"Perhaps not," Juzao said. "But it seems to me it certainly negates their justification for carrying a weapon in the first place."

"The Administrator is, of course, entitled to his opinion," the team leader said. "Nevertheless, our actions were perfectly legal."

"No!" Juzao said forcefully. "When Wakanreo signed the Articles of Confederation, we promised to proscribe certain governmental actions. One of them was detention without trial."

"Citizen Bellaire is not being detained on criminal charges," the Terran lawyer said. "She's being held in custody because she's no longer competent to make decisions for herself."

There was a stunned silence for about two seconds, and then Kuaron jumped to his feet.

"*Hur a mahar teinai da' fareesh da!*" he shouted.

Marochh blinked at this display of ferocity. "Sit down, please, *parundai*. You'll have a chance to speak in a moment."

Kuaron hesitated and then sat down reluctantly. Marochh leaned sideways toward Jared; a faint hum told Jared that the side conversation would be supressed in the transcript.

"What did he say?" the commander asked in a low voice.

Jared cleared his throat and spoke just as softly. "He called them a dirty name, sir. It was a double insult, because he not only compared them to the most repulsive animal on Wakanreo, he also implied they deserve to be what they are."

"I suppose it would be best not to demand an official translation, then," Marochh said. "Forget I asked."

"Yes, sir."

"Now," Marochh said, raising his voice as he turned back to the others, "before we proceed with an analysis of the situation, let's recap the facts so far. Are we all agreed that *Parundai* Du and Citizen Bellaire did indeed undergo a physiological reaction to each other that certainly resembles *shahgunrah*?"

"It is *shahgunrah*, Commander," Juzao said.

"We will concede that it certainly appears that way, Commander," the Terran lawyer said.

"Very well. And are we agreed that Citizen Bellaire wasn't engaged in any unlawful activity at the time in which she was taken into custody by the security forces of the Terran Embassy?"

"On behalf of the government of Fantar," the Terran team leader interpolated. "You've seen their written request, Commander, as has the Administrator himself."

"I have."

"That request in no way changes the fact that *Kantai* Bellaire didn't wish to go with those officers," Juzao said. "And as she wasn't on Fantar, her government had no right to force her to do it. She hadn't broken any Fantaran laws—or Terran laws, for that matter."

"But she had been acting in a manner that indicated a radical personality change," the lawyer said. "And that was why the Fantaran government asked us to take her into protective custody."

"Protective!" Kuaron shouted, jumping to his feet again.

His father turned and said a few curt words in a low voice. Again, Marochh leaned toward Jared.

"What did the Administrator say?"

"He told his son to shut up and sit down or he'd have him taken away."

"Humph!" Marochh said. "That's my call."

"Yes, sir."

Marochh smiled an abstracted smile. Jared always thought of an ancient Terran Buddha whenever the commander smiled like that.

"You like the *parundai*, don't you?" Marochh asked.

Jared was a little surprised at the question. "Yes, sir. He's a friend."

Marochh straightened up in his chair and spoke more loudly. "*Parundai* Du, I must ask you to refrain from further outbursts. As for you, citizen," he nodded at the Terran lawyer, "if you have a case for saying that Citizen Bellaire can't take care of herself, then make it. I haven't heard anything to support that yet."

"If you please, Commander," Juzao interrupted, "I haven't finished presenting my complaint yet."

"You've told us that *Parundai* Du and Citizen Bellaire both experienced *shahgunrah*, and that the Terran embassy staff abducted Citizen Bellaire. What more do you have to say?"

"Just this," Juzao said, drawing himself up to his full height. "*Kantai* Bellaire must be returned to her *shahgunrahai* immediately. If she's not released today, the Legislature assures me that the government of Wakanreo will issue a statement to the press denouncing the Terran government for holding a *parundai* hostage. Further, we will then formally request the Third Confederation to order the embassy closed."

There was an angry outburst at the Terran table. Jared looked from the ambassador's face to the assembled lawyers as they whispered noisily back and forth.

"Commander," the Terran spokesman said, "the government of Terra protests most strenuously! At no time did we ever hold *Parundai* Du hostage."

"I'm not speaking of my son," Juzao said. "I'm speaking of my grandchild."

There was complete silence that was finally broken by the mild voice of the Planetary Commander.

"I beg your pardon, Administrator" Marochh said politely. "I understood that *Parundai* Du was your only child?"

"That's true," Juzao said.

"As he has no children, how can you then claim to have a grandchild?"

"I'm speaking of my future grandchild," Juzao said, unfazed. "The child of my son Kuaron Du and the Terran woman known as Dina Bellaire."

Instead of silence, this announcement was greeted with a chaotic babble of many conversations uttered at once, as two of the Terran lawyers erupted into simultaneous speeches at the same time that Ambassador Inoue leapt to her feet and Commander Marochh tried to restore order.

Finally, Marochh resorted to turning up the volume the microphone in front of him. "Silence!" he intoned in a loud voice. "Everyone be silent!"

The noise stopped as abruptly as it had begun. Ambassador Inoue sat down, but she leaned over and whispered to the woman beside her, who then rose to her feet to speak.

"May I speak, Commander?" she asked politely.

"In a moment," Marochh said. "Administrator, do I understand you correctly? You are alleging that Citizen Bellaire is pregnant with a child who's half Terran and half Wakanrean?"

"I am," Juzao said. "And further, I'm pointing out that any child of Kuaron's will also be a *parundai*, just as he is."

Ambassador Inoue seemed unwilling to wait for her minion to be recognized. "Commander!" she said, popping out of her seat. "This is ridiculous! In the millenia that our people have traveled space, there has never been a case of a naturally occurring, cross-species hybrid birth."

Marochh twitched both ears and gave her his Buddha smile. "Madam Ambassador, if all that were required for a thing to be impossible was that it had never happened before, none of us would be here. At some point in time, our ancestors all did things for the first time. It may well be that here on Wakanreo, we're about to see a truly momentous event. Please resume your seat."

Ambassador Inoue sat down reluctantly and Marochh spoke to Juzao. "If you're finished articulating your complaint, Administrator, we will proceed."

Juzao bowed as gracefully as he had the first time. "That is all I have to say at this time, Commander."

He took his seat, and Marochh nodded to the leader of the Terran legal team. "Now, sir, if you would be good enough to continue, you said you had proof that Citizen Bellaire suffered from an incapacitating mental disorder. Please present your evidence on this matter so that we can either confirm or dismiss it."

The Terran rose and glanced at the Ambassador who nodded to him. "Very well, Commander. We'd like to call Citizen Arliana Cheng."

Kuaron muttered something under his breath, and his father gave him another stern look. Jared smiled to himself, as he thought he knew what his Wakanrean friend had said. A sharp glance from Commander Marochh made him tap out a few words on his terminal.

Marochh glanced down as the text was displayed on his own screen. He looked impassive as he read the words Jared had written: You don't want to know.

Arliana Cheng rose from the audience and walked to the front of the room. She took the same oath Kuaron had, but she looked a good deal more nervous as she did it.

As soon as she was seated, the Terran team leader asked his first question.

"How long have you known Dina Bellaire, Citizen Cheng?"

"Sixteen years," Arliana said. "Sixteen Standard years, that is."

The lawyer went on to ask a good many questions about Arliana's relationship with Dina. He established that Arliana had known Dina during the time she was married, that the two women had kept in touch after finishing their education, and that Dina had contacted Arliana when she knew she was coming to Wakanreo.

"And in all that time," the lawyer asked, "did Citizen Bellaire ever behave as impulsively as she has since she met *Parundai* Du?"

"No, never. Dina was always very cautious."

"And did she ever voice a desire to be otherwise?"

"No."

"Then to what cause do you attribute the change in her personality?"

Arliana looked a little uncomfortable, but after a moment's hesitation, she answered the question. "I guess I just thought Dina had gone round the bend, in a way. I mean, it was like she was a whole different person. She was such a prude before, and now here she was living with this enormous Wakanrean person she had just met. It was really creepy—like she'd been hypnotized or drugged or something."

Juzao Sadoc glanced at his son, who glowered but said nothing. The Terran lawyer went on to ask the specifics of what Dina had said and done when Arliana had seen her during her brief visit to her apartment during *shahkuun*. Arliana related Dina's conversation in great detail. She no longer looked nervous, and even seemed to relish the attention, as everyone listened intently to her description of Dina's appearance.

When the lawyer had finished, Juzao got to his feet and asked Arliana whether she had any Wakanrean friends.

"No," Arliana said. "I mean, I know lots of Wakanreans, of course, but I don't consider them friends in the sense—well, I mean, I don't spend time with them outside of work."

"I see," Juzao said. Very deliberately, he extended his right hand, flexed the tendons that exposed his claws, and then used the claw on his little finger to scratch himself under his chin. "So you've never seen a Wakanrean who was starting *shahgunrah*?"

Jared grinned to himself. Juzao had just illustrated Arliana's ignorance of Wisutan customs by insulting her.

"No," Arliana said, with a certain amount of distaste in her voice. "I haven't."

"If I might interrupt, Commander," the Terran lawyer said. "I'd like to challenge the relevance of this line of questioning. Citizen Bellaire is not a Wakanrean."

Juzao waved a hand. "As *Kantai* Bellaire was able to experience *shahgunrah*, I see no reason why she should be judged on purely Terran rules of behavior—or only by Terrans."

The lawyer began to protest, but Commander Marochh cut him off.

"This discussion has gone on far enough. We've heard what both sides have to say, and it all boils down to one question: Is Dina Bellaire competent to make up her own mind about where she wants to live and with whom? The answer is obvious. Bring her here, and I'll have a ThreeCon doctor—a Terran doctor—question her. That will settle it."

There was a stir among the Terran delegation as Marochh dismissed Arliana Cheng and she resumed her seat in the audience.

"Commander, I protest!" the lead lawyer said. "Citizen Bellaire is in the relative safety of the Terran embassy, and we cannot allow her to be removed from there."

"If you recall, you agreed to abide by my decision, and that is it," Marochh said. "If you renege on that agreement, then I'll have to forward a report to my superiors immediately. I think you know very well that the consequences could be grave."

The lawyer glanced at Ambassador Inoue. She glared angrily, but nodded. "Very well," the lawyer said. "We'll arrange for Citizen Bellaire to be brought here to ThreeCon headquarters."

Commander Marochh glanced at the wall chronometer. "You have one hour." He leaned back in his chair and let out a small sigh as if he were tired of sitting still. "This hearing is recessed."

# *Chapter Ten*

Glad as she was to get out of the cell-like room, Dina worried where they were taking her. She couldn't see anything through the thoroughly-opaqued windows of the flyter. The two uniformed guards who accompanied her didn't speak, even to each other, so Dina sat silently as the flyter traveled. Only when the vehicle set down and the guards opened the door did she venture to ask a question.

"Where are we?" she said, still sitting in her seat.

"ThreeCon headquarters," the woman said. "Come along, please."

Dina followed her, eager to find out what was happening. The flyter had landed in an open space in front of a large building. Before she had time to look around her, the guards hustled her inside. They went through a mechanical security check, and then Dina found herself facing a row of a half dozen people in the blue and brown uniforms of ThreeCon personnel. The fact that three of them were Milorans and another was a very small Shuratanian distracted her so much she didn't immediately see that one of the two Terrans was a woman and the other was a man with a familiar face.

"Citizen Bellaire?" the Shuratanian said.

Dina awoke to the meaning of the gold epaulets on his shoulders. "Oh! You're the Planetary Commander?"

The small being bowed and offered his hand. "I am indeed. Marochh shu Sstad at your service. It's a pleasure to meet you, citizen."

Dina bowed in return and looked up to find Jared Harlingen smiling at her. "Oh, hello, Jared. What's going on? Does this mean I'm free?"

"Not quite yet," Commander Marochh said. "The Terran government has prevailed on your home planet to declare you mentally
incompetent. I'm afraid you'll have to prove you're not before we
can cut you loose."

Dina clenched her jaw. "Ambassador Inoue is a first class bitch."

"I'm afraid I can't venture an opinion on that," Marochh said. "If
you'll come this way, please," he added, waving a hand toward the
end of the corridor.

He led the way, and Dina found herself in a small room furnished
as an office, with a desk in one corner and two chairs set close
together in the center of the room.

"Now," the Shuratanian said, nodding at the Terran woman,
"we're leaving you alone with Dr. Kwan Fang Li. Dr. Kwan is both
a medical doctor and a therapist. She's going to ask you a few questions. Just relax and answer her as honestly as you can, and when
she's done, we'll talk."

Dina glanced at the blank wall opposite the chairs and wondered
whether it provided a way to see into the room. It didn't really matter; ThreeCon could certainly have one or more cameras hidden,
even in a seemingly empty room. Dr. Kwan held what looked like
a small portable terminal, although Dina supposed it might be a
monitor for some other device.

"Fine," Dina said.

The Commander and the others left, and the doctor pointed
to a comfortable-looking upholstered chair. "Sit, please, Citizen
Bellaire."

Dina sat. She felt the warmth of the chair as she did so, and
the arms seemed almost to embrace her. She realized it must be
a therapist's chair that could measure her brain waves and other
physiological reactions during the session. Doubtless the monitor
the doctor held was keyed to the chair.

Dr. Kwan sat down facing Dina and smiled a professional smile.
"Shall we begin?"

"You'll have to start," Dina said. "I've never talked to a therapist
before."

"That's not a problem." She glanced at the monitor in her hand.
"Tell me a little about yourself."

Dina launched into a brief recital of her life to date. Dr. Kwan's
manner was encouraging, a nice mix of the briskly professional and
the warm and friendly. She took Dina through a series of questions

that elicited her previous close personal relationships, including her brief marriage, and then worked her way into what had happened at the embassy party.

Dina held nothing back. She wanted very much to get out of Terran hands, and if that meant she had to describe her most intimate feelings, she was willing to do it. She was a little surprised that Dr. Kwan didn't ask any questions about the sexual aspects of her relationship with Kuaron, but instead focused on how she felt about what had happened.

"Would it be accurate to say you're dismayed by this abrupt change in your life?" the doctor asked.

"No," Dina said. "I wouldn't say dismayed—at least not now. Maybe I was at first, but I've had some time to get used to it."

"And how do you feel about it now?"

"I'm still working that out."

"Would you say that you feel threatened by it?"

"Oh, no," Dina said at once. "If there's one thing I'm absolutely sure of, it's that Kuaron would never hurt me."

"Maybe not physically—"

"Not any way," Dina interrupted. "In fact, if anyone should feel threatened, it's Kuaron."

The therapist managed to convey surprise without so much as widening her eyes or lifting an eyebrow. "And why is that?"

"Because he's at a far greater risk. If I decide I don't like living with him as his *shahgunrahai*, I can leave and look for a way to end *shahgunrah*. I don't know that it would work, but I could try. That would leave Kuaron a lot more alone than I would be. I could find someone else and have a traditional Terran marriage, but Kuaron will never have another *shahgunrahai*."

"Do you think you'll do that?"

"I don't know," Dina said honestly. "It would be a drastic step that would hurt Kuaron terribly. I'm still exploring how I feel about being a *shahgunrahai* and how I feel about him. The only thing I'm sure of is that, for now, I don't want to leave him."

"And that hasn't changed even though you've been away from him for over a day?"

"Not at all."

Dr. Kwan nodded, as if she were checking off an item on a mental list, studied her monitor for a moment, and then went on to ask a few more questions about Dina's state of mind. When she got to her feet, Dina started to rise, too, but the doctor waved her back to her chair.

"Just wait here a few minutes, citizen," she said, starting for the door. "Someone will be right with you."

Dina sat back down. Now that the interview was over, she was nervous about the consequences.

Unable to stay seated, she paced the room. She found a clock on the desk, and noted the time. Some minutes later, she turned from her pacing when the door opened.

Jared stood there, grinning at her. "Come along, Dina. They're ready for you now."

"Who's ready?"

"Just about everybody involved," Jared said, his tone cheerful as he walked beside her.

They paused outside a set of double doors, and Dina was elated to feel Kuaron's presence nearby. She was scanning the room for him as she went through the doors, and she saw him at once. He was on his feet, facing the door as if he had known she was coming.

"Kuaron!" Dina cried.

His answer was inarticulate, but there was no mistaking the eagerness with which he lunged toward her. Only his father's sudden intervention kept him from sweeping the chairs from his path and rushing toward her.

"Kuaron!" Juzao said, grabbing his son with both arms. *"Na ha ibum!"*

Dina would have run to Kuaron, but Jared gripped her arm firmly. "The old guy's right," he said under his breath. "We're winning. Don't ruin it."

Dina held herself back. She took a deep breath and let it out in a rush, then turned to survey the room, and the people sitting in a cluster of three tables. The diminutive Planetary Commander sat at a small table in the middle of a sort of stage. Kuaron and his father had just resumed their seats at a second table. Opposite them, Ambassador Inoue sat at one end of a row of unknown Terrans at the third table.

"If you'll have a seat here, please, Citizen Bellaire," the commander said, indicating a chair that stood on the dais facing his table, "we're waiting to hear what you have to say."

Dina took her time walking across the room. She sat down and took her oath when asked, and then waited, making herself stay calm.

"Now," Commander Marochh said, "we've heard from Dr. Kwan that you're perfectly competent to make up your own mind. Tell us, please, citizen, what you want to do?"

"I want to go home," Dina said, "with Kuaron."

There was a buzz at the Terran table, and then the lead lawyer rose to his feet. "Commander, we reiterate our concern that Citizen Bellaire is not presently able to make a rational decision."

"Oh, shut up," Dina said, without waiting for Marochh to speak. She twisted around in her chair to glare at the Ambassador. "I'm as rational as you are. If I'm going to have the first interspecies-hybrid baby, I'd much rather do it with his or her father in the picture."

There was a momentary silence and then Ambassador Inoue blurted out what sounded like an epithet, but Dina didn't recognize the language. "You little witch!" the ambassador said, glaring at Dina. "You told us you'd had an affair with someone you met on the voyage here!"

"Of course I did," Dina said. "I knew if I told you the truth, I'd never get out of the damn embassy."

The room erupted in a babble of conversation, and Marochh had to resort to using the microphone to attain silence.

"Thank you!" the Shuratanian said when everyone was quiet. "It is the ruling of this tribunal that Citizen Dina Bellaire is mentally competent, and she herself has expressed her wishes. In accordance with the provisions of the ThreeCon Charter, we hereby declare her free to go. We also admonish the Terran government," he gave Ambassador Inoue a stern glance, "to remember that neither Citizen Bellaire nor her future progeny are in any way under their jurisdiction. This tribunal is dismissed."

Dina jumped to her feet, but she managed to take only two steps before Kuaron reached her. He enveloped her in a snug embrace that Dina found tremendously reassuring.

"Kuaron," she whispered. "We're going to be parents! Are you happy?"

"Yes," he whispered back. "Are you?"

She gave a little sigh. "I think so." And then she pulled out of his grasp enough to smile up at him. "I guess I'm not such a disappointment to your father after all?"

He smiled back, but there was an sharp edge to his relief and happiness. It took Dina a moment to sort it out, and then she realized it was fear. Kuaron was afraid.

"WELL, Kuaron," Jared said with a smile that was so satisfied he looked almost sleepy, "that went pretty well."

Kuaron drained his glass, set it down on the table, and then slipped his arm around Dina. The three of them were back at the cliff house, and he and Jared had partaken liberally of a bottle of Terran brandy. "It went well considering the *fareesh kualua* are still alive."

Dina decided it was time to assert herself. She put down her cup of *quascha* and let out an exasperated sniff. "All right! I've had enough of this! What the hell is a *fareesh kua- kualua?*"

"You're doing better with your pronunciation." Kuaron sounded pleased.

"A *fareesh* is a repulsive looking amphibian," Jared said, having just a little trouble with the sibilants. "It eats the droppings of other marine animals, and if you ever want to get your face clawed, just call a Wakanrean that."

"No, don't," Kuaron said. "I'd have to fight to protect you, and I might *jiewa* again."

"So what's *kualua?*" Dina said, not satisfied.

"It means dirty or foul," Jared said, his eyelids drooping. "Maybe you should start learning Wisutan?"

"Is that what you call Kuaron's language?" Dina said in surprise. "I thought it was Wakanrean."

"There's no such language as Wakanrean," Jared said, pouring another generous glass of brandy. "They speak Wisutan on most of this continent, but there are plenty of other Wakanrean languages and dialects. Before ThreeCon made contact, the Wakanrean Legislature conducted its business in Wisutan because the Planetary Capital is near here."

Dina watched him sipping his brandy. He had had three already, and she was a little worried. Kuaron had had five, but unlike Jared, he showed no signs of inebriation. "Don't you have to fly yourself home?" she asked Jared.

"The flyter has automated controls."

"He can sleep here if he needs to," Kuaron said, nuzzling Dina's neck.

She gasped in surprise; such close contact made it impossible for her to ignore his growing level of arousal.

"My father is right," Kuaron said, his voice muffled as he buried his face in her hair. "You are very dainty—almost delicate. Rather like a *guisha*."

"A what?" Dina said, moving a little away from him.

"A small animal often kept as a pet, much beloved by children," Jared said, lurching to his feet. "I can see it's time for me to go."

"You don't have to leave," Kuaron said. "We can go into the bedroom."

"No," Jared said in a determined voice. "It's time. Thanks for the brandy."

"Thank you for all your help," Kuaron said, rousing himself to stand. "And thank you for bringing us home."

"No problem," Jared said, tossing back the rest of his brandy and heading for the door with only a slight stagger. "I'll see you later, Kuaron. Dina, congratulations on being officially pronounced sane."

"Thanks," Dina said. "Are you sure you're okay?"

"I'm fine," Jared said, waving a hand over his shoulder as he opened the door. "Good night, furball."

"Good night, midget."

Dina watched her *shahgunrahai* sink back onto the sofa. "Do you two always insult each other like that?"

"Not always, but frequently." Kuaron reached out and pulled her close against him, and then nuzzled her neck. "Let's go to bed, *acubai*."

"Not just yet," Dina said, pushing him away as strongly as she could.

Kuaron allowed himself to be held back. "What's wrong?"

"I don't know. You seem okay now, but back at ThreeCon headquarters you were afraid. I could feel it. Tell me why?"

He grew instantly solemn. "I am afraid."

"Why?"

"Because I don't know what will happen. No one has ever had a half Wakanrean and half Terran child before. I don't know if it'll affect *shahgunrah*, and I don't know if it could be dangerous for you."

Dina met his eyes. "I don't know either."

Kuaron captured one of her hands. "Do you want to have this baby?"

She nodded. "I had time to think it over while I was locked up in the embassy. I never thought of myself as maternal, but I pictured the future with and without a baby, and then I knew I wanted to have it. For all I know, this is my only chance at motherhood, and I was terrified they might do something to stop it. That was one reason I lied to them. I did what I had to do to protect my baby—our baby."

Kuaron looked very happy at this statement, but before he could say anything, Dina held up a hand.

"Kuaron, stop and think a moment. Before you get your hopes up, think about this. We only know that right now I'm almost a couple of weeks pregnant. We don't know if this child will be viable—if he'll make it to term or survive outside the womb. We're talking about something that's never happened before."

"I do know it," Kuaron said. "We can only hope."

"Yes," Dina said. "We can hope."

THE next morning, Jared stood in front of the Planetary Commander's door and waited. In a few seconds, the door opened, and Jared stepped inside. He saluted smartly, but Marochh waved him to a seat.

"Sit down, Jared, and you can dispense with the military observance. It's just us, and anyway, you're officially in the Administrative branch."

"Yes, sir," Jared said, letting himself relax, but not going so far as to forget he was facing the supreme ThreeCon authority of Wakanreo. "You sent for me, sir?"

"I did. Have a look at the report on Citizen Bellaire's DNA."

He handed over a data slate, and Jared took it. A minute later, he lifted his head and stared at his commander. "I don't get it, sir. What does it mean?"

Marochh's eyes gleamed like two bright emeralds. "It means that either a coincidence of truly cosmic proportions has occurred, or a small part of this Terran woman's DNA is Wakanrean."

"How could that happen? Dina Bellaire is from a backwater colony world. She never set foot on Wakanreo until a few weeks ago."

"I'm aware of that. Nevertheless, the report makes it plain that several of her genes include material that does not appear to be Terran in origin. In fact, the suspect DNA matches very closely the same genes in a Wakanrean."

"What's her family background?"

"Believe it or not," Commander Marochh said, his tone wry, "ThreeCon doesn't actually have direct records on all our citizens. We rely on member worlds to supply them as needed."

"And what did Fantar say when you asked for hers?"

The Commander's left ear twitched. "They said they'd get back to me on it."

Jared grinned. "Am I correct in assuming that means 'don't hold your breath'?"

"I don't have your ear for languages, but I think I understand Terran idioms well enough to say yes. I think it would be best if you approached your friend's mate and asked her about her family."

Jared didn't answer right away. Marochh waited, and finally Jared looked up and met his gaze.

"Is that an order, sir?"

"No," the Shuratanian said. "If you prefer to stay out of this, I'm fully prepared to ask her myself."

Jared didn't comment, but merely leaned back in his chair. Marochh watched him for a moment, and then he put his hands on the edge of his desk and pushed so that he, too, was leaning back in his chair. "Are you regretting your involvement in this matter, Jared?"

"No, sir," Jared said promptly. "As a matter of fact, I'm regretting approximately half a bottle of Terran brandy."

Marochh's ear twitched again. "Do you need to visit the infirmary?"

"It's not that bad. I already took something for it."

"Ah!"

"I don't mind talking to Dina," Jared said. "But I wonder if it might be better if you were there, too, sir. I'm not comfortable representing ThreeCon's point of view."

Marochh smiled his Buddha smile. "I'm not at all certain ThreeCon has a point of view at the moment. We're not sure of anything, really. This Terran woman certainly appears to be pregnant, but her pregnancy hasn't been examined by a doctor yet. And even if she is pregnant, no one can say whether the child will survive. Just because a hybrid occurs naturally doesn't mean it's guaranteed to be viable."

"No, sir."

"I see what it is. You're worried about them."

"Yes, sir," Jared said, feeling almost as if he were admitting guilt. "Ambassador Inoue was right about one thing. I'm not a disinterested party."

"Ambassador Inoue has been right about a great many things," Marochh said, releasing the edge of his desk and letting his chair drop to a vertical position. "That hasn't stopped her from acting like an idiot."

Jared didn't comment, and the Shuratanian smiled. "You're learning discretion, Jared. I'm very pleased."

"Thank you, sir," Jared said politely.

"What about Citizen Bellaire's friend—the other Fantaran woman?"

Jared almost blinked in surprise. "Arliana Cheng? What about her?"

"I just wondered if you feel pulled in two directions, as her loyalties seem to be with her employer."

"I have no real relationship with Arliana Cheng," Jared said, trying to keep the annoyance out of his voice. "Or are you merely asking if I slept with her?"

Marochh chuckled. "You Terrans are so circumspect. What has sex got to do with slumber?"

"I always assumed the phrase came into use because for Terrans, both activities occur most often in bed," Jared said, making himself maintain his casual pose while every instinct told him to assume a more formal stance. There were times when Marochh could be annoying, and any time he took an interest in his subordinates' lives was one of them. The attention of one's superiors, Jared knew, was not always a good thing. "If you want to know, sir, why don't you ask me?"

"I thought Terrans considered it bad manners to reveal such information," Marochh said, the twinkle in his eyes betraying the gravity of his expression.

"I do, certainly," Jared said, letting some of his irritation show. "But when one's bed partner has already spread the news over most of the off-world sector, some license is allowed."

"Can I assume that means you did indeed consummate a sexual act with her?"

"Yes, sir."

"Ah!"

Jared held back a sigh. "There wasn't much to it, sir. She wanted a physical relationship, and I obliged. I called her the next day to be polite, but we didn't make any formal plans to see each other again."

"Haruum. That would have been the day before yesterday?"

"Yes, sir," Jared said, a little surprised that the Commander knew so precisely when he had met Arliana. "It's not like I feel any loyalty to her, sir. If you ask me, she sold Dina out."

"Perhaps," Marochh said. "But it may be that she sees it differently. She may well have been persuaded that her friend's best interests would be served by going along with the Ambassador's plans."

"That just makes her stupid."

Marochh waved one slender gray finger at him. "Tush! And here I just complimented you for learning discretion."

"Sorry, sir," Jared said, wondering if this discussion had some deeper meaning. Shuratanians were often inclined to take their time about getting to the point.

"Harumm!" Marochh said. "In any event, it seems you have no obligations other than your duty to ThreeCon and your friendship with the Wakanrean singer. Go call your friend now and arrange a meeting. They may be a trifle paranoid, considering what's happened, so we'll both go to visit them instead of asking them to come here."

"Yes, sir," Jared said, relieved that the conversation was finally over.

"THE Planetary Commander is just another bureaucrat," Kuaron said to Dina as they tidied up the main room, "like my father."

"It's easy for you to say that," Dina said, determinedly plumping every cushion in sight. "Your father is the Planetary Administrator, and your mother was a *parundai*. My family is considerably less exalted."

"Bosh!"

Dina stopped plumping and looked at him suspiciously. "What does that mean?"

"I assume it's like piffle." Kuaron's expression was bland, but Dina could sense his amusement.

"Watch it, buster," she said. "It's bad enough when you spew Wakanrean—I mean Wisutan. I have no intention of listening to you toss out Terran slang."

Before Kuaron could respond, the summit alarm sounded, and he had to go to the com panel to activate the lift for their visitors.

Jared led the way when they came through the front door, suggesting that perhaps this visit wasn't as formal as it seemed. He did wait for Marochh to take a seat first, however, so Dina wasn't entirely sure of everyone's role in the meeting.

Once they were all comfortable, she and Kuaron on a sofa and Jared and Marochh on chairs, Dina passed around a tray with cups of *quascha*. Everyone took a cup, and Dina sipped her *quascha* feeling that she had done her duty as a hostess.

"What's this about, Jared?" Kuaron asked. "You didn't really explain when you called."

"I asked Jared to call you," Commander Marochh said. "We got the results of Citizen Bellaire's genetic mapping, and we have some questions."

"Please call me Dina. The Terrans from the embassy kept calling me 'citizen,' and I don't care if I never hear the word again."

"What did you find out?" Kuaron asked.

"Ah!" Marochh said. "It's rather curious, actually. It appears as if a small part of Dina's genetic makeup is much closer to Wakanrean DNA than Terran."

Dina froze with her cup half way to her lips. "What? Are you talking about a mutation of some kind?"

"We don't know yet," Marochh said. "Mutation is always a possibility. But you should understand that Terran and Wakanrean DNA are very close, structurally, and virtually identical chemically, which, I can assure you is the only known instance of such similarity between two species from different planets." He nodded at Jared. "You explain it for them, Jared. You were there when the geneticist went over it, and you have a gift for translating technical jargon into plain Standard."

Jared cleared his throat and launched into what Dina recognized as his instructional mode. "Well, as I understand it, Terrans and Wakanreans both have paired chromosomes, the same number of pairs, in the identical double helix structure. Their DNA nucleotides even have the same four bases.

"People are fond of using percentages in describing DNA. They often compare Terrans with chimpanzees, for example, and say that the two species have ninety-eight percent of their DNA in common. This points out something a lot of people don't understand. We aren't really using all our DNA. A lot of it is like old computer code that no one wants to throw away. Or to use another analogy, if you think of DNA as the blueprint for a house, it's as if we moved from house to house but always took the floor plan of our old house with us every time we moved. Our DNA doesn't just represent the architecture of what we are now, but also what we were. That ninety-eight percent sounds incredibly high until you realize that humans and chimpanzees lived in a lot of the same houses."

"Where is all this leading?" Kuaron interrupted. "And what are chimpanzees?"

"Sorry," Jared said. "Chimps are Terran primates, para-sentient humanoid animals, who are closer to Terrans than any other species. And what I'm leading up to is that Wakanreans and Terrans may have lived in different neighborhoods in the past, but they seem to have arrived at the same address now. When you ignore the differences in archaic DNA, Terran and Wakanrean DNA are remarkably similar—and yet at the same time, there are significant differences. What's most interesting is that some of Dina's genes look just like the same genes in a Wakanrean."

Marochh looked at Dina with his eyes bright, and smiled a pleased but solemn smile. "So what we want to know now, Dina, is what is your family background?"

Dina looked at all their faces. She felt rather as if she were a magician who was expected to perform a miraculous trick. "I don't know if my family background is going to explain a whole lot. My mother is a first generation Fantaran. She was born on Fantar, but both her parents were born on Terra."

"Your mother is alive but your father is deceased?" Marochh asked.

"Yes," Dina said. "Dad was a prospector. His ship was lost when I was eleven."

"And what was his heritage?" Marochh said.

Dina shook her head. "Who knows? Dad was adopted. His birth mother arrived on Fantar on a refugee ship, and then died a few days later. Dad was only two, in Standard years, and only knew his first name. He was adopted by my grandparents soon after, but he was never able to find out anything about his birth family—not even a father's name."

"A refugee ship from where?" Marochh asked.

"Prashat," Dina said.

There was a sudden silence at this news. Finally, Kuaron said. "What is Prashat?"

Marochh's expression had become inscrutable. "Prashat was a Terran colony world. It was virtually destroyed some sixty years ago."

"Destroyed?" Kuaron said. "How?"

Marochh made an abrupt gesture with one hand, as if he were waving away something that wasn't really there. "It was the Lycandrians—the only known overtly hostile species in the galaxy."

"If your father's family came from there, Dina," Jared said, "we may never know more about him."

"That's what Dad always said," Dina said. "It never mattered that much, though."

"It matters now," Marochh said. "You studied history in university, Jared. What do you know about Prashat before it was destroyed?"

The liaison officer pondered. "Not that much, sir. It was a typical Terran sleeper world—except of course that it wasn't really."

"Explain," Marochh said. Dina thought she detected a note of impatience in his voice.

"Well," Jared said, "the term sleeper world is used to refer to Terran colonies that were founded before we had EFTL technology."

"What's EFTL?" Kuaron interrupted again.

"Effective faster than light," Marochh said. "It refers to traveling through folded space, which makes the distance shorter. The effect is that you're going faster than light, even though you're not. Go on, Jared."

"The thing is," Jared said, "sleeper has a double meaning. The colonists were usually literally 'asleep' in their ships in the sense that they were in suspended animation, but also the world itself was sleeping in a way, because it was cut off from Terra and the rest of the galaxy. Prashat was different because it was isolated for over two centuries, but the colonists didn't arrive on sleeper ships. Prashat was founded by one of the few expeditions to use generation ships."

"Oh!" Dina said. "I remember now. We covered that in history class. On a few missions, the ships were staffed by crews that were awake the whole time they were in space. Families were allowed to immigrate that way. The children grew up, and married and had children of their own. It took several generations to reach their destination."

"Precisely," Jared said. "It wasn't a popular method because most people wanted to immigrate in the hopes that they'd find a better life on a new planet. Not that many people were willing to condemn themselves and their children and even their grandchildren to a life spent on board a ship where the population controls were even stricter than they were on Terra."

"So how could the fact that Prashat was settled by generation ships have anything to do with Dina's DNA looking like Wakanrean DNA?" Kuaron asked Marochh.

"I have no idea," Marochh said. "But now that we have something to work from, we'll look into it."

"I hope you find something that accounts for this," Dina said. "Because I've had all the unexplained phenomena I can handle."

"Ah!" Marochh said. "Doubtless you're feeling a little shaken, Dina. However, now that it's not merely a matter of experiencing *shahgunrah*, but also being pregnant, it would be a good idea if you were to visit a doctor—or doctors—soon."

"I don't mind," Dina said. "Anyone but Dr. Mehtar."

"All in all," Jared said, "it might be best to have at least two doctors—one Terran and one Wakanrean. After all, you and your child may need both of them."

"We can arrange it for you," Marochh said. "Any time you like."

Kuaron put his arm around Dina and pulled her close against him. Again, she felt a twinge of fear.

"Soon would be good," Kuaron said.

Marochh nodded. "We'll make it soon."

DINA woke in the middle of the night when the alarm sounded. She was groggy, at first, and it was only when she realized Kuaron was sitting up beside her that she remembered why she had set the alarm in the first place.

"Kuaron, you don't need to get up, too," she said, laying a hand on his shoulder. "You can't do anything."

"Nonsense," Kuaron said, reaching for his skirt-like *xuschi,* which hung on its usual hooks on the wall. "Of course I'm getting up. It's always possible your mother will want to talk to me."

Dina considered it unlikely, but instead of answering, she pulled on a robe and found her slippers. She ran a comb through her hair, and then padded through the door to the main room with Kuaron right behind her.

"I'll make us some *quascha,*" he said, heading for the kitchen.

Dina sat down in a chair near the com terminal. Once she had activated it, she saw the timer counting down the minutes. She was a little early.

She sat back in her chair and mentally rehearsed what she had to say. She was fine; that was the important thing. Just because what had happened to her was unexpected didn't mean that it was to be deplored.

Dina felt Kuaron coming closer. When she glanced over her shoulder,he handed her a cup of *quascha.*

"Maybe it won't be so bad," he said.

"We'll see," Dina said, sipping from the cup. The *quascha* was hot and sweet, with just a hint of spices. "Mmm, thanks."

Kuaron sat down beside her. The counter on the com screen seemed to whirl faster and faster now. In a matter of seconds, it beeped. Dina put down her cup.

"Attention, attention!" said the automated voice. "A real-time transmission from the planet Fantar is now arriving for Dina Bellaire. Please log on and confirm identity."

Dina signed on and identified herself. When the fee acceptance statement flashed on the screen, the price staggered her, but

Kuaron reached over and hit the key to accept before Dina could even think about it.

There was the standard disclaimer that the signal could be lost at any time, a reminder of the inherent delay, and a warning that no refund would be paid, even if the quality of the image deteriorated during transmission. Dina acknowledged each warning and waited.

Finally, the screen blurred and formed a wavy representation of a familiar face.

Her mother's image was fuzzy at the edges, but clearly recognizable. There were the familiar deep-set brown eyes, the dark hair streaked with gray, worn just to her shoulders, the straight brows and short, straight nose.

Marie Dagostino looked worried. "Dina, are you there?"

"I'm here, Mother. How are you?"

"What's happened to you?" her mother demanded, without answering the question, and Dina realized she wasn't waiting the proscribed number of seconds to hear Dina's response. "I don't understand. Some people came here and told me you had gone crazy—run off with some alien or something. It didn't sound like you at all." Marie stopped talking suddenly. "How am I? How are you, that's the question!"

Dina took a deep breath and let it out for a few seconds. This wouldn't have been easy in person, but with a transmission delay, it was almost impossible. "Well, I don't agree that I've gone crazy, but it is true that I met someone—a non-Terran. He's a Wakanrean, in fact. His name is Kuaron Du." Dina waited, and after several seconds, her mother's expression told her she had heard Dina's words.

"What? You've only been there a couple of weeks!"

"I know," Dina said, trying to find the right words. "It's not just—it's not just a matter of I met him and liked him. There's actually a process Wakanreans call *shahgunrah*—did you listen to my express, Mother?"

"Yes, of course." Her mother looked impatient with the need to pause between question and answer. "I knew to call you, didn't I? Are you sure you can afford this, Dina? It must be very expensive."

"It is, but don't worry about it. Did you understand about *shahgunrah*?"

After the pause, her mother's face assumed an alarmed look. "Yes, but I don't see what it has to do with you. How could you start an affair with someone you just met? I thought I raised you to behave better than that!"

"It's not the same thing, Mother. It wasn't—I mean I didn't choose to do this. *Shahgunrah* is something that can't be stopped once it starts, and it seems that somehow I started it with Kuaron."

Marie looked anxious for a few seconds, and then her eyes opened wide. "What? Have you been to a doctor? Can they do anything to treat it?"

"It's not a disease," Dina said, trying hard not snap at her mother. "The thing is, I seem to have some Wakanrean DNA. The most likely source is from Dad. Do you know anything more about his background, other than what you've already told me?"

Once the delay was over, her mother's face was a study in amazement. "Wakanrean DNA? How could you possibly have Wakanrean DNA?"

"I don't know," Dina said, trying to hold on to her patience. "That's why I'm asking if you know anything about Dad's background that you never told me."

"Of course not. He was adopted. We told you that."

"And there was never any hint of anything different about him—anything in his medical records?"

Dina watched anxiously as her mother waited to hear what she had said. Marie opened her mouth as if to speak and then stopped. Her face had a curious expression, half reluctance, half distaste. She sat silently for so long that Dina knew she must have heard the question.

"Mother?"

There was another pause, and then finally her mother spoke. "There was one—one incident."

"What?" Dina demanded, once she had heard the response.

Reluctance was winning the battle in her mother's expression. "Do you remember when they finally found your father's ship?"

"Of course," Dina said, surprised. "I was fourteen."

"He lived for some time on that moon, but when he knew he was dying, he recorded a message for you."

"What?" Dina said, seething at the transmission delay. "How could you not tell me?"

"I didn't give it to you then," her mother said, without any pause. Obviously she hadn't heard the question. "You were too young to understand. I don't know if it would help now, but I'll send it to you in an express."

"Mother—"

"I have to go, Dina," Marie said. "This has all been very upsetting, and it's reminded me of a very unhappy time. I have to say goodbye now."

"Mother—"

The screen went blank.

Kuaron moved closer and put his arm around Dina. She laid her head on his chest and sniffed his familiar scent.

"What do you think your father said in his message?" he asked, his voice rumbling in his chest.

"I have no idea."

He patted her arm. "We'll find out in a few days, then."

Dina felt as if she had been subjected to a virtual thrill ride, where the rider experienced the sensory experience of danger while safely strapped into a seat. She had made the call because she felt she owed it to her mother, but she hadn't really expected to learn anything about her father. Her memories of him were hazy but warm—a father who was gone much of the time but who made up for his absences by cramming his visits home with fun activities and lots of hugs and kisses.

Kuaron gave her a gentle one-armed squeeze. "It can't be anything too terrible."

"No," Dina said. "No, I suppose not."

"Drink your *quascha* and let's go back to bed," Kuaron said. "You have to see the doctor tomorrow."

"You're right," Dina said, picking up her cup. "No sense wasting time trying to guess what's in the message. It could be anything."

Kuaron waited while she drained her cup, and then the two of them went back to bed. Dina lay there for a long time before she finally went to sleep.


THE next day, Dina visited ThreeCon headquarters and had her first examination by the team of Terran and Wakanrean doctors selected by ThreeCon. The examination wasn't obtrusive, but the doctors were extremely interested in her physiology, and they took an extensive medical history. Dina was relieved to escape from the examining room, but she was surprised, when she came out, to find Jared sitting in the waiting room next to Kuaron.

"Hi," Jared said, rising to his feet. "Do you feel up to a visit to the PC's office? He's got some news for you."

"The PC?" Dina asked.

"The Planetary Commander," Jared said. "Sorry. Sometimes I speak acronym."

"It's better than the piffle you usually speak," Kuaron said, unfolding himself from a chair meant for someone smaller.

Jared grinned. "Dina must have taught you that. I don't think I've ever heard a Wakanrean say piffle."

"We're learning from each other," Kuaron said, taking Dina's hand as they started for the door. "Dina has begun to study Wisutan."

"Don't get your hopes up, Kuaron," Dina said. "It's not an easy language to learn."

"It's a bitch, in fact," Jared said, leading the way as they navigated through corridors to the exit. "Wisutans must think that vowels get lonely. They seldom have one by itself, and sometimes they string them together without benefit of consonants."

"I don't mind that so much," Dina said, looking around at ThreeCon headquarters. "Some words are difficult to pronounce, but I can learn that. It's just that the syntax is so convoluted I have trouble making sense of the sentence."

"Wisutan is a very expressive language," Kuaron said, as if he felt compelled to defend his native dialect.

Dina was too busy getting her bearings to argue. ThreeCon headquarters was a compact cluster of buildings, much larger than ThreeCon headquarters on Fantar. She followed Jared as he led the way toward an imposing, centrally-placed building that Dina recognized as the site of her competency hearing.

Jared returned to the discussion as he walked though the entrance and turned down a corridor. "I have to agree with Kuaron," he said, opening a door and standing back to allow Dina to precede him. "I've been cussed out in a lot of languages, and I can tell you, Wisutan is right up there with the best of them."

"I'm sure you deserved it every time," Dina said, going through the door.

"Of course he did," Kuaron said, following her.

Jared came through last. "A prophet gets no respect in his own land," he said in a sad voice.

"That's often very true, Jared," said a small being standing beside a large desk.

"Commander!" Jared jumped to attention. He was too dark-skinned to show a blush easily, but Dina thought he looked chagrined. "I—I didn't expect you—that is—uh, I brought Citizen Bellaire to see you, sir, as you requested."

"Yes, I see that," Marochh said, smiling at Dina. "And *Parundai Du* is with her. Come into my office, please, and we'll talk."

Dina followed him past the desk where a very large Miloran woman sat in front of a terminal, and paused in the doorway. "Is Jared coming with us?" Dina asked Marochh.

"Would you like him to come with us?" the Commander said.

"Yes, I think I would," Dina said. "You agree, don't you, Kuaron?"

"Certainly."

"Come along then, Jared," Marochh said.

The four of them moved from the outer office into the Planetary Commander's private space. It was a large room, furnished with a desk and several chairs, and Marochh directed everyone to a seat before he sat down himself.

Dina noted that his chair was scaled to fit him and even had an opening in the back for his tail.

"Now," Marochh said, taking his seat, "I'd like to thank you for coming, Citizen Bellaire—Dina. I wanted you to see something."

"What is it?" Dina asked.

"This." Marochh turned in his chair. The air behind his desk seemed to thicken like a sudden indoor fog. It grew more and more opaque, then deepened quickly to a solid black. Tiny points of light appeared in rapid profusion, a glowing stream of lights, some much brighter than others.

"It's a star map, isn't it?" Dina said.

"Yes," Marochh said. "It shows the region of the galaxy where Terra is located, as it appeared a few centuries ago. That bright yellow light is Sol, Terra's sun. I've made it show considerably brighter than it is for demonstration purposes.

"Now watch carefully," Marochh said, as the image shrank in scale so that the yellow point of light that was Sol became a very tiny dot in a milky swirl of stars surrounded by blackness.

"The colonization missions that left Terra centuries ago always had specific destinations in mind," Marochh went on, "but the colonists didn't have precise information about the worlds to which they were headed. Consequently, every mission had at least five or six potential target planets. We don't have all the mission planning records, but here's what we do know about the route taken by the generation ships that colonized Prashat."

As Marochh spoke, a second star glowed brightly at the far end of the star map. This one looked orange against the whiteness of the other stars.

"That orange star is Signey," Marochh said, "Prashat's star. It's not really orange, but I needed to differentiate it. And this," another dot changed from white to bright green, "is Cobiou, the star that Wakanreans see in the daytime."

Kuaron got to his feet and approached the holo field. He studied it from different angles. "Wakanreo is close to Prashat?" he asked Marochh.

"I wouldn't say close," the Shuratanian said. "But if you consider the path the generation ships must have taken, you're definitely on the way." To illustrate his point, a red line appeared, starting at Sol and continuing to Signey, passing quite near Cobiou and Wakanreo.

"So where does this leave us?" Dina asked.

"Ah!" Marochh said. "It leaves us trying to find evidence of some contact between the Prashat colonists and Wakanreo."

"But," Kuaron argued, resuming his seat, "that's not possible, is it? First Contact was seventy years ago, and you said the colony had been there for some time when it was destroyed."

"I did indeed," Marochh said. "No, I was thinking of earlier contact. From what we can determine, the Prashat expedition would have come near Cobiou more than three centuries ago—shortly before Wakanreo had its industrial revolution."

"That far back?" Kuaron said.

"Yes," Marochh said. "What we did, *parundai*, was to ask a filtering program to scan all available Wakanrean literature and history and come up with anything that could represent contact between Wakanreo and one of the generation ships."

"And what did it come up with?" Dina asked.

Marochh looked at Jared. "Would you like to tell them, Jared?"

"Very well, sir," the Terran said, clearing his throat as if he were uncertain how his announcement would be received. "The program's best guess for some evidence of Terran-Wakanrean early contact was the Saga of Zaingour."

There was a moment of silence. Dina was lost by this reference, and she looked to Kuaron for enlightenment. She was perplexed because she sensed that he was amused.

"The Saga of Zaingour?" Kuaron said. "Are you joking?"

"No," Marochh said. "Not at all."

"But what *is* the Saga of Zaingour?" Dina demanded.

Kuaron patted her hand as if to calm her. "It's a *shainai taul*."

The phrase sounded familiar, but Dina couldn't place the words. "A what?"

"A fairy tale or a fable," Jared translated. "Wakanrean children's literature is full of stories of the supernatural. Many of them are about elf-like creatures called *kapuhai* who can take many forms. Sometimes they're giants, and sometimes they can fly or do amazing magic. But in every story, they bring trouble to any Wakanrean foolish enough to have dealings with them."

"So was Zaingour a *kapuhai*?" Dina asked.

"Oh, no," Kuaron said. "Let me tell the story, Jared. I used to love to have it read to me when I was little."

"Go ahead, then," Jared said. "I'm sure you know it better than I do."

Kuaron leaned back in his chair and let his voice fall into a story-teller's cadence. "Long, long ago, in the time of the Great Plagues, there lived a farmer named Zaingour. He was a hard worker and his farm did well, but he was lonely because he had not found his *shahgunrahai*. Zaingour was out in his fields one day when a magic silver boat appeared in the sky. It flew like a bird, but then came down in his field suddenly. Zaingour was astonished to see that the crops around the sky boat had been scorched, as if by a great heat. He ran to get help from the neighboring farms, but when the farmers approached the sky boat, it was too hot to touch. Finally Zaingour threw water on it, and it cooled down.

"There were strange markings on the side, and the other farmers were afraid to touch the sky boat because it might be evil magic. Zaingour was braver, and he rapped it with a stick. At this point, the farmers were amazed to hear cries from inside it. Zaingour found what looked like a handle, and twisted and pulled until finally a hatch opened." Kuaron smiled at Dina. "And who do you think was inside?"

"A Terran of course," she said. "What happened next?"

"Inside the magic sky boat was a single *kapuhai*. Once the farmers had pulled it out, they found that it was wearing peculiar coverings, all torn and bloody, because this *kapuhai* had been hurt in a battle with an evil *kapuhai*. They took it to Zaingour's house and removed the coverings, and they were even more shocked to find that the *kapuhai* was very like a *qatorai* except that it was smaller and had no fur and no claws. It was, however, clearly a female.

"Zaingour hoped that the *kapuhai* would recover and grant him a wish, so he tended her, nursing her back to health. As he cared for her, she grew stronger and stronger, and even learned a few words of his language. And then one day, when Zaingour was helping her to dress, his *shahgunrah* began. He was distressed to find that, although the *kapuhai* was quite willing to share *taal* with him, there was no *klunar* and no *haictor* for her. Nevertheless, he took the knocker from the door and pretended that they had a true *shahkuun*.

"And then, on the fifth day of the false *shahkuun*, a magic bracelet that the creature always wore began to speak to her in a tongue that only the *kapuhai* could understand. The *kapuhai* answered it and then she made it known to Zaingour, using signs and simple words, that she had to go.

"He was distressed, of course, and pleaded with her to stay, but she would not. She went out into the field and summoned another magic sky boat, bigger than the first one. It flew down from the sky and carried her off."

"What happened to Zaingour?" Dina demanded.

"He died a few days later. Some said that he had died from the plague but others said that he died from having his *shahgunrah* torn asunder."

"Very good, *parundai*," Marochh said. "You followed the story exactly as it was outlined in the databank."

"I read it often," Kuaron said, "and I have a good memory."

'It's very sad," Dina said. "And I can see that it does suggest some sort of space-going ship, but isn't it a fairly adult topic for a children's story, with that part about *taal* and everything?"

Kuaron shook his head. "Not to Wakanreans. Many *shainai taul*—fairy tales—are about *shahgunrah*. Wakanrean parents make a point to teach their children about it at an early age, so they're not surprised when it happens to them."

"Well, it sure puts 'The Sleeping Princess' to shame," Dina said dryly, pleased to note Kuaron was trying to use Standard words for her benefit. "Do you think the story could really be true, Commander?"

"Quite possibly," Marochh said. "And if it is, it suggests an interesting possibility."

"And what is that?"

"It suggests that you yourself are descended from this chance encounter. And if that's true, it may well follow that any Terran and any Wakanrean who had experienced *shagunrah* could produce a hybrid child, and that further, the child would—unlike most hybrids—*not* be sterile."

Dina stared at him a moment, and then she looked to Kuaron. "What do you think, Kuaron?"

Her *shahgunrahai* was looking overwhelmed. "I don't know what to think. The Saga of Zaingour has always been regarded as pure fantasy—something to tell the children before bedtime, to make their eyes open wide and their head crests stand up. I don't think anyone ever considered that it could be anything else."

"Wakanreo was pretty primitive back then, wasn't it, Kuaron?" Jared asked.

"Yes," Kuaron agreed. "Farmers, in particular, were very isolated. Paruian herself lived only a little more than a century before the Great Plagues. Her word was spreading then, but there was still sporadic warfare. Our civilization advanced quickly once we adopted her teachings, but back then communication was neither rapid nor sophisticated. Such an event could have happened and been seen as a miraculous occurrence. If it did, it could certainly have gone virtually unreported so far as the government was concerned."

"So," Dina said, "if this Terran pilot went back to her generation ship and had a half-Wakanrean baby, that child could have been my father's great-great-great-great-grandmother or something?"

"Yes," Marochh said. "Presumably, the event was seen as miraculous on the ship, also, but there was no way for them to communicate the news outside of it. Over the centuries, the Wakanrean DNA became so diluted that it was no longer noticeable in the pilot's descendants, and by the time Prashat was rediscovered, the whole event was ancient history."

"So that would explain how I have some Wakanrean genes, and how I came to experience *shahgunrah*."

"Precisely," Marochh said. "The only alternative explanation is that your father suffered either radiation or biological contamination in utero, and that that event produced a mutation in his genes. If that theory is true, it represents a less certain prognosis for the survival of your offspring, and less chance that he or she would be fertile."

"Well." Dina took a deep breath and clutched Kuaron's hand tightly. "All in all, Kuaron, I'm hoping for Zaingour as an ancestor."

"Yes," Kuaron said. "I think perhaps, *acubai*, that it would be best if we could bring ourselves to believe in fairy tales."

"Heck," Dina said, "I could believe in *kapuhai* if it would help."

# *Chapter Eleven*

After a few days spent closing up her apartment and moving all her belongings to the cliff house, Dina decided it was time to go back to work. She announced her decision at breakfast.

"It might be just as well," Kuaron said as he poured *quascha* into her cup. "I have a performance in three days time, and I must practice."

"Where are you singing?" Dina asked, sipping her *quascha*.

"At the home of the Prefect of Wisuta," Kuaron said, taking a bite of toast. "The audience will be quite small—not more than a hundred people."

"Can you make money singing to only a hundred people? How much are the tickets?"

"What tickets?"

"The tickets to hear you sing."

Kuaron looked offended. "No one buys a ticket. I'm not a lecturer, I'm a *qatraharai*."

Dina wrinkled her forehead. "Then how do you make a living if no one pays to hear you sing?"

"People pay, but there are no tickets. Most of my performances are for private patrons, wealthy people who hope to gain status for supporting the *qatrahs*. They ask me to sing, and then they invite their friends and business associates to the performance."

"How much do you charge these patrons?"

Kuaron folded his arms across his chest. "Nothing."

Dina put down her cup. "Nothing? I thought you said they gave you money in one of those figurine things?"

Kuaron nodded. "After I sing, the patron will give me a *guidros* that contains a gift of money."

"But," Dina said, still perplexed, "what determines how much money?"

Kuaron shrugged as if to suggest that the matter was of no great concern. "The reputation of the *qatraharai*, the formality of the occasion, the quality of the performance, the number of *qatrahs*, and the number of guests would all be considered in setting a fee."

"A fee? I thought it was a gift?"

Kuaron smiled. "It is."

Dina looked at him in annoyance. "It sounds pretty slipshod to me, Kuaron. What's to stop a patron from stiffing you—paying you little or nothing?"

"Well, if someone wants to earn status, they won't get it by not paying their *qatraharai*. And if anyone ever did that to me, I'd never sing for them again."

Dina chewed her toast and considered him. There was, she knew, no arrogance in his demeanor. He wasn't boasting, he was simply stating a fact. "Are you really that good or do you just think you are?"

"I'm very good. You'll hear for yourself in three days—if you come to the performance."

"I wouldn't miss it. And that's really the only way a *qatraharai* gets paid?"

"Not entirely," Kuaron said, reaching for another piece of toasted *juoin*. "There are also clubs made up of people who love the *qatrahs* but can't afford to be patrons. They pool their money and invite a *qatraharai* to sing in a large hall, and in that case the fee is settled ahead of time. Each of the members gets to invite a certain number of guests. Whether they choose to charge their guests for the privilege is up to them."

"Did you get started that way?"

"Yes," Kuaron said, licking crumbs from his fingers. "I have an aunt who belongs to two such clubs. She put me forward with one of them, and that was my first public appearance."

Dina was curious. "So can anyone join a club?"

"It depends on the club. Membership is often very competitive. Some clubs have been in existence for hundreds of years and memberships are passed on from parent to child. Others are newer and charge stiff entrance fees. There are some that are based on regional or religious affiliations."

"Do you still sing for these clubs?"

"Sometimes. Almost every *qatraharai* does. I was lucky, though. I made my name without having to sign an exclusive agreement with a club. If you do that, you're very limited in what else you can do until your contract runs its course."

"Well, it's all very interesting," Dina said, shoving her plate and cup into the cleaning hatch, "but I have to go to work."

Kuaron rose to his feet and hovered over her. "Be careful, *acubai*."

"I will."

DINA'S first day back on the job—her fourth day at Quafray—didn't start auspiciously. She took an autocab, and was admitted to the main entrance after showing her identification, but it seemed to her that the guards subjected her to a hostile inspection.

Once she was in her own section, her coworkers were polite, but even more formal and uncommunicative than they had been when she first arrived at Quafray. Dina admitted to herself that she might be over-reacting to Wakanrean manners, but still she found the atmosphere oppressive.

Her supervisor, in particular, was extremely reserved. She waved away Dina's apologies for her absence with a brief gesture and a half dozen words of dismissal. Dina got the impression that the woman wanted to say something very different, but couldn't bring herself to do it. Whatever the unspoken thought was, Dina didn't think it was complimentary. Hyral Brau looked as if she had bitten into something sour.

The only friendly face Dina saw was Shanour Taum's, the young technician who helped with her testing protocols. After Dina spent the morning reviewing the testing she had missed and assessing what was waiting in the queue, Shanour stopped by her cubicle. He bowed politely and asked if she wanted company at lunch. Dina found the gesture heartening, especially since she felt almost as if she were on trial again.

Since the lunchroom was only for employees and members, Dina was the only Terran in an ocean of Wakanreans. She felt many eyes on her as she sat down beside Shanour. Accentuating this sense of isolation was the need to avoid touching him, even through her gloved hands, which she found extremely irksome. The time she had spent with Kuaron had made her less careful, and it was difficult, now that she no longer saw Wakanreans as alien, to follow the no-touching rule.

The lab assistant reminded her how to operate the menu console. Their choices were limited, and they made their selections quickly.

"You seem familiar with our food already," Shanour said.

"I've been eating it for several days now," Dina said. "And my *shahgunrahai* is a good cook."

Shanour ducked his head in the Wakanrean equivalent of a blush, confirming Dina's first impression that he was inclined to be shy, at least with her. "I have no *shahgunrahai*."

Dina was a little at a loss. She didn't know what was considered a polite response to such a revelation. She decided to go with her instincts. "Are you looking forward to finding *shahgunrah*?"

"Oh, yes. I only hope I like her. And I hope it's a her, of course, because I want children."

Dina debated briefly about revealing the one bit of news about her circumstance that hadn't been widely circulated, but she decided that expecting Shanour to keep her pregnancy a secret would be too much to ask. "I wish you luck," she said, and then she added the Wisutan phrase for the same thing. "*Keiusha fa yin.*"

Shanour looked up in surprise. "You speak Wisutan?"

"Not really. I really only know a few phrases. It's a difficult language for a Terran to learn. Kuaron tried to teach me, but your syntax was too difficult, so I got a language program. I do much better with that because it doesn't slur the words like Kuaron does, and it can show me the printed words at the same time it says them."

"Oh," Shanour said, his eyes shining. His eyes were darker than Kuaron's, a golden-brown matrix with flecks of reddish color that matched his facial and body fur. "I think it's wonderful you're making such an effort."

"Well, it looks as if I'll be here a lot longer than I had planned."

Before Shanour could respond, the table chimed and the serving hatch opened to disgorge their trays. Shanour passed a tray to Dina and the two of them began to eat. Dina knew immediately that Quafray might subscribe to the Wisutan custom of providing the meal, but they didn't follow through on the idea that food should always be prepared by a sentient being. After several days of eating home-cooked food, the difference in texture was subtle but discernible.

"Your *shahgunrahai* is a *qatraharai*, isn't he?" Shanour asked.

"Yes. Do you like the *qatrahs*?"

Shanour looked embarrassed. "Not really, but my father is devoted to them. He told me he's heard your *shahgunrahai* sing several times. I never learned enough about the *qatrahs* to appreciate them."

"I haven't heard Kuaron sing yet. But that will change in a few days."

"And he's a *parundai*, too, isn't he?" Shanour said, with much more reverence than he had asked about Kuaron's career.

"Yes, he is. Are you a follower of Paruian?"

Shanour nodded once, emphatically, just as Kuaron always did. "Oh, yes. My family are all observant. My mother has made several pilgrimages to Paruianite shrines."

"Really?" Dina hoped asking questions wouldn't give offense. "What constitutes a shrine? Is it something that's built, or something that was there when Paruian was alive?"

"Both, in a way. Over the years, people built stone cairns to mark events in Paruian's life—where she was born, where she died, places where she preached, and places where she stayed for a long time. They go there to pray to her."

"I see."

Shanour stared intently at his plate as if he were afraid his food would crawl away. "My mother says it's a miracle that *Parundai* Du found *shahgunrah* with a Terran."

"I don't know that I'd call it a miracle, but it definitely has miraculous overtones. I certainly never expected it."

Shan looked up, his expression a mixture of curiosity and sympathy. "It must have frightened you when it happened."

"It did. But fortunately, Kuaron is a wonderful person. He was very kind and considerate."

"And is he a good lover?"

Dina almost choked on her food. She recalled how frank her conversations with Kuaron had been and realized she shouldn't have been shocked by the question, even coming from a man who was almost a stranger. "Yes," she said, as casually as she could. "Very good."

Shanour let out a sigh. "How nice for you."

Dina changed the subject to ask Shanour about his work schedule. Quafray didn't follow the standard Wakanrean eight day week but rather had employees rotate their work and rest days in cycles of four days of working followed by three days off. Shanour was currently assigned to the same shift cohort as Dina, and thus they both worked the same days. From there, they passed to a discussion of Shanour's studies, and the meal concluded with no further mention of *shahgunrah*.

By mid afternoon, Dina was tired. Her lab cubicle was well appointed, but small, and the walls were tall enough that she couldn't see over them. She was feeling confined as well as weary. She stood up and stretched as best she could, and then let out a sigh. She missed Kuaron rather badly; except for her incarceration at the Terran embassy, she hadn't been away from him for this long since she had met him.

"Are you well, Bellaire?" a voice said.

Dina jumped, and turned to find her supervisor standing in the opening to the corridor. "Oh, hello. I'm sorry, *Kantai* Brau. I didn't realize you were there."

"It's no matter," the Wakanrean woman said. "Are you quite well?"

"I'm fine," Dina said, well aware that all the cubicles in the room opened onto the same corridor and everyone could hear their conversation.

"How are you doing in your reading?"

"All right." Dina had been relieved to find Quafray's official records were in Standard, especially as many people seemed to speak Wisutan in their personal conversations. "I'm about halfway through the second section of the report."

"Very good," Hyral Brau said, without sounding at all pleased.

"I had a few questions—" Dina began. She stopped abruptly as she sensed that Kuaron was near.

"What is it?"

"Kuaron's here!" Dina brushed past her supervisor just as the door at the end of the corridor opened.

"Kuaron!" Dina said, rushing to meet him before he even appeared in the corridor.

In seconds he was there. He folded her into an embrace, and Dina felt again the reassurance that touching him brought to her. She hugged him tightly, and Kuaron bent down to whisper in her ear.

"Are you all right, *acubai?*"

"I'm fine," Dina whispered back. "I missed you, though."

"And I missed you."

Dina pulled back from him a little, and noted that he was wearing a visitor's badge. "How did you get in?"

Kuaron grinned a toothy grin. "It wasn't difficult. I do have identification."

Dina realized he was used to celebrity status. It dawned on her suddenly that her supervisor was waiting to be introduced.

"Where are my manners!" she said. "Kuaron, I'd like you to meet *Kantai* Hyral Brau, who supervises my work. *Kantai*, this is my *shahgunrahai, Parundai* Kuaron Du."

The Wakanrean woman's reaction to this introduction amazed Dina. She bowed deeply to Kuaron, hands behind her and head down, and then touched hands with him reverently.

"It's an honor to meet you, *parundai*," she gushed. "I had the great pleasure of hearing you sing once, at the Hall of Heroes."

"Thank you," Kuaron said. "Are you an admirer of the *qatrahs*, then?"

"Oh, yes! I go to performances as often as I can."

"It's always a pleasure to meet a *qatrahoinai*."

"Bellaire," Hyral said, turning to Dina, "are you sure that you want to start back to work on a full schedule? Many people prefer to work limited hours the first few weeks after their *shahkuun* ends. You do seem tired."

Dina had been staring, unable to believe this was the same woman who had been so stern and disapproving all day. "Um, thank you, *Kantai* Brau," she said, collecting herself with an effort. "I might like to do that for a few days."

"Take as long as you need," Hyral said. "Perhaps you should go home now, while the *parundai* is here to escort you?"

"Thank you," Dina said, flabbergasted. "I'll just sign off the system then, and we can go home."

Kuaron made conversation with the Wakanrean woman while Dina hastily exited the Quafray information system and secured her cubicle.

"Thank you again," Dina said politely, coming out of her cubicle.

"It's nothing," Hyral said. "It's company policy, in fact."

Dina refrained from asking why she hadn't mentioned it before, and took Kuaron's arm.

Kuaron bowed to Hyral, but when the Wakanrean woman stepped back to let him precede her to the door, he paused. "I had a thought, *Kantai* Brau. As it happens, I'm singing this *Unpaith* at the home of our Prefect. If you'd care for it, I could ask her to include your name on the guest list?"

Hyral looked as if she might burst from excitement. "That would be delightful, *parundai*! I would be honored by such an invitation."

"Or should it be two names?" Kuaron said.

Hyral ducked her head and admitted that her *shahgunrahai* shared her passion for the *qatrahs*. Kuaron gave her the address and time, and made his farewells with a formal bow.

Dina waited until they were in the flyter to speak. "Well! That was revolting."

"What was?" Kuaron asked. His eyes glittered with a strange light, and Dina sensed he was amused.

"My boss practically groveled at your feet, and it didn't seem to bother you at all."

Kuaron gave a Wakanrean shrug. "I'm used to it."

"Because you're a *qatraharai* or because you're a *parundai*?"

"Both. Some people are more impressed with one thing, and some with the other. Occasionally, I meet a religious *qatrahoinai* and their enthusiasm becomes excessive."

"Like Hyral Brau's wasn't?"

Kuaron laughed. "She wasn't that bad. I've met worse."

"You didn't see her before. She had a frown on her face every time she looked at me today—until you showed up."

Kuaron gave her a speculative look, but shook his head. "I think you're doing her a disservice, then. If she looked disapproving before, she most likely thought we weren't really *shahgunrahai*. When she saw you act like one, she changed her mind."

"Act like one? How did I act like a *shahgunrahai*?"

Kuaron smiled. "I'm sure you knew I was coming before I opened the door. And it looked to me like you nearly knocked her down to get to me."

"Oh, that. I suppose you could be right." She grimaced, a minor gesture compared to Kuaron's shrug. "I guess I was so revolted seeing *Kantai* Brau suck up to you that I don't want to give her credit for her motives. Why did you make that offer to have her invited to your performance? Is that allowed?"

Kuaron checked the destination control and leaned back in his seat. "Certainly it's allowed. It gives my patron something of an advantage in determining my fee, but it's my prerogative to ask to have a friend invited. Remind me to call the Prefect."

"So will we see Jared there? Since he's a *qatrahoinai*, too?"

Kuaron grinned. "You said that very well. No, I haven't asked the Prefect to invite Jared. If I asked to have him invited this time, he'd expect it next time. The man is insatiable where performances are concerned."

Dina leaned back in her own seat. "Well, anyway, I'm glad you came to get me. I was tired, and I was missing you."

Kuaron laid his arm on the back of her seat, and Dina knew instantly that he was becoming aroused. She gave him a questioning look.

He smiled but shook his head. "You're tired. It can wait until tonight."

"I'm not that tired."

"Are you certain, *acubai*?"

"Yes," Dina said, stroking his arm.

Kuaron's response was to pull her close and nuzzle her neck, and then to open her shirt. A few minutes later, they had moved to the more open space at the rear of the passenger cabin when the arrival alarm beeped.

Kuaron sat up and uttered something that sounded like a Wisutan curse.

"Just land the thing," Dina said, propping herself up on one elbow, "and then come right back here."

Kuaron scrambled over the seat and took the controls. In less than a minute, he was back beside her.

Dina lay down and pulled him on top of her. "Now," she said with satisfaction, "where were we?"

Kuaron said nothing, but Dina didn't insist on an answer.

DINA took pains over her appearance when she dressed for Kuaron's performance. She wore the same long red gown she had worn to the embassy party, and she wove bright blue and yellow Wakanrean flowers into the one long braid she wore down her back.

Kuaron wore a plain white *qatraharai's* robe trimmed in deep red. They were both ready when the Prefect's flyter landed on the summit and set off the alarm.

They hardly spoke at all in the flyter. Dina could feel that Kuaron was nervous; he gripped her hand the entire time. She watched him a little anxiously, unsure of whether she should try to make conversation, but she decided against it. Kuaron was concentrating, and she didn't want to distract him. When they arrived at their destination, the Prefect greeted them herself.

She was a tall woman, taller than Kuaron, with a distinguished shock of white in her black headcrest, and light amber eyes that glowed with anticipation. She wore an elaborate robe covered with intricate embroidery, and a long gold chain around her neck. She offered them refreshments, but both of them declined. Kuaron asked to go straight to the performance hall.

The Prefect obligingly led the way to a large room where several people were placing chairs in rows. Kuaron retreated to an alcove at the far end of the room. The entrance had been covered with a drape to provide some privacy. Dina knew he liked to meditate for a few minutes before a performance, so she didn't follow him when he slipped behind the curtain. When he came out, he smiled reassuringly at her. She was relieved that he seemed considerably less tense now that the moment of his performance was at hand. He showed her where he would be standing and asked her where she wanted to sit.

Dina glanced around at the rows of chairs. There was a small niche to the right of where Kuaron would stand. It wasn't in his direct line of vision, but she would be able to see him clearly without feeling like she was on stage herself, and without being surrounded by his Wakanrean admirers.

"How about there?" she asked.

Kuaron asked for a chair to be placed in the niche. Once it was there, Dina moved to it and sat down. She smiled at Kuaron, and he smiled back. Even from across the room, she could see that he was ready to start—not nervous any longer, but merely keyed up and looking forward to the opportunity to sing for an appreciative audience.

Kuaron moved to the position he had chosen at one end of the room, facing the hundred or so chairs that had been set up, and with his back to the alcove. There were no instruments or musicians or other singers. *Qatrahs* were always performed strictly as a solo, without any accompaniment. Kuaron stood quietly, not moving, and waited. There was a buzz of excitement around the room, and then the chairs filled rapidly as the guests arrived. Dina saw Hyral Brau come in with another Wakanrean woman. She nodded at Dina as they took seats in one of the back rows, but she didn't approach. A rush of people filled the room, and then once everyone was seated, the room became dead quiet. No one so much as moved in his chair.

Without warning Kuaron took a deep breath, filling his lungs until his chest strained the fabric of his robe. He put his head back and began to release the air, a little at a time, in a deep, slow, warbling wail. It grew steadily both louder and higher in pitch until Dina couldn't hear it anymore.

After a few seconds, Kuaron began to chant. It was a deep, sonorous chant, rising and falling to a definite beat. The chanting went on for some time, seeming to tell a story. At certain points Kuaron would hold out his arms or gesture, as if to emphasize the chant. Then, gradually, the chanting changed and became true singing, high lilting notes that filled the room. Finally, one note repeated several times, held for a moment, and then stopped. The *qatrah* was over.

There was total silence. Kuaron waited for several seconds and began anew. This *qatrah* started with whistling and clicking noises, slowly at first and then faster and faster, until Kuaron changed to singing. Dina was amazed at his vocal range. He could go from bass to soprano and back again in seconds.

The end of the second *qatrah* was also greeted with total silence. The third began soon after, with beautiful trilling notes, like a songbird, flitting up and down the scale, and then changed suddenly to harsh, guttural, angry sounds. Dina was suddenly reminded of Erik Kordes' comment comparing Kuaron's singing to torturing a small animal. Soon after that, Kuaron returned to singing a melody, and Dina realized she was hearing two notes at once, as if he were singing harmony with himself.

Kuaron sang seven *qatrahs*, two of them very long. After the seventh, he waited silently, as if he were finished. When everyone sat as still and soundless as statues for at least a full minute, he began an eighth *qatrah*, rapid, staccato sounds that changed to more chanting. After the eighth song, he bowed his head and stepped back a few paces. Still no one moved or spoke. They sat in total silence for a good five minutes. Dina was glad Kuaron had told her what to expect or she would certainly have thought it was over.

Suddenly, Kuaron stepped forward again. He put his head back and began to sing a low despairing wail; it was a profoundly sad and unhappy sound, like a child who has lost his mother. The melody repeated a few times, and then suddenly Kuaron's voice lifted in jubilant triumph, rising past Dina's range of hearing and dipping back again. His voice soared across the room in a joyful burst of pure sound. It exploded in Dina's ears like some kind of happy cannon. She smiled just to hear it.

When Kuaron finished this *qatrah*, there was still silence. This time he bowed from the waist and stepped back all the way into the alcove. Still no one moved or spoke.

Dina studied the audience. She saw Hyral Brau and her *shahgunrahai* sitting as still as everyone around them, both their faces rapt and blissful. Dina was surprised to see a distinctly Terran face a few rows in front of Hyral. She hadn't noticed any Terrans coming in, so she leaned forward to get a better look. It was Jared Harlingen. He sat motionless on the edge of his chair, looking every bit as attentive as any of the Wakanreans.

After a few more minutes, Kuaron came out of the alcove and took his place again. This song was quieter, more like a lullaby than anything else. There were a few clicks and trills in the middle but mostly it was a simple, sweet melody, with only the power of his voice to make it more than an ordinary song.

When he finished, he bowed twice, deeply, and returned to the alcove. Kuaron had told her that this was his signal that he would sing no more encores, so Dina expected the audience to move, but no one did.

Dina sat in her chair like all the others, waiting to see what would happen. After several long minutes, the Prefect came out of the alcove. There was a disappointed murmur from the crowd, and then she held up her hand for silence.

"*Parundai* Du has asked me to convey to you his deep appreciation of your response," she said raising her voice to carry over the crowd. "He's very tired, but if you can wait just a few moments, he will perform one—and only one—more *qatrah*."

She stepped back into the alcove. A quiver of anticipation ran through the audience and then the silence resumed, absolute and tomb-like.

Finally, Kuaron returned. He stood for a moment, as if to compose himself; then he drew in a deep breath and let loose a shriek that would have given the devil pause. Dina almost cried out, it startled her so. This was followed by a deep, reverberating hum, as if someone had struck a gong. The hum was repeated in various pitches and then it changed to trilling, rapid and high. Kuaron began to sing a melody that went all over the scale.

The melody changed to a dirge, sad and bleak. At first Dina thought it would end there but after a slight pause, it began to rise and become more upbeat. The melody went on for some time, often going beyond Dina's range of hearing; the rhythm changed several times from fast to slow and back again. Finally, Kuaron hit one high, clear note and held it for at least two minutes. When he stopped, the note hung in the air for just a fraction of a second. Then he bowed again, twice, and left the room.

There was a brief, respectful silence, and then a murmur went through the crowd and swelled to loud chattering. People began to leave their chairs and gather their belongings, talking and gesticulating all the while.

The Prefect nodded and smiled at her guests as she sailed through the departing crowd, like a boat cresting the waves. Dina jumped to her feet and zig-zagged past the Wakanreans to follow in the Prefect's wake. She entered the alcove right behind the Wakanrean woman and found Kuaron sitting on a chair with his arms hanging loosely at his sides. He looked exhausted, but Dina was reassured.

The Prefect was ecstatic. "That was wonderful, *Parundai* Du. The *Shahgundal* was the best I've ever heard. And to close with the *Cregamekano*—what a performance!"

"I'm glad you enjoyed it, Prefect," Kuaron said. "I hope you'll understand, but I must go home now."

Far from arguing, the Prefect was all solicitude, showing them out through a door that opened directly to a corridor so that Kuaron didn't have to face his audience. She ordered her flyter and, after leaving them alone for a few minutes, she walked them to the roof port herself. At the last minute she pressed something into Kuaron's hand.

"Well," asked Kuaron as they lifted off, "what did you think?"

Dina was well aware that he would know if she lied. "It was interesting."

"Only interesting?" Kuaron said.

Dina could tell he was hurt. "I'm sorry, Kuaron. I can recognize you have a powerful, trained voice, but I'm not good at music—any music. And I don't know anything about the *qatrahs*."

Kuaron sighed. "Ah, well. You may not realize it, but that, my *guisha*, was the performance of a lifetime." He studied the object the Prefect had given him. It looked like a small cast metal figurine of a strange animal except the head seemed to be detachable as Kuaron unscrewed it from the body.

"Is that a *guidros*?" Dina asked, eager to change the subject.

"Yes," Kuaron said. "I think it's supposed to be a *culahin* but it's too stylized to be a good likeness."

"So you have another *guidros* for your collection?"

"I expect I'll keep this one, even if it's not valuable. Tonight was a good performance, and it was the first time I sang after finding *shahgunrah*."

He turned the body of the animal upside down and tapped it. A slip of thermaplast fell into his hand. Dina recognized it as a deposit receipt.

She could tell Kuaron was very pleased with what he read on the slip. He chortled as he slipped it back into the *guidros* and screwed the lid closed. "At least my patrons appreciate my talent. If I can keep this up, we'll be rich."

Dina tried for a conciliatory note. "I liked the happy song the best. Was it about *shahgunrah*?"

This comment seemed to appease Kuaron, as satisfaction flowed from him as he leaned back in his seat. "You could tell that? That's good. I did it right then." He closed his eyes. "Wake me up when we get home. There are over six hundred *qatrahs,* and I feel like I've sung them all."

# Chapter Twelve

The next day, Kuaron spent the morning scanning the news for reviews of his performance. Dina was glad that she didn't have to work, so she could watch him as he eagerly flipped from screen to screen. It was a revelation to her to see him so vulnerable to other people's opinions.

Kuaron was pleased when the first review he read was favorable, but Dina sensed his sheer elation when he read the second.

"You should read this," he said. "It mentions you, if only indirectly."

Dina reached for the monitor but one glance made her tisk with annoyance. "It's in Wisutan!"

"Sorry. Do you know how to turn on translation?"

"Yes. I've got it now." Kuaron still watched her intently, so Dina read the review out loud.

"Last night, *Kantai* Lanoc Dre, our Prefect, treated over one hundred of her friends to a wonderful performance of the art of the *qatrah*. The Prefect invited a renowned *qatraharai*, *Parundai* Kuaron Du, to sing at a gathering at her home. This intimate setting proved to be ideal for the distinguished *qatraharai* to prove that his recent *shahgunrah* had in no way diminished his voice or his technique. In fact, his rendering of the *Shahgundal* left his audience deeply moved. No one in hearing could doubt the validity of his experience or question that it was reciprocated. The very essence of *klunar* poured from his throat during the *Shahgundal*.

"After a simple but moving encore of the *Truo*, *Parundai* Du went on to astound everyone with a final encore of the *Cregamekano*.

167

This most demanding of the *qatrahs* was rendered in perfect detail, in spite of the fact that the *qatraharai* was clearly exhausted. Those of us who were privileged to attend owe a debt of gratitude to the Prefect."

Dina pushed the monitor back to him. "Why don't you stop reading them? You're not going to find one better than that."

Kuaron grinned happily, but she noticed that he kept searching for reviews.

"Shall I make more *quascha?*" Dina asked, when she had poured the last cup.

"Why don't you?" Kuaron said. "Jared will be here soon."

Dina was surprised. "Did he call? I didn't hear the com."

"No, but he always comes to see me soon after's he's been to a performance, and I know he doesn't have to work today."

"I was surprised to see him last night. I thought you said you didn't ask for him to be invited?"

"I didn't. He got there on his own initiative. I plan to ask him how he did it."

"If there's one thing Jared Harlingen has plenty of, it's initiative."

A short while later, the summit alarm beeped, and Kuaron's prophecy was fulfilled when Jared's face appeared on the com screen.

"Good morning, Kuaron," he said cheerfully. "Is this a bad time?"

"No, midget," Kuaron retorted. "We're quite used to company coming in with the dawn."

"Aw, now, Kuaron," Jared protested. "It's not *that* early."

"Just land and come see us," Kuaron said, flicking a control on the security panel. "The *quascha* is ready."

When Jared came through the door a few minutes later, he was carrying a small bouquet of Wakanrean water blossoms. They were deep blue in color with darker blue stems; bright yellow and orange tendrils hung from the center of each globular blossom.

Jared bowed low in front of Kuaron and handed him the bouquet with both hands. "For you. Someday I'll tell my grandchildren how I was privileged to hear you sing."

Kuaron accepted the flowers with a nonchalant air, but Dina knew that he was pleased.

"Don't be a *nyesh*, Jared," he said.

"What," Dina said, interrupting in exasperation, "is a *nyesh?*"

"A boot licker," Jared said. "A suck-up. Someone who flatters excessively. I know I am, Kuaron, but I can't help myself. You were good before, but last night you joined the ranks of the immortals."

This was too much even for Kuaron's sense of self worth. "Now you're really going too far." He put the flowers in the sink while he got a bowl from the cupboard.

"Really, Jared!" Dina said. "I have to live with him."

"Lucky woman!" Jared said, grinning. "Wasn't it an amazing performance?"

There was a brief silence, and then Kuaron spoke as he filled the bowl with water. "Dina thought it was very interesting."

"Argh!" Jared said, clutching his chest as if he were in pain. "Interesting! She said it was *interesting*! My god! It's as if Leonardo da Vinci married a woman who was color blind!"

"Who is Leonardo da Vinci?" Kuaron asked, before Dina could protest.

"He was a great artist and inventor on ancient Terra," Dina said. "Cut it out, Jared! Just because I'm not musical is no reason to treat me as if I were a complete idiot."

Kuaron was sprinkling a silvery powder into the bowl of water. "After all, I know next to nothing about chemistry."

"What's chemistry compared to such glorious art!" Jared said.

"It's pretty damn useful if you need to turn a few tons of biomass into edible food," Dina said. "Or even if you want to build a house like this." She waved one arm to indicate the walls around her. "Wakanrean chemists invented the acid that ate away the rock and made this kind of house possible."

"It's also useful," Kuaron said as he dropped the blossoms into the bowl one at a time, "when you want to keep cut flowers alive longer." He set the bowl on the table, then watched the blossoms drift into clumps and twine their stems together.

"Bah!" Jared said.

"Sit down and drink your *quascha*," Dina said severely. "I'm losing patience fast."

Jared laughed, grabbed her swiftly, kissed her cheek, and then let her go to drop down into a chair. "No, really, Kuaron, you were great. Have you seen the reviews?"

Dina burst out laughing as she sat down next to him. "Has he? He hasn't looked at anything else."

"I don't blame him," Jared said. "It was wonderful. I do have a couple of questions—"

"Only two, midget?" Kuaron said, an incipient smile tugging at his mouth. "What are they?"

This proved to be all the invitation Jared needed. He launched into a recital of the specifics of the performance, demanding an explanation of Kuaron's timing, inflection, and phrasing on three different *qatrahs*.

Dina was lost in the details. She had no understanding of the techniques involved in singing the *qatrahs*, but she could tell from Kuaron's responses that Jared did.

After a while, she left them to their discussion and went into the bedroom to tidy it. She took a moment to study herself in the mirror Kuaron had bought for her. It seemed incredible, considering that she was only about three weeks pregnant, but it looked as if she was showing already. There was a slight bulge in her silhouette when she turned sideways. Dina was certain it hadn't been there the day before. She sighed and went back to the main room.

"So," Kuaron was saying, "how did you manage to get yourself invited? I didn't think you were close friends with the Prefect?"

"I'm not," Jared said, as Dina sat down. "I only know her officially."

"Well?"

Jared grinned. "As it happened, I called on her about a cultural program I'd heard she was sponsoring. After I finished lauding her efforts at promoting Wakanrean culture, I suggested including some Terran events in her program. I even asked her to attend a ballet with me—that's a Terran form of dance—so she'd know what they're like. Unfortunately, the Prefect had to decline as she was hosting your performance that night. She regretted she couldn't invite me as I was already committed to go to the ballet."

"And then you realized you had the date wrong, and she was stuck?"

"Precisely," Jared said, looking smug.

"You're terrible," Dina said. "Is there even a ballet?"

"Of course there's a ballet," Jared said. "Never lie outright. It's very dangerous."

"And will you go to it?" Dina asked.

"Certainly," Jared said with virtuous solemnity. "And I'm escorting the Prefect and her *shahgunrahai* to it in three days. I might well need her again, you know."

Kuaron laughed. "You should have been a politician."

"I am, in a way. That's what they call the Admin branch of ThreeCon—bureaucrats in uniform."

"I've never seen you in civilian clothes before," Dina said, suddenly realizing that he was wearing an ordinary gray shirt and trousers.

"What can I say?" Jared said. "I'm just a guy with a strong sense of duty."

His tone was facetious, but Dina suspected that he was serious. "Is that why you joined ThreeCon?" she asked.

"Partly," he said. "And I wanted to see more of the universe. I signed up right out of university, and I got my wish."

"It's a ten year enlistment isn't it?" Dina said. "You must be ready to get out soon?"

Jared shook his head. "Nope. I finished my first enlistment right before I came here, and I re-upped."

"You've done very well here," Kuaron said. "Not many Terrans bother to learn the local language—let alone learn to appreciate the *qatrahs*."

"Speaking of the *qatrahs*," Jared said, "about the third *cair* in the *Shahgundal*—"

Dina laughed and stood up. She started to say she would leave them to the intricacies of the *qatrahs* when suddenly she felt dizzy. "Kuaron—"

Her *shahgunrahai* looked up, froze for a second, then jumped to his feet and moved to her side. "What's wrong? You don't look well."

"It's very strange," Dina said, sinking into her chair. "I feel almost like I'm going to faint."

Jared had crossed the room, too. He looked down at her now and frowned. "You do look pale. Maybe you should lie down?"

Dina didn't answer him; she was too absorbed in the fact that his and Kuaron's faces seemed to have blurred.

Kuaron bent over her, his face looming close, his expression anxious. He took her hand. "Shall I carry you to bed?"

Dina wanted to tell him not to be silly, but she couldn't quite get the words out. She gave a little sigh instead, and then shut her eyes and slumped down in the chair.

WHEN Dina came to herself, she was lying in bed, and Kuaron was holding a cold compress to her forehead.

"Kuaron," Dina said, moving the compress. "What happened?"

"You fainted," Kuaron said. "How do you feel?"

"I'm fine." She propped herself up on her elbows. "I'm just a little woozy, that's all."

There was a knock at the door, and Jared came into the room.

"There'll be a medical team here in fifteen minutes," he said to Kuaron.

"Jared, no!" Dina protested, trying to sit up. Kuaron pulled her upright, then sat down next to her to prop her up. "It's ridiculous," Dina said. "I'm pregnant, and I fainted. That's all there is to it."

"No sense taking chances," Jared said. "How are you doing?"

"I'm fine. There's no need to make a fuss."

"Yes, there is." Kuaron put his arm around her.

Jared started for the door. "I'll wait by the com to let the med team in when they come."

"Thank you," Kuaron said.

Dina sighed. "This is absurd, Kuaron. I don't need a doctor. Don't Wakanrean women ever faint when they're pregnant?"

"It's not usual," he said. "I'm glad Jared was here to tell me that it was more common among Terran women, or I would have panicked."

Dina resisted the temptation to tell him he was panicking by allowing Jared to call a doctor. She felt suddenly dizzy, and Kuaron knew instantly that she was distressed.

"You should lie down," he said.

"I'm all right." Dina reached for a pillow. "Really. I'd rather sit up."

Wisutans didn't usually sleep with pillows in their beds, but Kuaron had bought several when he discovered that Dina was more comfortable sleeping with one under her head. Now he took the pillow from her, laid it against the wall, then pulled her back so that she was supported by it.

Dina smiled at him. "You do realize you're treating me as if I were a child?"

"You're not well."

"I'm fine."

"You don't look fine."

Dina waved a hand to signal defeat. "Okay, you win. I'm sick. I'll just sit here for a while until I feel better."

"Until the doctor comes," Kuaron said.

Dina gave him an annoyed look. "I never knew Wakanreans could be so damn stubborn."

Kuaron laughed and kissed her forehead. "You haven't even seen stubborn. Wait until my father hears about this."

Dina sighed, leaned her head against him, and sighed again.


THE medical team arrived with no fanfare, and Dina was relieved when they didn't fuss over her unduly. The Terran doctor was the same one she had seen the week before at ThreeCon headquarters, and Dina had liked him then. The Wakanrean was new to her, but she seemed pleasant enough.

The Terran doctor was reassuring but firm. "Your blood pressure dropped drastically. It's not unusual, but there's no sense in being careless. Wear the monitor *all* the time. Water won't hurt it, so don't worry about the shower or the bath. If anything goes wrong, we'll be notified by telemetry."

"All right." Dina felt the smooth acrylic of the monitor bracelet under her fingers. "I'll wear it if one of you will tell Kuaron it's okay for me to go to work."

"Going to the office shouldn't be a problem," the Terran doctor said. "But we would like you to check in with us once a week."

Dina wanted to protest that this was too restrictive, but she was too much a scientist to argue against caution in the face of the unknown. "Once a week it is."


LATER that evening, Dina was immersed in her Wisutan studies when the com chimed with a loud insistent sequence of notes. Dina looked up in surprise. She was in the main room, with Kuaron sitting across from her.

"It must be the express from your mother," Kuaron said. "I never got one before. I don't know anyone off-world."

"I'm sure you're right," Dina said. For some reason, she was reluctant to move.

"Do you want to listen to it here or in the bedroom?" Kuaron got to his feet. "*If* you feel up to it now?"

"I'm not going to faint again if that's what you mean," Dina said, galvanized into action by his concern. "I'll play it on the com here."

"I'll wait in the bedroom, then." Kuaron started for the door.

Dina grabbed for his hand. "Don't go, Kuaron. Stay here while I listen to what my father said."

"Are you sure?"

Dina nodded, and Kuaron sat down again. He took the com screen from the nearby side table and put it on the low table in front of her. "Here, you can log on with this set."

The screen was already on, activated by the incoming call. Dina turned it to a more comfortable angle and pressed her thumb against the ID panel.

"Interplanetary express message for Dina Bellaire from Marie Dagostino," the machine said. "Activate when ready."

Dina pressed the switch, and in a fraction of a second the screen lit with her mother's face. The image was crystal clear this time, and her mother looked tired.

"Hello, Dina," she said. "Here's your father's message. I listened to it when it arrived, along with the one he left for me. Maybe once you hear what he has to tell you, you'll understand why I didn't want to give you this message when you were fourteen."

The screen blanked for a few seconds, and then lit again with a less clear image.

Her father looked older than Dina remembered. His hair was liberally streaked with gray and he had a shaggy gray beard. His face was brown, lined, and weather-beaten. She couldn't see much of his clothes, but what little was visible looked grimy and ragged.

"I'm leaving this message for my daughter, Dina Annya Bellaire," he said. "I only hope someone finds this while she's still alive to hear it." He went on to give details about Dina—where she lived and her date and place of birth.

"Dina, honey," he said, "I'm sorry, but it looks like I'm going to let you down one last time. I thought I could hold out here indefinitely, but two days ago I stepped on what looked like a tree root, and it reared up and took a chunk out of my ankle. Now my foot's swollen up like a *cassora* plant, and I don't think I'll be around much longer." He reached down as if he were adjusting something, flinched in pain, and then kept going.

"If the chronometer's working, and I'm not entirely sure it is, I've been on this godforsaken moon for almost two years. That means you're thirteen now. I know your mother's done a good job raising you, and I know you're a good person. That was apparent when you were small. I hope you're happy. I hope you get to live out your dreams, big and small. I want you to know that nothing in my life has brought me as much joy as the times I spent with you."

He took a deep breath and squared his shoulders. "I also have to tell you what happened to me—it's not an excuse, I just want you to know why I was away so much of the time.

"It happened while you were a baby, Dina, while I was away on a trip. Before I started prospecting, I used to work as an engineer, and occasionally I had to make site visits. I was visiting an ocean thermal power plant on an island a few hundred miles from home. The supervisor at the plant was a woman named Peri. I had met her a couple of times before. She was a nice enough person, attractive in an ordinary sort of way. She was married and had a couple of kids—kept their holos on her desk, that sort of thing."

Dina's father ran his fingers through his hair as if he were having trouble finding the right words. "I can't account for what happened, honey, and believe me I've had time to think about it. Peri and I spent some time together going over the plans for an addition to the plant. I guess the best I can say is that I went crazy. It started when I scalded myself with hot coffee, and Peri put some medicinal cream on my arm. Wherever she put her hands, it seemed as if it was burning me again. I went hot all over; I felt flushed as if I had a fever, and then I felt light-headed, dizzy almost. I can still remember it, as clearly as if it were yesterday."

Mickul shook his head. "It was terrible after that. I wanted her so badly I could taste it. I tried to persuade her to come with me to the hostel. She looked at me as if I were insane. I think maybe I was. I wouldn't stop—I couldn't leave her alone. Finally, she called plant security, and they threw me out. I suppose I was lucky they didn't have me arrested."

"I went back to the hostel and I was sick, physically sick. The next day, I staggered back to the plant and tried to see her, but the security staff wouldn't let me in. I went back to the hostel again and locked myself in, this time. I tried drinking booze, but it didn't help much. I'm not sure to this day how long I was in that room—seven or eight days at least. It seemed like forever. Your mother called me several times, but I wouldn't speak to her. "

He took a deep breath and went on. "Finally, Marie came to the hostel to see me, but I wouldn't let her in. I didn't eat, I barely drank anything. For a while I thought I would die—I hoped I would die. Finally, I felt a little better, well enough to leave. I tried to see Peri one more time—I lied and said I wanted to apologize, but she would only speak to me on the com. I fell apart and begged her to see me. It frightened her, I could tell. She threatened to have me arrested if I came near her again. So finally, I went home."

He paused, as if to compose his thoughts. "As you might expect, your mother was very angry. But she was worried, too. My company had fired me, and I didn't care. That scared her as much as the rest of it. She insisted I see a doctor." He shrugged. "I was scared myself, so I went. They told me I had a psychosis induced by a hormonal imbalance that they had never seen before. They tried to level it out, but they weren't very successful.

"But," he said with a sigh, "I learned to cope. Your mother forgave me, and I looked for another job. Prospecting appealed to me because of the long periods of time spent alone. With my engineering background, I had no trouble qualifying.

"We never told you about it, sweetie," he said, looking straight at the cam as if he wanted to make eye contact with Dina. "I didn't want to frighten you or make you think your old man was a crackpot. But I want you to know now. I was gone all the time because I was afraid to be with people too much. I never felt truly normal after that. I came to realize that I still loved your mother, but it wasn't enough. Whatever it was that happened to me, it's still there. Even now, on this miserable excuse for a moon, I think of you and your mother in the daytime, but I dream of Peri at night."

Mickul Bellaire winced as if he were in pain. He reached forward, seemed to fiddle with something and then he sat back again. "This recorder won't last much longer. I have to go, dearest Dina. Remember what I said. I love you."

The image faded abruptly. Dina sat and stared at the blank screen.

Kuaron waited, as if to give her a chance to speak, but when she said nothing, he slipped an arm around her. "Now you know."

"Yes. Now I know. My father started *shahgunrah* with that woman."

"Not *shahgunrah*," Kuaron corrected. "*Glashunrah*. She felt nothing. Your father suffered what Wakanreans fear most from Terrans."

"But how?"

"It must be in your genes. I think perhaps we have to believe that the *Saga of Zaingour* is true. One of your ancestors did start *glashunrah* in Zaingour. He was the first Wakanrean to experience it, but not the last. It's even possible that many of your ancestors suffered the same fate."

"I suppose it is." Dina still stared at the screen. "But it wasn't just my father who suffered. My mother was obviously hurt by what happened, too."

"Yes, but she went on to find someone else."

Dina shuddered, overwhelmed by sudden horror as the implications of her father's story hit her.

"What's wrong?" Kuaron demanded, holding her close.

"I just thought—oh, Kuaron! What if I had been in love with someone when I came here? What if I had had children with him?" She clutched him in an attempt to find comfort in closeness. "What would have happened when I met you?"

"The same thing that did happen," Kuaron said, nuzzling her cheek.

"Maybe that night. But it would have been terrible the next morning."

"It didn't happen that way. The gods of fate were kind to us."

Dina threw her arms around his neck and clung to him. They sat there for a long time until finally Dina pulled away, and they went to bed.


DINA went to work the next day, but she wasn't surprised when Kuaron called her twice and picked her up at the end of the day. He was solicitous for the next several days, and he insisted on going with Dina to her next medical appointment.

"You're not going to do this every time, are you?" Dina said.

"Not necessarily," he said as he landed the flyter in the open space near the medical building. "If you can manage to go a few weeks without being ill or fainting, I might skip a time or two."

"Hmph!"

"I could ask my father to take you if you find my presence obtrusive?"

"Ha!" Juzao Sadoc had come to see them twice in the past week. During most of both visits, he had alternated between gloating over Dina's pregnancy and nagging her to take better care of herself. Dina hadn't cared for either experience. "I don't think there's any way the Planetary Administrator would be less obtrusive, especially not when it's your father we're talking about."

"How about Jared?"

Dina was surprised by the suggestion. "Jared? No thanks."

"Don't you like Jared?"

"Of course I do. He's been a good friend to you—to us. But the fact is, I'd just as soon go to the doctor's alone. I don't need a babysitter."

Kuaron smiled his feral smile. "That's what you said the day you got kidnapped."

Dina opened the flyter door. "Can we go now?"

"Certainly."


THE exam was very brief. Dina was glad the doctors had already asked all the questions they needed to ask, and all she had to do was allow them to take a blood sample, and submit to a medi-scan. She was a little surprised when the Wakanrean doctor pulled a second scanner forward after the first scan was complete.

"What's that?" Dina asked.

"It's a micro-image scanner," the Terran doctor said. "You're doing just fine, but we'd like to get a better image of the baby. He seems to be growing very rapidly, even for a Wakanrean baby."

Dina tried to keep from tensing up at this news, but she didn't entirely succeed. Kuaron was standing near the examining table, and Dina knew he was aware of her tension. He took her hand as the micro-image scanner passed over her abdomen and paused.

"Hmmm," the Terran doctor said.

"What?" Dina demanded. "What is it?"

"It's nothing bad," the Wakanrean doctor said. "Really. It's just, it looks as if there are two babies."

"What?" Kuaron almost shouted. "It's twins!"

"It certainly looks that way," the Terran doctor said. "Is there any history of twins on either side?"

"Not that I know of," Dina said, swallowing hard as she tried to catch her breath. For some reason, she felt as if she had been running for several minutes. "What about your side, Kuaron?"

"No." Kuaron didn't say anything more, and Dina sensed that he was upset at this news.

"It's all right," she said to him. "Is there any reason we can't handle two babies?"

"I don't like it. Twins are bad luck. It used to be a curse—'May you conceive twins!'"

"That's just superstition," the Wakanrean doctor said. "Before we had artificial wombs, carrying twins to term could be dangerous. But we have them now, and *Kantai* Bellaire would have probably had to use one anyway, as it would be difficult for someone her size to deliver even one Wakanrean baby."

"We'll talk about it later, Kuaron," Dina said. "Can I see the image?"

"Of course," the Terran doctor said. He pressed a switch on the micro-scanner and turned it to face Dina. "Have a good look."

Dina stared eagerly at the image frozen on the screen. The two fetuses were clearly visible, but neither of them looked very human or even very Wakanrean.

"They're very tiny right now," the Wakanrean doctor said. "We enlarged the image so we can see what's going on. Each baby has a placenta, and your uterus has expanded rapidly to accommodate the pregnancy."

"When will you transfer the babies to an artificial womb?" Kuaron asked.

"It's too early to make that decision," the Wakanrean doctor said. "Generally, the survival rate is higher if the fetus remains in the womb at least three Standard months. We'll track their progress every week, and see how they're doing."

"I want to wait as long as I can," Dina said. "I don't like the idea of an artificial womb."

"We'll do whatever is safest for you," Kuaron said.

"And safest for the babies," Dina said.

There was a brief, awkward pause, and then the Terran doctor moved the scanner out of the way. "We're all done here. We'll see you next week."

Dina climbed down from the table, a little concerned because she could sense that Kuaron was still upset. She waited until they were back in the flyter to bring up the subject of her pregnancy.

"So," she said as Kuaron leaned back in his seat after releasing control of the flyter, "you're really upset about the fact that it's twins?"

Kuaron turned to look at her before he answered. "I suppose I am. We're not used to thinking of twins as a good thing."

Dina considered this. "I don't know that Terrans are, either. They're more work, certainly, because you have to do everything twice. On the other hand, if you want only two children, you get it all over with at once. I guess we see them as a mixed blessing."

She reached over and patted his arm. "I'll be fine, Kuaron. At some time in the last few hundred years, a Terran woman successfully gave birth to a half-Wakanrean baby or I wouldn't be here today."

"The baby must have survived, but we know nothing about what happened to his or her mother."

Dina could sense Kuaron's apprehension, and for the first time she felt her own small twinge of fear.

Kuaron put his arm around her abruptly. "I'm a fool. Don't worry. Everything will be fine."

Dina leaned against him. "I hope so."


HIS father looked every bit as alarmed as Kuaron had felt at the news.

"Twins?" he said, when Kuaron told him that night after dinner. "They're certain it's twins?"

"Yes." Kuaron leaned across the table to clear his father's place and slide the dishes into the cleaning hatch. "Quite sure."

"Hmph," Juzao said. "I suppose it doesn't really matter—not like it used to matter."

"I guess not," Kuaron said.

"Bosh!" Jared said as he got to his feet and slid his own plate into the hatch. "You're both giving way to superstitious twaddle! If the two of you go around looking all gloomy like that, poor Dina will take to her bed from sheer depression."

Juzao looked vaguely affronted, but he merely nodded once. "There's something in what the midget says, Kuaron."

"That's me!" Jared said, undeterred by the slur on his height. "Short but perspicacious."

"Who's perspicacious?" Dina said, coming in from the kitchen with a tray of fruit tarts and a pot of *quascha*.

"I am," Jared said, taking the tray from her hands and setting it down on the table. "I say twins are good news."

"I agree with you," Dina said, reaching for the *quascha* as she sat down next to Kuaron.

Kuaron could tell she was telling the truth. She had been cheerful ever since they got home. "I'm not overly concerned," he said. "But it's not something I would have wished for."

"Bah!" Jared said, slapping Kuaron on the back. "Everyone knows Wakanreans are so tall, their nervous systems can't make it all the way from their brains to their claws."

"Do they?" Kuaron retorted. "Then they also know Terrans are puny, naked, unevolved beings with no more sense than a *chundin*."

Jared shrugged as he accepted a cup of *quascha* from Dina. "Suit yourself, furball. You're the one with a Terran *shahgunrahai*."

Juzao laughed heartily at this riposte as he took his own cup. "He has you there, Kuaron."

"Ah," Kuaron said, recovering, "but Dina is not one hundred percent Terran."

"Yeah, but even your kids will be almost half Terran." Jared dropped back into his chair as Dina handed him a fruit tart. "Just think of it—two half-Terran *parundai*!"

Juzao looked suddenly solemn. "I said as much at the ThreeCon hearing, but it will be up to the Disciples of Paruian to decide whether my grandchildren are truly *parundai*."

"There, you see, sir!" Jared said. "You used the plural. You're getting used to the idea of twins already."

Juzao blinked in surprise and muttered something under his breath.

Dina smiled. "You'd better watch it, *Quayzanai*," she said, using the Wisutan word for a *shahgunrahai's* father. "I'm learning fast, and I don't think that comment was entirely polite."

Juzao managed to look both pleased and embarrassed at the same time, and then changed the subject.

Kuaron smiled, but he wished he could dismiss his worry as easily as Dina had.

DINA spent the next several weeks in a state of nervous excitement. Kuaron didn't help by fretting over her any time she was away from him. She fainted one afternoon at work, and after that, he insisted on flying her to and from the office.

That incident combined with the fact that Dina was rapidly gaining weight soon made her pregnancy public knowledge. Hyral Brau took her aside to inquire if she planned to continue working after she gave birth. Dina said honestly that she didn't know.

"It's twins, you see," Dina said. They were sitting in her supervisor's office, and the door was closed. "Kuaron is worried, because two half-Wakanrean babies will be too much for me to carry to term."

Hyral Brau blinked in surprise. "Half-Wakanrean babies?"

"Oh, yes," Dina said, flushing slightly. "Kuaron is definitely their father."

Her supervisor seemed stunned. "Half-Terran *parundai?*" She added something else in Wisutan, but Dina didn't understand any of it except the word incredible.

"It is incredible," Dina said, "but it's also true."

Hyral said no more on the subject, but Dina knew soon afterwards that word had spread throughout Quafray. People who had been content to observe her from across the lunchroom made a point to walk by her table and study her covertly. Even Shanour, who ate lunch with her almost every day, tended to stare at her as if he couldn't quite believe what he saw.

Dina found it all rather wearing. She also found that she tired easily. Two months after they had learned about the twins, Kuaron picked Dina up at work for her weekly doctor's appointment, and she fell asleep in the flyter.

She came awake when Kuaron shook her arm gently and called her name.

"Dina!"

"What?" Dina sat up and looked around in surprise. "Where am I?"

"We're at ThreeCon headquarters," Kuaron said. "I just landed the flyter."

"Oh," Dina said, a little embarrassed. "I guess I fell asleep."

"You certainly did."

Dina was worried by the severity of his tone. "Is anything wrong, Kuaron?"

His expression softened, and she felt the warmth of his affection for her. "No, nothing's wrong. But you can't go on like this. If you want to keep working, we should ask the doctors to transfer the babies now."

Dina laid a hand across her swollen abdomen. "Not just yet. It's early."

"It's been three months since *shahkuun* ended."

"That's early. I'm not that big yet, am I?"

Kuaron looked at her before he answered. "I don't know. I was never around a Terran woman who was pregnant. To me, you look overwhelmed by this pregnancy."

"I am, a little, but that's more psychological than anything else."

Kuaron didn't answer, but merely opened the door for her and helped her out. He didn't say much at the doctor's office until the examination was over and Dina was struggling to her feet.

"When can you do the surgery?" he said to the Wakanrean doctor. "Is it safe to do it now?"

The woman looked surprised. "I suppose so. It's rare for a Wakanrean woman to transfer such a young fetus, but Terrans do so routinely, don't they, Doctor?"

Her Terran counterpart nodded. "Starting at about three months, yes, certainly. Many women find pregnancy limiting, and an artificial womb provides a safe environment for the child to develop."

"But we don't need to do it so soon, do we?" Dina protested. "I mean there's no medical reason why you need to take the babies now?"

The two doctors exchanged glances. "No," the Terran said. "Assuming the fetuses continue to grow at the same rate they are now, we estimate you could go another six weeks at the very least before the pregnancy became dangerous for you."

"Why wait?" Kuaron said.

"Because I want to wait," Dina said, laying a hand on the rounded form of her abdomen. She was a little alarmed at his insistence. "I don't want to stop being pregnant so soon."

There was another awkward pause, and then the Terran doctor spoke in a carefully neutral tone. "You two will have to talk it over and decide. Let us know when you're ready, and we'll set it up."

Dina waited, but Kuaron didn't mention transferring the fetuses on the trip home. It wasn't until they were clearing away the dishes after dinner that he brought up the subject.

"You look tired, *acubai*," he said as he took a platter out of her hands.

"I'm okay." Dina sensed that he was anxious, so she wasn't entirely surprised by his next words.

"You should have the surgery very soon. It's safe for the children now, and it would be better for you to do it soon."

"I'm perfectly capable of deciding what's best for me," Dina said, checking to see that the kitchen servoid was doing its work. "ThreeCon said so, remember?"

She could tell Kuaron was a little hurt at the brusqueness of her reply, but she wasn't willing to relent. There could be no compromise about something as important as who decided when she had surgery.

"Is it so difficult for you to understand that I'm worried about you?" Kuaron said as they moved to the main room.

"No, not at all." Dina eased herself onto a sofa. "But worrying about me doesn't give you the right to run my life."

"I'm not trying to run your life," Kuaron said, his concern growing more overt in the face of her persistence. He was still standing; he seemed reluctant to relax enough to sit down. "We're *shahgunrahai*, and *shahgunrahai* share decisions like this. Don't married couples?"

"I don't really know. I never had to make a decision like this."

Kuaron took a step forward to put his hands on her shoulders. "I don't want anything to happen to you. I don't know if I could go on living if I lost you now."

Dina could tell he was perfectly sincere, and it rocked her to know he was so oppressed by worry for her.

"Nothing's going to happen to me," she said with determination. "I'm going to be fine."

Kuaron said nothing. He simply stood looking down at her, intense concern in his expression and anxiety radiating from him like heat from a fire. Dina suddenly recalled how difficult it had been for her to read Wakanrean facial expressions when she first arrived in Wisuta. It seemed incredible now that Kuaron had ever been a stranger to her.

"All right!" she said sharply. "Three weeks. I'll do it in three weeks. Will that make you happy?"

She felt an easing of his distress, but he didn't smile. "I'll be happy when you're safe, and not before."

Dina sighed. "I don't know if any of us is ever truly safe, Kua-ron. When I think about all the things that could go wrong for our half-Terran, half-Wakanrean children, I get the shivers."

He sank down beside her and pulled her to him in a warm, com-forting embrace. "We can only hope they'll grow strong and healthy."

She clutched him back and took comfort in the knowledge that he would never leave her of his own will.

# Chapter Thirteen

For Dina, the next three weeks passed very quickly. Kuaron didn't mention her promise directly, but she was aware that he was keeping track of the days. On the afternoon just before the three weeks were up, Kuaron picked her up at work.

"Did you remember to remind *Kantai* Brau about the surgery tomorrow?" he asked as Dina took her seat in the flyter.

"Yes," she said. "You needn't sound so pleased because you're getting your way."

Kuaron maintained his composure as he took the flyter to cruising altitude. "I'm not getting my way. I'm getting our way. If I had gotten *my* way, you would have had the procedure three weeks ago."

She gave him an annoyed glance. "Have you been hanging around with Jared recently? That sounds like his kind of answer."

Kuaron grinned his wolfish grin as he activated the destination controls. "Yes. He came over this morning while you were at work."

"Hmph!"

"What does that noise mean?"

"It means," Dina said, well aware that she sounded cross, "that I'm not entirely convinced Jared Harlingen is a good influence on you."

Kuaron looked grave. "Are you trying to choose my friends for me—perhaps even trying to run my life?"

Dina wasn't deceived by his somber countenance, as she could sense his amusement. "Don't give me any of that guff!"

"Guff?"

"*Puoulgaio*," Dina translated. Very deliberately she switched to Wisutan. "And don't try to tell me you don't look like a *chundin* that just swallowed a *juija*, either."

Kuaron let out a laugh. "Very good, little one," he said in the same language. "My father will be pleased at your progress."

"I'm getting there. But the journey isn't always easy."

"No one said it would be. In fact, Jared warned you it would be difficult."

"He was right."

"He usually is. It's a very annoying habit of his." Kuaron checked the controls and then glanced at her. "Are you ready for tomorrow?"

"Yes," Dina said, changing back to Standard. "As ready as I can be." She patted her bulging stomach. "I'm going to miss having them this close all the time. In that way, being pregnant is just a tiny bit like *shahgunrah*."

Kuaron stroked her arm. "It's for the best, *acubai*."

"I suppose so."

He bent over to nuzzle her neck, and Dina let herself enjoy the sensation of his nearness.

"Let's go home," she said. "I want to go home and bask in my last night of being pregnant."

"We'll be there soon. Have you thought about what the doctors said last time?"

"You mean about birth control?"

Kuaron nodded.

"I've thought about it. I think it's a good idea for me to have an implant. Inoculations don't seem to work well against *shahgunrah*-induced hormones."

"I've thought about it, too. I think I should get an implant, also. It's better to be safe than to worry."

Dina looked at him curiously. "If everything goes well, Kuaron—if the twins are born viable and healthy—do you want more children?"

"I don't know," Kuaron said, and Dina could tell from the speed of his response that he must have thought about it before. "I can't decide if it would be a good idea or not."

"Did you want a large family?"

"I suppose I did. I was an only child and I missed having siblings."

"I did, too. But I don't know if I could ever have any more. Getting pregnant without planning it was one thing. Bringing a hybrid child into the universe on purpose would be much more difficult for me to square with my conscience."

"Square with your conscience? You mean you see it as a bad thing that we're having children?"

"No, not exactly," Dina said, sensing his shock. "I don't think it's immoral, or anything like that. It's just that it won't be easy to be half Wakanrean and half Terran. Aside from the possibility of social ostracism, I'm worried that people will try to turn the twins into research subjects. I'd hate for our children to live their lives under a microscope."

"So would I. In fact, I won't allow it."

Dina didn't answer and in a few minutes the landing alarm beeped. It was only as she went through the front door of Kuaron's house that it occurred to her that they had both spoken as if they could have children only with each other.

THE transfer of the twin fetuses went off without any problems. The procedure itself took less than an hour from start to finish. While the surgeon was closing the incision, Dina gripped Kuaron's hand and they both stared at the monitors on each of the two tanks that now held their twins. The fetuses, each drifting slowly in its own sac, had huge heads and tiny limbs.

The prenatologists were checking the readings from the fetal monitors and comparing notes as the surgeon completed her work. A medtech propped Dina up to get a better view just as the Terran doctor approached Dina and Kuaron

"Everything appears to be normal," he said.

A wave of relief washed over Dina.

"The babies' vital signs more strongly resemble Wakanrean fetuses than Terran," he went on, "but it's not definitive. It's too early for body fur or claws, in any case."

Dina looked at Kuaron. "Well, it looks like I've done my part. Now we both watch and wait."

Kuaron squeezed her hand. "Now we wait."

AFTER a few days of recuperation, Dina went back to work, but she made it a practice to visit the hospital every day. During her work week, she took the transit system to ThreeCon headquarters every afternoon, and then rode home with Kuaron after they both spent some time observing the developing fetuses. On rest days, she and Kuaron went to the hospital in the mornings, and then spent the remainder of the day doing errands or visiting Kuaron's many relations.

Every time she visited the hospital, Dina put one hand on the side of each twin's tank and held it there until she could feel the warmth of the synthetic amniotic fluid through the flexible membrane. She spoke to the children often, too. Kuaron did so rarely—at least when Dina was there—but she was quite comfortable talking to them. She and Kuaron had already picked out names.

"Are you certain you want both of them to have Wakanrean names?" Kuaron had said on his last visit.

"Yes, I'm sure. They'll both have my last name, so they should have a Wakanrean first name to even out the Terran surname."

"We could give them extra names. We don't do that much in my family, but it's common in other regions."

"No," Dina said firmly. "Just one personal name apiece, like you have, Kuaron. Our daughter will be Yulayan for your mother, and our son will be Kifarao for your father's father."

"Yulayan Bellaire," Kuaron said. "Kifarao Bellaire. I like both names. They balance, and balance will be important for our children."

"Yes," Dina had agreed, sliding her hand over the elastic membrane of the tank in as intimate a caress as the technology would allow. "Balance is important."

One night Kuaron suggested stopping somewhere for dinner on the way home from the hospital. They were both tired, and the idea of preparing food had no appeal. Kuaron proposed eating at a restaurant he had frequented in the past.

"Did you come here alone or with someone?" Dina asked him as they left the flyter and started for the door. The restaurant was in the outer suburbs, a small, cozy-looking building surrounded by a large flyter park. The only restaurants she had been to on Wakanreo had catered to Terrans, so she was curious to see what this one was like.

"Sometimes one, sometimes the other."

"I never liked going to restaurants alone," Dina said as they walked through the front door into a vestibule. She noted that the front door was in plain view, and realized Wisutans only hid the entrances to their homes, not their businesses.

"Why not?" Kuaron asked, pausing by a credit console set into the wall.

"What are you doing?" Dina asked, ignoring his question in favor of her own pursuit of information.

"Paying for our dinner."

"Really?" Dina asked, intrigued. "Are all the meals the same price or did you order something already?"

"Order?"

Dina didn't answer this question either. She was studying the interior of the restaurant.

There were no privacy booths like those in the restaurants on Croyzan, or even private tables like she was used to from Fantar. Instead, forty or fifty people were seated at four very long tables. They were all Wakanreans, and they were all talking as they ate, and helping themselves to various dishes placed on the middle of the tables. The din was deafening.

It died down to almost total silence in a matter of seconds, as people looked over and saw her standing beside Kuaron. Dina was conscious of being the center of everyone's attention. Some of the stares seemed merely curious, but others were rude to the point of hostility.

Kuaron moved very close but didn't put his arm around her. "There are two seats over there," he said, indicating two vacant chairs near the end of the table on the far right side of the room. Dina noted that there were places already set for each empty chair.

"All right." In spite of an intense desire to turn around and run for the flyter, she made herself walk to the chair on the near side of the table. Kuaron hovered, as if he were reluctant to leave her side long enough to walk around the table.

"It's all right," Dina murmured, sensing that his uneasiness was growing to match her own. She sank into her seat.

Kuaron didn't answer, but he walked swiftly around the table to sit down across from her.

Dina couldn't say later what she had eaten. Kuaron passed her serving bowls and platters, and she ate the food she put on her plate, but it was too difficult to concentrate on the taste of food in the midst of such palpable hostility.

Around her, the room went back to a semblance of normality. People resumed their conversations as servers brought full dishes and removed empty ones; the servers also brought washing bowls when requested. Several diners left and were replaced by new arrivals. But always Dina was conscious of a prickle on the back of her neck, as if people's stares were energy weapons aimed at her. When the man next to her rose and moved his plate to another table, Dina felt as if she had been struck physically. A server came over and put a new place setting there, but no one sat down to use it.

She could tell Kuaron was also affected. No one moved away from him, but Dina could sense his anger and distress at the insult to her.

Finally, after she had eaten enough, she looked at Kuaron. "Can we go now?"

He rose to his feet at once. The silence resumed as they made their exit. Dina breathed a sigh of relief when they got into the flyter.

"I don't think I want to eat out again, Kuaron," she said.

He reached across the seat to embrace her; Dina felt a warm reassurance that eased the tension of the last several minutes.

"We can eat at home for every meal," Kuaron promised.

Dina agreed, but the unspoken thought that weighed on her mind was the fear that she and Kuaron would never be able to go out in public together without facing overt hostility.

# *Chapter Fourteen*

As time passed, Dina found herself more comfortable in her interactions with Kuaron's huge extended family. Wisutans, she discovered, loved to party. Any positive change in their lives was an excuse to invite family members to celebrate with them. About two months after the twins were transferred to their artificial wombs, Dina and Kuaron attended a party hosted by his aunt, to show off her recent home renovations.

"At least we didn't have to get dressed up," Kuaron said as he parked the flyter that evening. "Parties like this are never formal."

Dina patted the decorative hair clip she wore above a single long braid, to be sure it was secure. She had debated about wearing her hair loose but decided against it. She was strange enough to Wakanreans without a mane of hair around her shoulders. "What renovations did your aunt make?" she asked, surveying the house. It was located a good forty kilometers from the outskirts of Wisuta, in the midst of rolling countryside. The house, a one-story, rambling structure, was nestled into the curve of a hill. With the light of two of Wakanreo's three moons, it was easy to see not only the house but the line of skimmers and flyters that formed a half circle around it. It was the first house Dina had visited that could be called rural, and she noted that the roof was peaked, rather than flat.

"They redesigned the main room," Kuaron said, opening the flyter door. "And they added on a large bathing room, with a pool."

They had to walk around the house to find the front door tucked into a niche in the facade. Kuaron's aunt opened the door herself. She was a tall, handsome woman, with jet black body fur and a

striking headcrest as white as Kuaron's. Even her clothes were distinctive—a long tunic of deep red with billowing sleeves, worn over
silky black trousers. Her *shahgunrahai* looked pedestrian beside
her. Short and plump, he was the fattest Wakanrean that Dina
had ever seen. His body fur and headcrest were both a nondescript
brown, and his tunic-style shirt was the same gray-green as his
trousers.

Both of them greeted Kuaron with enthusiasm and Dina with
politeness.

"Come inside," the aunt said after the introductions were made.
"And have some food."

There was quite a crowd in the main room, but Dina was reassured that she recognized most of them. Several people said hello
to her by name, and that made her feel more at home. Some of the
children gave her curious glances, but no one said anything rude.

The aunt made sure they had food and then moved away to see
to her other guests. Her *shahgunrahai* stayed behind, helping himself to a stick of broiled *juija* from a table loaded with food.

"I like what you've done to the house, Jeikeich," Kuaron said to
him. "This room came out well."

Their host smiled warmly at this praise and began to relate the
travails of remodeling. Dina studied the room as she nibbled a vegetable pastry. It did look nice. The high ceiling added to the feeling
of openness, and a loft above half the room made extra space for
party guests. The walls were all a pleasing shade of pale green, and
two of them were lined with windows.

"The bathing room took even longer," Jeikeich said. "Come and
see it, both of you."

Kuaron looked interested, so Dina followed along as they made
their way through the press of people, everyone moving out of the
way as Dina approached.

The new bathing room was located at the back of the house. It
was huge, almost as large as Kuaron's, but the blue-green walls
were tiled only waist high. There were two showers against the far
wall, and a skylight in the ceiling showed a clear view of one moon.
Two very young Wakanreans, a boy and a girl of about twelve, were
soaking in a large, oval pool. Both were naked, and two sets of
clothes hung on the row of pegs between the showers.

"Ah ha!" Jeikeich said. "Here's where you are, Tuutho! Why
aren't you out entertaining our guests?"

"I'm entertaining one of them, *Ayzanai*," the boy said. "My cousin wanted to try out the pool."

The girl smiled a shy smile, and Jeikeich laughed.

"An excellent idea!" he said, ripping open his shirt and kicking off his sandals at the same time. "I don't know why I didn't think of it. Come along, Kuaron. You and your *shahgunrahai* can join us. There's plenty of room."

He stepped over to the wall and hung up his shirt, then pulled off his trousers. His smile as he hung them up was patently pleased. Dina fought a blush. She looked at Kuaron in mute appeal.

"Perhaps we should get back to the party," Kuaron temporized. "Won't my aunt miss you?"

"Nonsense," Jeikeich said, slipping off his undergarments. "A short soak never hurt anyone." He was naked now. He looked even plumper with his clothes off.

There was an awkward silence as he stood waiting. It came to Dina that if she hadn't been there, Kuaron would certainly have had his own clothes off by now. There was nothing he enjoyed more than soaking in a pool of warm water. A quick glance at Jeikeich's expectant face told her his feelings would be hurt if she refused to try out his new pool. And after all, she decided, it was a good thing that he wanted her to join them. He could as easily have been reluctant to have her use his pool.

"I don't think anyone will miss us, either, Kuaron," Dina said, reaching up to unfasten her shirt. "Not for a few minutes, at least."

Kuaron blinked in surprise.

"We'll be right there," Dina said, pleased that her voice sounded reasonably normal. "You go ahead," she added, walking over to the pegs on the wall as if she undressed in front of naked strangers every day of her life.

Her host stepped into the shower and turned it on. Kuaron moved to Dina's side and spoke quietly.

"You don't have to do this, *acubai*."

"It's all right. I don't mind," Dina said as she hung up her trousers. She managed not to look at her host as she pulled off her underclothes and hung them up, too. Kuaron turned on the shower while Dina twisted her braid into a knot and secured it onto the back of her head with her hair clip.

She and Kuaron showered very quickly, and then walked to the pool. Dina was conscious of three pairs of eyes watching her. She felt a surge of gratitude, first that she was small-breasted and second that the scar from her premature delivery was almost invisible.

Their host, his son, and the girl were all sitting on the underwater ledge that ran around the circumference of the pool. Jeikeich rested his arms along the pool's tiled edge. With water drops glistening on his fur, he reminded Dina of a holo she had once seen of a Terran sea animal. A walrus, was it? Except he had no fangs.

"The water is perfect," he said. "Come in, come in!"

Dina cast a sideways glance at Kuaron. He seemed quite at ease. He sat down on the edge of the pool and reached a hand up to her.

Dina took his hand and sat down beside him, slipping into the water before she could change her mind about the whole thing.

The water temperature was indeed perfect, warm and inviting. It felt good against her skin. Kuaron slid in beside her, letting himself sink up to his chin and making a small tidal waved.

The girl was staring at Dina. "Your hair is so long," she blurted out.

Dina was too relieved that the girl had commented on her hair and not her breasts to be offended. She unfastened the hair clip to let her braid drop down onto one shoulder. "Yes, it is, even for a Terran. Would you like to touch it?"

The girl looked tempted, but she merely ducked her head. "No, thank you anyway."

Dina moved to the opposite side of the pool, where the ledge was higher, so she could sit without having to hold her chin up out of the water.

"Doesn't it get in the way?" the boy asked.

"Sometimes," Dina said, pinning the braid back up. "I'm thinking of cutting it shorter."

"I like it long," Kuaron said, sliding onto the ledge beside her.

Dina smiled at him. "Well, I have no definite plans to cut it."

"Don't you get cold?" the boy asked suddenly. "I mean, with no fur, you must be cold often."

"Frequently," Dina said. "I wear special clothes that can keep me warm, even when it's brisk enough to make Kuaron shiver."

Jeikeich was looking impatient. "So, tell me, Kuaron, where have you sung lately?"

Kuaron answered with the names of a four recent venues, and Jeikeich's response told Dina that he was a fan of the *qatrahs*. He and Kuaron engaged in a polite but spirited debate on the merits of various *qatraharai*.

The two children were looking bored when Jeikeich said, "I got to hear Triascou lu Huaic sing the other night. She performed a wonderful *Pularain*."

"She always did well with that *qatrah*," Kuaron said. There was no strain in his voice, but Dina could tell he was tense at this mention of his old friend. She wondered whether Jeikeich knew of the breech between the two *qatraharai*; his pleasant face, almost round for a Wakanrean, showed no sign of guile.

"She didn't do nearly as well with the *Shahgundal*," he continued. "Nowhere near as good as you, Kuaron. The critics say you've made that *qatrah* your own."

"Critics have been known to exaggerate," Kuaron said, some of his tension easing. "As I have cause to know."

Jeikeich laughed, but whatever reply he might have made was lost as his *shahgunrahai's* voice spoke from the doorway.

"There you are, Jeikeich—and Tuutho, too!"

Both the males she named assumed guilty expressions as Kuaron's aunt walked into the bathing room and stood looking down at them. It seemed to Dina that she had a curious expression on her face, rather like a cook who lifts the lid on a pot and finds something totally unexpected.

"Hello, *acubai*," Jeikeich said, still looking guilty. "Are you coming in, too?"

"*I* have guests to look after," she said. And then her face softened as she looked down at him. "You stay here and entertain my nephew and his *shahgunrahai*."

Jeikeich's warm smile in response was almost childishly engaging. "Certainly, certainly. Whatever you wish."

Dina was so involved in watching the interplay between the two *shahgunrahai* that she almost forgot she was naked in a pool with three relative strangers. When Kuaron's aunt left, Dina found herself in the position of having to remain in the pool to give Jeikeich an excuse to stay, also. Kuaron gave her a droll look, and turned back to engage his young cousin in conversation.

Dina had just decided to plead skin dehydration when another group of three Wakanreans strolled into the room.

"Hello, Jeikeich. Hello, Uncle Kuaron," the youngest one said. He was a slender boy of about fifteen or sixteen. The other two were a little older, one male and one female. "Is there room for us?"

Kuaron stood up and put both hands on the edge of the pool. "There will be," he said, lifting himself out. He reached one hand down to help Dina. "We're getting out now."

Dina took his hand eagerly, too grateful to have an excuse to put her clothes on to worry about the added presence of more Wakanreans.

There was too much milling about as the three newcomers disrobed and showered for anyone to pay attention to Dina. She dressed as fast as she could and followed Kuaron back to the main room just as the three new arrivals slid into the water with much splashing and happy cries about the perfection of the water temperature.

Kuaron pulled Dina into one corner of the room. "That was very brave of you, *acubai*."

"Nonsense," Dina said. "There was nothing to be afraid of— except maybe hurting Jeikeich's feelings."

Kuaron looked solemn. "I think it was brave. I know you don't like to be naked in front of anyone except me."

"It could have been worse."

Kuaron grinned his wolfish grin. "Of course it could. Fortunately, my father was too busy to come."

Dina flushed red at the thought of soaking in a pool with Juzao Sadoc, and Kuaron laughed and kissed her cheek.

IT was only a few weeks later that they were invited to yet another family gathering.

"I swear, Kuaron," Dina said as she started to dress. "I've been to more parties in the months since we became *shahgunrahai* than I had gone to in my adult life before I came to Wakanreo."

He smiled at this, and fluffed his headcrest. "Wisutans don't need much of an excuse to host a party."

"And this one is for your cousin Gwionu because he just qualified as a veterinarian?"

"Yes," Kuaron confirmed as he pulled on a clean shirt. "Gwionu found *shahgunrah* during his university years. He and his *shahgunrahai* had a child, so he dropped out of school to work. After his *shahgunrahai* finished her education, Gwionu went back to school,."

"I don't think I remember him," Dina said, pulling open drawers in search of the blouse she wanted. "What does he look like?"

"He's average height," Kuaron said, "and dark—like my father's coloring. You met him at my removed cousin Jhaguith's gift-giving."

Dina thought for a moment. "Was that the party where the boy's parents had such a nasty fight?"

"Yes. Jhaguith's mother Oiganna is my first cousin. She and her *shahgunrahai* have never been happy together."

Dina slipped a blouse over her head and tucked it into her trousers. "I'll say. If I recall, they didn't get along at our own gift giving. Why don't they separate if they can't at least be friends?"

"They tried living apart some years ago, but they weren't happy that way, either."

"Well, I hope they won't cause a scene tonight. It wouldn't be fair to Gwionu."

"I don't know if they're even coming," Kuaron said, brushing the fur on the back of his hands. "I haven't seen Oiganna much lately. But I do hope everything goes well for Gwionu's celebration. It wouldn't be an auspicious sign to start his life in Wisuta with a family squabble."

"I thought he was from Wisuta," Dina said, looking at herself in the mirror as she combed her hair. "Didn't you say the house is only a short ride away?"

"Gwionu and Wairfian plan to move to Wisuta to be near the zoo, because he just got a job there," Kuaron explained. "The party is at my uncle's house—my uncle Hushi."

"Hushi?" Dina said, pausing to consider the unfamiliar name. "Have I met him?"

"I don't think so," Kuaron said, stepping into the closet and pulling open the shoe drawer. "He wasn't at our gift-giving. He's one of my few maternal relations, my mother's younger brother—her only sibling, in fact. Since he's a *parundai*, my father couldn't call him up and order him around."

Dina smiled at the thought that there was someone Juzao Sadoc couldn't bully. "So why is your mother's brother giving this party for your cousin Gwionu on your father's side?"

"Hushi and his *shahgunrahai* are no direct relation to Gwionu, but Gwionu's parents knew them well, and they asked them to be his *quyarunai*."

Dina turned to collect her jewelry from its case and saw that Kuaron was sitting down to pull on his sandals. "What does *quyarunai* mean?" she asked as she slipped on an ear cuff. "Is it one of those Wakanrean things there's no equivalent for in Standard?"

"I suppose the closest term is foster parent." Kuaron walked to the wide rectangle of dense stone that hung on the wall and lifted his hands. "Gwionu is the eldest child in his family," he said, bringing both hands down in a swift motion that sharpened all ten claws at once. It made a dreadful screeching sound, but Dina had grown used to it. "Because Gwionu hadn't found a *shahgunrahai* when his younger sister reached maturity, he had to leave the small town where his family lives and be a *yarunai*."

"A which?"

"A foster child." Kuaron assumed the intent look he got whenever he was discussing something important. "It's almost a universal custom on Wakanreo. Virtually everyone practices *yarun*."

"Why?" Dina could tell he was concerned, so she stopped her preparations to stand in front of him.

"Because of *shahgunrah*." Kuaron took both her hands in his own. "Think, *acubai*. *Shahgunrah* doesn't respect blood relationships. Any two people who are *toshugai* and physically mature can become *shahgunrahai*. Everyone knows this, so they're very careful to always separate any of their children who are at risk."

"Oh," Dina said, understanding dawning. "So we'll have to do that with the twins?"

Kuaron nodded. "Yes. That's another reason it's bad luck to have twins. There's no chance that the elder one will find *shahgunrah* before the younger one is mature. One or both of them must go away to another city until one of them finds *shahgunrah*."

"Both of them?"

"Some people don't like to favor one child over the other, so they foster both of them."

Dina sighed, and then a thought struck her. "What happens if someone is careless and siblings do become *shahgunrahai*?"

Kuaron looked grim. "They become *shahgunrahai*. No one can stop it once it's started."

"But are they allowed to stay together?" Dina insisted. "Or is the incest taboo stronger than *shahgunrah?*"

"Nothing is stronger than *shahgunrah*. It's frowned upon for siblings to have children, but no one makes them separate."

Dina shivered at the thought. "It sounds horrible to have to send your child away just when he needs guidance, but I suppose it's better than taking a risk."

"Yes," Kuaron said.

"Well, I'm not going to worry about it now," Dina said, turning away from him for one last check in the mirror. "The twins are still in their artificial wombs."

Kuaron smiled, and Dina could sense his relief. "That's wise. We have plenty of time to worry about it."

Dina glanced at the time displayed on the com panel. "Yes, we do. Are you ready?"

Kuaron was ready, and he led the way to the flyter. As she took her seat, Dina couldn't help thinking about the intricacies inherent in her situation. She was soon to become a mother to two half-Wakanrean children without having a really good idea of what it was like to be Wakanrean.

She watched lights come on in the city below; in the darkness it could have been a Terran city, but it wasn't. She could never have anticipated, when she left Croyzan, what her life would become on Wakanreo.

Their journey wasn't long, but it started to rain about half-way there. Kuaron's uncle lived in the outer suburbs, in a small house surrounded by a well-tended plot of land and bracketed by neighboring houses. Kuaron parked the flyter at the end of a row of similar vehicles, and they each sprayed on a little water repellent before they started for the house.

Dina was glad Kuaron had been there before, as she couldn't even see the door until he led her quite close to it. It was in plain sight, but the rough, stucco-like surface of the door matched the surrounding walls perfectly, and there were no visible hinges, fittings, or indeed, anything to indicate a door except a small oval-shaped smooth spot about a meter above the ground. A carved stick painted exactly the same color as the wall hung near it, and Dina realized it was the traditional door knocker.

Kuaron applied his hand to the oval spot, and in a few seconds, the door opened inward.

"Kuaron!" a brown-furred Wakanrean said. "It's good to see you! And our welcome to your *shahgunrahai*, also. Come in out of the rain!"

"Good evening, Uncle Hushi," Kuaron said, stepping through the doorway to shake himself dry before he embraced his uncle.

Dina followed him, but settled for brushing the rain drops off her hair and clothes. She was glad it was summer, or the rain would have made her cold, even with her thermal clothing.

Dina didn't recognize Hushi, but she did note that he looked to be about Juzao Sadoc's age, and he wore a *heicha* just like Kuaron's. He was an otherwise very ordinary-looking Wakanrean of average height, build, and coloring.

Her host bowed politely and offered his hands. Dina bowed back and extended her own gloved hands, fingers curved inward and knuckles touching. She stopped short of actually making contact with Hushi, but he closed the distance himself, brushing his hands very lightly against hers in proper Wakanrean fashion.

"I'm happy to meet you, *Parundai* Du," Dina said. It sounded strange to address this man in exactly the same way as Kuaron was addressed.

"Please," Hushi said, straightening from his bow, "I hope you'll join Kuaron in calling me Uncle Hushi—or at least Hushi."

Dina wavered momentarily, wondering if this was merely a polite gesture on his part, or if he genuinely disliked being formally addressed. She recalled that few of Kuaron's relatives ever called him *parundai*, so she smiled. "I'm happy to meet you, Hushi."

He smiled back. "And this is my *shahgunrahai* Teleun Maar."

The taller, lighter-furred Wakanrean man beside him also bowed and offered his hands.

As she bowed back, Dina tried to recall if Kuaron had told her Hushi's *shahgunrahai* was a man. She didn't think so, but on the other hand, she had never asked him if he had any same-sex *shahgunrahai* in his family.

Neither man seemed ill at ease with her. Either they were comfortable with the idea of a Terran in the family, or they were very good at dissembling.

"Is Gwionu here yet?" Kuaron asked.

"He's in the main room," Hushi said. "Everyone came inside when it started raining. We might be a little cozy tonight if everyone comes."

"If it gets really tight, some of us will have to get wet," Kuaron said.

"It shouldn't be that bad," Teleun said. "I keep telling Hushi that we should break down the wall between the main room and the second spare bedroom, but he hates to have to say no when family ask to stay with us."

"We might one day," Hushi said. "But I'd rather enlarge the house—especially if Gwionu and Wairfian have more children."

They had all moved from the tiny entrance hall to a wide doorway. As soon as they stepped through it into the long, narrow main room, a wall of noise hit them.

"On second consideration," Teleun said cheerfully, "maybe it will be that bad."

"Kuaron!" a man's voice called, and Dina recognized the plump man in the corner as Jeikeich, Kuaron's aunt's *shahgunrahai*. He stood with nine or ten people clustered into a circle. "Come and talk to us about the story in the *Untulao*," Jeikeich said, waving his arm in a peremptory gesture. "We need an expert opinion."

Dina wasn't particularly interested in standing through a long, involved discussion of a *qatrah*, so she smiled at Kuaron and let go of his arm to move to a table where glasses of amber wine were set out, while her *shahgunrahai* went off to discourse on his favorite subject.

She took a glass and sipped slowly, enjoying the wine's fruity fragrance as she surveyed the room. It was a pleasant room, with a wall of windows at the far end, that must overlook the garden. The remaining walls were painted a pleasing shade of pale gold, with an occasional geometric design in brown and green breaking the sameness of the surface. The most distinctive feature of the room was the high, vaulted ceiling. Either Hushi or Teleun must have had a passion for ceiling ornaments, because the entire space was crowded with them. Mirrored geometric shapes hung every ten or twelve centimeters, and sprinkled here and there were delicate crystal spheres and spirals.

The room was very crowded. Dina stepped into a sort of niche beside the wine table so she could stay out of the traffic pattern as people milled around her. There were at least thirty people in the room already, and Hushi and Teleun went off to answer the door again as she watched, returning with four newcomers. As usual, Dina was the only Terran.

Dina decided the guest of honor must be the man in the dark
shirt and striped trousers, because he was only man present who
had Juzao Sadoc's coloring and was the right age. Besides, he
seemed to be with a young woman who held a toddler in her arms.

"This is the easy part," a voice said in Dina's ear.

Dina jumped, considerably startled as she hadn't realized a
Wakanrean woman had stepped close beside her. She let out a
breath of relief when she recognized Kuaron's cousin Oiganna Jin.
"Oh, hello," Dina said, trying to regain her composure. "I didn't see
you there."

Oiganna nodded her head at Gwionu and his *shahgunrahai*. "They
don't know it yet, but this is the easiest time to care for a child. It
gets much harder once they have minds of their own."

"I can believe it."

"You're going to have twins, aren't you?"

"Yes. But not for a few months."

"Ah!" Oiganna said, as if this were somehow significant. "Twins!
They're bad luck, you know."

"So Kuaron said. I don't let myself dwell on it. I'm not particularly superstitious."

"A lot of Wisutans are," Oiganna said, picking up a glass of wine.
"It's a common failing to appease the *midanai*." She drank half the
wine in one long swallow.

"What are *midanai*?"

Oiganna laughed. "Hasn't Kuaron told you about the *midanai*?"

Dina shook her head back and forth and then realized Oiganna
might not understand the gesture. "No, I don't think so."

"He's probably embarrassed to admit he gives them any cre-
dence," Oiganna said, swaying ever so slightly. "*Midanai* are the
little gods, who listen behind doors, and punish anyone who brags
or boasts, or weighs his *muuin* before it's picked."

"Oh," Dina said, as light dawned. "So that's why Kuaron doesn't
like to talk as if anything in the future is assured?"

"Of course not." Oiganna drained her glass and reached for the
wine pitcher. "The *midanai* might hear. That's why Wisutans always
hide their doorways—to fool the *midanai*."

"So they're like the *kapuhai* in children's stories?"

The Wakanrean woman waved her hand in a dismissive gesture.
"Only children believe in *kapuhai* but lots of people worry about

*midanai*, even once they're grown. It's ironic in a way," she added, sipping her wine. "Aunt Yulayan was determined that Kuaron shouldn't be swayed by religion, but she forgot to check what stories the child watcher was telling him."

"Many cultures have that kind of superstition," Dina said, wondering if a child watcher was a nanny or just a babysitter. Oiganna seemed to have had too much wine. Dina had never seen a Wakanrean get truly drunk.

"Now Heingeon has other failings," Oiganna said, staring straight ahead at where her *shahgunrahai* was conversing with an elderly lady in a dark red gown. "You're lucky you have Kuaron."

"Yes, I am," Dina said, feeling as if she were on shaky ground. A couple of people passed so close, Dina had to pull back to avoid having them brush against her, and she decided to change the subject. "It's a very crowded party, isn't it?"

"Yes. Hushi and Teleun both have big families. They need a bigger house to entertain like this."

"Hushi said he wanted to build onto this house."

"He might, one day. He's a carpenter, after all."

"I didn't know that," Dina said, glancing across the room to where her *shahgunrahai's* uncle was passing around a plate of food.

"Yes. So is Teleun. That's how they met."

Dina remembered Kuaron telling her he had hoped to find *shahgunrah* at the *qatraharai* school. "That seems very convenient. You have a lot in common that way."

"Yes. Heingeon and I met at the market. We were both shopping. *Shahgunrah* seemed exciting at the time, when *taal* was strong. It took me years to realize how truly dull he is." Oiganna tossed back the rest of her wine.

"I think I had better go get something to eat," Dina said, opting to detach herself from Oiganna. The conversation didn't seem at all promising, and the last thing she wanted was to be part of a scene.

In a matter of moments, however, she had no choice about it. Oiganna didn't protest when she left her, but a few seconds later, Dina nearly bumped into a very young Wakanrean woman wearing almost nothing but high-waisted trousers.

Dina had seen young people going topless in Wisuta before this. Kuaron had told her it was a style among young radicals to assert their Wakanreanness by rejecting off-world influences and wearing fashions not seen in Wisuta for decades. Not wearing shirts was the most distinctive feature of the radical dress code. Second was carrying a knife, usually on a sash worn diagonally across the torso with the knife scabbard over one hip.

This young woman had adopted the fashion completely. Her blue sash sported a long leather scabbard with a black-handled knife, and her baggy black trousers were belted right below her bare chest.

As bare as a Wakanrean chest could be, Dina reminded herself. Between the woman's brown body fur and the fact that she had no visible breasts, it was difficult for Dina to feel shocked, especially after her experience in the bathing pool at Jeikeich's house.

"Excuse me," she said, bowing slightly.

The young woman frowned at her. "I didn't think you would dare to come," she said, her tone angry. She spoke in Standard, but even so, Dina wasn't quite sure she had heard her correctly.

"Pardon?" she said, blinking in surprise.

"We don't want *fijazhai* in this family. If you have no shame, then you should at least have some sense." She put one hand on the knife at her hip in a suggestive fashion.

Dina was too shocked to be afraid. All around her the room had gone quiet.

"It's you who should have shame, young woman!" a stern voice said.

Dina looked around and saw that Oiganna's *shahgunrahai* Heingeon Krou had left the elderly lady and was fast approaching. He stepped forward until he was between her and the young radical.

"Bah!" he said, in an angry voice. "Have you no manners at all? How can you act this way at a family party?"

Dina heard a rustling behind her. Kuaron pushed his way through the crowd, an anxious look on his face. He moved beside Dina and caught her up in a one-armed embrace at the same time.

"Mind your own business, old man!" the young woman shouted at Heingeon.

"Joislu!" One of the hosts, Teleun Maar, moved from behind Heingeon to confront the shirtless woman. "Joislu, what are you doing? How can you treat my guest this way?"

"Your *guest*?" She made the word into an epithet by her inflection. "It's your *guest* who has behaved badly, Uncle Teleun. She behaved badly when she chose to disport herself with a *parundai*."

"I have had enough!" Teleun roared. "You will leave now, Joislu! And you will not come back to this house again until you learn some manners."

His niece curled her lip in a magnificent sneer, bowed to Kuaron, and stalked off toward the door. Halfway there, Hushi appeared, and Joislu stopped just long enough to bow to him, too.

"I must ask you to excuse me, *parundai*," she said in Wisutan.

Hushi frowned, but didn't answer. The crowd parted to let Joislu through. Dina heard the door open and close as she left the house.

"Please accept my apologies, *kantai*," Teleun said, bowing deeply to Dina and then to Kuaron. "And you, too, Kuaron. My sister told me Joislu had turned radical, but I had no idea it had gone that far."

"None of us can choose his family," Kuaron said, bowing back at the same depth, but still holding Dina's arm. "Perhaps we should go?"

"Nonsense," said Hushi. "You just got here."

Kuaron looked down at Dina. "Do you want to go, *acubai*?"

Dina could feel a tremor of anxiety coming from him. She stroked his arm reassuringly. "Of course not. I'm fine. Thank you for your concern, *kentai*," she said to Teleun. "I hope I haven't caused a rift in your family."

Teleun waved an arm dismissively. "It's not your fault. The young often need something to distinguish themselves from their parents. It seems that Joislu has chosen bad manners."

Kuaron also offered his thanks to both of them, and then led Dina away.

"That was unexpected," he said, still holding her by one arm as they walked. "I thought we were safe here."

"I think we're safe from physical harm, but I don't know if there's anywhere on Wakanreo that we're truly safe from that kind of verbal abuse. People have very strong opinions about you and me, Kuaron. Do you remember the restaurant?"

"Of course I do. I know there are people who still don't believe in our *shahgunrah*."

Something in his tone made Dina look at him speculatively. "Has something happened that I don't know about?"

He shook his head. "Not really. Nothing to worry about, at any rate. It's just that recently I tried one more time to send Triascou a message. She finally answered me."

Dina could feel his unhappiness rising. "What did she say?"

"She said," Kuaron said, his voice pitched low so no one else could hear him, "that the only thing worse than watching a friend suffer through *glashunrah* was watching a friend who was a *parundai*."

"Oh. That does sound conclusive, doesn't it?"

"Yes."

"I'm sorry, Kuaron. I know she was a good friend."

He pulled her tight against him. "Not nearly good enough."

# *Chapter Fifteen*

Dina scanned the analyzer screen. This set of samples looked much better than the last. In a way, she was lucky she had the kind of job where she had to keep her mind to her work. It had been three months since the twins were transferred to their artificial wombs, and when she wasn't busy with something, she found herself worrying about them.

"How does it look so far?"

Dina looked up from her analyzer to find one of the senior chemists watching her. "It looks pretty good for everything except the highest temperature ranges. There's some molecular disintegration when ambient temp gets above two hundred degrees, but it's the best we've seen yet."

"Good," the senior chemist said, moving further into the room. The lab was basically a long, windowless room with workbenches full of testing and other equipment occupying most of the space. "We're running out of time on this project."

"The schedule isn't my concern, *kentai*," Dina said, politely moving from behind the workbench to come closer to him. "Each sample either makes the cut or it doesn't. That's my job."

"Of course," the senior chemist said.

"Excuse me," Shanour said, setting a crate of small coded beakers down on another workbench. "Are you almost done, *kantai*? I'm ready to set up the next batch."

"Almost, thank you, Taum," Dina said. She spent almost every lunch hour with Shanour, and she had difficulty remembering to call her friend by his last name when others were present.

"If you could finish today," the senior chemist began. Whatever he was going to say was lost when Hyral Brau came into the lab, a party of six people behind her, all of them wearing visitor's badges.

Dina, Shanour, and the senior chemist all turned to face her and bowed. Dina had learned to remain silent in such circumstances, and let the senior person speak.

"Good afternoon, *Kantai* Brau," the senior chemist said.

Hyral returned the bow and the greeting, and introduced her companions as university students on a tour of Quafray. She named each one, and then introduced the three members of her team by name and title.

Dina bowed when her name was called, but Shanour barely nodded.

"I was hoping you could show the students the museum, Taum," Hyral said. "And perhaps a few more of the labs."

Shanour didn't answer. He stood very still, but Dina noticed that he was breathing rapidly, and his headcrest was erect. His attention seemed fixed on one of the students, a brown-furred Wakanrean woman with a black headcrest, who stood equally transfixed.

No one spoke. Dina was a little worried that her friend had somehow forgotten company etiquette.

"Shanour?" Dina said. "Is anything wrong?"

The young man still didn't answer.

"Shanour?" Dina said again, starting around the workbench toward her friend.

Hyral Brau stepped forward as if to intercept her, but stopped short of making contact. "He's fine. Nothing's wrong. It's perfectly natural."

Understanding dawned for Dina, and she glanced back at Shanour. Her friend had taken several steps and was now facing the Wakanrean woman who stood as if entranced in front of him. The other Wakanrean students had pulled back toward the wall as if to clear a path between the couple.

Dina let out a breath she had not known she was holding in. "Oh."

"Yes," Hyral said, very quietly. "*Shahgunrah* has found him."

"I'm happy for him. He wanted it to be a woman so he could have children."

A brief spasm of some strong emotion crossed Hyral's face. "He's lucky, then. Not everyone is."

Dina couldn't tell if the emotion were unhappiness or merely irritation. Before she could say anything more, Shanour and the stranger clasped hands. He bent his head down and spoke, and she answered. Dina couldn't hear what either of them said, but in a matter of seconds, they both started for the door, without even a word to Hyral or the other students.

Hyral let out a sigh. "The Legislator's daughter. He's doubly lucky." She seemed to come alert with a start. The other members of the tour were waiting expectantly. Hyral looked from them to the senior chemist to Dina.

It was, Dina realized, an awkward situation. Office protocol dictated that jobs such as showing visitors around the facility should go to the least senior team member, and yet, if Hyral followed the rules, she would have to put Quafray's only Terran employee in charge of a tour.

"Hiof," she said to the senior chemist, "perhaps you could show our visitors the museum while I notify Taum's family about his *shahgunrah?*"

"Certainly, *kantai*," the senior chemist said, bowing again.

"Good," she said, starting for the door. "Once I let Taum's parents know, I'll find someone else to lead the tour of the other labs."

As soon as the team manager had gone, the senior chemist began to herd the reminding students into a clump.

"Now, now," he said. "It's all very exciting to see *shahgunrah* find your friend, but after all, it happens every day. Life goes on, doesn't it? Let's move now, please. Move along. Through the door and to your left."

He stopped long enough to speak to Dina in a low voice. "Do you think you could set up the next test yourself, Bellaire?"

"Why, yes, *kentai*," she said, a little startled. The senior staff rarely used her name, preferring to get by without addressing her as anything at all. "I can manage."

"Good, good," he said, sounding pleased. "Mustn't let the schedule lag for a little thing like this."

Dina blinked, still stunned by the suddenness of this change in her friend's life. "How often does *shahgunrah* happen at work?"

He gave a convulsive shrug. "It's hardly an everyday occurance, but it's frequent enough that there's a protocol for what to do."

"I see," said Dina, thinking that she would ask Kuaron about it when she got home.

As it happened, she didn't have time to mention Shanour's finding *shahgunrah*. When she called Kuaron to be sure he would meet
her at the hospital, she saw that her *shahgunrahai* had changed
into a suit of dark red cloth.

"Oh," Dina said in surprise. "Are we going out?"

"I have to go," Kuaron said, looking a little grim. "If you can
come with me, it would be nice, but it means not visiting the hospital today."

"What's wrong?" Dina demanded. Neither *klunar* nor *haictor* had
any effect over the com, but she knew him well enough now to tell
from his expression that he was upset.

"I have to go to my Uncle Torzeiv's house. Oiganna died yesterday."

"Oiganna Jin? Your cousin?"

Kuaron nodded.

"Of course I'll come," Dina said. "What happened?"

"I'll tell you when I pick you up."

Dina cast an anxious glance at her own clothes. She had no
idea of the proper etiquette for a condolence call. "Am I dressed all
right?" She stepped back from the com so he could see her shirt and
trousers.

Kuaron considered her briefly. "I'll bring your red jacket, and
you can take off the scarf."

Dina concluded that dark red must be a mourning color, as the
only red jacket she owned was almost as dark as Kuaron's suit.

"I'll be there as soon as I can," Kuaron added.

He signed off abruptly, and Dina was left to ponder his news for
several minutes. Oiganna Jin was a year older than Kuaron, but
had found her *shahgunrahai* at a much younger age, and in consequence, her children were already grown and living on their own.

Dina recalled the last time she had seen Oiganna at Kuaron's
uncle's house. She had gotten a little drunk that night, but she
hadn't looked ill.

Dina scanned the latest news from the com in her office; there
was no mention of any fatal accident or anything else that might
account for a relatively young and healthy woman's death.

After work, Dina waited on the Quafray roof port. Kuaron was
cleared to land in the employees' section, so it was crowded where
she waited. One of the clerks from the accounting department came
over to Dina and bowed slightly.

"Forgive the intrusion, *Kantai* Bellaire," she said. "I heard the news about Oiganna Jin. Will you please convey my sincere condolences to *Parundai* Du?"

"Certainly," Dina said, a little surprised. "How did you hear about it? It wasn't on the bulletins."

A flustered look on the woman's face told Dina that she had committed a solecism by mentioning the possibility.

"No, of course not," the woman said. "As it happens, Heingeon Krou was my father's cousin."

"I see," Dina said. "I'll be sure to pass on your sentiments to Kuaron."

The clerk bowed and walked away before Dina realized that she had used the past tense in referring to Heingeon.

The com in Dina's pocket beeped, and Dina looked up to see Kuaron's flyter approaching. Kuaron had to hover for a moment, waiting for a gap in the flow of departing flyters until he could set down.

When Dina got into the flyter, she could tell immediately that Kuaron was troubled. She waited until he had brought the flyter to cruising altitude and set the destination controls before she asked any questions.

"Kuaron, what happened to your cousin," she said finally, when he had leaned back in his seat.

"She killed herself by taking drugs."

"Oh, Kuaron, no!"

"Yes. They did it last night."

"They?"

"She and Heingeon both took drugs. The police investigated, and they said it was clearly *naishagundah*."

The word was totally new to Dina. "What is *naishagundah*?"

"It's something no one likes to talk about," Kuaron said, looking out the windows as he spoke. "Sometimes, over time, two people find *shahgunrah* such a burden for them that they can't face life as *shahgunrahai*. If they try living apart and find it unsatisfactory, they agree to take their own lives—usually together."

"Oh, my! Were Oiganna and Heingeon really that unhappy together?"

"Yes. We all knew it. Their quarrels never got better over time. If anything, the last few years were much worse.

"Everything Oiganna valued in life was unimportant to Hein-geon. Everything he considered meaningful, she despised. She wanted to express her creativity, to spend her time in artistic pursuits, to live a spontaneous life free from the drudgery of habit. He wanted security, a comfortable routine, a life without surprises. Even their religions were at odds. She was a devout *Paruhuanhai*, and he believed in *Oishah*. Life had become a misery for them both."

Dina shivered, and Kuaron immediately slipped an arm around her.

"It won't happen to us," he said. "It could never happen to us."

Dina didn't answer, and a moment later, the arrival alarm beeped. They were hovering over the roof port of a large, suburban house where a gray flyter with the official seal of Wakanreo on the side was taking off.

"Your father must be here already," Dina said.

Kuaron murmured an affirmative, but he was busy with the landing because the roof port was already occupied by half a dozen other flyters.

"I think I had better send the flyter into a holding pattern," he said as they opened the doors. "Most of my cousins won't be able to do so, and there's not much room left."

Dina waited while he used the remote to direct the flyter to take off. She watched it as it climbed higher and higher, well beyond normal cruising altitudes, and turned to find Kuaron holding her jacket.

She slipped it on, then pulled off her scarf and stuffed it into her pocket. They went down a flight of gracefully curving stairs to the sprawling house Dina had visited once before.

They found that most of Oiganna Jin's relations had assembled in the *zagathua*n. The outdoor space was defined by a beautiful carpet and furnished much like the main room of Kuaron's house. There were sofas, hassocks, comfortable chairs, small tables, and a number of appliances including a sound system, a servoid, and a com console.

The servoid dispensed cups of *quascha* as they arrived. Kuaron's cousin Aermainna Jin, Oiganna's eldest sister, acted as hostess and welcomed them.

"Thank you for coming, cousin," she said to Kuaron as she embraced him. "Uncle Juzao is here already. He's in the house with

Father and Mother. It meant a lot to them that he left work to come here."

"I came as soon as he called me," Kuaron said, "but I had to pick up Dina from her work."

They were speaking in Wisutan, but Dina could follow the conversation without difficulty. She returned both Aermainna's bow and her tentative embrace, and murmured her own condolences after Kuaron had voiced his.

Aermainna seemed sad but composed as she replied, and Dina wondered if she had known this tragedy was coming.

"Where are the children?" Kuaron asked. "How are they taking it?"

"They're all inside with Father and Mother," Aermainna said, "except for Jhaguith and his *shahgunrahai*. They were on a trip to Zanliun, and won't be here until tomorrow. Apparently, Oiganna and Heingeon didn't give any warning—just a timed message to his brother to call the police this morning."

"*Naishagundah* is always hardest on the children," Kuaron said.

"Yes," Aermainna agreed. "But at least Oiganna and Heingeon were able to wait until all of them were grown. Even Hesquith has left school and is working."

Before Kuaron could reply, another cousin arrived, and Aermainna was called away to make her welcome. Kuaron and Dina circulated among the assembled relations and made quiet conversation, most of it about the sadness of two lives cut so short and the sorrow of the grown but suddenly orphaned children.

It seemed to Dina that although everyone grieved openly, no one expressed real shock about the *naishagundah* itself, as if it were an expected outcome rather than a surprise.

The daylight faded and light poles sprouted from the ground, illuminating the *zagathuan* with soft luminescence. The servoid dispensed food as well as drink. Dina found the gloomy atmosphere oppressive. Most of the family were dressed in some variation of the dark red color that Kuaron wore, and that combined with the hushed tones of their conversations was enough to depress Dina's spirits.

When they were ready to go home, they had to walk a little ways from the house to find a space large enough to land the flyter, and Dina recalled leaving the embassy party with Kuaron in much the same way. She shivered again, in spite of the fact that the temperature control in her jacket had activated and the garment kept her toasty warm. Kuaron slipped an arm around her and pulled her close.

"It's okay," Dina said, switching back to Standard with a sense of relief. "I'm not cold."

"I know," Kuaron said in the same language. "But you're worried."

"I suppose I am, a little. It was a pretty scary afternoon, Kuaron."

"Because my cousin committed *naishagundah?*"

"Because a Wakanrean man and a Wakanrean woman who grew up expecting *shahgunrah*—and most likely welcomed it when it happened—couldn't live happily, either with each other or without each other. What chance do we have, as different as we are?"

"But we respect each other's differences. Neither Oiganna nor Heingeon could bring themselves to value what was different in the other. He was a good person, but she thought of him as small-minded and dull. She was compassionate and intense, but he saw her only as flighty and impractical. You may not understand the *qatrahs*, but you don't denigrate them. I may not know anything about chemistry, but I respect your skill and knowledge."

"That's true," Dina said, considerably heartened at the thought.

"We may be of different species, but in some ways we're more alike than they were. We both prefer small parties to large ones; we like to read; we like to go on picnics; and you've even come to appreciate home-cooked food."

"That's true, too."

Kuaron bent his head down and nuzzled her cheek. "Don't let this depress you too much, *acubai. Naishagundah* is very sad, but it's also rare."

Dina felt cheered enough to nuzzle him back, but she was very quiet on the ride home.


DINA stayed home from work the next day, as Kuaron said it was customary as a sign of respect. Kuaron himself canceled a performance he was supposed to have given that night. It was to have been an out of town trip, and Dina was glad to have him home with her.

"What about a funeral?" Dina asked over the breakfast table. "Do Wakanreans have funerals?"

"Not like a Terran funeral," Kuaron said. "The immediate family will bury the bodies very privately today or tomorrow. Then, twenty days from the death, both families will hold a memorial service.

"Both families?"

"Yes. Heingeon's family and ours will share in the expense and the planning of the service. It'll be quite long—several hours at least because it's for two people—but a memorial is considerably less somber than the burial will be, or even the *pliquin* yesterday. We try to make it a celebration of what was accomplished in life rather than an expression of regret for what's been lost."

"But both families will participate—even though it was *naishagundah*?"

He seemed troubled at her difficulty in accepting the circumstances. "Yes, of course. It's not as if it were *aifshagundah*."

"What's *aifshagundah*?"

"Well," Kuaron said, hesitating as if he were unsure of what he wanted to say. "Sometimes two *shahgunrahai* are very unhappy, but only one of them is truly desperate enough to want to die. In that case, sometimes one of them will kill the other and then commit suicide. We call that *aifshagundah*."

Dina felt a cold chill at the thought. "How often does this happen?"

"Not that often."

"So it's rarer than *naishagundah*?"

"No, actually, it's a little more common. In a city like Wisuta, there might be four or five cases of *aifshagundah* in a year, and only two or three of *naishagundah*."

Dina was surprised. "How can you know that? I thought you said it was never in the news bulletins unless it happened to someone famous."

"It's not, but they publish statistics on it." He leaned across the table and stroked her arm. "Don't let it upset you, *acubai*. It's sad, but it shouldn't worry you."

Resolutely, Dina changed the subject. "So, can we still go to the hospital today?"

"Certainly," Kuaron said, looking relieved. "I have to help my father with some arrangements, but I'll be free this afternoon. We can go then."

"I'll wait for you here. Or if your errands run late, call me and I'll meet you at the hospital."

Kuaron agreed, and he left soon after they had cleared away the breakfast dishes. Dina occupied herself with catching up on her Wisutan studies, even attempting to read a book in Wisutan.

She was well into it when the summit alarm sounded. When she answered the com, she saw Jared's face on the screen.

"Hello, Dina. I was on my way back from a business appointment, and when I realized how close I was, I thought I'd stop by. Is Kuaron home?"

"No. His cousin died the day before yesterday, and he's out making arrangements with his father."

"I heard. In fact I thought he'd be home since the *pliquin* was yesterday."

"Why don't you come stay for a bit," Dina suggested. "Kuaron could be home any time. I don't know how long he's going to be."

Jared hesitated for just a fraction of a second, and then nodded. "All right. Set the lift tube to admit me, and I'll be right there."

"I'll put the kettle on for *quascha*," Dina said, and she cut the connection.

She was putting the cups out as Jared came through the door.

He inspected the plate of homemade *juoin* bread Dina had put out beside the cups, and made noises of approbation. "That looks good. Did you make it or did Kuaron?"

Dina gave him a look. "Please! You know very well Kuaron is the cook in this house. Help yourself."

He took a slice and began to eat while Dina poured the *quascha*.

"Thanks," he said, accepting the cup. "How did it go yesterday—at the *pliquin* I mean?"

"It was pretty grim," Dina admitted, waving him toward the main room. She carried the plate along with her cup, and put it down in front of Jared. Then she sat down across from him and put her feet up on a hassock. "Wakanreans like to have parties, so I had been to a lot of gatherings, but never one that was sad. I felt bad for Oiganna's family—her children and her parents. It must have been a tremendous loss for them."

"I'm sure it was," Jared said, joining her in putting his feet on a hassock. "*Naishagundah* is bound to cause grief, even when it's not a surprise."

Dina studied him covertly over her cup. She wondered whether he had really been on the way back from a call or whether he had planned this visit. He was wearing his ThreeCon uniform but that didn't mean much as he seemed to work very flexible hours. Had he come to see Kuaron or her?

"You know a lot about Wakanrean customs, don't you, Jared?"

"In the Wisutan region, I do," Jared qualified. "Things are very different on other parts of Wakanreo. Since my patch covers only this region, that's what I've concentrated on learning."

"What exactly does a liaison officer do? We didn't have any on Fantar."

Jared grinned at her. "Will you hit me if I say we liaise?"

"I might," Dina said, trying to sound severe. "Don't tempt me."

"Okay." Jared put down his cup. "Here's the drill. When a home-world or even certain types of colony worlds join ThreeCon, we always make sure any visitors to that planet go through a liaison office. That's why I was at your orientation when you arrived. I do similar stuff for tourists and business travelers, but with them I continue to check on them. With immigrants I leave the follow-up to the Wakanrean Off-world Residents Office, since they're the ones who make the rules for folks like you."

Dina nodded. "I remember. All the immigrants on my ship were off-loaded separately from everyone else. They divided us up by species and scheduled us all for an orientation. And they found a furnished apartment for me—although I wasn't in it for long."

"Well, my office is a little different. Whenever off-worlders want to come to Wakanreo, they have to file a request with ThreeCon. If their purpose is strictly tourism—and there is a small amount of that—then the request goes to a Wakanrean bureau that gives them the information it wants them to have. If their visit is for business, then their application goes to the liaison office for what-ever area they want to visit. For most of this continent, that means me.

"I check them out—find out what they plan to do, where they plan to stay and how long, and try to make sure they don't do any-thing that might offend local sensibilities."

"So who comes to Wakanreo?" Dina asked, sipping her *quascha*. "Besides tourists."

"People who work for Terran chemical and trading companies—scientists and business people, mostly. We get the odd cultural group now and again and a few social scientists, but mostly it's people who want to study Wakanrean advances in science, or people who want to make money buying and selling stuff."

"So that's why you learned so much about the customs here, and the language?"

"Well," Jared said, as if he were making an admission, "even if I were here as something else—maybe in security or the finance office—I'd probably still have learned about Wakanreans and picked up some Wisutan. My job justified the time I spent doing it, but I've always been curious about other worlds and other people. It's one reason I joined ThreeCon."

"So being in ThreeCon gives you the chance to be nosy, and being a liaison officer gives you a good excuse."

"You've got it," Jared said, not visibly disturbed at her characterization.

"How about being friends with Kuaron?"

Jared shook his head. "I told Kuaron the truth. At first it was business, but I really do like him, and I value his friendship."

"And having Juzao Sadoc's ear doesn't play any part of that?"

"No." Jared put his feet down and sat up straight in his chair. "Look, have you got a problem with me and Kuaron being friends?"

Dina debated her answer. "Not really," she said at last.

Jared cocked his head to one side. "What does that mean?"

Dina held her hands out in a gesture of inadequacy. "I'm not sure what I mean. It's just that, before he met me, everything Kuaron knew or thought he knew about Terrans came from you."

He grinned at this, and leaned back in his chair as if he were no longer worried. "I see what it is. Kuaron and I have got a buddy thing going, and you're afraid I'll warp his view of our species by only giving him the male perspective."

Dina considered this assessment and admitted to herself there was something in it. "Maybe that's true. You don't seem to have had any compunction about presenting your view of the universe as fact."

Jared put his feet back on the hassock. "And you do?"

Dina had to smile. "Okay, I admit to a bias for my opinions. I'm sure I'm just as guilty as you are."

"Almost everyone is, at one time or another. And you're not giving Kuaron enough credit. He's no fool, and he knows me pretty well. I'll bet he has a good idea of when I'm just spouting off and when I'm talking factually."

"I suppose he does."

Jared grinned. "You say that like it's terrible to have to make that admission. What are you worried about? *Shahgunrah* gives you a real advantage over any other Terran influences in Kuaron's life."

"I'm not worried," Dina said, trying not to sound defensive.

"Yeah, right. So, would you mind telling me more about the *pliquin?*"

Dina was startled by the sudden change of subject. "I already told you, it was grim."

Jared shook his head. "No, I mean would you tell me the details—what was said, who was there, how long did everyone stay—that kind of thing."

Dina blinked in surprise. "Why do you want to know?"

"Because I'll never get the chance to go to one. Unlike the memorial service, the *pliquin* is always limited to family—relatives by blood and by *shahgunrah*. You're the first Terran ever to attend one."

"Really?" Somehow the thought had never occurred to Dina.

"Yes, really," Jared said, taking out his pocket com. "Would you mind if I record your answers?"

"Yes, I'd mind," Dina said, considerably miffed. "It was a private occasion. I would no more tell you what went on at a family gathering than I'd tell you the details of my *shahkuun.*"

Jared slipped the com back into his pocket. "Sorry. My mistake. Sometimes my zeal for knowledge gets the better of me."

Dina gave him an appraising glance. "So, you're positive Kuaron is really a friend and not just a source of information?"

"Ouch!" Jared shook his head. "I suppose I deserved that."

"You certainly did."

Jared moved forward on his chair. "Look, Dina, cut me some slack here. I'm officially a liaison officer and unofficially Kuaron's friend—and yours I hope. I've done my best to help you learn about Wakanreo, but I'd have done it even if I hadn't known Kuaron before he met you."

Dina studied him overtly this time. "Just a benevolent busybody, trying to help me fit in?"

"Sure." Jared swallowed the last of the bread and licked his fingers. Dina realized she had forgotten the hand-washing bowl. "ThreeCon wants the situation here on Wakanreo to get better, not worse," he said. "I don't know if you understand how important you are to the state of Wakanrean/Terran relations?"

Dina opened her eyes wide at this comment. It was worded like a statement, but Jared's intonation made it a question. "I didn't realize I was a part of ThreeCon's plan for Wakanreo."

Jared lifted his arms wide in an expansive gesture that took in the whole room. "How could you not be? You're the first Terran who's ever experienced *shahgunrah*. The ramifications of that are still sifting down to us. Kuaron's position accentuates your importance, but it would be there even if he were a ditch digger with no family."

"Even if he were a female ditch digger?"

Jared waved a hand dismissively and lifted his cup. "If Kuaron were female, you'd still be important, but you wouldn't be pregnant."

"I'm not actually pregnant," Dina said dryly.

"Expecting, then," Jared said, sipping his *quascha*. "Technology allows you to be one without the other."

"I suppose it does."

There was a brief, awkward pause, and then Jared sighed, put his feet down, and sat up. "I think I'd better be running along. You're not the only one who has role problems, you know."

"What?" Dina said, confused.

Jared shook his head dolefully. "I don't know quite how to act with you. If you remember, I met you before you started *shahgunrah* with Kuaron. After that, I tried to think of you as my best friend's wife, but you're not really Kuaron's wife, or even a Wakanrean woman."

Dina didn't know what to say.

Jared didn't wait for her to think of a reply. "Mind if I ask a personal question?"

"No," she said. "But I don't guarantee to answer it."

"Fair enough. Did you ever date outside your species before you met Kuaron?"

She shook her head.

Jared smiled a peculiar, sardonic smile. "I thought not." He got to his feet. "You know, one consequence of *shahgunrah* is that Wakanrean men and women are much more likely to be friends—truly friends, not potential lovers—than a Terran man and woman ever would be."

Dina thought it over. "I can see that. In fact, I've noticed it at work. The only Wakanrean at Quafray who's been really friendly to me is a man. We eat lunch together, and we chat when we're working alone."

Jared held out his hand. "Let's you and me be friends, then—you and me, not just me and Kuaron?"

Dina stood up and took his hand. "Friends," she said, shaking it firmly. "Just friends."

Jared grinned at this. "I can take a hint." He started for the door. "Tell Kuaron I stopped by, will you? And give him my condolences. Tell him *Ka ainianee iyio kiorda*."

"Your thoughts go with him?"

"Very good," Jared said, slapping her on the shoulder as he let go of her hand. "See you later, buddy."

Once he was gone, Dina sat down with another cup of *quascha* and tried to determine what, if anything, the conversation had signified.

# *Chapter Sixteen*

Dina was intrigued to know how Shanour's *shahgunrah* was progressing, but she had to wait for some time before she was able to speak to her friend. Eleven days after Shanour left Quafray, word spread through the office that his *shahkuun* was over. Dina and Kuaron went to the gift giving the next day and presented the new *shahgunrahai* with a dozen crystal glasses, selected by Dina with Kuaron's guidance.

They found Shanour surrounded by a host of friends and relations. He fairly glowed with happiness as he introduced the tall, dark-furred Wakanrean beside him as Argiantur Diow, his *shahgunrahai*. Argiantur also seemed pleased in her *shahgunrah* and comfortable with Shanour's somewhat unusual friends. She went through the motions of touching hands with Dina without making actual contact, just as most of Kuaron's relatives did, with no shyness or hesitation. Argiantur's relations, on the other hand, stared very curiously at the only Terran in the house. Even her mother, the Legislator, made no effort to be friendly.

Rather than try to get Shanour alone, Dina decided to wait until her friend was back at work to talk to him. Dina and Kuaron stayed at the gift giving only as long as good manners necessitated, and left with a sense of relief.

Three days later, Shanour returned to Quafray. He wasn't at all shy about his experience, as the first thing he said to Dina once they had a chance to talk was that he had found *shahgunrah* to be both pleasurable and fulfilling.

"So tell me about Argiantur," Dina said as they sat together in the lunchroom. She had just tapped in their choices for lunch, and they were waiting for their food to be delivered.

"She's a little younger than I am," Shanour said obligingly. "Well, you knew she's still in university. She wants to be a *puoustahai*."

"Whatever is that?" The word was new to Dina, and unlike many Wisutan words, she couldn't determine an obvious root for it.

The console chimed, and Shanour removed their trays from the serving hatch. "It's a sort of combination artist and philosopher." He handed Dina her tray. "A *puoustahai* studies a topic, meditates on it, and then writes a brief comment in old-style script, and embellishes it by drawing a picture around it. They're often displayed on the wall or sometimes the ceiling and they're called *puousta*. Each one is supposed to be both beautiful and thought-provoking."

"Oh, yes. I know what you mean now. One of Kuaron's aunts has several of them in her house."

"Many people collect them," Shanour said, taking a bite of grilled vegetables. "Argiantur has done several that are very good, but of course, she hasn't produced anything original yet, because she's still studying and copying the masters."

"I see. And you spent *shahkuun* at your house instead of hers?"

"Yes. It was a little awkward because my roommates had to leave so suddenly, but it was better than going to her parents' house. Her family is illustrious but not wealthy, and their house is always crowded."

"That was obliging of your roommates," Dina said, thinking that she was lucky Kuaron could afford to live alone.

Shanour blinked. "Well, of course they had to move out temporarily. It's expected."

"Of course." Dina prodded her leaf vegetable casserole with her fork and took a tentative taste. Kuaron's cooking had spoiled her for synthesized food. "So, where will you live now?"

"We found a place yesterday. We're moving in the day after tomorrow."

"It's lucky you found somewhere so fast."

"Yes. I've been very fortunate. First because I found my *shahgunrahai* without having to wait for years and years, and second because she's a woman so we can have children."

Dina smiled reflectively as she remembered the conversation in which Shanour had first expressed his sentiments about *shahgunrah*. "And is she a good lover?"

"Oh, yes! In fact, I don't see how she could be any better."

"You enjoyed *shahkuun*, then?"

"Very much," Shanour said promptly. "Didn't you?"

"Most of it—once I got used to the idea."

Shanour's expression grew very solemn. "When we first heard what had happened to you and the *parundai*, my mother said that you had been blessed by Paruian. I didn't understand what she meant at the time, but I do now."

Dina felt a jolt of disorientation. It was disconcerting to have a friend link something intrinsic to his religious beliefs to Dina's own experiences—as if Dina had suddenly found herself part of Wakanrean theology. "I'm glad *shahgunrah* is working out for you."

"So am I," Shanour said happily as he sliced his broiled *juija*. "It's nice that sex is as wonderful as people told me it would be. It's disappointing when you hear something described with superlatives and then it turns out to be quite ordinary."

Dina agreed, but changed the subject to Argiantur's studies, and the young couple's finances. Shanour revealed that with his salary and her student stipend, they could just get by in their new apartment.

"Unless, of course, Argiantur is already pregnant," Shanour said. "My parents said if that happens, they'll be happy to help us out. Still, I'd have to put off completing my advanced degree for a few years."

Dina wasn't surprised, as she had learned from her Wakanrean doctors that it wasn't unusual for women to get pregnant during *shahkuun*, when their systems were flooded with the hormones induced by *taal*.

"Will you bring the twins to the center here at Quafray after they're born?" Shanour asked.

"We're still debating what to do," Dina said. "I plan to take four months off, and Kuaron, too. After that, Kuaron is home a lot during the daytime, but he has to rehearse a good part of every day, and he can't be disturbed during that time. We may keep the babies at home when we can, and use the childcare center here when he has a busy schedule."

"He travels a lot, doesn't he?"

"Yes. He's gotten even more well known in the last few months, and he's had a lot of invitations to sing in other cities. He had a performance in Jitsin last week, and another in Zanliun two weeks before that."

"Do you go with him?" Shanour asked as he chewed his *juija* steak.

"If I don't have to work the next day. I went to Jitsin but not to Zanliun, not this time. Fortunately, he's never gone longer than over night."

Shanour gave a little sigh. "That would be very difficult. I can't imagine being separated from Argiantur, even for one night."

Dina recalled her own experience of *shahkuun* and the days immediately after it and held back a blush by changing the subject again. "So, have you heard who transferred to the Solvents Team?"

Shanour was diverted, and the conversation passed on to all the events at work that Shanour had missed.


THE memorial service for Oiganna Jin and her *shahgunrahai* was every bit as long as Kuaron had predicted. It started early in the morning and lasted well into the afternoon. A good part of it was sung, as Paruianite rites dictated. The songs were sung in Wisutan, and were much more like Terran songs than any *qatrah* Dina had ever heard.

Another segment of the service was silent; Heingeon Krou's *oishah* faith, which Dina had learned was mostly a form of nature worship, required a period of quiet meditation. Next came an elegy for each of the deceased. Friends and relations then related anecdotes about the departed, illustrating their good qualities. Many people had worn Oiganna's brightly-colored creations to the service, and at one point, several of them paraded past the assembled guests to illustrate the dead woman's talent. One of them was a tall woman in a long robe like the ones Kuaron wore to perform, except that hers was brightly painted, with an elaborate pattern of flying insects intertwined with abstract shapes. She was striking even without the robe, as her coloring was almost like Kuaron's—pale gold body fur combined with an even paler golden headcrest.

She displayed her garment with the others and then, as the promenade ended, she walked past the row of chairs where Kuaron and Dina sat. Dina was admiring her robe when she caught the woman glaring at her.

Dina flushed, disconcerted by the overt malice in the other woman's gaze. She was used to a certain amount of curiosity, even rudeness, from strangers, but few people took the trouble to make their animosity so obvious. Certainly, no one else at the service had made any openly hostile gestures. This woman lifted her head as she passed and put her hand up to brush her neck with a quick, backhanded stroke that nicked her chin with her claws.

Dina had no idea if the gesture was significant, but beside her she heard Kuaron draw in a sharp breath. She could feel anger coming from him, and something else she couldn't identify—regret or sorrow, perhaps.

She took his hand and held it, not letting herself look back over her shoulder. The fact that the woman had passed them meant that most likely she was seated behind the rows reserved for family. Whoever she was, she was probably no relation.

Dina found the remainder of the service wearing, and she was glad when it was over.

"Who was that woman in the insect robe?" Dina asked Kuaron as they walked to their flyter.

"That was Triascou lu Huaic."

"Oh," Dina said, digesting the news. "Was it rude of her to scratch herself under her chin like that?"

"Yes, very."

"Hmmm. How long has she been a friend of yours?"

"Ever since we were at the *Quhom* together. We both debuted at the same club, a few days apart."

"Well, I have to say, Kuaron, that I think she's pretty tacky to insult me at a memorial service. I mean, she could have waited for another time."

Kuaron laughed and gave her a one-armed hug. Dina could tell his amusement was genuine. "I think so, too, *acubai*."

Dina let out a sigh. "Let's go home. We don't want your relations to think I'm some rude Terran who leaves her guests on their own."

Kuaron smiled and held the flyter door open for her. They hurried home to the cliff house, to prepare the evening meal for the several cousins who were staying with them. By the end of the day, Dina was weary enough to join Kuaron and his relations in the soaking pool with barely a twinge of embarrassment. There was, she found, something companionable about relaxing in very warm water that made up for any of the awkwardness that came from being naked. She went to bed too tired to worry about rudeness from Kuaron's old friend.

DINA went to the hospital the next morning instead of waiting until afternoon. Kuaron couldn't come with her, as he had to fly to Fargaj for a performance that afternoon, so she went alone, taking the new flyter Kuaron had urged her to buy so she wouldn't have to depend on autocabs and the transit system.

She wasn't entirely surprised to find Jared Harlingen waiting for her when she came out of the nursery.

"Hello," he said. "How are you holding up?"

"Good morning," Dina said. "I'm fine. Why do you ask?"

He fell in step beside her as she started for the exit. "The memorial was yesterday. I thought it might have tuckered you out."

"It did, a little," Dina confessed. "But that was mostly because we had several of Kuaron's cousins staying with us."

He nodded understanding. "I know exactly what you mean. Wisutans are big on family obligation. When they travel, their relatives are stuck with them. If you have a big enough family and live in a popular place to visit, you might as well be in the hotel business."

Dina smiled at the simile. "It's not as bad as that. They were all very helpful and undemanding. It was just that there were nine of them."

"So, did Kuaron head out for Fargaj?"

"Yes," Dina said, glancing at him as they walked. "Did he tell you he was performing there or did you find out on your own?"

"I have my sources."

"And you follow his career closely?"

"Yup. It's a career that's going to be pretty spectacular before he's done."

Dina frowned a mock frown. "You're being a *nyesh* again."

Jared shook his head. "No way. Believe me, Kuaron is good at what he does—one of the very best. And you should know his career has taken off since his *shahgunrah*. He was always good—technically good—but now his singing has a depth of emotion that wasn't there before he met you."

Dina smiled at this. "You're flattering me. You know Wakanreans well enough to know *shahgunrah* isn't something you can take credit for, any more than you can take credit for gravity. It's a force of nature."

"Of course I know that. Anyway, all this is beside the point. If all your *shahglynai* are gone and you're alone in the house, do you want to have dinner at my place tonight?"

Dina was flustered by the invitation. Except for the reference to her *shahgunrahai's* relatives, it sounded almost like a request for a date. "They all left this morning," she said, to give herself time to think. "Kuaron took them to the air terminal with him."

"Well, then?"

There was nothing at all lover-like in his expression, and Dina decided to trust in his friendship with Kuaron. Besides, she hated eating alone. "All right. I'll come for dinner."

"Great! Kuaron's not the only one who can cook, you know. I've learned a few things since I've been on Wakanreo."

"More than a few," Dina said. "I've learned some things myself."

He got a peculiar look on his face—something between compassion and distress. "More than a few," he repeated her words back to her. "I'll see you tonight. I have to get back to work."

Dina noticed that he was in uniform. She knew his work schedule was more variable than her own. "What time should I come?"

He consulted his pocket com and flicked through a couple of screens, as if he were checking his appointments, and then named a time early in the evening.

"I'll be there." Dina waved a hand at the hospital flyter park. "I've got my own transport now."

Jared glanced at the small, sleek flyter sitting gracefully on its struts. "Very nice."

"I try not to be too proud," Dina said with mock humility. "I never owned a flyter before. I never had this much disposable income. Kuaron owns his house outright, and he won't let me pay for anything except a third of our food."

"Wisutans don't go in for mortgages. And Kuaron probably eats more than twice as much as you do."

Dina shook her head. "It doesn't seem right."

"Kuaron can afford it." Jared slapped her on the back. "See you later."

He headed back toward the main complex at a brisk pace. Dina watched him go, and wondered if she had made a mistake in accepting his invitation.

DINA'S fears were eased that night at dinner. Jared's manner bordered on the fraternal as they ate and then cleared away the dishes. It was only after they sat down in the main room with cups of *quascha* that his tone grew confiding.

"If you're wondering if I had an ulterior motive in inviting you to dinner, you're right."

Dina looked at him warily. He was sitting across the room from her, but his apartment wasn't large, and even the main room was small enough to be called cozy.

Jared burst out with a laugh. "Don't look at me like that. I'm not going to make a pass. I just wanted to tell you some things I wasn't sure Kuaron was ready to hear."

"Like what?"

"Like ThreeCon has been doing its own research on how *shahgunrah* happens. Like we hope to have a vaccine ready within a few months that could ensure that no Terran would ever induce *glashunrah* in a Wakanrean."

Dina was stunned. "Really?"

Jared nodded. "Ambassador Inoue may be an ass, but she was right about the need to guarantee that Wakanreans won't be hurt by contact with Terrans."

"You'll forgive me if I don't consider that sufficient justification for what she did."

Jared grinned. "Neither did the Terran government. In fact, Inoue has been recalled. They're sending a new ambassador, but quite frankly, I don't expect he or she will last long. Wakanreo is fed up with Terran high-handedness. They've already asked ThreeCon to order the embassy closed. The ThreeCon Assembly will probably get around to granting that request, once the Terran bloc is through haggling about it."

"The Terran bloc?"

Jared shook his head. "Oh, come now. I know you grew up on a backwater world, but you went to an excellent university on Croyzan. Surely you know the reason why Terra pushed to reform the Second Confederation into the Third?"

"I thought it was because they wanted to use Terran Standard as the official language instead of the Shuratanians' common dialect?"

"That was part of it," Jared conceded. "But mostly they wanted more say in how ThreeCon was run. The old order was controlled by homeworlds. Terra was one of eight planets with a vote. When the Third Confederation was formed, the primary difference—aside from using Terra as the standard for language, time, and distance measurements—was that the Assembly is a bicameral legislature. The Gipatuur is based on population—one delegate for every ten million people on the planet, with a one delegate minimum. But in the Senate, it's one world, one vote."

"So the many Terran colony worlds gave our species a bigger voice?"

"Sure. That was the point. It was an even bigger difference at first; there are a lot of Terran colonies because there were so many sleeper missions. But what's happened is that when sleeper world colonies are rediscovered, they don't necessarily worry about what Terra wants. And even the newer colonies don't always toe the Terran party line. Once they become truly independent, they tend to allow other species to settle there. Very few non-sleeper colonies are all one species."

"So that's why Terra is still creating new colonies like Fantar?"

"Exactly," Jared said, sounding pleased at her perspicacity. "The newer colonies tend to vote with Terra."

"They never mentioned that in school on Fantar."

"I don't suppose they would," Jared agreed, sipping his *quascha*. "Not with Terra still paying their bills. You would have found out about it on Croyzan, if you'd taken anything besides graduate level science classes."

Dina ignored this hint that he had pried into her life history. "I'm surprised we got away with it. Creating the Third Confederation, I mean."

Jared shrugged a quick, restrained shrug, reminding Dina how different Terran gestures could be from Wakanrean. "It's not that difficult to understand. After all, there are really only three species that interact on a wide-spread basis and have colony worlds."

"The Triad," Dina said. "Terrans, Milorans, and Shuratanians. Even I know that."

"Right," Jared confirmed. "Except for Wakanreans, Tryffs are the only other humanoid oxygen breathers of a reasonable size. Tryffin is a full member of ThreeCon because they're well represented in ThreeCon's enlisted personnel, but Tryffs are mostly limited to ships and space stations—and of course, planets where the gravity is too light for everyone else."

"So," Dina said, thinking as she talked, "neither the Milorans nor the Shuratanians minded the change in ThreeCon's structure?"

"Well, Milorans tend to have their own view of things. They consider Milora a sacred planet for their species and as long as no one tries to mess with it, they're happy. The Articles were written to assure special status for homeworlds."

"And what kept the Shuratanians appeased?"

"For one thing," Jared said with a slight smile, "Senators are elected for life. And since Shuratanians live three times as long as Terrans or Milorans, that gives them a big edge in the seniority department."

"So everyone got what they wanted?"

"The Triad did. I don't think the Tryffs are unhappy. Shuratanian is a very difficult language to learn, and they can't even articulate it. And the other species don't interact much, for one reason or another."

"You mean they're xenophobic, like the Xuxa?"

"Or the Wakanreans, for that matter."

"I never studied other species that much," Dina said. "I mean, it was in the news when ThreeCon made First Contact on Xuxan ten years ago, but other than that, I never paid much attention."

"Kind of ironic, isn't it?"

"Yes." Dina remembered abruptly how the conversation had started. "So, how does *shahgunrah* work? If we can prevent it, does that mean we know?"

"We know some of it," Jared said leaning forward in his chair. "It all starts with pheromones."

"Pheromones?"

"Yes, you know, pheromones—a hormone-like substance excreted by animals. One of their main purposes is to attract the opposite sex."

"I know what a pheromone is," Dina said tartly. "I may have opted for industrial chemistry over biochem, but I know the basics."

"Good. Okay, here's the deal. Wakanreans and Terrans both make pheromones, but in Wakanreans they're much more important, and much more complex. In fact, every Wakanrean produces a unique combination of pheromones—sort of a biochemical fingerprint, if you will.

"Wakanrean pheromone combinations can also be categorized, much like Terran blood types. There are a dozen major categories and hundreds of subcategories. Each type can react only with specific other types."

"By react, you mean start *shahgunrah*?"

"Precisely. Generally speaking, each category is either male or female, but there are a few subcategories that are ambiguous. Those folks can attract either a male or a female. That's why sometimes Wakanreans start *shahgunrah* with a person of the same sex.

"Now, the thing is, it doesn't usually take much to set off *shahgunrah*. Wakanreans have a very keen sense of smell, and once a mature Wakanrean gets a whiff of someone nearby with the right pheromone combination, they start *shahgunrah*. So long as they make physical contact within a short time after that, *shahgunrah* is fully developed—there's no stopping it."

Dina also leaned forward on her chair. "So Kuaron and I have compatible pheromones?"

Jared nodded. "Not only compatible, but rare. According to our biochemists, this is why some Wakanreans don't find *shahgunrah* until they're older—if they find it at all. About twenty percent of the population have dead common combinations—they're compatible with a huge number of people. Of the remaining eighty percent, most have fairly unusual combinations—compatible with about five to ten percent of the population. A small percentage have very rare combinations. Apparently, the fact that Kuaron's mother reached middle age without finding *shahgunrah* was a tip off that it could happen to him, too."

"But his father was younger?"

Jared held out his hands. "That's how it works sometimes. See, a couple of the pheromone combinations are like universal blood donors—those people can bond with almost anyone of the opposite sex. And on the other hand, some combinations require proximity to someone with a very rare pheromone combination. Compatibility isn't the same as equality. It's not that two *shahgunrahai* have the same combination of pheromones; it's that they have compatible combinations."

"How can ThreeCon know all this?"

"Ah!" Jared said, looking inscrutable. "They've had seventy years to do the research, and all they needed was access to Wakanreans. They've been gathering data for decades, and then when you came along, you gave their research a real leg up."

"Okay," Dina said. "If ThreeCon knows so much, how does *glashunrah* happen?"

"Well," Jared said, leaning back, "it turns out Terrans produce a more limited set of pheromones that can sometimes mimic a Wakanrean combination, even though they're weak by comparison. Fortunately, we've found a way to tweak Terran body chemistry so that that can't happen, but until we get the vaccine in production, it's still a risk.

"Anyway, one of the Terran combinations is very like a Wakanrean type and that caused the first cases of *glashunrah*. Once ThreeCon figured that out, we started screening for it, but it turned out that there are more potential copycat combinations than we first realized, and some Terrans slipped through to cause problems. Luckily, the fact that the Terran pheromones are so weak meant that they don't kick in unless physical contact happens."

"So the no-touching rule worked most of the time?"

"Yes."

"Except for me and Kuaron?"

Jared looked suddenly inscrutable again. "Yes, but what happened to you wasn't *glashunrah*."

"That's true," Dina said reflectively. "I suppose it was an amazing coincidence that I happened to come here."

"Maybe not."

Dina studied him. His expression had gone from inscrutable to smug. "What makes you say it wasn't entirely a coincidence?"

"For one thing, you're a damn good chemist. And Wakanreo is noted for its chemists."

Dina wrinkled her brow. "Are you suggesting that, minute as it is, the Wakanrean part of my DNA made me a good chemist?"

"Who knows?"

Dina shook her head in mock despair. "I don't think that's likely. Kuaron is one hundred percent Wakanrean, and he knows nothing about chemistry and cares even less."

"True. I'll concede that part is mere speculation. But there's more to my theory."

"More?"

"You were interviewed on Croyzan, weren't you?"

Dina nodded. "Quafray sent a hiring agent. He was the first Wakanrean I ever met."

"Yes, and you were the only Terran who smelled right to him."

Dina opened her eyes wide. "What?"

"Think about it," Jared urged, his eyes lighting with a peculiar light. "Quafray was determined to hire a Terran chemist to prove that they weren't prejudiced against other species—they do have a few Shuratanians and Milorans working at sites other than Wisuta, by the way, but no Terrans. They went off-world to hire those folks, too, so they didn't risk picking an industrial spy. They always sent a member of the corporation, not just an employee, which meant their agent had already found *shahgunrah* and was not at risk. And in your case, when the Quafray agent met a handful of young Terran chemists on Croyzan, one of them actually smelled like a Wakanrean."

Dina laughed. "Kuaron said the same thing, and so did his father when he met me." She cocked her head to one side and regarded him with a rueful smile. "So it wasn't my grades, my test scores, my work experience, or even my personality that got me the job, it was my body odor?"

"Not entirely. If you hadn't been qualified, you wouldn't have been hired. But it wasn't like they were looking for a genius—far from it. All they wanted was a junior chemist to join the Quafray ranks and put a Terran face in their work force. You were in the top ten percent of your class, but you weren't *the* top applicant. The Quafray name was enough to draw some very talented—and more experienced—chemists."

"And it was enough to make me nervous enough to sweat during the interview," Dina added. "That probably did me more good than any of my recommendations."

"Probably," Jared agreed.

Dina smiled. "I refuse to be depressed about this. If Quafray was looking mostly for a token Terran to review quality testing, why shouldn't it be me?"

"No reason. In fact, Quafray has stood by you. They came under some pressure from a few of their more fanatic members, you know—the ones who saw you as contaminating a *parundai*. The top brass refused to fire you. Your boss stuck up for you, too."

"Really?" Dina asked, amazed. She thought it over for a second, and she nodded. "They know—certainly Hyral Brau knows—that *shahgunrah* is never anyone's fault."

"Yes."

It was said flatly, and without any intonation. Dina gave Jared a speculative look. "You sound almost as if you disapprove of *shahgunrah*."

"No." He made a sudden abrupt movement, as if to shift the focus of her attention away from their conversation. "Do you know if people recognize you when you go out?"

Dina blinked at this change of subject. "Not usually—not unless I'm with Kuaron."

"I suppose seeing the two of you together gives it away."

"I suppose it does," Dina agreed. "For one thing, he always wears his *heicha*. He only takes it off to bathe."

"And his coloring is unusual, too. Be careful, Dina. Fortunately, Kuaron has the resources to travel privately, and you live in a very secure house."

"We're thinking of buying a new house. Kuaron says—and I agree with him—that the cliff house isn't really a good place to raise children. We both want neighbors, and he'd really like a house with a *zagathuan*."

Jared heard this news in silence. His expression had become inscrutable again, and Dina wondered what he was thinking.

"When?" he said finally. "I mean, when would you move?"

"Not for a year or so," Dina said, a little embarrassed to reveal her *shahgunrahai's* weakness. "Kuaron feels that it's bad luck to buy a house for the children until they're old enough to need the room—that if we went ahead and moved for them, we might as well ask for something bad to happen to them."

Jared nodded absently. "A lot of Wisutans subscribe to that superstition—appeasing the *midanai*, they call it."

Dina didn't refute the charge. She waited instead for Jared to explain his question, and when he didn't, she asked her own. "Why did you want to know when we might move?"

Jared drew a deep breath. "Because there's been a lot of rumbling from certain groups in Wisuta and the surrounding region. Some people aren't pleased about you and Kuaron. The ones who aren't won't be any happier once the twins are born."

Dina felt a cold fear tightening in her throat. She recalled the young fanatic who had threatened her at Hushi's party. "You think they might hurt the children?"

"They might try. The thing is, there are some equally fanatic groups who see your finding *shahgunrah* with Kuaron as a miracle. If we're lucky, one group will keep the other in check."

"And if we're not lucky?"

"Then they might try something," Jared admitted. "But fortunately, Kuaron's not an easy man to find."

"He gives public performances!" Dina protested.

"Yes, but he himself isn't likely to be a target. It's you I'm worried about—you and the children."

Dina drew in a breath and tried to let it out slowly. "If you're trying to scare me silly, it's working."

"I am—a little, anyway." Jared leaned across the low table between them and took her hand. "Take it easy, Dina. You live and work in a secure place, and you don't take public transportation. That should cut down on the risk right there."

"What about Kuaron's performances?" Dina said, pulling her hand away.

"Hmmm. It's too bad Administrator Sadoc doesn't care for the *qatrahs*."

"It's true he much prefers a good wrestling match. I don't think he's been to one of Kuaron's performances since I've been here. But why does it matter?"

"Because," Jared said, with a regretful sigh, "as Administrator, he usually travels with an armed escort."

Dina couldn't stop herself from shivering. "Now you're really scaring me."

Jared frowned ever so slightly. "Do you go to every performance?"

"Unless it's too far away."

His frown deepened. "I'll talk to Kuaron when he gets back. It might be best if you stayed home."

"Even when he travels? I mean, is the danger only in Wisuta?"

"I don't think we can say." Jared smiled and lifted his eyebrows as he asked a question. "Did you go to Zanliun with him?"

She nodded. "I did on one trip. Why?"

"Nothing. I just wondered what you thought of the city."

Dina wasn't fooled by the general nature of the question. "You mean, what did someone from a provincial planet like Fantar think of the fact that hardly anyone in Zanliun wears much in the way of clothing?"

"That's it exactly," Jared said, his tone cheerful.

"I suppose I would have found it a lot more embarrassing if Quafray had hired me to work in Zanliun and I had gone there my first day on Wakanreo," Dina admitted. "But as Kuaron pointed out to me, Wakanreans are never truly naked." It suddenly occurred to her that Jared was distracting her from her earlier worries. She got to her feet. "I'd better go now, Jared. I have to work tomorrow."

He rose slowly, as if he were reluctant to see her go. "Be careful, will you?"

"Of course I'll be careful," Dina said, collecting her bag. "Thanks for dinner. It was nice to eat Terran food for a change."

Jared stepped in front of her as if to block her way. "Dina, are you happy?"

"What?" she asked, astonished that he would ask her such a personal question.

"Are you happy?" Jared repeated. "Are you glad you found Kuaron and *shahgunrah* or do you wish you could go back in time and undo it?"

Dina was distressed to realize she was breathing rapidly and her face was flushed. "I don't know! You're asking me to make a hypothetical decision, anyway, because I can't go back in time."

"But what if there were a way to undo *shahgunrah*? What if ThreeCon finds a way?"

"Look," Dina said fiercely, "I'm not prepared to talk about this with you. Thank you for dinner. I'm going now."

She stepped around Jared and made for the door. Jared made no move to stop her, but she saw him watching from the window when she got into her flyter.

# *Chapter Seventeen*

Dina was at work when Kuaron arrived back from Fargaj, early the next afternoon. He called to tell her he was at home, and she was pleased *klunar* didn't work over the com or he would have known she was still upset by what Jared had said.

"Have you talked to Jared?" she asked him, after confirming that the performance had gone well. "He cooked dinner for me last night."

Kuaron looked surprised. "Jared came over to cook for you?"

"No, I went to his house—his apartment, rather."

Kuaron smiled. "Well, you survived, so he must have cleaned it since I was there last."

"Are you saying he's a slob?"

Kuaron didn't look as if he knew the word, but he certainly understood the context. "He's not the tidiest person I know."

"Neither am I," Dina said. "Anyway, it was nice of him to fix dinner for me. I've been spoiled for synthesized food."

"Everyone should be. Should I meet you at the hospital this afternoon?"

"Yes, of course. I'm getting excited, Kuaron. The doctors said the babies will be ready to come home in only three weeks!"

Kuaron nodded. "We have work to do, then."

"You mean I can buy the cribs now?"

"Well," Kuaron hesitated, "we can pick one out, but let's not have it delivered until the day before the children are born."

"Good enough," Dina said with enthusiasm. "Let's go virtual shopping as soon as we get home."

"I don't want to shop that way. I like to see the real thing, not a simulation. Besides, there's an excellent baby goods market on our way home from the hospital."

"This one time, you might be right about virtual shopping. Okay, we'll go tonight."

Kuaron agreed and signed off. Dina went back to work, in a better mood than she had been in when she arrived that morning.

THE baby goods market was enormous. Dina and Kuaron stood at the entrance and stared at row after row of merchandise stretched out before them. Customers—all Wakanreans—strolled up and down aisles scrutinizing every kind of infant need—furniture, clothes, toys, educational electronics, and even food.

"Wow!" Dina said. "This is one hell of a lot of stuff, Kuaron."

"Yes," he agreed. "But tonight we need only to pick out an infant bed. We can worry about the other things later."

Dina started forward down an aisle of baby clothes. It was very tempting to stop and inspect them, but she knew Kuaron would be distressed if she bought anything for the twins to wear before they were even born.

Instead she walked resolutely past a legion of infant wraps designed to swaddle a child in warm comfort, even in the coldest Wakanrean weather, and pressed on until she came to an intersection bordered by child-sized furniture. After two aisles, they finally found a selection of sleeping accommodations advertised to safely confine small children in comfort. They were larger than Dina had expected, and she realized it was because Wakanrean babies were larger than Terrans of the same age. There were also at least forty of them.

"My goodness," Dina said. "What a selection!"

"Naturally," Kuaron said. "People are less likely to buy something if they think it's common—that their neighbor may have one just like it."

Dina looked around and noted that there were a few non-Wakanrean customers in sight—a Shuratanian couple and one Terran woman—but they were looking mostly at toys rather than baby furniture. She turned back to examine a compact crib with storage space under it. "This one looks well designed."

Kuaron looked it over skeptically. "It's not large enough for two babies."

Dina sighed. "You're serious about that? You really think it's a good idea to put them both in the same crib?"

"Why not?" Kuaron said, obviously astonished at her reluctance to adopt his plan.

"Won't they keep each other awake?"

"I'd rather they keep each other awake and not us." Kuaron eyed a much larger model with a well-padded interior and a built-in entertainment system, including a sound system that wouldn't have disgraced a family parlor.

Dina wondered if the expense of buying two cribs was a stumbling block; Kuaron wasn't stingy, but he was careful with his money. It couldn't be a lack of space, as the bedroom they had selected for the twins was spacious enough to hold several cribs.

"I like this one," Kuaron said, patting the side of the well-padded crib.

Dina checked the price. Clearly money wasn't the reason for his decision, as the crib cost more than any piece of furniture she had ever bought. "Are you sure we want to spend that kind of credits on something they'll grow out of in a few years?"

"Before they grow out of it, they'll have spent countless hours in it."

Before Dina could answer, a young Wakanrean woman approached them. She stared from Dina to Kuaron and then back to Dina as if she couldn't decide which of them to address.

Dina recognized the confused look as one she had seen often. Except at Kuaron's performances, many Wakanreans they encountered when they were together tended to assume the same bemused expression. They couldn't quite believe she and Kuaron were truly together as a couple.

No situation could make it more obvious, Dina decided, than shopping for baby furniture.

"May I assist you in finding something, *kantai?*" the woman finally said, opting to speak in Standard and to aim her greeting at Dina.

"You may," Dina said, trying not to let her anxiety show. "We need a crib—or possibly two cribs."

"One large infant bed," Kuaron said. "For twins."

The woman's eyes flared open, her pupils opening wider as she grasped their identity. Her quick glance at Kuaron's *heicha* revealed that she knew who he was. "Certainly, *parundai*," she said, her voice still uncertain. "Have you made a selection yet?"

"Tell me about this one, please," Kuaron said, patting the large model that had captured his fancy.

The saleswoman launched into an exhaustive discourse on the features available in Kuaron's choice. Dina listened with half her attention. She had a feeling of unease—as if some sound just below her level of hearing were distracting her. It took her a moment to associate it with the silence around them.

The store had been noisy when they first entered it, and now it was very quiet. The saleswoman's voice, almost the only sound they heard, held a practiced effortlessness as she rattled on, but a slight quaver betrayed her nervousness. Dina glanced around and saw that many other customers, all Wakanreans, had stopped their own shopping to gather a few meters away and stare at her.

Kuaron's arm slid around Dina's waist. As soon as he touched her, she could feel the echo of her own fear. He knew she was afraid, and he pulled her closer to him. The saleswoman's spiel trailed off to vague, inconsequential details.

"We'll think about it and come back another time," Kuaron said.

The woman made no effort to persuade them to make a purchase as they started back the way they had come. A crowd of thirty or forty Wakanreans blocked the aisle. Most of them were adults, but there were almost a dozen children among them, including one infant in her mother's arms.

Kuaron and Dina stopped abruptly.

"Will you allow us to pass, please, *kentai?*" Kuaron said to the tall man who stood closest to them.

The tall man stared first at Kuaron, and then his eyes shifted to Dina. "You're the *parundai* who claims *shahgunrah* with a *fijazhai*— this *fijazhai!*"

Dina could feel Kuaron's anger rise at these words. Kuaron had spoken in Standard, but the tall Wakanrean had answered in Wisutan. Dina darted a quick glance around the store and saw that even more people were moving toward them.

"Let us pass!" Kuaron said in Wisutan.

"She should have been deported!" the tall man said angrily. "She's polluting you—polluting the sacred blood of Paruian with her off-world body! And now she'll bring her twin *tuzouwai* into the world. It shouldn't be allowed!"

Dina fought a rising sense of panic at these words. They didn't go unchallenged by the crowd, however. A woman a little to the left of the tall man gave an angry exclamation.

"Are you a fool or merely a *bwaion*?" she demanded of the tall man. "If Paruian has seen fit to grant this miracle, who are we to challenge Her will?"

"Miracle?" the tall man retorted. "It's not a miracle, it's a disgrace!"

There were angry words from spectators on both sides of the two, and Dina was soon lost in trying to follow the many conversations shouted back and forth in loud, rapid-fire Wisutan.

She peeked over her shoulder and saw that there were more Wakanreans behind them, moving slowly closer.

"Kuaron!" she said in a whisper. "Let's get out of here now!"

He nodded absently, but didn't speak to her. Instead he took a step toward the crowd in front of them and raised his *qatraharai*-trained voice in a loud call for silence.

The shouting died down to a few rumbling murmurs.

"I must ask you to let us pass," Kuaron said. "Immediately!"

No one moved for a few seconds, and then a path began to form as people stepped back against the shelves to leave room. The tall man moved closer, however, and glared at Dina.

"Run away, *fijazhai*," he said, lifting one hand to scratch under his chin with the claw on his little finger. "Run as far away as you can."

Dina felt Kuaron flush with anger. "No, Kuaron," she said in perfectly audible Wisutan. "Let it go. There are children here."

The crowd reacted with surprise, and a number of people looked down at their children as if they had forgotten they were there.

"You're quite right, little one," Kuaron said, also in Wisutan. "We'll go now."

He tightened his grip on her waist and pulled her around to his other side, so that he was between her and the tall man. The two of them moved forward, and this time everyone moved back to let them through.

A hushed tide of whispers swelled from the crowd as they passed, and a small childish voice wailed above it.

"Mommy," it said, "why does that *fijazhai* sound like a person?"

A woman bent down and made hushing noises, and Dina fought a compulsion to giggle.

The crowd also seemed to feel that this infantile utterance had broken the tension. Dina saw a few smiles as she passed.

In a matter of seconds they were at the door. Kuaron kept Dina close as they exited the store and made their way down the street, walking rapidly without actually running. He didn't stop until they came to an open space a few blocks away, where both vehicular and pedestrian traffic had thinned out considerably.

Dina let out a breath. "My god, that was scary!"

"Yes," Kuaron said, looking up. "But we'll be home soon."

Dina realized he must have used the remote to activate the flyter. A moment later it appeared in the traffic lane above them, and she watched with relief as it glided slowly downward.

They had started toward it when a sudden movement behind them made Dina glance around.

The tall man from the baby goods market was lunging right at her with something in his hand.

Dina jumped back against the flyter, and at the same instant, she felt a hot blast of anger from Kuaron. He let out a roar of inarticulate rage and surged at the man so fast that Dina was too stunned to react.

Instead she simply stood with her back against the flyter and watched in horrified immobility as Kuaron knocked whatever the tall man held to the ground. The man stepped back half a step, but Kuaron didn't allow him to retreat. He grabbed the taller man by the throat with one hand and slashed at his chest with the other.

Kuaron's claws were out, and he drew blood. His anger was so intense that it was the only emotion Dina could sense from him. There was no fear, no caution, and no compassion. There was only a blinding frenzy of rage.

Kuaron raked the tall man's chest with his claws, shredding clothing and leaving five trails of blood as the man struggled against Kuaron's grip, swatting with his own claws at Kuaron's face and hands.

Dina darted forward to try to bring Kuaron to his senses. "Kuaron! Stop!" she cried, laying a hand on his shoulder.

A middle-aged Wakanrean woman pulled her back by her jacket. "No, leave them alone, *kantai*. He's *jiewa* now, and the other one is fighting for his life. If you try to bring your *shahgunrahai* out of it, you could get him killed."

Dina stood indecisively. Kuaron and the other man were down on the ground, grappling each other with claws extended and teeth bared.

"Someone has to stop this!" Dina said, looking around frantically for help.

A crowd had gathered. The Wakanrean woman beside her still held her sleeve. "The police have been called," she said. "We'll see if they get here in time."

Kuaron gave a fierce cry of triumph and sat astride his prostrate opponent. He held the man's throat in his hands and choked him, while the man beat ineffectually against Kuaron's wrists.

"Kuaron!" Dina cried, pulling forward against the Wakanrean woman's grip. The tall man's blows were getting weaker. "Stop it!"

Before she could say or do anything else, two Wakanrean men in police uniforms pushed their way through to the front of the crowd. They took one look at the scene before them and then both men pulled weapons from their belts and fired at both Kuaron and his opponent.

There was the faint hum that Dina remembered from the ThreeCon stun guns. Kuaron jerked convulsively, and loosened his hold on the tall man's throat. As Dina watched helplessly, Kuaron toppled over and lay senseless on the pavement, half sprawled on the erstwhile attacker.


DINA sat in the hospital waiting room and fought the temptation to pace. The room was crowded with Wakanreans, none of them at all familiar, and she had no wish to draw any more attention to herself than she had already, just by being a Terran.

She had been waiting for some time, and she was now worried as well as restless. When she looked up and down the corridor there was no sign of Kuaron's doctor, but a familiar figure in ThreeCon blue and brown was coming closer.

"Well," Jared said in a cheerful tone, as soon as he was close, "you have had a bad day, haven't you?"

"Don't play the fool with me, Jared, " Dina said, looking up at him. "I'm not in the mood."

He dropped into the empty seat beside her. "Sorry. How are you holding up?"

Dina let out a sigh. "I'd be a lot better if that doctor would just come out and tell me Kuaron will be fine."

"I'm sure he will. I checked out the official report on the way over. Kuaron wasn't badly hurt, and the stun gun won't have any lasting ill effects."

Dina realized belatedly that he had gone to some trouble on Kuaron's behalf. "Thanks for coming. I appreciate it, and I know Kuaron will, too."

"No problem." Jared glanced around the room as if he were evaluating the other occupants. No one was close enough to overhear them. "Where's Administrator Sadoc?"

Dina held back another sigh. "Gone. He rushed over when I called and told him what had happened, but he said it would be improper of him to get involved, and so he left."

"There, you see? If Kuaron were in any danger you can bet his father would still be here."

"I suppose so."

Jared cocked his head to one side and studied her. "You're really down about this, aren't you?"

"Yes."

"Because Kuaron *jiewa'd* and damn near killed someone?"

Dina shook her head. "That's only one reason. It was terrifying to watch him change so quickly and so thoroughly, but it happened because he was protecting me."

"Like he tried to do in that doctor's office in the Megato Complex?"

"Yes, except that was over so fast I never had time to realize what was happening to him. This was much scarier."

Jared patted her hand. "So is there another reason you're so upset?"

Dina stared down at her hands. "Did you hear what happened?"

Jared frowned. "Yeah. Some guy jumped you as you were getting into your flyter. Kuaron went *jiewa* and attacked him. Fortunately, there was a civil servant in the crowd who was wired. She called for help and some nearby munis—municipal police—answered the call."

"There was a little more to it than that," Dina said, looking up at him. "We were shopping—for a crib—and people recognized us. They all gathered around to stare at us, and then this man insulted me. A woman argued with him, and then the whole lot of them started shouting. Kuaron and I decided to get out. They let us go, but the man must have followed us.

"When he lunged at me, he didn't have a weapon, Jared. All he was holding was a bottle of paint from a child's paint set. He must have planned to mark me in some way—as a protest or something."

"I see." Jared's frown deepened. "I don't think the fact that he had paint instead of a weapon will hurt Kuaron's case. *Jiewa* is a recognized defense, and it doesn't need an actual assault to occur. All that has to happen is for someone to think there's a danger."

"You don't understand. The man hated me! He had never seen me or spoken to me, and yet he hated me enough to risk his life trying to hurt me. And he'll hate my children even more."

Jared took her hand. "He's a definite minority, you know. Many people see what happened between you and Kuaron as a good thing—almost a miracle. It's just that they're not knocking on your door to tell you that."

Dina wasn't reassured. "That man wasn't the only one in the store who hated us. How can I raise my children in a city where people hate me so much?"

There was a long pause before Jared answered. "You could leave Wisuta," he said finally. "You could even leave Wakanreo."

Dina let out a deep sigh. "I don't know if Kuaron could ever be happy away from Wakanreo."

Jared didn't answer. He patted her hand again and then released it.

"*Kantai* Bellaire?" a voice said.

Dina looked up and saw a Wakanrean man in a doctor's tunic standing only a few meters away.

"Yes?" she said, rising to her feet.

"We're ready to release *Parundai* Du," the doctor said. "If you'll just come this way—"

"I'll be right there." Dina turned to Jared. "Will you wait for us here, Jared?"

"Sure thing."

Dina followed the Wakanrean doctor with a sense of relief mixed with trepidation. She couldn't shut out the mental image of her last view of Kuaron. He had looked gory—splattered with his opponent's blood and bleeding from various gashes on his face and arms. But most of all, there had been the terrible brutality of his anger, that hot, overwhelming fury that had surged from him like smoke pouring from a fiery building.

And then the door opened and Kuaron stood there, looking over his shoulder as she came into the room. He was clearly expecting her and clearly his usual calm self.

"Dina," he said, his pleasure evident. "They said you weren't hurt, but I was worried."

"I'm fine."

And she was.

Kuaron finished fastening his shirt and bent to kiss her cheek. The familiar gesture did much to make Dina feel at ease.

"Are you in trouble, Kuaron?"

He made a dismissive gesture with one arm, and sat down to slip on his sandals. "I hope not. My father is getting me an advocate, but he didn't sound worried on the com."

"He didn't tell me that," Dina said, surprised.

"He said you seemed upset and he didn't want to worry you further."

"Humph!" Even though she was no longer pregnant, Juzao still tended to treat Dina as if she were fragile.

"In any event, I'm sure the advocate will be able to tell me where I stand."

"Jared didn't seem to think you'd have any problem."

"Jared?"

"I called him," Dina said, suddenly embarrassed at her own apprehension. "He's waiting outside."

"There was no need to trouble him." Kuaron began to transfer his belongings from the bedside table to his pockets. "But I'm not surprised he came running over. Jared always likes to know what's going on."

"Yes, he does." Dina studied the cuts on Kuaron's face. The lacerations themselves had already healed but thin strips of his facial fur had been shaved to allow them to be treated, and that made them very noticeable. "How do you feel?"

"I'm fine. I hated lying still under the healing accelerator, but I'm not in any pain."

He reached out to take her arm, and Dina felt a warm flush of reassurance.

She sighed. "You scared me, Kuaron."

"I know." He pulled her close against him. "I'm sorry. It was so sudden; I had no time to evaluate the situation. I simply reacted as anyone—any Wakanrean—would."

She held him tightly for a moment, and then pushed him away. "If you're ready, then let's go home."

Jared was waiting when they came into the corridor. He looked Kuaron over head to toe and then smiled. "You look okay to me, furball."

"Thanks for your concern, midget." Kuaron shook his head in mock dismay. "You're still in uniform. Does that mean you were at work when Dina called?"

Jared's smiled widened to a grin. "Nope. I just wear this to bars because it attracts women."

"Pish tosh," Kuaron said.

Jared flung one arm over Dina's shoulders and pulled her close in a loose embrace, as if she were a drinking buddy he wished to confide in. "You're going to have to teach him some new Terran expressions, Dina. He's overusing the ones he knows."

Kuaron laughed and slipped his arm around Dina's waist to pull her closer to him and away from Jared. "Now you're talking piffle."

"See what I mean?" Jared let go of Dina. "I think I'll run along now."

"No, don't go," Dina said. "You came all this way just to reassure me. Why don't you come out to the house and have a meal with us? I've just realized I'm starving."

When Jared hesitated, Kuaron added his own invitation. "I'll fix some *duiko* the way you like it."

"All right," Jared said. "You've convinced me."


BACK at the cliff house, Dina and Jared pitched in, under Kuaron's direction, and helped him chop up the fruits and vegetables for the *duiko*. When they had most of it ready, Kuaron poured a large measure of cooked grain into the serving bowl and added the right mixture of spices, oils, and a small amount of wine.

"How's this?" Dina asked, holding up a platter of chopped *muuin* fruit.

"Fine," Kuaron said. "Toss it in."

Jared added the remainder of the vegetables, and Kuaron stirred the whole thing with a huge spoon.

"You made too much," Dina said as they all moved into the dining room. "We'll never eat all that."

"I wanted leftovers," Kuaron said as he spooned a serving into each of the waiting bowls. "It tastes better the next day."

"It tastes great right now," Jared said, tasting his. "You're a good cook, Kuaron."

"Thank you."

Dina could tell that Kuaron was pleased at the compliment. Resolutely, she turned the subject. "How long will it be until they hold the hearing?" she asked Kuaron as she poured glasses of water flavored with amber wine.

"Not long," Kuaron said, sitting down beside her.

"How long is not long?" Dina asked.

"Between one and two weeks, usually."

"Hmmm," Dina said. "Before the twins are born, then?"

"Yes," Kuaron agreed.

"I really don't think you need to worry," Jared said. "I'm something of an expert on the legal situation in regard to *jiewa,* because I have to warn off-worlders about it. In this region it's always been recognized that *jiewa* can happen to anyone, and someone who provokes it on purpose has to live with the consequences." He broke into a sudden grin and laughed.

"What's so funny, midget?" Kuaron said, taking a bite of *duiko.*

"I was just thinking, furball," Jared said, his eyes still laughing. "In her hearing, Dina had to prove she was sane to go free. In yours, you'll have to prove you were temporarily crazy."

"Very funny," Dina said. "Now eat your *duiko.*"

Jared assumed a solemn demeanor. "You sound like a mother already."

"You need a mother," Dina said severely. "In fact, you need a minder."

Jared chuckled. "You're not the first one to suggest it."

"Actually, I'm a little worried about becoming a mother," Dina said. "It's not like I've had a chance to practice."

"Didn't you two go to some classes or something?" Jared asked.

"Six sessions," Kuaron said. "Everything from bathing and feeding them to how to tell if they're sick."

"I needed that one," Dina said. "It's difficult to feel someone's temperature from a forehead covered in fur."

"I'm sure you'll both do fine," Jared said.

"I hope so," Dina said with a sigh. "But somehow I have a feeling it's different with your own child than with a simulated baby."

"I should hope so," Jared said.

"And besides," she went on, "taking care of their physical needs isn't really the part I'm worried about. Having children is a tremendous step to take—even without the interspecies aspects. You have to really grow up once someone else depends on you for everything. You can't be selfish anymore."

"You're not selfish," Kuaron said. "You've never been selfish."

Dina shook her head. "Sometimes I am. Do you know, I figured out my birthday in Wakanrean time, and I was worried it might happen on the same day the twins were born. I didn't want to share it."

Jared laughed at this, but made tisking noises. "Wisutans don't make much of a fuss over birthdays. It wouldn't matter if it did come on the same day."

Dina sighed with resignation. "I've noticed that, but I still didn't want to share my birthday."

"But it would only affect their first one," Jared pointed out. "Unless you plan to switch over to counting in Wakanrean years, your next Terran birthday would come on a totally different day."

"No, thank you," Dina said firmly. "I'm getting older fast enough. No need to rush things by counting in shorter years."

"Perhaps you should give the twins two birthdays?" Jared suggested. "You could count their ages in Terran years as well as Wakanrean?"

"It's a thought," Dina said. "In fact, I rather like that idea!" She glanced at Kuaron. "What do you think?"

He shrugged in the convulsive Wakanrean manner, but Dina had become used to it and no longer saw it as an extreme gesture. "I think that will be fine so long as you don't rely on my father going along with keeping track of his grandchildren's ages in Terran years. He'll most likely ignore anything that relates to the Terran half of their heritage."

"I don't care if he does," Dina said. "So long as he doesn't ignore me."

"He won't do that," Kuaron said. "I wouldn't let him if he tried."

Dina gave him a warm smile, and Kuaron responded with an intense glance.

"So," Jared said. "Who's your advocate, Kuaron?"

Kuaron picked up his drinking glass. "Shukanao Liaz. She's supposed to be very good."

"She is," Jared said. "I've heard her argue. I've also heard she's damned expensive."

Kuaron smiled and set down his glass. He stirred his *duiko* with his fork. "My father offered to pay her fee."

"It seems a waste of legal talent," Jared said. "She won't be allowed to do much except sit there, and ask a few questions if she doesn't think you're getting a fair shake."

"What?" Dina demanded.

"Those are the rules," Jared explained. "The judge will ask all the witnesses and the participants to relate what happened. He'll give Kuaron and the other guy a chance to state their perception of the events. Then he'll make a decision."

"It sounds a lot like what ThreeCon did at my sanity hearing," Dina said. "Where does the advocate come into it?"

"She'll coach Kuaron on his statement—make sure he's clear on what he's going to say—and she'll be there just to make sure no one tries anything illegal, like stating hearsay as fact. And she can ask questions if she thinks they need to be asked."

"I suppose it's worth getting a first class advocate, then," Dina said. "Are you really going to let your father pay for it, Kuaron?"

"No, of course not," her *shahgunrahai* said. "I told him so at once."

Jared was munching on a large mouthful of *duiko*. "Umumph," he said, swallowing. "Wow, Kuaron! That's a pretty large chunk of change you're turning down."

"*Toabatu ko araihou si maali din,*" Kuaron said.

"'The size of the animal doesn't change its species,'" Dina translated. "Are you saying the principle is the same regardless of the fee?"

"Yes. It's not my father's place to pay my advocate. It's not as if I'm penniless."

"Is your father well off, Kuaron?" Dina asked. "It never occurred to me to wonder about his circumstances. I mean, he lives in an official residence, surrounded by guards and servants, so I have no clue as to how well off he might be."

"His salary is a matter of public record," Kuaron said, "and he's well paid. But most of his money comes from my mother. She was a corporate executive at a large conglomerate. Their salaries depend on how well the company does, and her company did very well indeed."

"And she left it all to him?"

Kuaron shook his head. "It wasn't a question of leaving it to him. In this region, *shahgunrahai* own everything together. If I die first, all this," he waved an arm, "will be yours."

Dina felt a cold chill at the thought.

"Let's not get maudlin," Jared said at once. "I'm sure the hearing will go fine, Kuaron."

"I hope so," Dina said. She needed to stop worrying. "Pass the *duiko*, please, Kuaron."

THE physical setting for the hearing did nothing to allay Dina's apprehension. The large, round room at the municipal hall seemed innately confrontational, with both parties and all the witnesses sitting in a large circle facing inward. Kuaron and Dina's chairs were side by side, directly across from Iotuwan Murail, the tall man from the baby goods store. The judge, an elderly Wakanrean man, stood outside the circle and opened the proceedings with a brief summation of the legal process. He finished with a reminder that Standard was the legal language of Wakanreo, which Dina found reassuring. The judge stayed standing, walking around the circle from time to time, in order to face the witnesses, who rose when he called them to speak.

Shukanao Liaz turned out to be a middle-aged Wakanrean woman, taller than Kuaron, with dark brown body fur, a tan headcrest, and a deep voice. Dina had learned enough about how Wakanreans judged appearance to realize that Shukanao's facial features could be called homely. This didn't in any way detract from her commanding presence. She was very sure of herself, and on the two occasions when she rose from her chair to speak, she commanded instant silence from everyone in the room.

The first time was when a witness related seeing Iotuwan Murail lunge at Dina with a bottle of paint in his hand.

"If I may interrupt, judge," Shukanao Liaz said.

"Certainly, *kantai*," the judge said, moving to stand opposite her.

"You could tell it was a bottle of paint, *kentai*?" she asked the witness.

The man looked nervous, but he nodded. "Yes, of course."

"And yet you were standing some distance away?"

"Yes."

The advocate maintained an impassive expression, but she studied the man intently. "You have normal vision, I suppose?"

"Yes."

"And when did you first see the bottle of paint in *Kentai* Murail's hand?"

For the first time the witness hesitated. "It was inside the baby goods store," he said after a moment. "I saw him pay for it. And he was right beside me as I went through the door."

"So when he rushed away toward *Kantai* Bellaire, you already knew exactly what he held in his hand?"

"Yes," the witness said with some reluctance.

"Thank you," Shukanao Liaz said, resuming her seat.

The witness sat down, and the judge reminded everyone that it was their duty to give their testimony fully, with no attempt at obfuscation.

The hearing proceeded with no more recalcitrant witnesses, until Iotuwan Murail himself rose to speak. It was clear he was in the grip of strong emotion as he made his statement. He admitted buying the paint with the intention of flinging it in Dina's face, and the glare of hatred he shot at her as he said the words made her shiver.

Kuaron put his arm around her.

"Did you stop to think that *Parundai* Du might *jiewa*?" the judge asked.

"*Jiewa*?" Murail practically spat out the word. "How could he *jiewa* from protecting a *fijazhai*?"

"Surely you've heard about *Parundai* Du finding *shahgunrah* with a Terran woman?" the judge said.

"I heard the rumors," Murail said. "Disgusting, I call it. For a *parundai* to suffer *glashunrah* is bad enough, but for him to dress it up like *shahgunrah* is beyond the boundaries of what I can forgive."

Dina felt Kuaron stiffen at her side. "Kuaron," she whispered before she could stop herself.

"Excuse me, *Kantai* Bellaire," the judge said. "Remember there must be no private conversations. Everything must be said out loud or not at all."

"Yes, judge," Dina said, abashed.

The judge directed Murail to continue his narration. After the man described what had happened when he lunged at Dina, the judge told him to sit down again.

"Very well," the judge said. "We progress. We now know what happened up until the point of the attack itself. Now we will ask *Kantai* Bellaire to tell us her perspective on these events."

Dina was surprised, as she had not expected to be called before Kuaron spoke. Kuaron patted her arm reassuringly as she rose to her feet.

"Now, *kantai*," the judge said. "Where you afraid when this man came at you so suddenly?"

"Yes. Actually, I was already afraid from what had happened in the store."

"Afraid for your life?"

Dina hesitated. "I don't know," she said honestly. "I don't think I was expecting to die at any moment. I was just afraid."

"I see. And doubtless your fear communicated itself to *Parundai* Du?"

"We were both uneasy in the store," Dina said.

Shukanao Liaz rose to her feet. "If I might ask a question, judge?"

The elderly man nodded consent, and Dina turned to face her *shahgunrahai's* advocate.

"*Kantai* Bellaire," the Wakanrean woman said, "what did you feel when you saw *Parundai* Du attack this man?" She waved a hand at Murail and waited for Dina to speak.

Dina hesitated. It seemed foolish to admit that her primary fear had been that Kuaron would murder the man on the spot. And then Kuaron looked up at her, and she knew she had to tell the truth. "I was terrified. I thought Kuaron would kill him."

"Why did you think that?"

Dina blinked. She began to suspect where this was leading. "Because it was like Kuaron had gone away from me. One second he was standing there beside me, a little worried but perfectly calm, and the next second there was this raging beast. It didn't

look like him, and it didn't feel like him. All I could sense was blind
fury with no compassion, no worry for what he was doing. It was
like Kuaron wasn't there at all."

"Thank you, *kantai*," the advocate said, resuming her seat.

Dina turned back to face the judge.

"I have no more questions to ask you, *kantai*," the man said. "You
may sit."

Dina sank into her chair with relief.

"*Parundai* Du," the judge said. "Will you stand, please."

Kuaron rose to his feet.

"I have only one question, *parundai*," the judge said. "Were you
*jiewa* when you attacked *Kentai* Murail?"

"Yes," Kuaron said. Dina could tell he was surprised.

"Thank you." The judge held out both arms. "Does anyone wish
to say anything further?"

There was a long pause, but no one spoke.

"Very well," said the judge, lowering his arms. "This hearing
finds that *Parundai* Kuaron Du was indeed *jiewa* during this incident. Further, we find that *Kentai* Iotuwan Murail provoked him to
this state deliberately, by attacking his *shahgunrahai* in a manner
that couldn't help but cause fear. *Kentai* Murail therefore suffered
the consequences of his own actions, and the law has no cause to
intervene."

Dina could feel Kuaron's euphoria as the room erupted in a buzz
of conversation. Dina reached up to embrace Kuaron. Remembering
Jared's joking words, she whispered in his ear, "Congratulations on
being found crazy, Kuaron."

He let out a deep sigh, half relief and half satisfaction. "Congratulations on being proclaimed my *shahgunrahai*."

Dina hadn't thought about this aspect of the verdict, but she
realized it was true. She let go of Kuaron to look him in the face. "I
guess it's official now?"

"Yes," he said, looking down at her. "It's official."

# *Chapter Eighteen*

Aweek after the hearing, Dina came home from doing errands to find the house strangely silent and Kuaron nowhere in sight.

"Kuaron?" she called as she walked through the main room into the kitchen. She was sure he was in the house. Aside from the fact that his flyter had been in the landing port when she parked her own flyter, *haictor* told her he was nearby.

"Kuaron!" she said louder. It occurred to her that he might be in his rehearsal room. It was soundproofed, and he would never hear her call.

She started down the corridor, but as she passed the door to his study, she knew at once that he was in that room.

"Kuaron?" she said, opening the door.

"Surprise!"

Dina blinked and stared at the assembled group. On one side of the desk, Kuaron and his father looked slightly anxious, and on the other Jared grinned at her from where he stood next to Shanour Taum and Shanour's *shahgunrahai* Argiantur Diow. In between Kuaron and Jared, an elaborately decorated cake occupied a prominent place on Kuaron's desk.

"Good heavens!" Dina said. "What—"

"Happy birthday, Dina," Jared said. He looked inordinately pleased with himself.

"I hope you like surprises," Kuaron said, stepping closer.

Dina caught a twinge of uneasiness from him and realized he was uncertain of her reaction.

"Oh, my!" she said, reaching out a hand to Kuaron. "This is wonderful! It's so kind of you all to make a fuss over my birthday."

259

He took her hand and pulled her close to him. She could sense his relief instantly, as he felt the truthfulness of her words.

"It was Jared's idea," he said.

Dina smiled at her *shahgunrahai's* friend. "Thank *you*, then, Jared."

"You're welcome."

Dina turned to study the cake, and noted with further surprise that on the desk behind it stood a vase of flowers that had not come from Wakanreo. "Meadow bells!" she said with delight. "How did you ever find meadow bells on Wakanreo?"

"They're a gift from Jared," Kuaron said.

Dina leaned over the desk and sniffed the faint, delicate scent. Meadow bells grew in the lush grasslands of many of the Fantaran islands. Long loops of cascading, bell-shaped blossoms tumbled down from thick, woody stalks. The petals were pale blue with faint tints of deep violet at the edges.

"They're beautiful," Dina said, sniffing. The musky scent brought a wave of nostalgia for Fantar, so strong she could almost smell the sea with it. "Thank you so much."

"Do we give it to her now?" Shanour asked Jared.

"Sure," he said. "Any time."

"What?" Dina said. "Give me what?"

"This," Shanour said, pulling something from behind him.

Dina recognized it at once. It was a *puousta*. This one was small, and made of a thin sheet of coppery metal, burnished to a dull sheen and fastened to a slate backing. The picture depicted a landscape at night, with all three moons high in a cloudy sky over the cliffs of Wisuta. Only when she looked closely could Dina discern the words in the sky, written in Wisutan, in a flowing script that made it difficult to read, even without the camouflage of the clouds.

"Oh, my goodness!" Dina said. "Did Argiantur make this?"

"Yes," Shanour said with pride. "It's etched. Can you read it?"

"I think so," Dina said, peering at the many curlicues and loops that made up the letters. "Does it say 'Time is the greatest gift'?"

"That's it," Argiantur said. "I hope you like it. It's only my third original work. I wanted to make something to thank you for being such a good friend to Shanour."

"I'm honored," Dina said, running her fingers over the varied textures of the picture. "And I like it very much. Thank you both."

There was a short, awkward pause, as if no one else knew what to say.

"Are we going to eat the cake?" Shanour said. "Or is it purely decorative, like the flowers?"

"Oh, let's eat it," Dina said.

Wordlessly, Juzao moved a stack of plates from the top of a nearby table to the desk. Kuaron produced a knife and utensils, and Dina cut her cake and then served everyone a piece.

"I'm sorry I couldn't find any candles," Jared said.

"Don't worry about it," Dina said. "Once you reach a certain age, it's just as well to forgo the candles. Where did you find the meadow bells?"

"There's a shop in the Megato Complex that specializes in off-world flowers," Jared said, shoveling a piece of cake into his mouth. "They have a warehouse full of seeds from all over the known universe. So long as you give them enough notice, they can usually provide a bouquet of flowers from any planet that has such things."

Dina was intrigued. "How did you hear about it?"

Jared looked mildly embarrassed. "I've bought a number of bouquets there over the years."

Dina couldn't hold back a smile. "You mean you buy flowers for your lady friends there?"

Kuaron chuckled. "Of course he does. He said Terran women almost always like flowers as gifts."

"He's right," Dina said. "Don't Wakanrean women like to get flowers?"

"All Wakanreans like to get flowers," Argiantur said, nibbling at the crumbs on her plate. "Not just women. Why wouldn't they?"

"I can't think of a reason," Dina said. "In fact I'll have to remember that the next time I need a gift for Kuaron."

"Hmph," Juzao said. "You're giving him the best present there is in three days time."

Dina smiled and put her arm around her *shahgunrahai's* father. "That's the sweetest thing you've ever said to me."

Juzao didn't look entirely comfortable with this degree of closeness, but he didn't pull away, either. When everyone had finished their cake, Dina carried her flowers and the *puousta* while Kuaron took the remains of the cake, and they all trooped into the kitchen. Kuaron put down the cake and reached for the *quascha* kettle.

"Where shall we put my *puousta*, Kuaron?" Dina asked, holding the plaque at arm's length.

"How about on the ceiling in our room?" Kuaron said, adding the *quascha* leaves to the boiling water. "We have nothing there now. It looks very bare, in fact."

"Yes, but hardly anyone else would get to see it there," Dina said, propping the gift up on the counter.

"Then let's put it by the windows in the main room—if we can find a surface smooth enough for it." Kuaron moved to the row of cups his father had put out.

"It's good to see you using that kettle," Juzao said, looking pleased as he watched his son pour the *quascha*.

"I like having it," Kuaron said, "but I can see a problem one day when I have to decide which of my children will get it."

"You never know," his father said, sliding onto the bench seat next to Shanour. "It may be that one of them will care nothing for tradition while the other one does. That would solve your problem."

"What if neither of them cares for tradition?" Jared asked. He was leaning against the edge of the stove watching Dina pass around the cups. "They might not, you know—especially when they're young."

"Once they're old enough to appreciate a true heirloom, I'm sure they'll both want it, Kuaron," Dina said, moving from the table to slip an arm around her *shahgunrahai's* waist. "We may have to flip a coin."

The four Wakanreans looked blank.

"She means you'll have to break an *eirouth*," Jared translated.

"Oh," Kuaron said. "Well, so long as they both have the same chance."

"Some people give preference to the eldest child," Shanour said, sipping his *quascha*. "But that hardly seems fair in this instance."

"Very true," Dina agreed. "The doctors will determine their birth order, not nature."

"They've already decided Yulayan will be born first," Kuaron said, one arm encompassing Dina in a single-sided embrace. "They says she's slightly larger and looks stronger than Kifarao."

Dina couldn't hold back a shiver. "I hope everything goes well."

"I'm sure it will," Shanour said. "They're doing so well in their artificial wombs, I'm sure they can survive on their own."

"I hope so," Dina said with a sigh. "It seems so strange to be having babies this way. In some ways, Fantar is very backward."

"Shanour and I are considering whether to use an artificial womb," Argiantur said, her eyes cast down in a demure but satisfied smile.

"Shanour!" Dina said, pulling free of Kuaron. "Is Argiantur pregnant?"

Her friend nodded. "Yes. We've known for a week but we wanted to wait until we had a chance to tell her parents before we told anyone else."

Dina started to lean across the table to give her friend a hug but stopped herself just in time. "I'm happy for you both!"

"Thank you," Shanour said.

"Do you really think you would use an artificial womb?" Juzao asked. "The little one needs it because she's so small, but Argiantur is a healthy Wakanrean woman with a fine figure."

Dina couldn't resist exchanging a quick glance with Kuaron. He looked quite bland, but she could sense a certain amusement in him.

"Thank you, Administrator," Argiantur said. "I'm flattered, but also I'm practical. An artificial womb offers some distinct advantages, especially because I work with chemicals in creating my *puousta*. I don't want anything to go wrong with my pregnancy."

"That's true," Juzao said, looking much struck. He gave Dina an appraising glance. "I never thought about that."

Dina could foresee even more nagging to take care of herself. She shot Kuaron a pleading look.

"I'm sure Quafray takes all necessary precautions, *Ayzanai*," he said. "They've been in business for over two centuries."

Juzao didn't answer him, but Jared put in his own comment.

"Artificial wombs are perfectly safe, sir. And they allow a woman a lot more freedom from worry. She doesn't have to be so careful what she eats or drinks, or restrict her activities at all."

Juzao snorted in a peremptory fashion, as if to suggest that Jared's opinion was of little value. "It may be safe, but it's not natural."

"Dying in childbirth is perfectly natural," Jared said. "That doesn't mean women should have to do it."

Juzao stiffened in his seat, his headcrest standing up straight and his pupils narrowing to slits. "What?" he said, his voice gruff enough to suggest a roar.

Jared didn't look worried. "I said—"

"I heard you!" Juzao tapped the table top in front of him with one claw. "Don't try to put words into my mouth, you young *bwaion*."

"What's a *bwaion*?" Dina said, as much to lighten the tension as to satisfy her curiosity. "I've heard people called that before, and the dictionary says it's a sort of brick."

"It's a very dense brick," Jared said. "Basically, the Administrator just called me a blockhead."

"You always were good with language, Jared," Kuaron said. "It's one of your strengths."

"Unlike diplomacy," Jared said. "I'm sorry if my efforts to persuade you sounded offensive, Administrator."

Juzao studied the younger man for a moment before he finally nodded. "I accept your apology, then."

"*Ayzanai*," Kuaron said, "Jared is a guest in my home."

Juzao barked an abrupt laugh and bowed ever so slightly in Jared's direction. "And I apologize for calling you a *bwaion*."

"Apology accepted," Jared said, straightening up. "I'd better go home before I get myself into more trouble."

"Thank you again for the flowers and the cake," Dina said, letting go of Kuaron to offer her hand to Jared. "I really appreciate it."

Jared's face lit in a smile of genuine warmth. "I'm glad you liked them."

"I did—very much." On an impulse, Dina bent toward him and kissed his cheek."

Jared's complexion was dark enough that it was difficult to see if he blushed, but Dina thought he looked just a little red.

"Happy birthday, then," Jared said. "Don't let Kuaron finish off all that cake by himself."

"I won't. Goodbye, Jared."

"Goodbye, midget," Kuaron said. "Thank you for your help."

"No sweat, furball," Jared said.

He gave a broad spectrum wave to the other Wakanreans still seated at the kitchen table and headed for the door.

"He's very interesting," Shanour said when he had gone. "Are all Terran men like him, Dina?"

"No," Dina said. "Unfortunately, they're not."

"Just as well," Juzao said. "Now that he's gone, Kuaron, let me tell you that he's a *nyesh* to you and a *cirac* in my heel."

"I liked him," Argiantur said. "I never met that many Terrans before I met Dina. They're not what I expected."

Dina smiled at this. "Are you saying you were surprised that I'm not pushy and overbearing?"

Juzao opened his mouth, but Kuaron spoke before his father could say anything. "Some of the more aggressively commercial Terrans who came here have gotten a lot of attention and made it difficult for other Terrans to make friends with Wakanreans."

"The no-touching rule makes it damn difficult," Dina said. "It's very tiring to have to be so careful not to touch anyone. Several times I've almost slipped up at work."

"I know," Shanour agreed. "I find it hard, too."

"Why do you bother to continue observing the law, *guisha?*" Argiantur said to Shanour. "You've found *shahgunrah* with me. You're in no danger from contact with Dina."

"I know that, of course," Shanour said. "But I wouldn't want either of us to get into trouble. Quafray is very conscious of their public image."

"And besides which," Juzao said, "the law is the law."

"Balderdash!" Dina said. "You hug me all the time, and you don't object when I hug you."

"That's different," Juzao said. "You're family."

"What is balderdash?" Kuaron asked. "Is it like piffle?"

"Yes, only more so," Dina said.

"In any event," Shanour said, "I wish someone would invent a way to prevent Terrans from starting *glashunrah* in Wakanreans so we could repeal the law."

Kuaron glanced at his father. "Is that at all likely, *Ayzanai?*"

Juzao frowned. "Why don't you ask your Terran *nyesh* friend?"

"Why do you keep calling Jared a *nyesh?*" Dina said in exasperation. "Just because he admires Kuaron's singing is no reason to malign him."

"She has a point, *Ayzanai,*" Kuaron said. "Don't you admire my singing?"

Juzao's frown grew thunderous. "We've had this conversation before, Kuaron. We don't need to have it again."

Kuaron laughed. "Come now, *Ayzanai!* Many people prefer watching a wrestling match or a game of corner ball to attending a performance of the *qatrahs*. It's no disgrace to admit you know nothing about them."

"I certainly don't mind admitting it," Dina said. "And I've been trying to study them. I just don't have an ear for music."

Shanour smiled, but rose to his feet. "It's time we were going, too. I'll see you at work, tomorrow, Dina."

"Yes," Dina said. "My last day for a few months, at least."

Shanour nodded as he slipped an arm around his *shahgunrahai*. "It hardly seems worth your while to go to work for one day of our shift."

"I thought about skipping it," Dina admitted, "but since I procrastinated on cleaning out my queue, I need to go."

Shanour commiserated with her and then made respectful goodbyes to Kuaron and Juzao, which Argiantur endorsed. Dina thanked them again for the *puousta*. When the two of them headed for the lift tube, the old man rose to go.

"I'll say goodbye, also, Kuaron. Thank you for having me at your birth day celebration, little *guisha*."

"We're glad you could come," Dina said, returning his farewell embrace. "I'm glad there are at least two Wakanreans I can hug."

She was sensitive enough to Wakanrean facial expressions to see that Juzao was very pleased at this comment, but he merely made inarticulate noises as he went out the door.

"He likes you a lot," Kuaron said, folding Dina into an all-encompassing embrace as they returned to the kitchen.

She chuckled. "How can you tell?"

"I know him," Kuaron said. "Besides, if he didn't like you, you would know it by now. He can keep up a pretense only so long."

"I'm surprised he went into politics, then," Dina said, pulling away from him to rinse out the kettle.

Kuaron cleared all the plates into the cleaning hatch. "He's not a politician; he's appointed, not elected. And one reason he likes his job is that the Planetary Administrator is specifically forbidden to engage in anything that smacks of politics. He can't so much as petition the Legislature."

"We would still call him a politician."

"One of our many differences." Kuaron put the remains of the cake in the larder. "Like birthdays."

"Yes. Thank you for making my birthday special, Kuaron. It was nice."

He pulled her close against him. "One familiar thing in the midst of so much strangeness?"

"Yes," Dina said, pleased that he understood. "Did *klunar* tell you that I felt that way?"

"No, Jared did."

"Oh."

Kuaron tilted her chin so that she looked up at him. "You're disappointed that I didn't know that without help from a Terran?"

"Maybe a little," Dina admitted. "You know me so well in some ways, it disconcerts me when you don't realize how I feel about something." She studied his face and let *klunar* tell her he was uneasy."Don't you ever feel that way about me?"

"Perhaps sometimes. But I have the advantage of being surrounded by a large family and many friends and acquaintances who all look like me."

"Except for Jared?"

"Yes, but even he is an advantage for me. I knew a Terran long before I knew you."

"True."

Kuaron hugged her tightly. "*Klunar* isn't enough. We still have to talk—to tell each other when something is wrong. My father told me it would be so."

"Did he?"

"Yes, he did."

"Then that's one Wakanrean I've truly won over."

Kuaron radiated worry, and Dina sighed.

"I'm looking forward to staying home with you and the babies for a while," she said to distract him.

"So am I."

"You'll miss performing, though."

"It's only for a few months. Will you miss your work?"

"I'm not sure," Dina said. "I guess I'll find out."

THE next day, Dina arrived at Quafray earlier than usual. She logged onto the system and cleared two projects from her queue before she even stopped for *quascha*. By the time Shanour came by to ask if she wanted to go to the lunchroom, she was ready to take a break.

"Whew," Dina said as they walked through the corridors. "It'd amazing how much you can get done when you know you don't have any more time."

Shanour laughed. "I know what you mean."

"Have you told *Kantai* Brau that your *shahgunrahai* is pregnant?" Dina asked, lowering her voice as they entered the lunchroom.

"Not yet."

"How long does it take a Wakanrean woman to show?"

Shanour looked blank as he started for their favorite table. "Show what?"

Before Dina could answer, a large Wakanrean man walked right up to her and stared down into her face. He looked vaguely familiar, and she saw that he wore a Quafray member badge.

Dina stopped abruptly. She was unused to Wakanreans coming this close except for Kuaron and his father. Also, this man looked extremely agitated, and he was glaring at her in a manner that bordered on threatening.

"I beg your pardon," she started to say.

Before she could go any farther, the man hissed at her, a strange, hostile, sibilant sound. "Don't come back," he said in Standard. "Don't come back, *fijazhai*. We don't want you here!"

"Go away!" Shanour ordered. "Stop bothering us. It's not up to you to say who works here."

The man erupted with an angry burst of Wisutan curses.

"*Fareesh!*" Shanour shot back at him.

A crowd had gathered. Dina was reminded of being surrounded by Wakanreans in the baby goods market—except that she knew many of these people.

"Shut up, Jukais!" someone shouted in Standard. "No one wants to hear it."

"Better a *fijazhai* than a *bwaion* like you, Jukais," someone else shouted in Wisutan."

Dina couldn't sort out all the comments muttered in two languages, but she could sense that the majority seemed to be on her side. This, coupled with the security cameras in every corner of the room, gave her the courage to confront her detractor.

"Why are you so afraid of me?" she said in Wisutan. "I'm only one person. Surely you don't think what happened to me is going to happen again?"

Jukais stared at her in surprise, as if the last thing he had expected was calm argument in his native language. "It's not right," he almost stuttered. "A *parundai* should never find *shahgunrah* with a *fijazhai*," he added, his voice trailing off at the end.

Dina laughed out loud. "Does anyone ever get to choose the person with whom they find *shahgunrah*? I'd like to know how they do it!"

Hyral Brau pushed her way to the front of the crowd around Dina. "What's going on here?" she said in Standard. "What are you doing, Tumao?"

Thus addressed, the man mumbled an incoherent defense that consisted mainly of a claim that he had done nothing wrong.

"You're causing a disturbance," Hyral said sternly. "Go on about your business and don't bother other people while they go about theirs."

Jukais Tumao didn't even argue. He turned and shouldered his way through the crowd without a word, leaving the lunchroom by the same door that Dina and Shanour had just entered. As soon as he was gone, the clumps of people who had been lingering began to disperse.

"Are you all right?" Hyral asked Dina.

Dina nodded. "I'm fine. He didn't do anything but shout at me."

Hyral looked grim. "Sometimes that's enough. We'll have to review the security tapes to see if we need to take disciplinary action."

"I don't want to get anyone fired," Dina said in alarm.

"He can't be fired," Hyral said. "He's a member of this Corporation. But if he threatened violence, he can be bought out."

"He didn't threaten me," Dina said. "He just doesn't like offworlders in general, and me in particular."

"That doesn't give him the right to harass you in the lunchroom," Shanour said.

Dina noted that his headcrest was erect and there was a steely light in his eyes. "Calm down, Shanour. It's over. Let's go get lunch."

"Yes," Hyral agreed. "The two of you should eat now. It'll be time to go back to work soon enough, and you have a lot of work to finish today, Bellaire."

On an impulse, Dina gestured towards the table. "Will you join us, *Kantai* Brau?"

"Thank you, but no," Hyral said. "I have other plans."

She walked away abruptly, and Dina and Shanour sat down at their usual table.

"I hope that wasn't out of line to ask her to eat with us," Dina said.

"If out of line means improper, then it wasn't," Shanour said. "Although I'm sure you've noticed she doesn't often eat with her staff."

"I've seen her with Dubrao and Carshain."

"Yes, but they were all friends before *Kantai* Brau was promoted," Shanour said, studying the order panel.

"What are you looking at that for," Dina said. "You know very well it'll have the same choices it has every *Twerpaith*."

Shanour smiled but continued to study the panel. "Tomorrow you won't have to worry what day of the week it is. And you can ask your *shahgunrahai* to fix whatever you want to eat."

"That's true. But it's not fair to Kuaron to let him do all the cooking, and since he absolutely refuses to eat synthesized food, I've started learning to cook."

Shanour punched in his choice and swiveled the panel toward Dina. "And do you like it?"

Dina punched in her own choice, then pushed the panel out of the way. "I think I like cooking, but I don't like *having* to cook, if you know what I mean."

Shanour nodded. "I understand perfectly. I feel that way about work, sometimes."

Dina agreed, and they ate lunch with no more discussion of the incident with Jukais Tumao.

THAT night at dinner Dina told Kuaron what had happened in the lunchroom.

Kuaron frowned at his plate as if his food were somehow at fault. "Were you afraid of this man?"

"No," Dina said, helping herself to braised vegetables, "not for more than a second. For one thing, there are cameras all over the lunchroom, and for another, I had a lot of supporters. Shanour looked ready to jump him if he had taken another step closer."

"He's a good friend," Kuaron said, beginning to eat.

"Yes, he is."

"It's too bad he doesn't care for the *qatrahs*. I could ask him to my performance tomorrow night."

Dina smiled as she cut up her food. "From what he said, he didn't enjoy the one performance he went to with his father."

"Ah, well. I'll find another way to show my appreciation for his friendship."

"So," Dina said, "tomorrow night's performance is a big deal?"

Kuaron tried to look nonchalant, but *klunar* told Dina it was an act. "Not that much. But the Grienshasa is a very old and respected club—and very large. They own their own hall, and it seats over ten thousand people."

"So, you get a big fee?"

"Respectable."

Dina knew quite well his idea of a respectable fee was very generous indeed. "Just as well, since you won't be performing for a few months."

Kuaron wasn't worried. "We can afford to take the time off."

"You know," Dina said, aware that he might not like what she was about to propose, "we could use this time to look for another house."

He frowned again, at her this time. "The children won't need more space for a year or two."

Dina held back a sigh. "But I don't want to move just for the twins. It's lonely up here, Kuaron. It's a long way to a hospital or a police station. I'd like to have a garden, and you said you'd like a house with a *zagathuan*."

Kuaron considered. "It might be nice to live in the city again—or at least the suburbs. It's a long way for my family to come for a visit."

Dina laughed. "Now you sound like you're trying to talk me out of moving."

Kuaron smiled back at her. "Let me think about it, *acubai*."

"All right, I will. What are you going to sing tomorrow night?"

He took a sip of water before he answered. "I haven't decided all of the program yet. I thought I'd open with the *Pularain* because that's always a good show, and then go to something more emotional, like the *Untulao*."

"The *Pularain* is the one with all the animal noises?"

"Yes. It's basically some ancient Wakanrean's description of a hunt."

"So what's the *Untulao*?"

"It's the story of a man who loses his *shahgunrahai* to a marauding animal, a *culahin*. It makes him very sad."

"Did he at least have children to console him?"

Kuaron shook his head. "His *shahgunrahai* was another man, so they had no children to raise. Instead, the man spent his life trying to kill every *culahin* in the world, until he realized the beast was only acting according to its nature, just as he had done."

"Why don't *shahgunrahai* who are the same sex adopt children?"

"Sometimes they do," Kuaron said, helping himself to a wedge of bread. "But Wakanreans—or Wisutans at any rate—are very strongly family oriented. Orphans are rarely adopted outside of their own family, so unless tragedy strikes, there might not be children available."

"Then why don't they have children artificially, with a donor egg or sperm as needed?"

Kuaron looked uncomfortable at this suggestion, and Dina knew that he was indeed uneasy. "Artificial conception isn't popular even among *shahgunrahai* who are of opposite sexes but need help conceiving. People tend to see it as unnatural. And when two people of the same sex become *shahgunrahai*, it would be seen as defying a divine plan for them to try to have their own children."

"But they're not urged to separate?"

"No, of course not. If *shahgunrah* finds them, then they're meant to be together. In fact, same-sex *shahgunrahai* are often asked to be *quyarunai*."

"Oh. So they get to be foster parents because they have no children of their own?"

"Yes. There are no cousins with whom the *yarunai* might find *shahgunrah*."

"But, doesn't that mean these folks don't have much experience with children?"

Kuaron smiled. "From what my father says, caring for a child during his early years doesn't really prepare you for dealing with him once he becomes an adolescent."

"My mother said something similar," Dina admitted. She took a bit of *shuishfa*, the meat and vegetable pudding Kuaron had served at their first meal together. "Since you won't be singing again for a few months, how about if I go to this performance?"

Kuaron didn't frown, but he got that inscrutable look that she knew so well. "You don't really enjoy the *qatrahs*. Why take the risk?"

"I don't dislike them," Dina argued. "And I'll never learn to appreciate them if I can't study them."

"I'll let you listen to my recordings."

"I thought the Society of *Qatraharai* didn't allow that?"

"They'll never know if you don't tell them."

Dina shook her head. "No, Kuaron. That's not the only reason I want to go. It came to me today in the lunchroom at Quafray. I won't let narrow-minded people make me a prisoner in my own home, and I won't let them keep me away from your performances. Why should I have to stay away?"

Kuaron thought it over for only a few seconds, and then he nodded. "All right. I'll call the *jioshai* tonight and tell her to reserve a place for you.

Dina felt a sense of triumph as she scooped up the rest of her *shuishfa*, and then she had a thought. "Will Jared be there?"

Kuaron smiled. "I don't know. I didn't ask for him to be invited, but I would never bet any credits that he won't be there."

Dina smiled back at him. "I wouldn't, either. What's for dessert?"

# *Chapter Nineteen*

Dina went to some effort in preparing for Kuaron's performance at the Grienshasa Hall. After she had bathed and sprayed herself with perfume, she braided her hair and pinned up the braids in an elaborate pattern, then fastened a few of the meadow bells into her hair with gold hairpins.

"Very pretty," Kuaron said.

Dina looked at herself in the mirror and then flicked the view control so it showed the back of her head. "I'm glad you like it," she said as she studied the pattern of woven hair laced with delicate blue flowers. "It's very non-Wakanrean."

"Is that why you wore it that way?"

"Maybe." Dina turned off the mirror and lifted her chin to stretch herself to her full height. "I'm feeling just a little confrontational— like this is me, and I'm not changing into someone else just to blend in better."

"Terran and proud of it?"

"You've got it." Dina gently prodded a meadow bell blossom into a more secure position. "Or maybe Fantaran and proud of it."

Kuaron sniffed delicately. "You even smell Terran, for once."

Dina grinned. "I have a whole bottle of perfume, and I never wear it to work."

He stroked her cheek with the back of his hand, and Dina felt a sudden rush of passion mixed with affection. She wasn't sure whether it had started with her or with Kuaron.

He laughed. "It's too bad it's time to go."

Dina looked down at herself. She was wearing just her undergarments. "One more thing, Kuaron."

"I suppose you have to wear the dress," Kuaron said as she lifted her arms and slipped an elaborate gown of shimmering silver fabric over her head, carefully avoiding her coiffure. "But if you really wanted to flaunt your differences, you could go without it?"

Dina smiled as she fastened the side of the gown. "If you had ever been on Fantar, you'd know better than to suggest it. We even wear clothes to go to swimming at the beach."

Kuaron shook his head. "We don't usually go to the sea shore for recreation. The tides make it too dangerous. But if we did, we would never wear clothes to go in the ocean. We certainly don't to go in a lake or a pool."

"I think I'll skip any invitations to swimming parties. Bathing at your aunt's house was embarrassing enough." She looked Kuaron up and down. He was wearing a pearly white *qatraharai's* robe trimmed with silver braid on the hem and on the cuffs of his sleeves. Above the braid, the fabric was embroidered with the pattern of flying insects that Dina had learned was a symbol of the *qatrahs*. "You look very nice, too, Kuaron."

"Thank you. Are you ready?"

"Yes. Are you sure you want me to fly us there?"

He nodded. "I'm always too tense to fly myself to a performance and too tired to fly myself home. My private patrons send a flyter for me, but for club performances I usually hire one."

"I don't mind piloting the flyter, but I hope I can find the place."

Kuaron grinned. "You won't be able to miss it."


DINA hadn't believed him, but Kuaron was right. The Grienshasa Hall was enormous—the largest structure for kilometers in any direction. On the huge circular roof, colored tiles formed the same pattern of flying insects that Kuaron wore on his robe. It was the largest mosaic Dina had ever seen. A huge parking structure for ground vehicles stood next to it, as well as a large area for flyters.

"Wow, this is a big place," Dina said as she set down the flyter in the area Kuaron had indicated. "I hope they have a good sound system so everyone can hear you."

"Sound system?" Kuaron said as he opened the flyter door. Dina could tell he was horrified at her question. "Certainly not! No *qatraharai* ever needed artificial amplification. *I* certainly don't."

But, Kuaron, it's so big!" Dina protested, getting out and locking the flyter. "How could you possibly sing so that everyone can hear you?"

"The acoustics are perfect," Kuaron said, starting around the flyter toward her. "Better even than my rehearsal room. I assure you everyone will be able to hear me."

"Excuse me," said a Wakanrean voice speaking in Standard.

Dina turned and found herself almost face to face with a Wakanrean man in a dark green coverall. He was looking from her to Kuaron, not so much in confusion as in uncertainty. His expression cleared as soon as his gaze rested on Kuaron's *heicha*.

"I thought it might be you, *parundai*," he said. "I was told to wait for you, to show you the way."

"Thank you," Kuaron said, and Dina could sense his gratification at this courtesy. "I've been here many times, but I've never sung here."

The man bowed in Kuaron's direction. "We're honored to have you, *parundai*."

"I'm honored to be here," Kuaron said, answering the bow as well as the words. "This is my *shahgunrahai* Dina Bellaire."

The man sketched another bow in Dina's direction. As she bowed back at him, Dina took in the stripes on one sleeve and the emblem on the other and realized he was wearing a uniform. A discreet bump on one side of his belt suggested he was armed.

"Do you work for the Grienshasa Assembly?" she asked.

"Not directly, *kantai*. I'm employed by a security firm. The Assembly hired us to keep an eye on things."

Kuaron's surprise was evident to Dina even without *klunar*. "Security firm?"

"Yes, *parundai*."

"Is that normal for performances here?" Dina asked.

"No, *kantai*. But the Assembly wanted to ensure that nothing goes wrong."

Dina could feel tendrils of worry seeping from Kuaron, like warm drafts from a smoldering fire. She slipped her arm through his and tugged at her glove. "Shouldn't we get going?"

"Dina," Kuaron said.

"No!" Dina answered before he could ask the question. "I do *not* think I should go home now. Nor do I think I should skulk off into the background. I came to see a performance, and I intend to see one."

Kuaron's golden eyes warmed in appreciation, but he shook his head once in mock despair. "Most people would say they came to *hear* a performance of the *qatrahs*."

Dina smiled up at him. "I'm not most people."


THE performance hall was enormous, but not as large as Dina had expected after seeing the building from the air. Much of the seating was provided by two broad balconies, one stacked above the other, that cantilevered over the main floor.

"There are a couple of rehearsal halls," Kuaron said when she asked him about the rest of the building, "and a few meditation rooms for *qatraharai* to use before they perform. And you'll notice the lobby is even bigger than the hall. No one is allowed in before the *qatraharai* is ready to sing, so the audience needs somewhere to wait."

Dina looked out at the vast expanse of chairs. They were standing in the middle of a small, round stage placed at the center of a semicircular auditorium. The hall was designed so that only the closest seats were below the level of the stage. After a dozen rows, the floor sloped upward, and the two balconies were likewise slanted to give every member of the audience a good view of the stage.

"It must take awhile for everyone to get to their seats," Dina said. "What about people who are late?"

"No one is late if they can help it. They won't be seated if they come after I start to sing. They'll have to listen from the lobby. The ushers will leave one door open so they can hear. It's called the Stragglers' Gate."

Dina squinted, trying to see if the seats were numbered in any way. She saw no signs or numbers, but she noted that the color scheme seemed significant, as the chairs were arranged in a rainbow pattern with the color changing every eight chairs. "Is the seating assigned or will there be a stampede once the doors open?"

"The seating is strictly assigned based on seniority with the club," Kuaron said nodding at the first row. "Every block of eight chairs belongs to a particular member. He or she can bring up to seven guests—or he can even sell all eight seats if he wishes. The Grienshasa doesn't forbid its members to do that, like some clubs do."

Dina pointed to a spot near the middle of the center section, only a few rows in front of where the first balcony began. "Someone's getting cheated. There are only four white chairs there."

"Those are the seats reserved for the *qatraharai's* guests."

"Oh," Dina said, trying not to sound apprehensive. "I guess I'll be right in the middle of things, then."

"Yes," Kuaron said. "But you won't be alone."

"Who's sitting with me?"

"My father."

Dina had to laugh. "How did you ever persuade him to come to a performance?"

"He told me you insisted on coming, *guisha*," said a familiar voice.

Dina jumped, and turned to find Juzao Sadoc, resplendent in a formal suit of dark blue velvet, standing at the edge of the stage. Behind him stood two Wakanreans in the red and gray uniform Dina recognized from her excursion to the Planetary Administrator's Office.

"*Quayzanai!*" Dina said in surprise. "You're here very early."

"It seemed best not to take chances with the traffic," Juzao said. "I didn't want to end up listening to my son's performance at the Stragglers' Gate."

"Perhaps you can wait with Dina, then, *Ayzanai*," Kuaron said. "I need to meditate for a while."

"Certainly," Juzao said, smiling at Dina.

"And this," Kuaron said, looking over at the side of the stage where a Wakanrean woman was mounting the stairs, "is the *jioshai.*"

It took Dina a moment to remember that a *jioshai* was the person in charge of a club. The woman on the stairs didn't look especially authoritative; she was shorter than Dina, shorter than any full grown Wakanrean Dina had ever seen, and she was smiling a warm smile. She was very formally dressed, however, in a quilted robe of gilt fabric belted with a jeweled sash. Her black headcrest was dusted with gold glitter, a fashion quirk Dina had never before seen a Wakanrean adopt.

Kuaron made the introductions, and the *jioshai* was extremely gracious in greeting both Dina and Juzao.

"The reception room is open if you'd like to wait there, Administrator," she said. "And you, too, of course, *kantai*."

Dina murmured her thanks and followed Juzao as he walked beside the *jioshai*. She cast one quick glance over her shoulder at Kuaron, but he was already on the way to the meditation room.

Dina didn't pay much attention to the conversation as they walked, as Juzao and the *jioshai* seemed to have a mutual passion for wrestling. Instead, she day-dreamed about bringing the twins home from the hospital. She was taken aback as she entered the reception room to hear her name called by someone already there.

"Dina!" the voice said insistently.

She came out of her mental fog and looked around in surprise. The room wasn't large, but it was well furnished with clusters of sofas and tables. A bar set against the wall held glasses of amber wine and trays of food, and several people were helping themselves. At one end of the bar, Jared Harlingen was standing next to a Wakanrean woman who looked vaguely familiar.

"You've met the Prefect, haven't you, Dina?" Jared asked.

"Why, yes," Dina said, bowing to the woman. "We met at Kuaron's performance at her house." She decided their brief association didn't merit the intimacy of touching hands; it would be presumptuous to assume the relationship would develop beyond a casual acquaintance.

The Prefect surprised her by offering her hands. Dina immediately held out her own gloved hands. The Prefect almost but not quite brushed her knuckles against Dina's.

"It's a pleasure to see you again, *kantai*," the Prefect said to Dina. "And you also, Administrator."

The second greeting was addressed to Juzao, who had left the *jioshai* to join Dina, his two guards following silently in his wake. He looked as if he were not entirely pleased to be bowing to Jared, but he did so with enough depth to avoid bad manners. "I'm happy to see you, too, Prefect," he said with a deeper bow in her direction.

Jared grinned and winked at Dina, but didn't ask the Administrator whether he was glad to see him. "You're looking well, sir," he said instead.

"Thank you," Juzao said. "I wasn't aware that you were a member of the Grienshasa Assembly."

"I'm not," Jared said with cheerful candor. "The Prefect invited me."

"Yes," the Prefect said. "My *shahgunrahai* greatly enjoyed the Terran dance performance to which *Kentai* Harlingen escorted us. He suggested we return the favor."

A bored-looking Wakanrean man walked up carrying two glasses of amber wine. He handed one to the Prefect, and Dina realized this must be her *shahgunrahai*. "Hello, Administrator," the man said to Juzao. "How is everything on Wakanreo?"

"Well enough, well enough," Juzao said. "Is there wine?"

"Certainly," the man said with a wave of his hand toward the bar.

While Juzao went off to procure wine for himself and Dina, the Prefect performed introductions between Dina and her *shahgunrahai*.

"I don't think I saw you at Kuaron's performance at your house," Dina said, after going through the motions of touching hands.

"I missed that one," the Prefect's *shahgunrahai* said. "I was out of town on business."

Something in his tone suggested to Dina that he hadn't minded missing the performance. She recalled Kuaron's saying that many Wakanreans didn't appreciate the *qatrahs*, and she understood that this man was among them.

Of course, so was Juzao Sadoc. When the Administrator returned with a glass of wine for himself and another for Dina, she sipped gratefully and studied her *shahgunrahai's* father. He seemed content enough, but not especially eager for the performance to begin. He took no part in the animated discussion between Jared and the Prefect on the finer points of Kuaron's performance of the *Shahgundal*. Instead he began a conversation with the Prefect's *shahgunrahai* on the current wrestling season. In the middle of a heated debate on which of two wrestlers was more likely to win the championship in their weight class, the Prefect's *shahgunrahai* glanced over at Dina and smiled.

"But surely we're boring *Kantai* Bellaire?" he said.

"No," Dina said. "Not at all." Hoping to change the topic of the conversation, she glanced around the room. "Isn't this room rather small for a reception hall? It's a large club, isn't it?"

"Oh, yes," agreed the Prefect's *shahgunrahai*. "But the room is open only by invitation from the *jioshai*."

"I see," said Dina. She didn't see the *jioshai* anywhere, so presumably the woman had gone off to check on other arrangements for the performance.

Before Dina could think of another general comment, Juzao broke in with a question about a wrestling match that had taken place a number of years before. At the same time, Jared turned to the Prefect and asked her opinion of a particular *qatrah*.

Dina sighed and sipped more wine. By the time the *jioshai* appeared in the doorway to signal that Kuaron was ready, Dina was so bored she could have screamed.

They filed into the main hall in an orderly fashion. Most of the chairs were already filled. Dina took her seat between Juzao and one of his guards, and glanced around to study the rest of the audience. The Prefect and her guests were very close. Jared sat two rows ahead of Dina and only six seats to her left. In the center of the bare stage, Kuaron stood waiting.

There were rustling noises and chairs scraping as everyone got comfortable, and then the room got very quiet. When the silence was absolute, Kuaron took a step forward and began to sing.

Dina recognized the song as the *Pularain*. It was one of the few *qatrahs* in which she felt any interest because she enjoyed the parts about the animals that were the object of the hunt. The ancient language in which the *qatrahs* were sung was unintelligible to her, but the animals' sounds were represented clearly with growls, roars, grunts, and chirps. When the *Pularain* was over, there were several seconds of complete silence, and then Kuaron began the next *qatrah*.

The *Untulao* was particularly long, and rather dirge-like in places; by the time it was over, Dina had to fight the urge to yawn. The third *qatrah* was even longer. Because Kuaron had tutored her on the *qatrahs* in the program, Dina knew that it related the history of a friendship between two people on opposite sides of a war. She tried to listen attentively, but the part in the middle that described a battle scene was particularly repetitive, and she found it difficult to concentrate. Instead her gaze drifted to where Jared sat.

The liaison officer looked entranced. He sat back in his chair as still and attentive as the Prefect beside him. In fact, both of them nodded their heads in unison, as if to punctuate Kuaron's chanting of the roll call of warriors.

The Prefect's *shahgunrahai*, on the other hand, looked as if he, too, were having trouble concentrating. As Kuaron punctuated the song with a fierce wave of his hand, the Prefect's *shahgunrahai* stretched and sat up in his chair as if he were weary. He cast a bored glance over his shoulder and his eyes met Dina's.

She flushed, and he smiled the faintest of smiles. A slight lift to his chin suggested a nod of recognition, as if he wanted her to know he understood her situation.

Dina looked away resolutely, fearful that it would be disloyal to Kuaron to smile back at the man and suggest that she, too, was bored. It occurred to her to wonder if Jared had been invited to keep the Prefect occupied enough that her *shahgunrahai* could ignore the performance.

The *qatrah* moved into high gear as Kuaron arrived at the battle scene in which the two friends found each other fighting face to face and hand to hand. Kuaron's voice rose in volume and pitch as he related how one friend struck the other down and then dropped his weapons, allowing himself to be killed so that he could die with his friend.

The *qatrah* ended abruptly on this tragic note, and there was the traditional silence. When Kuaron opened his mouth again, he began the opening wail of the *Shahgundal*. Just as he lifted his voice in the triumphant cry that signaled the start of *shahgunrah*, Dina was startled by a sudden scream from above.

She turned in her chair and was horrified to see a shirtless Wakanrean man jumping from the balcony. He landed with a crash only a half dozen rows behind her, knocking chairs and people left and right. The man quickly regained his footing and stood holding a knife in his hand. His face was contorted in a grimace of anger and hatred, but Dina recognized him easily. It was Jukais Tumao.

"Die, *fijazhai!*" he shouted, attempting to clamber over the chairs toward her.

Dina leapt to her feet, and one of the two guards threw himself at her, taking her down to the floor with him. The other one jumped in front of Juzao and pulled her weapon, but she couldn't get a clear shot through the crowd.

From the stage, Kuaron shouted Dina's name. There were more cries from the audience and another scream.

Dina couldn't see well, and in spite of her fear, she felt an intense need to know what was going on. She struggled against the guard's grip, and when the man abruptly let go of her, she got to her feet successfully.

Kuaron was running up the nearest aisle, but it was clear that he was too late to have any effect. Most of the audience were standing, and many of them had surged into the aisles. In the midst of an area clogged with chairs tilted at every angle, Jukais Tumao lay stretched face down across a broken chair, his neck flexed at an odd angle. A tall woman in a formal gown stood over him, blood dripping from a gash in one bare arm. She didn't seem to realize that she was bleeding. Instead of binding her wound, she wiped her hands on her dress as if they were dirty.

"Don't trouble yourself, *parundai*," she called out to Kuaron. "I took care of him for you."

Dina stared in amazement. She was still not good as judging Wakanreans' ages, but she could see this woman must be at least middle aged and possibly older. She was a very large woman, muscular as well as tall.

"Oh," Dina said faintly.

Beside her Juzao studied the scene with satisfaction. He appeared to know the woman with the wounded arm as he bowed to her. "Our thanks, Nuskara," he said in a loud voice. "Well done."

"Dina!"

Dina turned around and found Jared on one side of her as Kuaron approached from the other. Jared put a hand on her shoulder as if to reassure himself that she was unharmed.

"I'm fine," she said. "There's no need to fuss."

Kuaron rushed up, gulping air. Dina could sense a rapidly fading rage as he neared her, and she realized it was the remnants of another attack of *jiewa*.

"Are you sure?" he demanded, putting an arm around her waist and pulling her close. Jared stepped back a pace.

"Yes," Dina said, brushing dust off of her dress and then trying to remove it from her hands. "Absolutely fine. They need to do a better job of cleaning the floors in here."

"You seem awfully cool considering someone tried to murder you," Jared said.

"I'm getting used to being attacked," she said. "What happens now?"

"A good point, *kantai*," the Prefect said, approaching the group. "Are you unhurt, also, Administrator?"

"I'm fine," Juzao said, watching as one of his guards inspected the fallen attacker's body while the other aided the woman with the bleeding arm. Jukais wore the same kind of high-waisted trousers Dina had seen on radicals in Wisuta, and a brightly colored sash crossed his bare chest. The scabbard that hung from it was empty. "But I think your police will have only a corpse to arrest."

"Yes," the Prefect agreed. "It seems that way. The medical team will let us know once they get here. Still, there will have to be an investigation. I've already called the central office."

Kuaron's breathing was still rapid, but Dina could feel his fear and anger dissipate as he held her. Around them the mood in the room evolved into relieved chaos as people milled about talking over what had happened.

"Perhaps, Prefect," said the *jioshai*, materializing at the Prefect's side, "we could take the *parundai* and his *shahgunrahai* off to one of the meditation rooms while you do your investigation?"

"How long will the investigation take?" Dina asked. "Can the performance continue?"

Juzao gave a small crow of laughter. "Well done, also, *guisha!* You're small but sturdy!"

"Administrator, a man has died here," the Prefect said in stern tones.

"I'm well aware of that, Prefect," Juzao said. "He died trying his best to kill my son's *shahgunrahai* and disrupt this performance. I see no reason why he should succeed with the one goal while he failed in the other."

The Prefect seemed struck by this sentiment, and the *jioshai* cleared her throat. "If *Parundai* Du is willing to continue," she said, "we can move everyone out to the lobby except those needed in here for the investigation. Once all your questions are over and the, uh, body is removed, is there any reason the performance can't be resumed?"

"I'm willing," Kuaron said, "so long as I have some time to meditate again."

"Oh, you'll have time," the Prefect said. She paused, and then nodded once, emphatically. "Very well. Clear the room except for the security staff and the Administrator's party, and we will begin the investigation. Once we're done, you may continue, *parundai*."

Kuaron looked solemn. "I think that will be the best course, *kantai*."

Dina said nothing, but she was glad for Kuaron's arm around her. It was going to be a long evening.

# *Chapter Twenty*

The next day, Dina slept well into the afternoon. When she finally awoke and saw the time, she suffered a pang of guilt for sleeping so late. Still, she was too enervated to do more than sit up in bed.

Kuaron was nowhere to be seen. A few seconds later, *haictor* told her that he was approaching. She waited expectantly as he came through the bedroom door carrying a large tray.

"Good morning, *acubai*," he said, putting the tray on her lap. "I brought you breakfast."

"That's very nice of you," she said, inspecting the tray. There was a bowl of fruit compote, a plate with several strips of braised *juija* and two slices of toasted vegetable root smeared with fish paste, and a cup of *quascha*—her favorite breakfast. "But lunch would be more like it."

"It may be time for lunch, but it's the first meal of the day so it's breakfast."

"Past time," Dina said, taking a bite of vegetable root. She had a sudden stab of fright. "We're not too late, are we—to go to the hospital, I mean?"

Kuaron shook his head. "I called an hour ago. They got our message, and they'll wait until we get there to begin."

"I should hope so," Dina said, munching away. "As if our children could be born without their parents being in the room!"

"I thought that was the point of an artificial womb?"

"Tcha!" Dina picked up her *quascha*. "The point is to make childbirth safer, not to miss it altogether."

"How do you feel today?"

"I'm fine." Dina put down the cup to slice her *juija*. "I know I got the shakes last night, but I'm fine now, really."

Kuaron brushed her cheek delicately with one fingertip. "You frightened me."

"I know."

"You were so brave at the Grienshasa—asking for the performance to continue. It took me by surprise when you broke down like that."

Dina shrugged. "I suppose I felt safe enough at home to quit pretending."

"You weren't pretending. I would have known if you were."

"Maybe pretending is the wrong word," Dina said, taking a bite of *juija*. "I was making myself relax and not worry in the midst of a crowd of mostly strangers. That was a lot of work. Once I was home with just you, I let my guard down, and the fatigue hit me all at once."

Kuaron still looked anxious. "Are you sure you don't want to postpone the twins' birth? The doctors said we could, for a day or two."

Dina shook her head vehemently. "No, absolutely not! I can't wait another minute, Kuaron. It's not like I was actually hurt. Your father's watchdogs took good care of me, and that amazing woman made sure that lunatic won't put me or anyone else in danger ever again."

"We were fortunate Nuskara Yipiou is a fanatical *qatrahoinai*," Kuaron said. "And fortunate that her seats are so close behind the *qatraharai's* section."

"I wouldn't mind if she came to all your performances," Dina said brushing crumbs from her lap. "Was she really a major star in the wrestling circuit?"

Kuaron nodded. "She's been retired for some years now, but she was the champion in her weight class, three years running. She was very wealthy by the time she quit competing."

Dina frowned as she thought about the attack. "I still wish we knew how Jukais Tumao found out I'd be there last night. I haven't gone to any of your recent performances, and I certainly didn't tell anyone at work I was going to that one."

"Ah! I can answer that question. The Prefect called earlier to tell me the results of the investigation."

"And?"

"And Tumao didn't know. It wasn't planned at all. His *shahgunrahai's* father is a member and often invites them to performances. But his *shahgunrahai* is sure Tumao didn't plan the attack. She said he had always been hostile to off-worlders, and recently he joined a radical group. When he saw you sitting there with my father, he got angry. He worked himself up to a rage—his *shahgunrahai* knew it even though he hadn't said a word—and then he jumped over the rail."

"And he just happened to be carrying a knife?" Dina asked, unconvinced.

"Apparently he often carried it. They're in style with radicals."

In spite of the reassuring words she had spoken to Kuaron, Dina felt a shiver of fear as she recalled the events of the night before. "Nuskara won't get into trouble, will she?"

"I doubt it very much. Tumao wounded her, after all. She tried to disarm him, and he attacked her. The magistrate will almost certainly find her actions reasonable."

"I should hope so."

He patted her arm. "Finish your breakfast, and let's get going."

Dina looked down at her half-empty tray. "You must have been up for hours if you cooked all this, ate your own breakfast, and called the hospital, too?"

Kuaron looked almost sheepish. "I wanted to read my reviews."

Dina suddenly realized she had forgotten about his performance. "Oh, Kuaron, how could I forget? How were they?"

He grinned his wolfish grin. "They vary. Some critics didn't care for my treatment of the *Untulao*, while others deplored my handling of the *Pularain*, but they were united in admiration for my *Cregamekano*, and they hailed me as the greatest interpreter of the *Shahgundal* in living memory."

"That's wonderful!"

Kuaron made an effort not to look smug, but Dina could sense his satisfaction. "The *Shahgundal* has become my signature *qatrah*. I'll have to sing it at every performance."

"I think it's amazing you did so well, what with the attack and having to wait for the police to finish questioning everyone."

"I was able to meditate again. That's essential to any performance."

"Well, congratulations, Kuaron," Dina said, finishing her fruit compote. "I'll bet your father is very proud."

Kuaron's eyes twinkled. "If he reads the reviews. I doubt that he will."

"I'll have to read them later. Remind me if I forget."

"You can do that any time." Kuaron made hurrying motions with his hands. "Finish eating. We have a lot to do today."

Dina gave him a sour look as she crammed the rest of the vegetable root into her mouth, chewed, and swallowed. "That's what happens when you leave everything to the last minute."

Kuaron looked unrepentant. "It was safer this way."

"Hah!"

He smiled and took a bite of her *juija*. "It's the way Wisutans do things. The stores are used to it. They'll deliver the crib tomorrow, and the clothes you selected will come the next day. We still have to pick out the other furniture, though."

Dina pushed the tray off of her lap. "Okay, I'll get going."

THREE hours later, Kuaron and Dina stood to one side of a delivery room in the hospital at ThreeCon headquarters. The room was full of a mixed group of Wakanrean and Terran medtechs and doctors. Dina glanced around the room, taking in the details of the place where her children would be born.

The two artificial wombs sat upright, each on a separate table made for this purpose. The Wakanrean doctor who was in charge of the team was checking their readouts one last time before beginning. Across the table from her, medtechs stood ready with every conceivable piece of life support equipment in case the twins had any difficulty breathing or otherwise maintaining life on their own.

Dina found she was holding her breath as the doctor stepped up to Yulayan's tank, unlocked the safety lock, and then turned the spigot at the bottom of the tank. The artificial amniotic fluid began to trickle out of the drain and into a channel in the table that led to a holding tank. Dina knew it would be recycled later.

She couldn't help thinking that the process was not only less painful than a natural birth, it was tidier. There was no blood, no sweat, no mess of any kind.

As the fluid drained away, the membrane sac that held Yulayan changed shape, became less round and more baby-shaped. Once the sac was empty of fluid, the medtechs laid the frame on its side and loosened the clamps that had held it closed. They pulled the top half away to reveal the tiny infant squirming inside the flexible membrane. A Wakanrean neonatologist stepped forward to pull the sac away, and then lifted Yulayan from the artifical womb. The baby let out a wail of protest.

Dina laughed with relief. "Listen to her, Kuaron!"

"I am, *acubai*. She sounds very healthy."

The doctor immediately took a reading with a medi-scanner. "Everything looks good. Let's give her a minute in the spotlight, and then we'll birth the boy."

A medtech clamped off the umbilical cord, severed it, and then wiped the baby clean of the fluid. When she wrapped the newborn in a loose sort of sack, the garment promptly shrank to fit.

Dina held out her arms and the medtech handed her her daughter. "She's perfect," she said, studying the tiny infant.

Golden downy fur covered Yulayan's face; it was still damp from the fluid, and it stuck to her skin, reminding Dina of how Kuaron looked after a bath. Her face was vaguely triangular, like Kuaron's; her tiny nose was more prominent than on a human child; and the short, stubbly hair of her incipient headcrest was silver white.

"She looks like you, Kuaron," Dina said, pleased.

Kuaron held one finger in front of the baby's cheek and nudged her gently. The child yawned and stretched her head back, opening her eyes for just a fraction of a second. "Her eyes are more like yours. The irises are smaller, and very murky. I wonder what color they will be?"

"You hold her now." Dina handed him the well-wrapped bundle.

Kuaron took his daughter carefully but with confidence. "She's beautiful."

"She is, isn't she?"

A Terran medtech hovered near by. "If I could just get a blood sample?"

Kuaron held the baby within his reach. After the man had pulled down the covering to bare the baby's arm, he pressed a small blood sample cube against her furred arm. Yulayan seemed not to care for the experience, as she cried a tiny, mewling cry when he moved the cube. Dina fought the urge to demand that Kuaron return the baby to her.

Yulayan was quiet in a moment, and Dina was reassured.

"That's it," the Wakanrean doctor said cheerfully. "She's been an only child long enough. Time to bring her brother into the world."

The procedure was identical for Kifarao, except he didn't cry when the doctor picked him up.

"Let's just make sure his lungs are as sound as his sister's," the neonatologist said, after she had taken a reading. She pinched his arm tightly, and instantly, Kifarao let out a wail of protest.

"Fine, fine," the doctor said, handing the baby to the medtech to detach the umbilical cord.

Kifarao was also cleaned, wrapped, and delivered into Dina's waiting arms.

Dina studied him anxiously. His features, as they had noted earlier, were more Terran than his sister's. His face was almost as oval as Dina's and, just as on every Terran baby Dina had ever seen, his nose was little more than a bump in the middle of his face. His fur and headcrest had the same downy look as Yulayan's, but the color was a darker brown, more like Juzao's coloring than Kuaron's.

"I think you're beautiful, too," Dina whispered to him.

The baby opened his eyes and looked at her, blinking as if he found the light intrusive.

"Oh," Dina said, "Kuaron, he has Wakanrean irises—and they're golden like yours."

"Yes." Kuaron seemed to swell with pride. "I'm very happy today, *acubai.*"

Kifarao wriggled in her arms, and Dina rocked him gently. "Me, too, Kuaron. Me, too."

AFTER eight days with no sign of distress from either child, and with Dina nursing successfully, they were allowed to pack up the babies' supplies and the myriad small toys sent by well wishers. They were going home at last.

As Kuaron helped her lift the children out of the flyter, Dina couldn't help but recall how she had walked with him down the winding corridor the first night she had met him. And then Yulayan opened her mouth to wail a protest at being awakened, and Dina had no more time for introspection.

The new family settled into a routine. Dina would rise first and nurse the babies, then shower and dress. Kuaron would have breakfast ready when she came out of the bedroom. Before they ate, he would fetch the children in their day beds, basket-like cots that could fold up when they weren't in use. Dina liked to keep her children nearby, and the twins didn't seem to mind the level of noise in the kitchen.

In addition to the crib, the day beds, an enormous quantity of clothes, toys, and baby furniture, Kuaron had bought two nursery servoids, specially programmed to carry the day beds safely, and rock them like cradles if desired. Dina had thought it an unneces-sary expense, but she had to admit, with two children to handle, it was convenient to be able to direct the nursery servoids to carry them around the house.

Juzao came to visit their first day home, and returned three days later. Dina could tell he was bursting with pride as he looked at the sleeping twins, but he declined to hold them.

"Not now," he said, when Kuaron urged him to pick up Yulayan. "When they're older, perhaps. They're too small now."

"Very well, *Quayzanai*," Dina said. "But in a month you won't get out of it so easily."

"In a month," Juzao said, bending over Yulayan's day bed to tickle her chin.

Dina was so busy caring for the children, she had no time to think about work or even to ponder the outcome of any debates that might be raging about her *shahgunrah*. She was too absorbed in the two new lives under her care to worry about philosophical differences between various religious sects.

Juzao called and told them the result when the hearing was held on the death of Dina's assailant. Dina was relieved to hear that the death had been ruled self defense, and Nuskara Yipiou was in no legal difficulty.

About two weeks after the twins came home, Dina was surprised when Kuaron told her they would have an unexpected visitor.

"Who?" she asked. They were sitting in the main room with the twins asleep in their day beds. She had her feet up on a hassock, and Kuaron had just come in from the kitchen.

"The Planetary Commander," Kuaron said, sitting down beside her. "He'll be here in an hour."

"Really?" Dina said, alarmed. "Is anything wrong?"

"I don't think so. He said he wanted to see the babies."

Dina glanced around the room and decided it was tidy enough for company. "Well, that we can arrange."

Yulayan and Kifarao didn't cooperate, however. After sleeping peacefully for hours, both babies broke into a wail of complaint when the summit alarm sounded.

"Wouldn't you know it," Dina said, picking up Kifarao as Kuaron went to the security panel to allow their company use of the lift tube. "Sleeping angels right until company arrives."

Kuaron came back and picked up Yulayan, holding her against his shoulder. "I doubt the Commander will be surprised. Jared says he has a large family himself."

"When is Jared coming to see us?" Dina asked, trying unsuccessfully to shush her son. "I would have thought he'd come by now."

"He said he doesn't want to intrude," Kuaron said, having no more success with quieting Yulayan. "He'll come in a few weeks, when the babies are older."

Dina had started to say Jared sounded rather like Juzao, when there was a knock on the door.

"Come in," Kuaron said, raising his voice to be heard above the wailing of the children.

They stood up, still holding the babies, to greet the Planetary Commander. Dina was surprised to see a very familiar Terran figure following the small Shuratanian. Both of them wore the blue and brown ThreeCon uniform.

"I hope you don't mind," Commander Marochh said with a polite smile. "I prevailed upon Jared to bring me since he knows the way so well."

"Certainly not." Kuaron bowed first to Marochh and then to Jared. "Jared is always welcome here, as he knows."

The Commander returned the bow and offered his hand to Dina, who shook it briefly.

"Sit down, please," Dina said, resuming her seat and placing Kifarao in her lap to rock him on her knees. His cries subsided to whimpers as he stared at her with his golden eyes.

Instead of sitting, Marochh crossed the room to peer down at Kifarao.

"A beautiful child," he said, smiling warmly. "I congratulate you, *kantai,* and you too, *parundai.*"

"Thank you." Kuaron cradled his crying daughter in his arms. "But you mustn't ignore Yulayan."

Marochh turned to look at her, and Dina caught Jared watching her with a curious expression on his face. He looked almost sad.

"Don't you want to see the babies, Jared?" she said.

"Of course." He moved across the room to where she sat. "So this is Kifarao?"

"Yes." Dina smiled down at her son. "This is Kifarao. Kuaron says the nickname is Farao, but for now we're calling him by his full name."

"Interesting." Marochh turned from his examination of Yulayan. "My people don't often use nicknames. But then, I think Terran and Wakanrean naming customs are closer than Terran and Shuratanian, wouldn't you say, Jared?"

"Yes," Jared said. "Certainly, sir."

"Why don't you both sit down," Dina said. "Kuaron made some wonderful cookie things. Would you like some with *quascha*?"

"No, thank you," Marochh said. "We really don't have time to stay. I just wanted to see how the children were doing."

"They're fine," Dina said, jiggling Kifarao on her lap. The baby's whimpers changed to gurgling sounds as he stared at his mother. "Noisy at the moment, but fine."

Marochh's smile was serene. "I can tell. They sound perfectly healthy."

"They do indeed." Kuaron was having less success with Yulayan, who still produced a higher volume of noise than was comfortable.

"Allow me, *parundai*." Marochh held out his arms.

Kuaron hesitated, then stood up and handed Yulayan to the Commander. The Shuratanian held her on his chest and made peculiar clicking noises; the child stopped crying instantly.

"How amazing," Dina said with relief. "You could hire out as a nanny, sir."

"It's nothing," Marochh said. "As it happens, I have a lot of experience with babies."

"It shows," Dina said.

"Yes," Marochh said. "My people have always valued families. One reason we've immigrated to so many colony worlds is because almost all of us want to have a family of our own, and our homeworld imposes population controls. Do you think you'll have a family one day, Jared?"

Dina was surprised by the personal nature of the question. Jared seemed even more taken aback, as he jerked his head up and stared at the commander.

There was a brief moment of silence, and then Jared seemed to recover his composure. "Who knows?" he said in his usual flippant tone. "Anything is possible, sir."

"Then perhaps you should get some practice," Marochh said, handing Yulayan to Jared.

The liaison officer put his hands up as if from reflex. "What—" he started to say, and then he grabbed the baby more securely. He sat down precipitously and clutched her to his chest as if he were terrified of dropping her. Yulayan didn't seem to appreciate his efforts as she let out a howl of protest.

"Be careful, Jared!" Dina ordered.

"I'm trying," Jared said. "How long do I have to do this?"

"Let me take her," Kuaron said, amusement in his voice.

Marochh watched as Kuaron extracted his daughter from Jared's nervous hold, and then finally the Commander sat down near Dina.

"Everything is going well, then?" he asked her.

"Yes, just fine," Dina said, wondering if he was leading up to something.

Marochh darted a swift glance at Kuaron and then looked back to Dina. "Actually, I had another reason for coming, *kantai*, besides seeing your two amazing children."

"And what is that?"

"I wanted to let you know ahead of the public announcement— our scientists have solved the problem of false *shahgunrah*. They have discovered a vaccine that prevents a Terran from producing the pheromone combinations that mimic Wakanrean pheromones. It's guaranteed. So long as the Terran is vaccinated, he or she will be no danger to any Wakanrean."

Dina drew in a breath in shock. "I see. And what will ThreeCon do with this new vaccine?"

"They'll give the formula to the Wakanrean government. And in a month or so, Wakanreo will require all Terran visitors to be vaccinated. It's quite safe. They don't anticipate any problems with side effects."

Dina swallowed convulsively. "Maybe not in the average Terran. I'm not average."

"Quite true. You are, in fact, a tiny part Wakanrean."

"So what will they do?" Kuaron demanded. "Will ThreeCon also require Dina to take this vaccine?"

"Actually, ThreeCon's rules apply only to tourists and other travelers. Immigration to this planet is controlled by Wakanreo," Marochh said.

"You mean it's the government of Wakanreo who will impose any restrictions on Dina?" Kuaron said.

"Precisely," Marochh said.

"Does my father know about this vaccine?" Kuaron asked.

"The Arbiter of the Legislature was informed about two hours ago, so I expect word will have filtered down to the Administrator by now."

Kuaron got that abstracted look that Dina recognized as meaning he was worried. "Do the ThreeCon scientists know what the effect of this vaccine would be on Dina?"

"No," Marochh said. "They built a computer model of her, based on her DNA and medi-scans, and subjected the model to the vaccine. Unfortunately, the program refused to yield a result. It said there was no basis for reaching a conclusion with even a fifty percent degree of certainty."

"I see," Dina said. "So if I have to take this vaccine, there's no telling what effect it would have on me—on my *shahgunrah*, I mean?"

"Precisely," Marochh said.

"What about the opposite?"

Marochh blinked. "I'm not sure I understand."

"What if I don't take it? Can ThreeCon say whether or not I'm capable of inducing *glashunrah* in a Wakanrean if I never take the vaccine?"

"That's a good point," Kuaron said. "One reason other Terrans are a problem is they're never *shahgunrahai*. Once someone is *shahgunrahai*, they can't start *shahgunrah* in someone who's still *toshugai*."

"That's quite true," Marochh said. "However, we still don't know that much about the mechanics of how *shahgunrah* actually happens. We don't know what it is about a mated Wakanrean that prevents them from mating again with someone new. There's no way we could guarantee that it would never happen."

"How about your best guess, then?" Dina asked.

Marochh looked inscrutable. "Our simulations suggest that whatever mechanism caused *shahgunrah* in you must be close, or even identical, to what causes it in a Wakanrean. Therefore, it would be unlikely that you could provoke *glashunrah* in someone else after starting *shahgunrah* with *Parundai* Du." The Shuratanian said the Wakanrean words carefully, as if he found them difficult to enunciate.

Dina looked over at Jared, to ask for his take on the situation. She was surprised to see he was staring at Kuaron. His expression was neither friendly nor hostile, but rather guarded.

"What do you think the Wakanrean government will do, Jared?" she asked.

He jumped as if he hadn't expected to be addressed. "What? Oh, I don't know. It'll be up to the Legislature to make any new laws, and they're not even in session now. And once they are, it usually takes them weeks or even months to agree on anything."

"I concur with that assessment," Marochh said. He rose to his feet, and Jared immediately stood, also. "We have to be going. Thank you for allowing us to visit."

He started for the door, and after a few seconds hesitation, Jared followed in his wake.

Dina stood up to follow them, and Kuaron joined her.

"Thank you for coming," she said. "And for telling me about the vaccine."

Marochh bowed farewell to her. "I hope I haven't distressed you, but I thought you should know."

He bowed again to Kuaron and turned to go. Jared merely waved and called a quick goodbye before following Marochh through the door.

"Well," Dina said when she and Kuaron were alone with the children. "That was unsettling."

"Yes. What do you think we should do?"

Dina let out a long, thoughtful sigh. "I don't think there's anything we can do, Kuaron. Except maybe wait."

WHEN the summit alarm beeped the next day, Dina went to answer it. She was surprised to see Jared's face on the com screen. "Hello. That was quick. I didn't know you'd be back so soon."

Jared's mouth was set in a grim line. "Is it a bad time? I need to talk to Kuaron."

"It's not a bad time except Kuaron's not back yet," Dina said, activating the admission control. "He went out to do some shopping. He could be here any time, though. Why don't you come in and wait for him?"

Momentary indecision flashed in Jared's expression, and then he nodded. "I'll be right down."

Dina cut the connection and put the *quascha* kettle on to heat. She had a tray ready by the time Jared walked through the door, and she carried it into the main room so they could sit in comfort.

"Thanks," Jared said absently when she handed him a cup. "I'm going to miss this."

"What?" Dina said, confused as she sat down across from him.

"*Quascha*. You can't get it anywhere but Wakanreo."

Dina figured it out as she watched him put his head back and drink half the *quascha* in one gulp. "You're leaving Wakanreo?"

He nodded as he set down his cup. "I just got orders out. They're sending me to Xuxan."

"Good lord! That's on the other side of the galaxy!"

"Yes," he agreed with grim finality. "It'll take me two months just to get there."

"Oh, Jared, I'm going to miss you. When do you have to go?"

"In four days."

Dina blinked in astonishment. "Four days! Isn't that incredibly short notice?"

Jared barked a harsh laugh. "Short notice, but not incredibly so, apparently. ThreeCon has been known to work even faster. The terms of my enlistment have been explained to me in exact detail. I'm leaving for Xuxan in four days time whether I like it or not."

"Oh, dear! Don't you want to go?"

He jumped to his feet as if he couldn't keep still. "I don't know. It'll be interesting, lord knows. The Xuxa are xenophobic enough to make Wakanreans look like galactic sophisticates by comparison. It'll be a hell of a challenge, and I'm always glad for that."

"Will you be a liaison officer there, too?"

"Not exactly," Jared said, pacing back and forth. "Xuxan doesn't allow visitors yet. In fact, my assignment is to evaluate the situation as far as the best way to implement a liaison office—or something approximating a liaison office. But they already told me to expect a change once I get it going."

"You mean you could come back here?" Dina asked hopefully.

He shook his head. "No. It would most likely be a new job on Xuxan—maybe in Security or something like that."

"Why Security?"

"Because," Jared stopped his pacing to look to the window, "as my boss just reminded me, I need experience in both the Military and Admin branches to qualify for a command position."

Dina got to her feet. "Well, if the job is something you want, then I'm glad for you, Jared. But we'll miss you."

He looked over his shoulder at her for a second, and then turned back to stare out the window. "And I'll miss you."

Dina was at a loss. The words were reassuring, but he seemed distant. She crossed the room to give him a hug. "Oh, Jared! This is going to be difficult for Kuaron, too."

Jared pulled away from her and moved closer to the window. "He'll be fine."

Dina was astounded. "Jared! What's wrong? Have I said something to make you angry at me?"

He turned to face her. "You? Hell, no, Dina! Don't be ridiculous."

"Then why are you so—so—wound up?"

He looked down at his hands and then back up to her, like he couldn't keep even his gaze still for long. "I don't know." His eyes darted around the room. "I guess maybe I'm nervous at the idea of such a big move—new world, new language, new customs, new job. You know how it is."

"Of course I know."

He looked her in the face and then turned back to the window, tugging at his hair as if he meant to pull it all out by the roots. "Of course you do. How stupid of me."

"Jared," Dina said, moving closer again. "Will you please tell me what's wrong?"

"What's wrong? What's wrong? Everything and nothing!"

Dina let out a sharp, exasperated snort of annoyance and moved so that she stood in front of him, blocking his view of the window. "Jared Harlingen, will you stop playing the fool and tell me what's wrong before I slap you silly!"

He took her hands as if to prevent her from putting her threat into execution. "Nothing is wrong, Dina. It's perfectly natural—it's just—it's just *shahgunrah*."

She stared at him. "What?"

He clenched her hands tightly. "It's just *shahgunrah*. You found *shahgunrah* with Kuaron, and I can't do a damn thing about it."

It took a second, but his meaning sank in. Dina felt her face flush hot. "Oh, dear."

"You had to know. You had to know how I feel about you—didn't you?"

"I—I wondered, sometimes," Dina admitted. "But you and Kuaron are such good friends—"

Jared let go of her hands and took a step away from her. "We were."

"Don't say that!" Dina said angrily. "You're still friends. Kuaron loves you like a brother."

"Maybe. What about you, Dina? How do you feel about me?"

"I don't know for sure," she said, a little reluctant to admit uncertainty. "But I do know that you're a dear friend."

"A dear friend," he repeated. "Just what every guy wants to hear from the woman he loves!"

"Don't!" Dina ordered. "Don't talk like that, Jared! You can't mean that!"

"Why can't I?"

"Because—because you're Kuaron's friend, too. Before you ever met me, you were Kuaron's friend."

"Yes, I was. But that hasn't stopped me from loving you." He stared at her face as if he felt a need to memorize every feature. "Are you happy with Kuaron?"

"That's none of your business," Dina snapped, before she could stop herself.

He shrugged. "Maybe not. But what if it's not a purely academic question?"

She frowned at him. "You're being quizzical again."

"I know." He took a step closer, snatched up her hands, and held them together. "What if the new vaccine could interfere with *shahgunrah* enough to free you from it?"

Dina felt a sudden lurching in the pit of her stomach. "What makes you say that? Do you know something beyond what Commander Marochh told us yesterday?"

"No. I'm simply asking the question."

She stared at him, wondering if this was the truth. "What about Kuaron?"

Jared shook his head. "Once a Wakanrean starts *shahgunrah*, there's no going back."

"So if I did something that canceled *shahgunrah* for me, he would still feel tied to me?"

"Most likely. Either that, or he'd feel that he'd become *jashugai*."

"As if I had died, you mean?"

"Yes."

Dina took a deep breath. "So, what's your question?"

"My question is, do you want to try the vaccine, Dina? Do you want to try to put your life back to where it was?"

She shook her head. "It's too late for that. There are two babies asleep in the other room who need a mother. That's me. I don't intend to go anywhere."

"Not even if you could bring them with you?"

Dina had to smile at this. "Think about it, Jared. Yulayan and Kifarao both look very Wakanrean. Can you honestly say it would be fair to them to try to bring them up anywhere but here?"

"So that's it? No matter what you might feel about me, you're tied to Kuaron because of the children?"

Dina hesitated. It was tempting to let the twins be her excuse for rejecting him, to avoid hurting his feelings. It would also, she knew, be completely untrue.

"No, that's not it—not all of it, anyway. I'm very fond of you, but I don't love you. I'm not saying I couldn't have fallen in love with you if I hadn't become Kuaron's *shahgunrahai*, but I did, so there's no question of that now."

"I see." Jared released her hands. "Letting me down easy but with no hope?"

"Yes."

He took a step closer and took her face in his hands. Dina wasn't in the least afraid of him, but her heart beat faster as she waited to see what he would do.

"Then I guess this is my only chance to do this," Jared said, and he kissed her on the mouth, delicately at first, and then with passion.

Dina didn't struggle. She was too busy sorting out her reactions to being kissed by a man of her own species—someone close to her height, whose skin was almost as smooth and hairless as her own—to take any kind of initiative. After months of intimacy with no one but Kuaron, the kiss felt strange and familiar at the same time.

"Goodbye, Dina." Jared started for the door, but she stopped him before he had gone more than three steps.

"Wait!"

He looked over his shoulder without turning. "What more is there to say?"

"You can't leave like this," Dina protested. "You haven't said goodbye to Kuaron."

He frowned for a moment, and she was afraid he would refuse, but then he nodded.

"All right. I owe him that. I'll come by tomorrow night if I have time, or the day after. I have a lot of packing to do." He frowned again. "I'd appreciate it if you didn't tell him about this part of our conversation, at least until after I've left Wakanreo."

Dina turned one hand palm up in a gesture of helplessness. "I'll try not to."

"I guess that's all I can expect." He turned and went out through the entrance hall.

Dina went to the windows and waited until his flyter lifted from the summit a few minutes later. She followed its progress toward Wisuta, with utter confusion in her mind.

She admitted to herself that she had suspected Jared had feelings for her. What she hadn't expected was that those feelings would be strong enough to overcome his friendship with Kuaron. And then off in the distance she saw another flyter approaching. When it came closer, she could see that it was Kuaron's.

Dina met him at the door.

"What's wrong?" Kuaron said as he kissed her cheek and then put his packages down on the kitchen table. "Are the babies well?"

"They're fine," Dina said. "It's Jared. You just missed him. He came to tell us he's been transferred to Xuxan. He's leaving in four days."

Kuaron looked shocked, and Dina could tell he was truly distressed. He slipped an arm around her and they moved into the main room. "Four days! That hardly seems time enough to pack for a short trip, let alone to make arrangements to move from one world to another."

"I know. Apparently, they really need him on Xuxan."

Kuaron looked perplexed. "That seems inefficient of them. How can they need one particular person so badly?"

"ThreeCon only made contact with the Xuxa ten years ago. The base there is small because Xuxan has opted not to join the Third Confederation, not even as an auxiliary member like Wakanreo. They don't really have a liaison office, and Jared said it would be a challenge for him to start one."

"It's too bad he has to leave us. But if it's an opportunity for him, it hardly seems fair for us to deplore his going."

"I know." Before Dina could comment further, there was a faint wail from the corridor that led to the bedrooms, followed almost immediately by a second, louder wail.

"I told you we should have put them in separate rooms," Dina said, starting for the corridor.

"I doubt it would have made much difference," Kuaron said, following her. "Maybe they're merely hungry at the same time?"

"I just fed them a bit ago," Dina said, walking through the open door to find both her children lying on their backs at opposite ends of their crib. Their eyes were scrunched shut, and their mouths were open as wide as they could go. Dina still felt a jolt of recognition every time she saw them. They were hers—her babies.

She picked up Kifarao and held him, nuzzling his neck and murmuring low, soothing sounds that had no language. Kuaron did the same for Yulayan, and both children were quiet.

Kuaron took a seat in the larger rocking chair and placed Yulayan on one shoulder. He held her there with one large hand on her back. "It's a good thing you were able to find these chairs. The babies seem to like being rocked in them."

"Yes." Dina sat down in the smaller chair. "I'm glad my mother suggested them."

Kuaron looked at her from over their daughter's head. "Do you think she'll ever see the children?"

Dina shook her head, genuinely confounded. "I don't know. It's a long way to Fantar, and interstellar travel is very expensive. I couldn't have moved here if Quafray hadn't paid my way."

"Could we afford to buy her passage?"

"Probably. But aside from the cost, there's the time, and the fact that I don't think Mother really wants to come here. She may have stopped urging me to leave you, but she's still not comfortable with what happened."

"You mean with our *shahgunrah*?"

Dina patted Kifarao's back. "No matter how much I tried to explain *shahgunrah* to her, Kuaron, she didn't really understand it. For a Terran who has never even seen a Wakanrean, it's not an easy thing to comprehend. To her, it's as if I chose to marry an—a non-Terran."

"An alien?"

"Yes. I'm sorry, but we're not very culturally responsive on Fantar."

"I don't mind being called an alien. It just means a foreigner."

"Like *fijazhai*?"

Kuaron grimaced. "That word is intended to rankle. It's been a pejorative almost from the beginning of its use."

Dina sighed. "I wonder if the twins will be called that?"

Kuaron glanced down at the tiny furred being on his shoulder. "I doubt it. Except for having smaller irises, Yulayan looks completely Wakanrean."

"It's interesting that Kifarao has Wakanrean eyes, and yet somehow he looks more Terran." Dina shifted the baby boy to her lap. "It's the shape of his face, I think, and his ears and nose."

"You may be right," Kuaron said. "Do you think we can put them down long enough to fix dinner?"

Dina smiled. "Only if you don't mind hearing screaming while you cook."

Kuaron wasn't visibly put out at the suggestion. "We can eat late, then." He nuzzled Yulayan's stomach with his nose. "If you don't mind waiting?"

"I don't mind," Dina said, glad that the subject had changed from Jared's leaving.

"And I'll have to do something for Jared before he leaves. Can you think of anything suitable?"

"Not at the moment."

"Hmm."

Kifarao started to fuss, and Dina was happy for the distraction he provided. Kuaron said no more about Jared, and eventually they got the twins back to sleep.

WHEN Dina went to bed that night, sleep wouldn't come to her. She lay still so as not to disturb Kuaron, but in her mind she kept thinking about her conversation with Jared. She wondered if she had somehow failed to see an obvious sign of the strength of his feelings, if she should have done more to discourage him, if it had been wrong to let him kiss her.

Suddenly, Kuaron's arm slid around her waist and drew her closer to him. "What's wrong, *acubai*?"

"Nothing," Dina said automatically.

Kuaron tisked disapproval. "Don't be silly. Of course there's something wrong."

"Not really wrong," Dina tried to cover her lapse. "I'm just sad about Jared leaving."

There was a long pause, and then Kuaron let out a small sigh. "I see. Finally, he told you that he loves you."

Dina rolled immediately to face him. In the dim light, Kuaron's face was a blur. "You mean you knew?"

"Of course."

Dina was astounded. "How could you tell?"

Kuaron made a small chortling sound, almost a chuckle. "I know you both very well. He always liked you, and he came to care for you more and more over time. In a way, it was like watching slow-motion *shahgunrah*."

Dina was a little irked at his calm amusement. "And it doesn't bother you that your best friend is in love with your *shahgunrahai*?"

"Not that much. Not unless my *shahgunrahai* is in love with my best friend."

Dina went from irritation to outright indignation. "What? Are you accusing me of being unfaithful?"

Kuaron sat up, and the lights came on. Dina could see that his expression was carefully neutral.

"Faithfulness in marriage is a Terran concept," he said. "*Shahgunrah* requires no rites or legal documents. You've made no promises to me."

Dina sat up next to him. "Maybe not, but we're still *shahgunrahai*."

"And you're still a Terran—just as Jared is a Terran."

Dina frowned at him. "What are you getting at?"

Kuaron traced the line of her jaw with the tip of one finger. "I suppose I'm asking how you feel about Jared. It seems to me that you're quite fond of him. And he seems to know things about you that I don't."

"You pointed out yourself that we're both Terrans," Dina said, trying to contain her wrath at what she still saw as an accusation. "That gives us something in common—besides the fact that you know us both rather well."

"No matter how well I know you, I know little about how Terrans love."

"I don't love Jared," Dina said flatly.

"Are you sure?"

"Yes."

"How can you know for certain?"

"Because," Dina said, blurting it out without really meaning to, "what I feel for him is nothing compared to the love I feel for you."

Kuaron blinked once, and Dina could sense his surprise. "You love me?"

"Yes."

He pulled her close and nuzzled her neck, then hugged her tightly. *Klunar* let her feel the warmth of his emotion as a physical heat. He glowed with warmth until Dina felt as if she were next to a blazing fire.

"You love me, too?" she said.

"Yes," he said, his face still buried in her neck. "Oh, yes."

Dina sighed a deep sigh of relief and then let out an awkward, nervous laugh. "It's almost funny. We've lived together for months, we have two children, but we're just now telling each other how we feel."

"I was afraid you couldn't love me," Kuaron said, pulling away to look at her. "We speak of many things, but we never talked of love before this."

"I know. I wasn't too sure Wakanreans even expected love to happen in *shahgunrah*."

"We don't talk about it often in my culture. *Shahgunrah* is so all-consuming that everyone defines the relationship in terms of it rather than of love, and yet love is often there for *shahgunrahai*, too."

"If they're lucky," Dina said.

"Yes, if they're lucky."

"Were your parents in love, do you think?"

"I know they were," Kuaron said. "My father told me only recently how much he loved my mother. I told him I loved you, but I wasn't sure of your feelings. He told me I should speak to you about it."

"He's a pretty smart guy."

"I know that now more than I've ever known it," Kuaron said. "When I asked him about love, he advised me to read a book of ancient poetry called *Inshatrah sa Triubith*."

"Love Songs from My Soul?" Dina translated.

"Yes. I found one verse in particular that I remember. The form is rigid and the language archaic, but I'll try to translate it for you:

"When *taal* fades to dull content,
"When sunlight dims in my eyes,
"Still will I hold thee deep within.
"Still will I count thee dearer than breath."

"It's a beautiful sentiment, Kuaron."

"It's how I feel about you."

"Oh, my," Dina said. Along with the warmth of his feeling for her she could feel the echo of her love for him; the emotion was so intense it almost seemed to scorch her. "It's very strange, but I don't think I've ever felt this way before."

"So, are you glad you went to the party at the embassy?"

Dina knew he hadn't asked the question frivolously. Her answer was important to him. "Yes, I'm glad."

He pulled her close again, and held her so tightly she squeaked in protest.

"I'm sorry," Kuaron said, easing his grip.

"It's all right," Dina said, nestling in his arms. "I quite like it here."

"I like holding you."

Dina let out a happy sigh. "This makes me very happy, Kuaron. Except for worrying about Jared, I couldn't be happier."

"Perhaps," Kuaron said, and Dina could hear his voice rumbling in his chest as he spoke, "it's for the best that Jared leaves us? He would only grow more and more unhappy seeing us together."

"I think so, too, in a way. But I hate to think his feelings for me are interfering with his friendship with you. You two have been such good friends to each other, I hate to see it end this way."

Kuaron was silent for a moment, and then he patted Dina on her shoulder. "I'll have to think of something."

"What do you mean?"

He shook his head. "I don't know. But I'll ponder it for a while, and it may be that a solution will come to me."

Dina leaned her head on his shoulder. "I hope so."

# *Chapter Twenty-One*

Jared looked out the flyter windows at the night sky above the sparkling lights of Wisuta. His situation was so awkward that he had no words to describe it. He hadn't meant to reveal himself to Dina the day before, and if he could go back in time to undo the fatal moment he would.

But time travel was beyond him, so here he was, making what he hoped would be his last trip to the cliff house. He had timed his visit for after the dinner hour, just so he wouldn't have to sit across the table from Dina and eat Kuaron's food as if nothing had happened.

He waited until he had set down on the summit to buzz the house com.

Dina's face answered him on the screen. She looked pleased to see him. "Hello, Jared. I hoped it was you."

"Is this a bad time?"

"No, no. It's perfect. We're just putting the twins to bed. Come on down."

Jared locked his flyter and came down the lift tube. Dina was pouring *quascha* when he came into the kitchen.

"Come in," she said as she set the kettle down on a tray. "Kuaron's with the babies. He'll be out in a minute."

Jared was intensely uncomfortable, but he attempted to make conversation. "How are they doing?"

"Fine." She picked up the tray. "Mostly they just eat, sleep, and mess their diapers."

"Sounds just like Terran babies."

"Yes," Dina agreed, starting for the main room. "Although I never had to take care of any myself."

Jared followed her reluctantly. Somehow the farther he went into the house, the worse he felt. "I never have, either."

"Come and sit down." Dina sank into a sofa.

Jared hesitated. "I can't stay long, Dina. I just wanted to say goodbye to Kuaron."

She looked up at him in surprise. "But you're not leaving for three more days!"

"I know, but I have a lot to do."

She frowned, but before she could speak, Kuaron came in from the corridor.

"Hello, Jared," he said, offering his hand. "I was distressed to hear you're leaving us."

"Hello, Kuaron." Jared shook the hand that was offered. "It can't be helped. When ThreeCon says go, I go."

"I've always known that. But we're sorry to lose you all the same."

There was compassion in his eyes, and Jared knew immediately that Dina had told him what had passed between them.

"I was just telling Dina that I can't stay," Jared said, determined to get out as fast as he could. "I'll give you a call before my shuttle takes off."

"Don't be ridiculous, midget," Kuaron said. "You can't be in that much of a hurry. Sit down."

Jared hesitated, unwilling to commit open rudeness by contradicting his host. Dina made it even more difficult by handing him a cup of *quascha*. Finding no graceful way out, he took the cup and sat down across from her.

"Dina," Kuaron said. "Would you check on the twins? They seemed very restless to me."

"Certainly," Dina said, getting to her feet.

She went through the entrance hall to the main corridor.

Kuaron turned to Jared. "I'll be back in a moment. I need something from the bedroom."

Jared sipped his *quascha* and waited resolutely, wondering how soon he could make his getaway. A few seconds later, Kuaron came back into the main room carrying a knife with a carved handle and a slender, wicked-looking blade.

Jared sat up in alarm. "What's that?"

Kuaron's expression was bland as he sat down in a chair across from Jared. "It's a knife."

"No, I mean what's it for?"

Kuaron placed the knife carefully on the low table between them. "It's for something I need to do before you go."

Jared was overcome by a strange sense of disorientation, as if he had just realized he was dreaming. "And what is it you need to do?"

"Did you ever hear of *glynunshah*?"

Jared blinked. "No, I don't think so. It sounds like it means 'blood kinship.'"

"It does—not kinship by blood in the sense of family relationships, but rather kinship through shedding blood."

"Whose blood?"

"In this case, yours and mine."

Jared swallowed hard. He wondered if he could somehow have gotten drunk and not remembered it. "How do you mean?"

"*Glynunshah* is an ancient ritual that dates back to when my people were given to fighting among themselves. We're more civilized now, but back then disputes could lead to blood feuds. Fighting to the death was common."

"The Middle Century."

"Exactly." Kuaron nodded once. "Back then, when two people were able to build a bond of friendship and trust, they wished to seal it with something formal. *Glynunshah* provided a means to do this. To make *glynunshah* is to promise, on the blood in your veins, that trust and friendship will continue so long as you both breathe."

"Really?" Jared stared at the knife. He was trying hard to maintain a sense of reality. "It sounds like a fascinating custom."

"I thought you'd be interested. You always liked to learn new things about Wakanreo." Kuaron reached into his tunic, pulled out a piece of folded paper, and handed it to Jared. "Read this, please." He started to roll up his left sleeve.

Jared read in growing amazement and then looked up at his friend. "What the hell is this, Kuaron?"

"It's a letter to my father. I thought you could read Wisutan?"

"I can read it just fine," Jared said angrily. "It says that you've discovered that I love Dina, that you're consumed by *jiewa*, and that you mean to kill me."

"You translated it perfectly."

"Kuaron," Jared said, still angry, "in the entire history of Wakan-reo, *no one* has ever sat down and written a letter saying that he was consumed by *jiewa*. Anyone who was wouldn't be picking up a pen."

"That's probably true. Still, it was the best I could do under the circumstances. Give me your left hand, please, Jared."

Jared stared at him. He was tempted to conclude that he was being mocked, but he couldn't imagine Kuaron ridiculing him in this fashion. Besides, the other man looked perfectly serious. When Jared looked into those golden eyes, there was no anger, no pity, no disdain. There was only affection and respect.

Kuaron was still waiting. Slowly, Jared extended his left arm. Kuaron leaned across the table and pushed up the sleeve of Jared's shirt. He turned Jared's hand so that it was palm upward and the inside of his forearm was exposed.

"The essence of *glynunshah*," Kuaron said, "is trust—trust and vulnerability. You deliberately make yourself vulnerable to show your friend that you trust him. We expose the arm because Wakan-reans have an artery just here" he ran one finger across Jared's wrist, "that's very large and close to the skin. One good, deep slash and without immediate treatment, you're done for. I understand Terrans are similar in this part of their anatomy."

Kuaron got a good grip on Jared's bare arm with his left hand and then with a sudden movement, he extended his right arm and flexed the tendons on the back of his hand. Five razor sharp claws shot out. Kuaron surveyed them with satisfaction. "I sharpened them for the occasion."

Jared watched in fascination as Kuaron carefully closed his hand, then turned his wrist so that only the long, curved claw of his thumb was over Jared's arm.

Jared couldn't stop himself from jerking his arm backwards, but Kuaron's grip held firm.

"Do you want your arm back now, Jared?" he asked.

Jared was dazed by the turn of events, but the golden eyes still held neither duplicity nor anger. "No," he said, hoping he wouldn't regret it. "Go ahead."

"When we make *glynunshah*," Kuaron went on, "we draw blood with our claws, to show that we would shed blood for our new kin."

Kuaron brought his thumb claw slowly down on Jared's arm until it punctured the skin. The pain was enough to make Jared flinch, but he gritted his teeth and said nothing. This was Kuaron's show, and all he could do was play his part.

Kuaron dragged his claw down to make a long but shallow incision, perhaps twelve centimeters long, on Jared's forearm. He lifted the claw and drew a smaller incision across the first so that it formed a lopsided cross.

The Wakanrean smiled at Jared. "This is the tricky part." He released Jared's arm. "It's your turn to mark me, but Terrans don't have claws, so you'll have to use this." He picked up the knife and handed it to Jared by the hilt.

Jared took the knife slowly, trying to determine what was happening. It was difficult to think because his arm was throbbing already, and his head felt as if it were stuffed with sawdust.

Kuaron held out his own bare arm. "Make *glynunshah* with me."

Jared hesitated. He stared from the knife to the letter on the table and back to Kuaron. Finally, everything clicked into place.

Kuaron waited without moving. After a few seconds of silence, he said, "There's only one way to break *shahgunrah*. You know that as well as anyone. You have the letter. It would be enough for ThreeCon to get you off. If you truly believe Dina is a prisoner of *shahgunrah*, you hold the means to free her in your hand."

Jared stared down at his own arm where blood oozed from the cuts Kuaron had made. Two red drops fell to the floor.

Kuaron still held his arm out, "Do it, Jared. Make *glynunshah* with me."

Jared took a deep breath and held it. He had a sudden sense of looking down on the scene, as if he were an observer watching through a holo camera. He saw Kuaron, calm but expectant, waiting with his bare arm for his friend to perform this ritual that seemed to mean so much to him. He saw himself, holding a barbaric-looking weapon and thinking murder in his heart.

And it would be murder. It would be murder because Kuaron had done nothing wrong.

Quickly, before he could think anymore about what he was doing, Jared touched the knife to Kuaron's arm. His friend didn't move. The point punctured the skin and Jared made a long, shallow cut. The incision hardly showed on Kuaron's arm because of his short, dense fur, but purplish-red blood flowed in seconds. Jared made a second cut across the first and then dropped the knife onto the table.

He covered his face with his hands and started to shake.

Kuaron got up and went to the kitchen. He came back with a cloth, a vial of medicine, a bottle of Terran brandy, and two glasses.

He sat down next to Jared and took his arm gently; he wiped the blood away and sprayed disinfectant coagulant on the cuts. He did the same for himself and then he poured two full glasses of brandy.

Next Kuaron put his arm around Jared and offered him a glass.

Jared sat up and wiped his eyes. He took the glass and downed half the brandy in one gulp. "Damn you, Kuaron, you *fareesh!*" he said, half choking on the brandy. "Why did you do that to me?"

"Because I wanted to be *glynunshahai* with you. Why else?"

"You know why else," Jared said, suddenly furious as the tension of the last several minutes pushed him into white hot anger. "You know how I feel about Dina."

Kuaron nodded. "I've seen you watching her. And lately I've seen you look at me, also, in a way you never looked at me before—as if I were your enemy."

"It wasn't fair to her! She had no choice."

"No Wakanrean has a choice. You know that."

"She's not Wakanrean."

Kuaron picked up his own glass of brandy and took a sip. "No, she's not Wakanrean. But she is my *shahgunrahai.*"

All at once, Jared was exhausted. He leaned back in his chair and stared at the cuts on his arm. "Yes. She is your *shahgunrahai.*"

Kuaron gave him a measuring stare that offered no apology. "And now you and I are *glynunshahai.*"

Jared let out a deep sigh and took a long drink of brandy. "So what the hell does that mean?"

Kuaron let out a deep bass chuckle. "Now is a fine time to ask."

Jared grimaced. "You didn't give me much of a chance before. You just asked for my arm and started cutting."

"I did. And you gave me your arm. You trusted me not to hurt you—not to really hurt you."

Jared touched the edges of the cuts gingerly. "It does hurt, though."

"Have some more brandy."

Jared took another long drink and drained his glass. "So what does being *glynunshahai* mean?" he repeated.

"It means we're sworn to defend each other. It means we've each pledged to aid the other when asked. And if anything happens to me, you have to look after Dina."

Jared could feel the brandy going to his head. He wished he had eaten dinner. "Yeah?"

"Yes."

"Damn right." Jared glanced around the room. "Where is Dina?"

Kuaron refilled his brandy glass. "She's in the children's room. She won't come in for a while yet. I asked her to leave us alone."

"So you could cut up my arm?"

Kuaron smiled. "That was one reason."

"And so we could talk about the fact that I love her?"

Kuaron nodded. "That was another reason."

Jared shivered. "You gave me the creeps, furball. I thought for a moment you were going to murder me."

Kuaron's smile widened as he took a healthy sip of his own brandy. "That didn't stop you from giving me your arm."

"I knew you wouldn't. Short of *jiewa*, you couldn't hurt anyone."

"And you didn't hurt me."

Jared gulped his brandy. "I thought about it, though."

"Thinking isn't the same as acting."

Jared shivered again. "Why? The rites of *glynunshah* aside, why did you do that?"

Kuaron put down his glass. "Because in a few days you'll leave this world. I don't know if you'll ever return. We may never see each other again. I wanted you to leave knowing that you would always have a friend here—a true friend, bound by blood, who trusted you with his life. And I wanted you to know your own heart."

There was silence as Jared thought about what he wanted to say. Absently, he drained his glass again. "This doesn't change what I feel for Dina," he said at last. "I won't lie to you about that."

Kuaron filled his glass. "I know that."

Jared cocked his head and considered the Wakanrean. "You trying to get me drunk?"

"Yes."

"Why?"

"You need to get drunk." Kuaron poured brandy into his own glass. "It makes it easier for you to talk about your feelings."

"You think so, huh?"

"Yes, I do."

"You may be right." Jared picked up his glass and drank deeply. "But it would serve you right if I got sick all over your floor."

Kuaron smiled. "Don't worry about it. We have a good servoid."

Jared drank again, more slowly. "Too bad. It would have been a good revenge if you had to clean up after me."

"I took care of your arm for you," Kuaron pointed out.

"So you did." Jared studied the neatly sprayed cuts. He looked up and found Kuaron watching him gravely. "So, I suppose you think this makes it all right?"

"No." Kuaron put the cap on the brandy. "I don't think that. For one thing, I never thought there was anything wrong."

Jared knew he was drunk. He could feel that familiar sense of not being in control—of not knowing quite what he would do or say next—that made being drunk a release for him. "You don't think it was a bad thing for a Terran woman to find herself tied forever to a man she had just met?"

Kuaron sat back in his chair; Jared was pretty sure the Wakanrean wasn't in the least intoxicated.

"You're forgetting something, " Kuaron said, "the same thing Ambassador Inoue forgot, in fact. The only person who can say if it's a good thing or a bad thing is Dina herself."

"Fat chance she has of making a decision."

"She made one already. She wants to stay with me."

Jared sucked in air, feeling just a little like he had been punched in the stomach. "You love her, don't you? It's not just *shahgunrah*. You love Dina, and she loves you."

"Yes."

Jared put one hand over his eyes. "I'm an idiot."

"Balderdash."

Jared barked a harsh laugh. "If I were sober, I'd be heading for the door right now. All this high-minded claptrap about *shahgunrah* and the need for choice, and what it boils down to is I fell in love with my best friend's wife."

"I can hardly fault you for that."

"You could if you were a Terran." Jared gulped his brandy. "You'd be throwing me out the door about now."

"If I were Terran, Dina might well have fallen in love with you rather than with me."

"Is that supposed to make me feel better?"

"I hope so."

Jared started to laugh but it came out almost as a giggle. "You know, Kuaron, if you're going to start trying to manipulate people, you have to get over this unfortunate habit of always telling them the truth."

"Why?"

Jared waved a hand. "It's counterproductive, that's why." He blinked as he realized he was not only tired but sleepy. It was a struggle to keep his eyes open, in fact. A sudden thought hit him. He swayed as he grinned at his friend.

"Can I ask you a question, Kuaron?"

"Certainly," Kuaron said with an answering wolfish grin. "What are a few questions between *glynunshahai*?"

"I was just wondering." Jared fingered the cuts on his arm. "Have you had your shots?"

Kuaron took a swipe at him, but Jared evaded the blow. "You're slowing down, furball," he said, chortling happily. And then the room swam around him and faded to black.

KUARON picked his friend up off the floor and made him as comfortable as was possible on the sofa. He cleaned up the brandy bottle and the glasses, and wiped away the blood and other signs of *glynunshah*. Then he turned out the lights and went to the children's room to tell Dina she could come out. She had fallen asleep in the big Wakanrean-sized chair. Kuaron carried her into to their own room and laid her down on the bed. Then he shed his clothes, lay down next to her, and went to sleep.

THE next morning the sound of her babies crying woke Dina. She was surprised to find herself fully dressed and in bed, but she didn't wake Kuaron to ask him about it. Instead, she fed the twins, took a shower, and started for the kitchen dressed only in a towel. One glance into the main room made her run for the bedroom to get dressed.

As soon as she had pulled on a shirt and trousers, she shook Kuaron awake. "Kuaron! Kuaron, wake up!"

Kuaron gave a little groan, and rolled over on his side toward Dina. She was horrified to see the cuts on his arm.

"What happened?" Dina demanded. "Why is Jared sleeping on our sofa, and how did you cut your arm?"

Kuaron sat up and shook his head. "Argh!" He stretched his arms out. "Good morning, *acubai*."

"Good morning to you, too," Dina said impatiently. "Now what gives?"

"I beg your pardon?"

"Don't you go all innocent on me, Kuaron Du. You know very well what I'm asking."

"I do indeed," Kuaron admitted, brushing her cheek with his hand. "Very well, Jared is asleep on our sofa because I got him very drunk last night. And I didn't cut my arm; Jared cut it for me."

"What?" Dina was horrified. "Did you two have a fight?"

"On the contrary," Kuaron said, flashing her a grin, "we became *glynunshahai*. Wait until you see *his* arm."

"What the hell are *glynunshahai*?"

Before Kuaron could answer, there was a loud groan of anguish from the main room. It was followed by a bout of cursing, most of which was in a language Dina didn't recognize.

Kuaron stood up. "I'll explain it later, *guisha*. Do me a favor, please, and look in the medicine box. I think we have something for a hangover. You'd better give Jared two of them."

Dina thought it over and decided that the fastest way to get an explanation was to comply with this request. When she brought Jared the capsules, he was sitting up on the sofa and cursing softly in Wisutan. He took them gratefully and popped them into his mouth.

Kuaron came out of the bedroom wearing his *xuschi* and carrying a robe over his arm. "Good morning, Jared."

"No it isn't," the Terran contradicted him. "Not until these things start working, anyway."

"Go get cleaned up in the bathing room, and you'll feel better," Kuaron said, handing him the robe. "You can wear this until I can get your clothes clean."

Jared took the garment and left the room without argument.

"If you're not going to explain right away, Kuaron," Dina said, "then you can go and get the babies. I changed them and fed them already."

"Of course."

Dina put the *quascha* on, and in a few minutes, Kuaron came back into the kitchen trailed by the two nursery servoids carrying the twins in their day beds.

"They're asleep again," Kuaron said. "They still sleep quite a lot."

"I know. From what Terran parents tell me, we're very lucky. Terran babies almost never sleep through the night as quickly as the twins did."

"Perhaps it's because they were in an artificial womb?"

"Perhaps," Dina agreed, handing him a cup of *quascha*.

Kuaron began to pull out pots and pans while Dina gathered together the ingredients for a casserole. Several minutes later, Jared came into the kitchen trying to hitch up the robe so that it didn't drag on the floor. Kuaron took his clothes from him and started for the laundry room.

Dina could empathize with Jared's efforts, having tried to walk in that particular garment herself. "Would you like some breakfast, Jared?"

"Thanks," Jared said, "but I don't think that would be a good idea just yet."

"How about *quascha*?"

"Okay, thanks."

She gave him a cup, and then crossed the room to check on the babies. They were indeed sleeping peacefully.

Jared laid his injured arm on the kitchen table and stared down at it. Even from the other side of the room Dina could see that his cuts were even worse than Kuaron's; they were jagged at the edges, as if they had been made with something rougher-edged than a knife.

"Kuaron," Jared said as Kuaron came back into the kitchen, "did I get this the way I think I did?"

Wordlessly, Kuaron held out his own arm.

Jared stared from his wound to Kuaron's. "I must have been drunker than I thought."

"We didn't have any brandy until afterwards," Kuaron said.

"Someone," Dina said, "had better enlighten me about what the hell went on here last night."

"I wouldn't mind knowing myself," Jared said.

Succinctly, Kuaron outlined the rite of *glynunshah*.

"It sounds barbaric," Dina said.

"It is, in some ways," Kuaron said. "In other ways, it's quite civilized."

"How?" Dina demanded.

"Don't you think it's civilized to celebrate friendship?" Kuaron asked.

"Can't you do that without shedding blood?"

Kuaron looked solemn. "Shedding blood is the whole point. The very marrow of *glynunshah* is that each person is willing to suffer for the other."

Dina waved a hand. "Okay, I give up. It's the greatest thing since the spatial fold generator."

"I can tell you're not really convinced," Kuaron said. "What about you, Jared?"

"I'm feeling a little better," Jared said. "Maybe I will have some breakfast, if that's all right with you?"

"It's almost ready," Kuaron said. "And that's not what I was asking."

"I know." Jared frowned and glanced at Dina. "I'd rather not talk about it now, Kuaron."

Dina could take a hint. "I think I'll take the children out to the main room so they can get some sunshine," she said, using a remote to direct the nursery servoids. "Call me when breakfast is ready."

She wondered, as she watched the two sturdy machines trundling along, what it was Jared didn't want to say in front of her.

"I WANT to apologize, Kuaron," Jared said. "I was out of line to tell Dina how I felt."

Kuaron didn't seem perturbed. "No, you weren't. Your rules of etiquette don't apply. Dina isn't my wife."

Jared gave a strangled laugh. "Like it's any more proper to tell someone's *shahgunrahai* that you love her."

Kuaron shook his head. "You know better than that. We don't have the same kind of constraints that you Terrans do."

"That's only because no one can steal someone else's *shahgunrahai*."

"Precisely my point."

Jared sighed and ran a hand over his eyes. "I still shouldn't have done it."

"I'm glad that you did."

Jared stared at him. "Why?"

"Because you needed to ask the question. And you needed to hear her answer."

Jared felt bile rising as he considered the implications of this comment. "You're pretty damn sure of yourself."

"In this case, yes."

"Because *shahgunrah* ties Dina to you?"

"No. Because *klunar* tells me that she loves me."

Jared's hostility left him abruptly. "I'm sorry. I shouldn't have said that. I think maybe it's a good thing I'm going to Xuxan."

"I think so, too, midget. But I'll miss you all the same."

Jared looked down at the cuts on his arm. "I still don't believe you did that, furball. What if I had sliced you up with that knife?"

"Well, then I would have looked pretty damn stupid."

Jared stared at him for just a second, and then he laughed. "Kuaron, where am I going to find someone like you on Xuxan?"

"I don't know," Kuaron said, smiling. "But breakfast is ready."

"I'll call Dina."

He stepped into the main room and saw her standing over Yulayan's day bed, looking down at her child with a tender expression. He stopped abruptly, and waited for her to look up before he spoke. "Breakfast is ready," he said when she did.

She smiled impishly. "Is it safe to come back, then?"

"Yes. No blood was shed this time."

"I'm glad."

"Dina, I—I—" He trailed off, unable to articulate what it was he wanted to say.

Dina didn't leave him hanging. "You don't have to say anything more. I know how you feel, and you know how I feel. Let's just leave it at that."

"All right."

"Let's go eat," Dina said, glancing down at the sleeping infants. "I'll leave the babies here for now."

It was a quiet meal. Jared ate steadily, and answered Kuaron's questions about Xuxan and his new job, but he didn't start any lines of conversation himself. Finally, Dina brought up the subject of *glynunshah*.

"So what does this ritual actually mean?" she asked Kuaron as she put down her fork. "Is it any kind of legal relationship or is it just a formality?"

"It's neither." Kuaron poured another cup of *quascha*. "It has no legal standing, but it's much more than a formality. *Glynunshai* owe each other loyalty and friendship. If Jared were to send me word that he needed help on Xuxan, I would go there at once."

Jared lifted his eyebrows. "If you send me the same kind of message, furball, you'll have to explain *glynunshah* to ThreeCon."

"I see," Dina said. "And how long does this relationship last?"

"Until one of us dies."

"I might never make it back to Wakanreo before that happens," Jared said.

"That makes no difference. *Glynunshah* is a promise that's not affected by time or distance."

"So how come I never heard of it?" Jared asked.

"It's gone out of fashion," Kuaron admitted. "I think my grandmother's generation was the last to practice it with any prevalence. But it appears frequently in old books and stories, so people still know about it."

Jared looked down at the marks on his forearm. "Maybe it's just as well I'm leaving, then. These cuts will be recognizable on Wakanreo,but on Xuxan they'll just be scar tissue."

"True," Kuaron said. "*Glynunshah* scars are very distinctive."

"Did women practice it, too?" Dina asked.

"Oh, yes. In fact, *glynunshahai* aren't always the same gender."

She looked intrigued. "Ah! And can you be *glynunshahai* with more than one person?"

Kuaron shook his head. "Not while your first *glynunshahai* lives. Otherwise, there might be a conflict of loyalty."

"What about *shahgunrah*, then?" Jared asked, interested in spite of himself. "What if your *glynunshahai* and your *shahgunrahai* are at odds?"

Kuaron looked solemn. "*Shahgunrah* is the only thing that takes precedence over *glynunshah*."

"Ah!" Dina said to Jared. "So I outrank you."

"I would try to keep on your good side, but it won't matter since I won't be around." Jared stood up and offered Kuaron his hand. "Thanks for breakfast, Kuaron. And good luck with your career. I know you'll do well because you've got the talent and the drive to be the best."

Kuaron stood up but ignored the hand. "You don't imagine that you're saying goodbye now, do you? You're not leaving for three more days."

Jared felt his face flush and was glad he was too dark-skinned to show a blush. "Let's not drag this out any, shall we? If you don't find this awkward, I do. Just give me my clothes, and I'll get going. I have a lot to do before I leave."

Kuaron gave him a toothy smile. "I know that. But if you expect me to hand over your clothes, then you had better be prepared to promise to come to dinner on your last night on Wakanreo."

Jared considered the long robe he wore and debated his options.

"Please, Jared," Dina said. "Come to see us one last time. We want to say goodbye properly."

Jared glanced down from his arm up to Kuaron's face. "How can you hold me up like this if we're *glynunshahai*?"

Kuaron's expression was bland. "How can you say no if we're *glynunshahai*?"

Jared snorted. "I never knew you had a devious side, Kuaron."

"I learned it from you," Kuaron said, still deadpan.

Jared debated. After all, it could hardly be more traumatic than the night before. "All right. You win. I'll come for dinner."

"Good!" Dina jumped to her feet. "I'll get your clothes now."

She headed for the pantry, and Jared couldn't resist following her with his eyes. He turned back to find Kuaron watching him sympathetically.

"You're a lucky man, furball. And if you don't treat her right, I'll come back here and make you sorry."

"I don't think you've quite grasped the concept of *glynunshah*, Jared," Kuaron said.


THE next day, Dina came into the kitchen to find Kuaron watching the news with a grim look on his face, and a faint but discernible aura of worry.

"What's wrong?"

He nodded at the com. "They've announced the news about the vaccine to prevent *glashunrah*."

She slipped an arm through his. "What's going to happen next?"

He pulled her close against him. "The Arbiter of the Legislature has called an emergency session to start in three weeks."

They watched together as a news reader interviewed a ThreeCon scientist about the effects of the vaccine. They listened as various Wakanrean dignitaries gave their opinions on whether this was a bad development or a good one. Finally, the sound of the babies crying made Dina come alert.

She took a deep breath and held it for a few seconds. "No need to worry yet. We'll wait and see."

He hugged her for a long moment, then let her go. "I'll get the babies."

ON the third day after Jared's visit, Dina had no time to worry about the vaccine. She and Kuaron spent most of the afternoon preparing an elaborate dinner of Jared's favorite Wakanrean foods. They had everything ready by the time their guest walked through the door. Dina handed him a glass of amber wine, and Kuaron offered a tray of *ishgua*.

"Wow," Jared said accepting the glass and an *ishgua*, "I'm glad I didn't wimp out and stay home."

"I would have come to get you," Kuaron said. "Sit down, Jared."

"I think I'd better," Jared said, relaxing on a sofa. He popped the *ishgua* into his mouth and chewed it up. "Delicious."

"I made them," Dina said with pride.

Kuaron gave her a tolerant look and smiled.

"All right, I know there's not a whole lot to preparing *ishgua*," Dina said. "You just clean them, broil them, and then frost them with mold, but I did it all by myself."

"You did a great job," Jared said. "Don't let Kuaron go all superior on you. He only knows how to cook because Wakanreans are so backward."

"And Terrans are so forward," Kuaron said, with a gleam in his eye.

Jared laughed, and Dina was relieved to see him so relaxed.

"It's just as well I'm leaving, furball," Jared said. "You're getting too good at comebacks."

"You've given me a lot of practice," Kuaron said. "It's too bad my father never got to know you better. I think you two could have been friends."

Jared snorted. "Not bloody likely. He's your father, and I have a lot of respect for him, but the man just doesn't like Terrans—except for Dina."

"He's changed his mind about a lot of things over the last year," Kuaron said.

"Maybe he has," Jared said, inspecting the tray of *ishgua*. "But I'm not one of them."

Dina pushed the tray toward him. "Well, you no longer need to worry about his opinion. The Planetary Administrator of Wakan-reo won't have a thing to say about your career on Xuxan."

Jared took another *ishgua*. "You've got a point there, Dina. Maybe it won't be so bad after all?"

"I'm sure it won't be," Kuaron said. "You'll make your own luck, Jared. You always have."

"Most of the time," Jared said with a glance at Dina.

Kuaron made no comment and went into the kitchen.

"You mind your manners," Dina said severely. "Kuaron has put a lot of work into tonight, and I won't have you spoil it by feeling sorry for yourself."

"Yes, ma'am," Jared said, looking surprised.

"And don't call me ma'am, ever again," she said, pleased with herself for being so assertive.

"Okay." He sat up straighter in his chair. "I'll be good."

He looked so much like a schoolboy caught in mischief that Dina burst out laughing.

"What's so funny?" Kuaron said, coming back into the room with a large bowl.

"Jared is," Dina said. "Is dinner ready?"

"Yes," Kuaron said. "Come and sit down."

They moved to the dining table where places were laid for three, Dina and Kuaron on one side of the table, and Jared on the other.

"Where are the twins?" Jared asked as he sat down.

"Sleeping," Kuaron said as he passed the bowl of *duiko*. "We timed this dinner very carefully. I'm hoping they cooperate."

Their luck held all through the meal, and it was only after they had moved to the main room for *quascha* that Dina was obliged to leave them to tend to the crying babies.

"You stay there, Kuaron," she said as she got up. "I know you have a surprise for Jared."

She walked into the corridor leaving the two friends staring at each other from across the room.

JARED cleared his throat. Everything had gone well, so far, but it would be better not to outstay his welcome. "I really should be going. My shuttle leaves very early."

Kuaron shook his head. "Not just yet, *glynunshahai*. I'm going to do something for you I haven't done in a very long time."

He moved to the middle of the room, and Jared felt a flutter of nervousness. "It's not another Wakanrean ritual is it? My arm still hurts from the last one."

"Don't worry. I won't be using my claws." Kuaron stepped back a pace and smiled. "I'm going to perform a *qatrah*—without being paid."

Jared gaped at him. "A private performance?"

Kuaron nodded. He put his head back and began the slow, wailing opening to a *qatrah* that Jared recognized as the *Saimuar*, the song of parting. Kuaron's voice could reach to the back rows of a large auditorium without amplification; it filled every corner of the room with a sad, haunting sound that made Jared want to weep. The *qatrah* detailed the sorrow of loved ones who parted, never to see each other again. Every trill, every quaver spoke of the sadness of farewell and the uncertainty of life. Only at the end did hope surface that one day there might be another meeting.

When it ended, Jared sat as still as a stone for several seconds, as a sign of respect for Kuaron's talent. When he did move, it was to stand up. "I have to go now."

Kuaron didn't try to deter him, but he embraced him warmly. Jared hugged him back.

When they let go, Jared took a deep breath to compose himself. "Thanks for a wonderful dinner." He held out his hand.

Instead of shaking it, Kuaron put his own hand into his pocket, and then he slipped something into Jared's palm.

Jared looked down at his hand and discovered he was holding an audio disk. "What—" he started to ask, and then it dawned on him. He looked up at Kuaron eagerly. "The *Shahgundal*?"

Kuaron nodded. "And the *Cregamekano* and about a dozen others. I've been working on it for the last three days."

"Wow!" Jared breathed reverently. "What about the Society of *Qatraharai's* rules?"

"I don't consider that their rules apply to my *glynunshahai*," Kuaron said blandly.

Jared broke into a grin. "Then it was worth the pain, furball."

"I'm glad you think so."

Jared looked at him and suddenly had to swallow. "I hope I can pay you back someday."

Kuaron shook his head. "I'm the one who's trying to pay you back, for all you've done for me."

"I—I don't know what to say," Jared confessed.

Kuaron grinned at him. "Then this is indeed a momentous day. I don't think I've ever seen you at a loss for words before."

Jared smiled back at him. "I've never had to say goodbye to my best friend right after trying to steal his wife."

Kuaron laughed. "And I never had to say goodbye to my *glynunshahai*."

Jared felt his throat tightening up again. "That's it, then. Goodbye, *glynunshahai*," he said, offering his hand a second time.

This time Kuaron shook it. "Goodbye."

Jared turned toward the door and found Dina in the way.

"Goodbye, Jared," she said, holding out her arms.

Jared hugged her fiercely, but couldn't trust himself to speak. He let go of her and headed for the door, wondering if he would ever see either of them again.

# Chapter Twenty-Two

"I hope we can manage as well with our one as you're doing with the twins," Shanour said as he laid Yulayan in her crib and then picked up her brother.

Dina smiled to see her friend handle the baby so gingerly. "You'll do fine, and so will Argiantur—that is if she's really pregnant. I swear she hardly shows at all. When I was less pregnant than she is now, I was a small house."

Shanour made a tisking noise. "Nonsense. You were never that big."

"Yes, I was. I remember it well." Dina picked up Yulayan and scrutinized her features, trying to remember how the child had looked when she was first born. "How can they be three months old already? It seems like only a couple of weeks since they were born, but in only a month I have to decide if I want to go back to work or not."

Shanour subjected Kifarao to the same scrutiny. "They do look older. Farao looks just a little like you, I think."

"He looks Terran, at any rate."

"Not just Terran," Shanour said. "I've gotten to know Terrans better now that there are two living in my complex. I can see that little Farao has your cheekbones."

Dina held one of Yulayan's hands and gently pinched it between her thumb and forefinger. Five tiny claws extended from the tips of Yulayan's fingers. "They're both more Wakanrean than Terran—in spite of Yulayan's eyes."

"Are you sorry for that?" Shanour asked.

Dina shook her head. "No. It's going to be tough to grow up neither one thing nor the other. I want them to be able to blend in with their world."

The security speaker on the wall beeped softly.

"Oh!" Dina said. "There's the port alarm. Kuaron must be home."

"I'd better be going, then," Shanour said, rising to his feet. He laid Kifarao on his back in the crib, and stood looking down at him. "Goodbye, little *guisha*."

Dina smiled as she put her daughter down beside her brother. "Kuaron's father calls me that sometimes."

"I know. It shows how fond he is of you."

"I wonder if he even thinks of me as Terran," Dina said backing up from the crib toward the door. She gestured to Shanour to come with her. "Let's go. If we're lucky, they'll amuse each other. They do that sometimes."

They stood in the corridor for a moment, but there was no noise from the twins' room.

Dina sighed with relief. "Let's see how long it lasts," she said, heading for the kitchen.

They met Kuaron in the entrance hall. As soon as she was near him, Dina could tell that something was worrying him.

"Hello, Kuaron," she said, slipping her arm around his waist. "Is anything wrong?"

He stared right at her, not even greeting Shanour. "My father called me while I was on my way home. The Legislature issued an edict that all Terrans with permanent resident status must get the vaccine on a regular basis. Any Terran who refuses has to leave Wakanreo."

Dina struggled to suppress the surge of anxiety this news provoked. "We expected as much."

"I'd better be going," Shanour said. "Will my pocket com work out here, Dina? I need to call an autocab."

"I'll take you back to Wisuta," Kuaron said, blinking as if he had just noticed the other Wakanrean was there.

"Don't bother, *parundai*," Shanour said. "You just got home."

"The security system needs to know—" Dina began, when a sudden wail from the twins' room interrupted her. She let out a Wisutan swear word. "It looks like they're not ready for a nap after all. Would you call an autocab, please, Kuaron, while I see to the babies?"

"I'll help," Shanour said.

"Thanks," Dina said, leading the way.

The two of them put the children into their day beds, and let the nursery servoids carry them back to the main room.

"The cab will be here soon, Shanour," Kuaron said as they came into the room.

"Thank you," Shanour answered, taking a seat next to Yulayan's day bed.

"Did your father say when the vaccination is supposed to start, Kuaron?" Dina asked.

"In ten days' time," Kuaron said. "The pharmaceutical companies have been manufacturing the vaccine ever since ThreeCon gave them the formula. They say they're ready, and the law will take effect then."

"There must be thousands of Terrans who will be affected," Shanour said. "Tens of thousands. How will they vaccinate them all at once?"

"It's to be done over several days," Kuaron said. "There are ten or twelve sites around Wisuta where the Terrans are to report. There's a schedule based on their surnames, so they don't all show up at once."

"It would be alphabetical," Dina said. "Bellaire. I'll be among the first."

"Will you go, then?" Shanour asked.

Dina looked to Kuaron. They had discussed it many times. "No. We agreed that if it came out as a formal requirement, I would apply for an exemption based on my tiny bit of Wakanrean DNA and my *shahgunrah* with Kuaron. I've already hired an advocate, and she'll write my appeal, and defend it if the court questions it."

"Who's your advocate?"

"Shukanao Liaz. She represented Kuaron during his hearing."

Shanour looked impressed. "I've heard of her. She's supposed to be very good."

"I thought so," Kuaron said. "She knows the law, and she presents herself well."

"Well, good luck," Shanour said. "I hope they let you out of it. It sounds pretty scary, otherwise."

"Thanks," Dina said. "I appreciate your concern,"

The summit alarm chimed, and Kuaron got to his feet. "The cab is here."

"I'll be going then," Shanour said, rising.

Dina jumped up to see him to the door. "Thanks for coming. It's difficult for us to get out these days, so we're grateful for our friends who visit."

Abruptly, Shanour threw his arms around Dina and hugged her. "I'm happy to be your friend," he said, releasing her just as quickly.

Dina was startled, but warmed by the gesture. Shanour had never touched her before. It came to her that he was as close to her as any girlfriend had ever been. "I'm glad, too, Shanour. It's meant a lot to me to have a friend at Quafray."

Shanour looked pleased at this recognition of their relationship. He murmured a respectful goodbye to Kuaron, declined his offer to see him to the summit, and left Kuaron and Dina alone with their children.

"Well," Dina said, pulling Kuaron close, "it's happened."

"Yes," Kuaron said. "It has happened."

"Do you really think my appeal has a chance?"

Kuaron was still for a moment, as if he were thinking. "I have to believe it does," he said at last.

It was, Dina knew, only half an answer.


SIX days later, Dina waited tensely in a circular courtroom, where the chairs surrounding the center table were packed with spectators. Several members of Kuaron's family—not including his father, who was taking care of the twins—had come in support; their familiar faces helped Dina to relax a little. In addition to his many relations, a few onlookers had offered verbal support before the hearing, which made Dina feel better about the many strangers who clearly had come hoping to hear her appeal rejected.

In a back row sat a spectator who was neither a stranger nor a well-wisher. Every bit as conspicuous in street clothes as she had been in her brightly-colored *qatraharai's* robe, Triascou lu Huaic's aloof manner as she stared at Kuaron and Dina made her opinion clear.

From her seat at the center table, Dina stared back at Triascou until the panel of three judges came in and took their seats. Dina took a deep breath. She wanted to take Kuaron's hand, but the two of them had decided that it would be best not to touch each other in such an adversarial situation. Instead, Dina clenched her gloved hands together. She could feel Kuaron's presence next to her even without looking at him.

On her other side, Shukanao Liaz waited with her usual calm demeanor. She sat almost motionless until the moment the chief judge rose to his feet.

Dina knew that unless the judges had questions for them, the decision would be announced now. The petition Shukanao had filed on her behalf three days before had been her only chance to present her arguments. There would be no hearing, no oral presentation at all. If the judges asked no questions, there would be only this pronouncement of the court's decree.

The judge waited for silence; when the courtroom finally grew quiet, he spoke. "This court has decided that we have no standing to grant an exemption to this edict."

Dina felt her stomach lurch with apprehension. She was so devastated she almost missed what the judge said next.

"The appellant may seek relief directly from the Legislature if she chooses, but we have no grounds to contravene their law."

Dina could feel Kuaron's disappointment as sharply as her own. The silence held until the three judges filed out of the room, and then a stir arose, a loud buzz of conversation that swirled around Dina like a whirlpool. People were leaving their chairs, talking and gesturing, arguing about what the judge had said. And through it all, Kuaron didn't move.

Dina tried not to let her shoulders droop as she turned to face him. "Well, what do we do now?"

"We appeal directly to the Legislature." Kuaron stood up to touch hands with a cousin of his who had stopped to pat him on the shoulder and offer sympathy, and then he turned back to Dina. "But first, let's get out of here."

She rose, too, standing straight so defeat wouldn't show in her pose. Kuaron made a herding motion with one arm as if to envelop her without actually touching her.

"Will you come talk with us, *Kantai* Liaz?" Dina asked, turning back to her advocate.

The Wakanrean woman looked to her *shahgunrahai*, the man who had approached from her other side. Stuikaz Deloun was both tall and very handsome, Dina decided. He had seemed quite pleasant when she met him before the hearing. Dina knew that he worked as a gardener, and had taken time off to come see the announcement.

Now he nodded his acquiescence. "Don't worry about me, Shukanao. I'll wait for you at the flyter."

"Nonsense," Shukanao said. "One of the benefits of *shahgunrah* is that your *shahgunrahai* is exempt from the restrictions placed on other third parties. You come with us."

If she hadn't been so upset by her situation, Dina would have smiled at the warm affection in Shukanao's voice.

Before they could proceed, a tall figure loomed in their way.

"Hello, Kuaron," Triascou lu Huaic said, with the slightest of bows.

Kuaron bowed back at the same depth. "Hello, Trias."

"It seems your new friend has lost her bid to rise above the law," Triascou said. "Perhaps you should take it as a sign of what's meant to be? Or even as a second chance. Other *huishfanai* have reclaimed their lives after they were afflicted."

It took Dina a moment to recall the meaning of *huishfanai*—the maimed ones, Wakanreans who had suffered *glashunrah*. She could feel a hot blast of anger from Kuaron.

"It doesn't matter whether she wins or loses her legal battle," Kuaron said, pulling himself up to his full height. "Dina Bellaire is my *shahgunrahai*, and I am hers. *That* is what is meant to be. If you can't accept that, then there's no need for you to speak to me again in this life."

Triascou's eyes flicked to Dina and then back at Kuaron. "It will be as you say, then, Kuaron Du," she said, her tone as cold as Kuaron's. "And when your alien tires of you," she continued in Wisutan, "may you remember that I, at least, tried to warn you that the day would come when you would have to face the truth."

"You're a fine one to speak of facing the truth," Dina burst out in Wisutan before Kuaron could respond. "You wouldn't know the truth if it sat in your lap." She was so angry that it didn't occur to her to stop and think whether it was wise to insult a noted *qatraharai* in such a public place. Instead, she deliberately ripped off one glove and scratched herself under her chin with her little finger.

Triascou gave a roar and lunged toward Dina, but before she could even come close, a powerfully built, dark-furred man grabbed her and pulled her back, muttering urgently in her ear. He half dragged the *qatraharai* into the milling crowd, while Kuaron stepped protectively in front of Dina.

"That was not well thought out, *kantai*," Shukanao said. "Nevertheless, I applaud your grasp of our language and customs."

"Trias is gone," Kuaron said, turning back to Dina. "Fortunately, her *shahgunrahai* was with her. He was always the one to calm her down."

"That does seem to be a *shahgunrahai's* job," Dina said brightly. She felt considerably better for having confronted the enemy. At least Triascou lu Huaic was a real person and not some vague and faceless foe.

Stuikaz gazed at her with admiring eyes. "You're very brave, *kantai*, especially for such a small person."

"I'm hell on wheels, in fact," Dina said. "Let's get out of here."


THEY went to a nearby *quascha* parlor that offered private rooms. After Kuaron poured everyone a cup of spiced *quascha*, they began to discuss the situation.

"The thing is, *kantai*," Shukanao said, "the Legislature is very slow. Look how long it took them to issue the edict on the vaccine, and there was very little opposition to that. You have only four days. The chance that they'll respond to an appeal in that time is virtually nonexistent."

"But what do you think they'll say when they do respond?" Dina asked.

"Who knows?" Shukanao said, with an expansive shrug that would have done Kuaron proud. "Who can say what politicians will do? They all answer to an electorate. Doubtless, each of them will try to please the voters in his or her region."

"That's what my father says is the problem with politics," Kuaron said. "You can't please everyone, and you compromise yourself trying."

"So what are my options now?" Dina said. "I mean, we'll definitively appeal to the Legislature, but what happens in four days if they haven't said or done anything?"

"Ah!" Shukanao leaned back and slid an arm around her *shahgunrahai*. "What happens then is up to you. If you comply with the law and report for the vaccine, then you keep your residency status. If you don't, the planetary authorities will almost certainly deport you."

Dina looked to Kuaron. He took her gloved hand in his own. "We'll have to decide soon, *acubai*."

"Yes."

"In the meantime," Shukanao said, "you should write your own appeal. What you're asking from them is not so much a matter of law, as of compassion. The appeal should be in your own words— from the stomach, as it were."

"Thank you for your efforts, *kantai*," Kuaron said. "And for your acceptance of us as *shahgunrahai*."

"Of course we accept you!" Stuikaz exclaimed, not waiting for Shukanao to answer. "When *shahgunrah* strikes, what else can anyone do but accept the consequences?"

"That's the traditional belief," Kuaron said. "But it appears that there are those who don't see it as universal."

He was thinking of Triascou, Dina knew. She wondered if the others saw the irony of a close friend being less tolerant of his unorthodox *shahgunrah* than two relative strangers, but she said nothing of these thoughts. "I'd like to add my thanks, also, *kantai*."

Shukanao smiled enigmatically as she lifted her cup. "We'll just call it my contribution to the cause of universal acceptance. And allow me to wish you luck, *kantai*."

"You'll need it," Stuikaz said. "After all, the Arbiter of the Legislature is one of the *huishfanai*."


THAT night Dina tried to compose an appeal to the Legislature, but she couldn't put Stuikaz's comment out of her mind. She sat in the main room with a portable terminal on her lap, unable to write a word.

"What's wrong, *acubai*?" Kuaron asked, dropping down beside her on the sofa.

"I can't quite get past the fact that I'm appealing to a *huishfanai* to let me walk around Wakanreo without the vaccine that prevents *glashunrah*."

Kuaron sighed. "I was afraid you'd think that. That's why I never told you about her."

"So everyone knows?"

Kuaron nodded. "*Glashunrah* struck her a long time ago, when she was young. It was with a Terran man who worked for a chemical company. He left Wakanreo within a few days of it happening."

"It's amazing she's not a radical," Dina said. "I don't know if I could be unbiased if something like that happened to me."

Kuaron stroked her cheek with one finger. "Don't worry about her. The Arbiter doesn't even vote unless there's a tie."

"But she controls who speaks and for how long."

"True." Kuaron made the admission with reluctance. "But Prokien Diow is known for being fair and even-handed. Even my father respects her."

It was, Dina knew, an accolade of the highest order, but it did little to reassure her. "All of this is beside the point, Kuaron. I'll send the appeal in as soon as I finish it, but we have to decide what I'm going to do in four days."

Kuaron was silent a moment. "What do you want to do, *acubai*?"

Dina held in a sigh. She didn't know how he was going to take her suggestion. "If it were just you and me, I'd say let's tell the Legislature what they can do with their vaccine and let them deport me. You're a ThreeCon citizen as much as I am; there's no way they could stop you from going with me. But it's not just you and me, Kuaron. We have the twins to think about. If we leave now, they might not let me come back. Do you want to raise two Wakanrean children somewhere like Fantar or Croyzan?"

"They're half Terran."

Dina smiled. "That half doesn't show very much." She looked at him gravely as she offered the other solution she had already rejected in her own mind. "Would you prefer to let relatives raise them here on Wakanreo—without us?"

Kuaron sat motionless for a moment. Dina could sense his unhappiness.

"You want to take the vaccine?" he said.

"I don't *want* to take it," Dina said, a little exasperated that he would put it that way. "But I think I *have* to take it. We don't have a lot of choice here. What's the worst that could happen if I take it?"

"It could destroy *shahgunrah* for us."

The anguish she felt from him as he said the words was mirrored in his voice. Dina put one arm around him and stroked under his jaw with the other hand, trying to dull the sharpness of his misery.

"That's possible. But even if *shahgunrah* fades, I'll still love you and want to be with you."

He responded by throwing both arms around her in a crushing embrace. Dina hugged him back as tightly as she could. When he finally relaxed his grip, she couldn't stop a sigh from escaping.

"Well, Kuaron? I think this qualifies as something *shahgunrahai* should decide together."

"You're right. We need to stay on Wakanreo—all four of us—even at this price."

Dina hugged him again, and the two of them sat locked together for several minutes, until Kifarao's thin cry sounded from his day bed, joined almost immediately by Yulayan's more robust wail.

DINA joined the line of Terrans, very glad that her face had never appeared in any news bulletin. No one paid her any attention. But then, she had insisted that Kuaron wait in the flyter.

The person at the head of the queue went through the door at the end of the corridor, and everyone in line shuffled forward a few steps. People got in line behind her. When the woman in front of her moved, Dina took a step automatically. It went on like that for several minutes, as the line grew behind her and shrank in front. Finally, the line of Terrans behind her snaked down the length of the corridor, while only a half dozen people separated her from the counter where a Wakanrean man recorded peoples' names on a terminal.

The door opened again, but this time it was because someone was coming out of it. Dina noticed the woman's bright blue, beaded vest before she looked at her face, and when she did, she was shocked into recognition.

"Dina Bellaire!" Arliana Cheng said, standing stock still only a few feet away. "So you're going to do it!"

Now everyone really was staring at Dina. She frowned at her former friend. "Hello, Arliana."

The other woman was looking her up and down as if to assess her appearance. "You look okay."

"Thank you so much," Dina said, not even trying to rein in her sarcasm.

Arliana didn't seem to notice. "So, you're going to have the vaccine like the rest of us?"

"I don't have much choice, do I?" Dina said, not pleased to be having the conversation in such a public place.

"You could go home to Fantar—*if* you wanted to."

Dina noted her emphasis. "As it happens, I don't want to go back to Fantar."

"Boy, you must be really far gone."

The line moved again, and Dina took another step forward, which brought her very close to Arliana. "I suppose it looks that way to you. But then, it seems we have very different views on a lot of things—like friendship."

Arliana flushed, and seemed, finally, to wake up to the fact that everyone was looking at them. "I did what I thought was best. You changed so fast, it scared me."

It was, Dina realized, the closest Arliana could come to an apology. "Perhaps you did act as you thought best. Now, if you don't mind, I'd just as soon do this with some semblance of dignity, thank you."

Arliana hesitated, and then held out her hand.

She was wearing gloves for once, Dina noted. Dina debated for a fraction of a second, and then she put her own hand out and shook Arliana's. It wasn't much of a gesture for two friends who had once been more likely to embrace than to shake hands, but it was something.

"Goodbye, Arliana."

"Goodbye, Dina," Arliana said, her voice grave. "And good luck."

"Thank you."

Arliana let go of her hand and walked away. Dina watched her go, and then turned back to find that everyone was still staring at her. The line moved up again, and this time when Dina stepped forward, the man behind her hung back a little, as if he didn't want to get too close.

Dina held in a sigh and made herself stand straight. No one said anything to her, but she could hear whispers from the people behind her.

In a few minutes, she reached the counter with a sense of relief.

"Name?" said the Wakanrean man, without looking up.

"Dina Bellaire."

That brought his head up. He gave her a piercing stare for a second, and then his hands moved on the terminal as he found her records. He rattled off her planet of origin, birth date, and resident alien registration number for confirmation.

"That's me," Dina said.

"Go through the door."

For just a moment, Dina froze. She knew what she had to do, but the thought of it was so frightening that it took a real effort to make herself walk through the doorway. She took a deep breath and let it out, and then she started walking.

BY the time Dina got back to the flyter, Kuaron was in a state.

"There you are!" he said, practically surging across the seat console as he reached for her. "What took so long? I was worried you had become ill."

"There was already a long line," Dina said, stroking his arm reassuringly. "Getting the vaccine didn't take long at all. Once they scanned my medical history card, they gave me an injection and that was it."

"How do you feel?"

Dina considered. "I'm a little shaky, but I think that's because I'm scared. I'm fine otherwise."

"I don't sense anything different."

"There won't be any effect for several hours at least, Kuaron. We knew that going in. Try to relax."

Kuaron said nothing in response, but he kept a firm grip on her arm.

"Do you want me to fly us home?" Dina asked.

"No." He let go of her to turn to the controls. "I'm fine. It's just that it upset me to wait here alone. I wanted to go with you."

"I know you did," Dina said, glancing around the flyter park for any sign that they were under observation. She saw no one, but she wasn't reassured. "I appreciate your being so reasonable about it. Now, let's go home. I want to be home."

THEY were almost to the cliff house when the com sounded. When Dina answered it, she was surprised to see Shukanao Liaz's face on the screen.

"Hello," Dina said. "What's happened? Is anything wrong?"

"Two things have happened," Shukanao said, without any greeting. "The first is that Administrator Sadoc resigned this morning."

"What?" Kuaron said from the pilot's seat.

"Your father resigned his position," Shukanao said, addressing Kuaron even though Dina had the screen turned toward herself.

Kuaron flicked on the autopilot and swiveled the screen to face him. "Did he give any explanation?"

"He released a public statement that he wouldn't assist in the destruction of your *shahgunrah*."

"Oh!" Dina said. "Oh, dear! I feel terrible!"

"Nonsense, *kantai*," Shukanao said in a brisk tone. "*Kentai* Sadoc is competent to make his own decisions. It was none of your doing if he chose to make such a sacrifice."

"But it doesn't serve any purpose," Dina protested.

"Perhaps it does to him," Kuaron said. "Thank you for telling me, *kantai*."

"You're welcome."

"Was there something else?" Dina asked. "Didn't you say you had two things to tell us?"

"I did, yes. The Legislature notified me that they have convened a special session just to hear your appeal. They meet in six days."

Dina put a hand to her mouth in revulsion. "Oh, my god!"

Shukanao frowned. "You already took the vaccine?"

Dina nodded. "Just a few minutes ago. I went early to avoid the crowds."

The advocate's frown dissolved into a look of bland neutrality. "So long as the results aren't too deleterious, it might be worth it. It could help your case. Taking the vaccine shows good faith on your part."

"I don't think we'll know how bad the results will be until tomorrow, or even later," Dina said, glancing at Kuaron. His jaw was set in a grim line, and she could sense his rapidly-growing unhappiness.

"We can only hope for the best," Shukanao said.

"Yes," Dina agreed. "Thanks for letting me know about the appeal."

The advocate disclaimed and broke the connection.

Dina stared for a moment at the blank com screen. "Six days. Who knew the Legislators could move so fast?"

"Not Shukanao Liaz, certainly."

"It wasn't her fault, Kuaron."

"No?"

"No. It was no one's fault. She was doing her best for us. How can she be expected to give advice in a case like this? It's not like she had any precedent to follow."

Kuaron was silent a few seconds. Dina could feel his anger ebb, but a profound unhappiness took its place.

"Six days," he said, echoing her words. "If only we had waited!"

"There's no saying for sure the municipal authorities wouldn't have deported me by then," Dina argued. "And anyway, we can't go back in time, so let's not reproach ourselves for what can't be helped."

"I know you're right," he said, letting out a large sigh, "but it's difficult not to regret the circumstance."

"Speaking of regret, I do feel bad about your father resigning."

The arrival alarm beeped, and Kuaron reached for the manual control switch. "We're home. We can go in and ask him about it."

He landed the flyter quickly, and the two of them made their way through the long corridor to the front door without speaking. Kuaron was still depressed, and Dina was suffering pangs of guilt that Juzao Sadoc had given up a position he could never again equal.

The former Administrator didn't seem to have any such qualms. They found him on his hands and knees in the main room, leaning over his grandson. Kifarao lay on his back on the floor. Juzao was shaking his head and making strange noises at the infant, who laughed and kicked his feet every time his grandfather moved his face close and burbled at him.

"Shwurfroo!" Juzao said, grinning fiercely. "Wuzza wuzza shwoof!"

Kifarao cooed with delight while his sister watched from her day bed, her expression solemn.

"Here's a fine state of affairs," Kuaron said. "What's Kifarao doing on the floor?"

Juzao scrambled to his feet. "Ah! I didn't hear you come in."

"Not with all this commotion." Dina scooped up her son and cuddled him. The baby cooed again, and reached for her chin.

"They're in those things all day long," Juzao said, indicating Kifarao's empty day bed. "They need to get out more."

"Do they?" Kuaron's voice assumed a serious tone, but Dina knew he was amused.

"Yes, they do." Juzao extended a finger to brush Kifarao's cheek. The baby grabbed at it with his own furred hand.

"Well, then, it's good you'll have more free time to spend with them, no?" Kuaron said.

Juzao shot a sharp glance at Kuaron. "So you heard the news?"

"Yes," Kuaron said. "Shukanao Liaz called us."

Juzao's expression was guarded. "Ah!"

"She also told us the Legislature will hear Dina's appeal in only six days," Kuaron said.

His father put an arm around him in a brief embrace. "Don't feel that it would have changed anything to have known that this morning, Kuaron. Prokien called me right after you left, to tell me that news. She also told me the municipal authorities would deport Dina immediately if she didn't report for the vaccine."

"You didn't call to tell me that?"

Juzao shook his head. "Prokien told me in confidence, as a courtesy. I was bound not to say anything until the official announcement."

"It wouldn't have mattered, anyway," Dina said, restoring Kifarao to his day bed. "Stop worrying, Kuaron."

"Ha!" Juzao said. "It would be the first time. He's just like his mother."

"I'm sorry I never got to meet her," Dina said, picking up Yulayan. She handed the infant to Juzao. "Here. Your granddaughter wants her turn."

Juzao took the baby girl in his hands and nuzzled her stomach, then laid her on the floor. He dropped to his hands and knees and began to burble at her just as he had at Kifarao.

"Baby talk sounds the same in any language," Dina said. "But I wish you hadn't resigned."

Juzao stopped and looked up at her, blinking. "Don't be silly, *guisha*. This is about family. Kuaron understands."

"Of course I do." Kuaron slipped an arm around Dina. "And thank you, *Ayzanai*."

"Wuzza whoofa shwufa," Juzao said, tickling Yulayan on her stomach."

Yulayan kicked her feet vigorously. "Ayya!"

"You see, Kuaron," Dina said, looking up at him. "How bad can it be if we're all still together?"

Kuaron said nothing, but as Dina hugged him, she could feel a tinge of anxiety still lingered.

Still on the floor, Juzao sat back on his heels and laughed. "Never ask a Wisutan how bad it could be."

THAT night, Dina took her time getting ready for bed. Kuaron was always ready before her, because he never did anything but shed his clothes, drop them into the laundry hatch, and chew a dentifrice tablet to clean his mouth.

Dina still liked to sleep in a nightgown, and she enjoyed using that brief period of time to herself to perform her nightly routine. She put away her jewelry first, undressed, then took her gown from its hook in the closet and put it on. She brushed her hair, washed her face and hands, and cleaned her teeth.

Kuaron watched her from where he lolled naked on the bed. "Why do your people wear clothes to sleep in? There's no one to see you in bed."

"It's warmer, and I'm used to it. Don't Wisutans ever wear clothes to bed?"

"Only if their *shahgunrahai* are away from them for a long time."

Dina was intrigued. "Why then?"

"Because it lets you send your *shahgunrahai* your scent. You sleep in a special garment, and when it has absorbed your scent, you seal it into an airtight bag and send it to him or her. Then your *shahgunrahai* can sleep with it."

"Oh! Well, the next time you perform out of town, you can take one of my nightgowns with you."

"I think I will."

"Wisutans have such interesting customs."

Kuaron came up off the bed in a flash, and caught her tightly in his arms. "That's not the only one that's interesting."

Dina could feel *taal* growing strong in him, and her own answering surge of passion was just as quick. "Umm," she said, as he nuzzled her neck. His fur was silky against her skin, his familiar scent strong and reassuring. "I've always appreciated Wisutan customs."

Kuaron pulled the straps of her gown over her shoulders and yanked downwards. Her nightgown fell to the floor. Dina expected him to touch her again, but instead he stood motionless.

"What's wrong?" she asked.

"I was just thinking," Kuaron said, and she could feel worry creeping in to taint *taal*, "what if this is the last time we can do this?"

"I refuse to believe any such thing," Dina said at once. "You said yourself that people who pair off after they're widowed can have sex. If people who were never *shahgunrahai* with each other can do it, I don't see why we couldn't, no matter what the vaccine does."

He didn't answer, but instead bent to nuzzle her neck again. Dina pressed against him, and after a few seconds of her stroking his back and sides, Kuaron picked her up and laid her down on the floor.

"Here?" she said, gasping a little as he began to fondle her breasts. "What's wrong with the bed?"

"Nothing. But I want it to be like the first time."

Dina laughed aloud. "All right, then. But you'll have to get me a pillow. I don't think I can hold that pose for long without it."

"You won't need a pillow. It won't take long."

Kuaron was quite right. In a very short time, Dina cried out in ecstasy. Kuaron persisted until she screamed again, and at the same time she felt his climax as a rush of cascading pleasure.

"Umm," Dina said, letting go of the chair legs she had used to support herself and collapsing onto the floor.

Kuaron dropped down beside her, gasping for breath.

"That was wonderful," Dina said, rolling over so that she nestled against him. "But I don't think I can move."

Without saying a word, he picked her up and carried her to the bed. Dina grabbed her nightgown as he lifted her, and clung to him as he put her down. When he pulled the bedclothes over them both, she let out a sigh.

"I'm glad I found you, Kuaron Du."

"I'm glad, too, Dina Bellaire."

As Dina's drowsed into sleep, her thoughts drifted. Foremost in her mind was a hope that the vaccine might have no effect on her life with Kuaron, but close behind that was the fear that such a wish might be too much to ask.

# Chapter Twenty-Three

Dina awoke the next morning with a sudden start. She sat up in bed, and tried to think what was so important that she had to remember it right away.

She felt Kuaron's warmth beside her, and it all came back to her. She had taken the vaccine yesterday.

Kuaron was still sleeping, but she could feel the familiar sense of his being close that came from *haictor*. The sound of Yulayan crying reminded Dina that she was still a mother as well as a *shahgunra-hai*. She slipped out of bed and pulled on her nightgown, added a robe, and then started for the twins' room.

She nursed Yulayan first, as always, and then Kifarao. After she laid the little boy on his back in the crib, his eyes drooped as he flung out a hand toward his sister. Yulayan was fast asleep already, dozing in sated complacence.

Dina left them and checked the bedroom. Kuaron was still sleeping in the middle of the bed, his arm curved around the place where she had lain.

She took a shower, and dressed, opening drawers quietly so as not to wake him. Once she had slipped on her shoes, she started for the door, but Kuaron's voice called her back.

"Where are you going?"

"Oh," Dina said, turning back toward the bed. "I didn't realize you were awake."

Kuaron frowned and sat up. "You can always tell when I'm awake or asleep, just like I know about you."

It was true, Dina realized. She waited, apprehension building with every breath, as Kuaron stood up and reached for his *xuschi*.

She thought of their first morning together as he walked toward her.

"*Shahgunrah* is gone!" Kuaron said, stopping in front of her.

Dina could sense deep despair coming from him, almost like a physical pain. "No, it's not! I can feel you. You're upset—distressed, even."

Kuaron shook his head. "I feel nothing—not even *haictor*. It's as if you're not really there."

Dina threw her arms around him. Kuaron's whole body went rigid, and Dina felt his shock.

"It's back—a little," he said. "*Klunar* is still there a little when we touch, not like it used to be, but there is something."

Dina held him tightly. "I can still feel you. I can feel everything, except there's no echo. I used to be able to sense an echo of my own emotions when you felt them."

"So it's gone."

"Not completely," Dina said, determined to put the best face on the situation.

"Bah! What remains is a frail wisp of *shahgunrah*."

His desolation washed over Dina like a wave on the shore, buffeting her almost off of her feet. Dina pushed it back, refusing to let herself be overwhelmed by the totality of his despair. For some reason, his sense of defeat made her angry. "Stop it! Stop it! Don't you dare feel sorry for yourself, Kuaron! And don't feel sorry for me, either."

Kuaron stepped back from her, and Dina sensed his surprise. "Don't you understand? I can feel almost nothing from you."

"Yes, I understand. You're the one who hasn't thought it through. We knew this could happen, and we made a choice. I still think it was the best choice. I have you, and you have me, and we both have our children. Even if *shahgunrah* is impaired forever, we're better off than if we had never known it."

Kuaron frowned. "You sound like a Terran."

"I am a Terran," Dina said, getting angrier. "I've always been a Terran. I was a Terran that first night at the Embassy when you came up to me. I can't be anything else but what I am."

"I understand that."

"You don't sound like you do."

A sharp pang of regret tugged at Dina, and she realized it came from him. "You said you were glad you found me, Kuaron. But I think perhaps you're wishing that I was Wakanrean."

"No!"

It was said with conviction, but Dina could sense an underlying doubt. "Are you sure?"

There was a long pause. "Maybe a little," Kuaron said finally. "I can't help but think it, *acubai*. If you were Wakanrean, this would never have happened to our *shahgunrah*."

"*Puoulgaio!*"

Now Kuaron was angry. He walked two quick strides away from her and then turned to face her. "Surely you can't think our *shahgunrah* would be crippled if you were a Wakanrean?"

"That's not what I mean!" Dina said, almost stamping her foot on the floor. "I mean stop acting like this change is the end of the world. Stop wallowing in self pity, and look at this as objectively as you can. What does this mean to us? What does it mean now that you can't sense my emotions?"

That caught him off guard. He blinked at her in that wide-eyed way he had that always reminded her of a wild creature. "It means *klunar* is gone."

"*Klunar* is gone, but I'm still here." Dina stepped closer. "You have an opportunity most Wakanreans never get—the chance to find out how you really feel about your *shahgunrahai*—without *shahgunrah* getting in the way."

"You call that an opportunity?"

"Damn right I do."

"Bah!"

"Oh, stop it!" Dina said, truly incensed now. She could feel that his anger was growing stronger than his sadness, and somehow that made her indignant. "If you want to feel sorry for yourself, go ahead, but I still say things could be a lot worse."

"How?" Kuaron demanded. "What could be worse?"

"I'll tell you," Dina said, searching her mind. She was, she realized, angry enough to think of whatever would hurt him most. "What if I hadn't gone to the Embassy that night? What if I had gone to the wrestling matches with Jared? He asked me. Did you know that?"

"No," Kuaron said, a peculiar look on his face. "I didn't know."

"Well,  he  did,"  Dina  answered  with  relish.  She  was  fairly
launched  now,  and  intent  on  doing  as  much  damage  as  she  could.
"What if I had gone to the wrestling matches with Jared and really
liked him? What if we had gotten to be good friends—maybe slept
together a few times? And then at some point, he had introduced
me  to  you.  What  would  have  happened  then,  do  you  think?"

"It  would  have  been  the  same,"  Kuaron  said,  but  his  voice  was
hollow.

"You  really  think  so?"  Dina  tilted  her  head  to  look  at  him.  "I
doubt  it.  Oh,  I  would  have  come  here  when  you  asked  me,  but  I
would  have  hated  you  the  whole  time,  and  I  would  have  hated
myself,  too.  And  if  Jared  had  tried  to  stop  me  from  going  with  you,
you  might  well  have  killed  him."

Kuaron's  chest  expanded  as  he  took  a  deep  breath.  When  he  let
it  out,  it  was  as  if  a  blast  of  pain  and  anger  came  with  it,  filling  the
space  between  them  with  a  cold  chill.  "You  told  me  you  didn't  love
Jared."

"I  don't,"  Dina  said,  flinching  from  his  anguish.  "I  never  did.  But
I  might  have  come  to  love  him  if  I  had  gotten  to  know  him  first.  And
where  would  we  have  been  then,  Kuaron?"

He  turned  away  again,  but  said  nothing.  She  could  feel  him
seething  with  anger  and  frustration.  She  could  feel  the  underlying
dull  ache  of  his  pain.

All  at  once  it  came  to  Dina  that  this  was  what  life  had  been  like
for  Oiganna  Jin.  Every  time  she  and  Heingeon  had  quarreled,  they
must  have  gone  through  this  misery—each  of  them  sensing  the
other's  suffering,  neither  of  them  able  to  stop  the  torment.  Life  had
been  one  long  sentence  of  suffering  without  any  chance  of  reprieve.
Finally,  Dina  could  understand  what  could  drive  Oiganna  and
Heingeon  to  take  their  own  lives.  The  revelation  left  her  feeling
drained,  empty  of  any  positive  emotion,  and  perversely,  she  was
angry  at  Kuaron  for  not  sensing  her  despair.

Kuaron  also  seemed  struck  by  the  bleakness  of  the  situation.  He
wheeled  around  and  headed  for  the  door  to  the  corridor.  "I'm  going
to  bathe."

Dina  waited  until  he  had  gone  through  the  door  before  she  let
out  a  sigh  and  started  for  the  kitchen.

KUARON was quiet for most of that day. He went off to his rehearsal room for several hours, but he didn't seem any more talkative when he came out of it. Nor could Dina sense any kind of conciliation or regret; there was nothing but anger and silence.

It was only in caring for the children that Kuaron was at all communicative. He cooed at Yulayan when he held her, and smiled at Kifarao when he played with him. He sang to both of them, a cheerful children's song with a simple melody that forced a smile from Dina.

Mealtimes, on the other hand, were terrible. From breakfast onward, each meal grew steadily quieter. Kuaron was laconic at lunch and almost wordless at dinner. Dina cleared the table with a feeling of gloom hanging over her. After she put the babies to bed, she sat in the main room and waited, but Kuaron stayed in his study and didn't come out.

Finally, she went into the bedroom and began to get ready for bed. Her nightly ritual offered no comfort. After she had taken her gown from its hook and slipped it on, she put her jewelry away, then stood in front of the mirror and brushed her hair. She stared at her image and tried to remember what her life had been like before *shahgunrah*. What had happened to that hopeful young woman who had stepped off the liner from Croyzan? She had been so eager to start work, to prove herself, to make a career in her chosen field. And now it had been days since she had even thought about work.

"Dina."

She jumped. Kuaron had never been able to sneak up on her, and his silent arrival took her completely unawares. She hadn't realized how important the echo of her own feelings was to *haictor*.

"Yes?" she said, turning. He stood in the doorway, several meters away.

"I do love you. I think this would be easier to take if I didn't love you, but I do. I want very much to stay with you and the children."

Dina drew in a breath. His truthfulness came through as clearly and as sharply as his pain. A rush of remorse and compassion overwhelmed her. "I love you, too, Kuaron. And I'm sorry I said such hateful things to you. I'm a terrible person when I'm angry."

"No. It was good that you said it. You reminded me of things I needed to remember."

Dina let out the breath she had been holding in. "I know this is difficult for you. I'm not trying to say it's easy or an unmitigated blessing. I'm just saying we can learn something from it."

"I have already. I know what it means to be Terran—to love without *shahgunrah*. To rely on trust instead of certainty."

"Then maybe it will be worth it?"

He said nothing, but instead he came closer and held out his arms. Dina stepped into them, and he embraced her fiercely. She could feel a rush of joy from him, and the faintest echo of her own relief. And then *taal* washed over her, and she felt it rise in him, also.

She laughed with sheer delight in the moment, and began to stroke his neck and jaw. "Maybe it won't be so bad?" She laughed again as he gently nudged her backward toward the bed.

He didn't speak, but kept pushing until she bumped into the bed and fell over on her back. She sank into the bed covers, and Kuaron launched himself onto the bed beside her.

"Ummm," was the only answer he made as he nuzzled her neck and pushed her gown up under her arms with one deft movement.

Dina gave a long, happy sigh. "Use your claws just a little, Kuaron."

Kuaron complied, and finally Dina felt whole again.


THE next few days, Dina did her best to help Kuaron relax and learn to live with the change in their situation. It was, she decided, just a little like learning to care for a sick person or a child. Kuaron needed constant reassurance as to the state of her feelings, and she often had to touch him to calm his fears.

Still, she found it a positive experience in that they did at least learn to communicate with only one-sided *klunar*. Once Kuaron was more at ease with her, Dina turned her mind to what she wanted to say in her address to the Legislature.

The night before she was to appear, Dina spent some time rehearsing her speech in her mind. She pulled a clean nightgown from the drawer and slipped it over her head, all the while debating how to address the legislators.

Kuaron was sitting up in bed watching her anxiously. "Is anything wrong, *acubai*? You look very solemn."

He wasn't used to relying on her facial expressions, Dina realized. "Nothing's wrong. I'm just trying to figure out what to say tomorrow."

She slid into bed beside him, and Kuaron slipped an arm around her to pull her close as they both slid down under the covers. Dina felt a pang of guilt as she took comfort in the concern she felt from him, knowing that he couldn't feel her own emotions nearly so well.

Dina gave his arm an affectionate squeeze as the lights dimmed. "How are you doing?"

He paused before he answered, and she knew he was evaluating his answer. "I'm better, I think. It's not so bad at times like this, when we can touch. I think it's worse when you're in the room but not right next to me."

"If we're lucky, it's only for a year." He didn't answer, and she stroked his arm, wishing she could see his face. "It will come back. I know it will."

He raised himself up so that she could feel he was right over her, and she realized he could probably see her even if she couldn't see him. "I hope so," he said. "But you were right. What matters most is that we're together. I can bear it if this is how our *shahgunrah* will be, so long as we can be together."

Dina moved her hand to caress his jaw, and then ran her fingers through his headcrest. "So you admit that love is more important than *shahgunrah*?"

Kuaron laughed, a deep, contented laugh. "I admit it. Does that make you happy?"

"You make me happy." A burst of *taal* rose in Dina, and she moved her hand down his back to stroke his buttocks.

Kuaron laughed again, this time a chortling noise. Dina was relieved to feel an answering flush of passion from him as he slipped her nightgown over her head and pushed it out of the way.

"Ummm," she said as he slid his hand down her bare torso. "Fortunately, *taal* seems to be intact."

He nuzzled her behind one ear, and his breath was warm on her neck as he spoke. "And fortunately, we have to touch to do this."

Dina didn't answer, but as she stroked his fur, she was distressed to note that although she could sense both arousal and desire coming from him, it didn't grow into the burning, overpowering need of *taal*. His breathing quickened, his erection grew, but still there wasn't the same urgency in his caresses. When Dina's climax flowed over her in a familiar flood of pleasure, she barely felt the smaller explosion of sensation when he achieved orgasm.

When it was over, she held him close and sighed. "I'm sorry it wasn't the same for you this time, Kuaron."

He was lying on his side, holding her snugly against him. "It wasn't that bad." She could feel his voice rumbling in his chest. "I think I know now what sex is like for Terrans, or for widowed Wakanreans who find a new partner."

"And how is that?" Dina asked.

"Nice, but not so intense."

"It didn't seem so—so—innocuous the other night."

Kuaron rolled over. He seemed to be looking at something on the bed. "I think this must be the reason."

"What?'" Dina asked.

"This is a clean gown," Kuaron said, and Dina realized he must be holding the nightgown he had pulled over her head. "The other night you wore one you had slept in before you took the vaccine."

Remorse surged through Dina. Things would only get worse as less and less of her natural scent lingered in the house. "I'm sorry, Kuaron! I'm so sorry!"

He kissed her cheek. "It's not your fault, *acubai*. We both agreed you should take the vaccine. We had no other choice."

"I know, but I still feel bad."

He rocked her back and forth a few times. "Don't let yourself dwell on it. Think instead about what you'll say to the Legislature tomorrow."

Dina pulled away, and propped herself up on one elbow. "Do you mind if I turn the lights on a little? I can't see you."

"I don't mind."

Dina sat up in bed and the lights came on until a soft glow illuminated the room. She saw that Kuaron had put his hand over his eyes. "That's better," she said.

Kuaron moved his hand and blinked. "Now, what is it that you're going to say tomorrow?"

"I was going over everything in my mind," Dina said, taking his hand. "In a way, I'm trying to remember what it was like when I came here—when Wakanreans were exotic creatures, and *shahgunrah* was an alien bond. It's difficult for me to recall how it felt because I'm so at home now."

"I'm glad. There was a time I feared you would never value our *shahgunrah* as I do."

"I think in a way I value it more, just because it was so strange to me. Instead of always expecting it, I had it handed to me as a total surprise—like a present when it wasn't my birthday. I spent a lot of time debating the nature of the gift."

Kuaron sat up beside her so they were face to face. "And what did you decide?"

"Well," Dina chose her words carefully, "I decided *shahgunrah* can be either a blessing or a curse. It all depends on your *shahgunrahai*."

"Whether the two of you get along, you mean?"

"That's only part of it." She stroked his chest fur right below his *heicha*. "It also matters whether you respect each other and come to love each other."

"You're thinking of my cousin Oiganna." Dina could tell he was troubled.

"Yes," she admitted. "In a way I can understand their committing *naishagundah* better now than I could then."

Kuaron's unease grew. "Why?"

"Because I know now how strong the bond between us is." She smiled to reassure him. "When I woke up this morning and saw you sleeping next to me, it came to me that I could never leave you. Even now, with *shahgunrah* crippled, I couldn't even make myself *want* to leave you. And because I love you and you love me, that bond is a good thing.

"But for someone who's tied to a person they dislike or can't respect, *shahgunrah* must be terrible, Kuaron. A Terran couple who marry and then fall out of love can end their relationship, but *shahgunrah* lasts until death. No matter if you live apart, the bond is still there, and for most Wakanreans, nothing can undo it. Wakanreans who are happy in their *shahgunrah* are very lucky, but Wakanreans who are unhappy are truly miserable."

"So, do you think Wakanreans are better off than Terrans?" Kuaron asked, his golden eyes blinking like some night creature's.

Dina thought about it. "It all depends. With *shahgunrah* you can't help finding out what your *shahgunrahai* is really like—right to their core. There are probably Terrans who are happy in their marriages because they don't know each other that well, but *shah-gunrahai* don't have that option. They know the truth—good or bad. Sometimes that's a good thing and sometimes it's terrible. Luck counts more in *shahgunrah* than in marriage."

Kuaron reached out an arm and embraced her, pulling her close against him. "Even with our *shahgunrah* disabled, I consider myself as lucky as a Wakanrean can be."

Dina chuckled into his chest fur. "And I'm luckier than any Terran has a right to be."

"Ah!" Kuaron said with a sigh. "Life is truly strange."

THE Legislative enclave was located over two hundred kilometers from Wisuta. The trip there took a while, even in a fast flyter, and Dina complained about it to Kuaron.

"They moved the enclave almost a century ago," he said. "The idea was to make politicians suffer for their power by forcing them to live in the middle of nowhere, but the arrival of the Third Confederation gave us new technology that negated the distance."

"It's still a hell of a commute from Wisuta," Dina said.

"That was the point," Kuaron said.

"At least your father never went in for real politics," Dina said, leaning back in her chair to study the view. "As an appointed official, he got to live in Wisuta." They were travelling over the foothills of the mountain range that stretched for most of the length of the continent, and some of the cliffs were spectacular. On their right Dina could see a series of bright colored boulders, red and purple and every shade in between, stacked in a kind of rough staircase. A deep groove in the rocks allowed a small river to course down the steps. At the bottom, the long cascade of waterfalls ended in a deep, blue-green pool. "What's that?" she asked.

Kuaron looked at where she was pointing. "That's the Duanlana. A glacier made it long ago."

Dina leaned over in her seat to see better as they moved past. "It's beautiful," she said, noting several parties of picnickers around the pool.

"It's a favorite spot for anniversaries and other celebrations," Kuaron said.

"Maybe we can go there for a picnic sometime, if everything goes well today?"

"Maybe."

There was reluctance in Kuaron's voice, and Dina knew his superstition made it difficult for him to make plans without waiting for good news first. "Let's see how it goes."

"Yes," Kuaron said. "Let's wait."

They rode the rest of the way with only desultory conversation.

Dina was relieved when they came in sight of a cluster of buildings. A central, domed structure dominated the landscape, with streets radiating out from it like the spokes in a wheel. The buildings closest to the dome were tall apartment buildings, while individual houses lined streets farther out.

"The big building in the middle is the meeting chamber," Kuaron said. "The other buildings are offices and residences for the Legislators and their aides."

Dina studied the beautifully-landscaped grounds, where trees and bushes separated the buildings to give them a sense of privacy. Every edifice had a garden, and a few gardens had stone bridges spanning a large stream that meandered though the area.

"It doesn't look to me like living here is much of a punishment," she said.

"Not now, certainly," Kuaron said, his attention on landing the flyter. "Although the Legislators live in the apartments. Their staffs get the separate houses because they live here year round." He brought them down in the middle of a large parking area. "That looks like my father's flyter," Kuaron said, indicating a comfortable-looking dark green vehicle parked nearby.

"He said he'd come if he could," Dina said.

They made their way up a paved path to the main entrance to the central chamber, where they had to go through a security check, showing their identification and submitting to both a retinal scan and a weapons scan. The uniformed guards were polite but thorough.

"They're not taking any chances," Dina said.

"It's not just us," Kuaron said. "Everyone goes through it."

Dina remembered the night she had been attacked at the Grienshasa and was reassured.

After they had passed through the tall doorway into a busy corridor crowded with people, they discovered Juzao Sadoc waiting on a bench beside Shukanao Liaz. Both of them got to their feet when Kuaron and Dina approached.

"Hello, *Ayzanai*," Kuaron said. "Thank you for coming."

"I'm sorry to have caused you so much trouble," Dina added.

"*Puoulgaio!*" Juzao said. "You never did, *guisha*. It's these dolts in the Legislature who are the problem."

"Now, *kentai*," Shukanao said. "Don't assume they're going to be unreasonable until it happens."

"Hmph!" Juzao said. "They knew about Dina when they wrote the edict. They could have exempted her without any of this commotion."

It was, Dina knew, what had been bothering Kuaron from the beginning. Resolutely, she stood up straighter. "I think *Kantai* Liaz is right. Let's not holler until we're hurt."

Shukanao looked intrigued. "Is that a Terran expression, *kantai*?"

"Well, we said it often on Fantar," Dina said. "I don't know where it comes from, but it fits the situation."

"I think so, too," Kuaron said.

"Let's go inside, then," Juzao said. "Might as well be comfortable."

He led the way, down the length of the corridor to where two tall Wakanrean guards stood on either side of a wide doorway, with a security gate in front of it. All four of them had to go through the gate one at a time, and then the doors opened and they passed through into the legislative chamber.

The room was octagonal, with the Legislators sitting on very plain circular benches that ringed a small podium in six concentric circles. The circles were not quite complete, as they were broken periodically by aisles, and by a gap at the back of the podium.

Slender steel arches spanned the open space above them, bracing the high vault of the ceiling, open all the way to the central dome. The delicate curlicue designs of the arches gave the room a fairy tale atmosphere at odds with the more prosaic decor of the furnishings.

Dina noted that the benches were made of stone and leaned over to whisper to Kuaron. "Those benches look very uncomfortable."

"They are," Kuaron said. "They're meant to be. It gives the Legislators an incentive to keep debates from running long."

In spite of the tension of the moment, Dina had to smile. She studied the room and the 260 Legislators, who did indeed look uncomfortable, or at least restless. "Not a bad idea."

"Fortunately, spectators and witnesses are allowed more accommodation," Kuaron said, waving a hand for her to follow his father to a place in the outermost circle.

Dina noted that the spectators' benches were well padded. She sank down into the cushions beside Juzao, and Kuaron sat down next to her. Several people turned to look them over, but no one spoke to them.

The elderly Wakanrean woman who stood on the podium in the center of the circle was in the midst of a speech. Dina recognized her as Prokien Diow, the Arbiter of the Legislator. She had seen her often in news bulletins; she was unmistakable because she was the ugliest Wakanrean Dina had ever seen. Her nose was crooked and much too big for her face, her upper lip was elongated, and her teeth had turned brown with age. Only her luminous amber eyes mitigated the plainness of her countenance. None of this seemed to weigh on her as she held one hand up to make a point in her speech.

"Can we allow this risk to our citizens?" she said. "We rejoiced when we heard that the Third Confederation had discovered a solution to the *glashunrah* threat. No longer did we have to choose between the benefits of allowing Terran visitors and immigrants, and the possibility of Wakanreans being maimed by *glashunrah*."

"We don't know for certain that the vaccine will work!" called a Legislator in the third row. "It may well be a failure."

Another Legislator in a back row jumped to his feet. "Their test results suggest otherwise."

Two Legislators from the other side of the room also jumped to their feet and shouted down the previous speaker. More loud comments rose from every part of the chamber. Finally, Prokien Diow raised her arms above her head, and the room fell silent.

"They're still at the open discussion stage," Kuaron whispered to Dina. "Once they've finished, the Arbiter will call for any witnesses to speak, and it will be your turn."

"I ask you again to consider the question of risk," the Arbiter said. "*Kantai* Bellaire has appealed for an exemption from our law. What you must all decide is: how much risk would this impose on our citizens?"

Several more Legislators gave their opinions on the reliability of the ThreeCon vaccine, and the chances that *shahgunrah* would make it impossible for Dina to cause *glashunrah*. Opinion seemed to be running in favor of caution when the Arbiter again raised her arms.

"I declare the open debate at an end."

The Legislators all sank back into their seats and an expectant hush pervaded the room.

"I call now for *Kantai* Dina Bellaire to present her case to us. If *Kantai* Bellaire is present, let her step forward."

Dina took a deep breath and stood up, still holding Kuaron's hand.

"Good luck, *acubai*," Kuaron whispered, squeezing her hand.

Dina squeezed back and then let go of him. Resolutely, she stepped away from Kuaron into the aisle, and then started toward the podium. With every step, she could feel countless Wakanrean eyes watching her. It came to her that in spite of all that had happened, she had been very sheltered in her life on Wakanreo. Except for work and shopping excursions, she had spent very little time with large groups of Wakanrean strangers. Now, for the first time, she was the only Terran in a room filled with Wakanreans who owed her no loyalty—a very large room.

She reached the podium, and Prokien Diow moved aside to allow her the central position. Dina turned to face the Legislators. She hadn't realized they would almost surround her.

Dina swallowed nervously. All at once her tongue seemed to be glued to the roof of her mouth. She took a deep breath and remembered what Kuaron had told her about performing in front of a group. She exhaled slowly, and then she made herself focus on the face of a legislator in the back row.

"I wish to say first that I appreciate the chance to speak to you personally," she said, trying not to rush through her speech.

"And second, I wish to tell you how much I value my *shahgunrah*. It may seem strange to you to hear a Terran speak of the importance of something as Wakanrean as *shahgunrah*, but the fact that I came here as an outsider makes me able to see the value of it clearly."

Dina made herself pause for breath. She was feeling more at ease now that she was launched into her statement. The hundreds of faces in front of her blurred into patches of gold, brown, tan, and black.

"You all expected, maybe even hoped to find *shahgunrah*. I never even suspected it could happen to me. For the first few months after *shahkuun*, I was too concerned with my pregnancy to really sort through how I felt about what had happened to me. But as the months passed, I learned more about the Wakanrean way of life—or at any rate, the Wisutan way of life. I met my *shahgunrahai's* many relations. I went to gift givings and other celebrations—saw new babies, visited relatives, and had them visit me. When Kuaron's cousin died, I attended the *pliquin*.

"It was all new to me. I confess that sometimes it seemed very peculiar. And yet, gradually, it became commonplace. I realized I was fitting in.

"And then my children were born—my two half-Wakanrean children. I knew then that I was tied to Wakanreo in a way that no Terran had ever been before. And when I thought about what had happened to the Wakanreans who had suffered through *glashunrah*," Dina paused in her speech, and dared a glance at the Arbiter. The Wakanrean woman stood a little ways to her left, her back ramrod straight and no sign of any emotion on her homely face. Dina took a deep breath and went on. "I understood their grief in a way that no other Terran can understand it—firstly, because my own *shahgunrah* has been crippled by this vaccine."

A surprised murmur rose from the assembly. For a moment it threatened to become a roar, and then it died down to nothingness. Out of the corner of her eye, Dina saw that the Arbiter had raised her arms for silence.

"Six days ago, I took the vaccine, as required by your law," Dina said. "The next morning, my *shahgunrahai* told me that *klunar* was very weak for him. I could feel his grief, but he couldn't feel my compassion. *Haictor*, also, is almost gone. *Taal* remains, a little, but it's not the same for us now. So you see, I do know something of *glashunrah*. Kuaron and I have our own form of it."

Dina paused again and made herself look back at the faces that were staring at her. "The second thing that gave me insight into the pain of *glashunrah* is that my father and possibly others of my ancestors suffered a similar fate. My father was happily married to my mother until he met a woman who started *glashunrah* in him. It destroyed the trust so essential to any' marriage. Because of my own and my father's experiences, I know the cost of *glashunrah*."

A childhood memory of her parents quarreling made Dina swallow hard. She glanced at Prokien Diow, who still stood silently a few meters away. Dina realized that a year ago she would not have known that the expression on the Wakanrean woman's face was compassion. Staring into Prokien's luminous amber eyes, Dina had an epiphany. Departing from her prepared speech, she extemporized to express her new insight.

"Not only does *glashunrah* rob you of your life's partner," she said, "but it subjects you to a truly horrifying encounter. Just when you expect to form a lifelong bond, to experience the wonder of *klunar*, you find instead that a stranger—an alien—views you with fear and revulsion. And you can sense his distaste, his repugnance as clearly as you can see his smooth hairlessness and smell his utter strangeness. The one time in your life that you expect happiness and total acceptance, you find instead, misery and rejection."

Dina took a deep breath. Almost done now. "I can't promise you that without the vaccine I would be no danger to the *toshugai*. I'm sure the ThreeCon scientists have told you what they told me: that since I found *shahgunrah* like a Wakanrean, most likely I'm no more able to start *shahgunrah* in another Wakanrean than any of you who are already *shahgunrahai*.

"But they can't guarantee that, at least not yet. Because we don't know quite how *shahgunrah* works, we don't know why it happens only once. And if we don't know why and how, then we can't say with absolute certainty that what holds true for you also holds true for me."

Dina took another deep breath. "So instead of making you a promise I can't keep, I'm asking you to weigh the reality of my *shahgunrah* against the theoretical risk of my body chemistry interfering with some poor *toshugai*. I will promise that once the vaccine wears off, I will wear gloves every time I go out. And if *glashunrah* ever did happen, I would either leave Wakanreo or take the vaccine again. I know enough of *glashunrah* that I will never have more than one *huishfanai* on my conscience."

Dina let out a small sigh. "And that's all I have to say," she ended in a rush.

There was silence for a few moments, and Dina was reminded of Kuaron's concerts. After a few seconds, the Arbiter stepped back onto the podium.

"Does anyone have a question for *Kantai* Bellaire?" she asked.

There was an even briefer pause, and then a man in the fourth row from the center stood up. "I wish to ask *Kantai* Bellaire what she will do if we do not exempt her from taking the vaccine every year."

The Arbiter looked at Dina. "*Kantai?*"

"If I have to take it again, I'll take it," Dina said. "Kuaron and I will always be *shahgunrahai*. We'll stay together because we love each other. And we don't want to raise our children anywhere but here. If the only way I can stay on Wakanreo is to continue to take the vaccine, then I will, at least until my children are grown."

"Thank you," the Arbiter said. "Are there more questions?"

No one else rose or spoke.

"Very well," the Arbiter said. "If the spectators will clear the room, we will now proceed to the closed debate."

Dina walked all the way back to where Kuaron stood waiting, without seeing anyone's face but his.


THEY waited for over two hours. Juzao was impatient.

"Stone!" he said, pacing in the small conference room that a staff member had offered for their use. "What's nice smooth stone to these fools? They should put broken glass on the benches."

"It's an important question, *kentai*," Shukanao Liaz said. "Surely you wouldn't want them to rush their decision?"

"Hmph!" Juzao said. "Those *bwaion* wouldn't know how to rush a meal, let alone a decision."

Dina had to hide a smile. "Aren't they the people who appointed you Planetary Administrator?"

Juzao waved an arm. "It took them long enough to make up their minds about that, too. I assure you I won't miss dealing with them."

"Are you certain you don't want to ask for your job back, *Ayzanai?*" Kuaron asked.

Juzao stopped pacing long enough to give his son a steely stare. "If they refuse to see reason, Kuaron, I'll have no hand in helping further the destruction of your *shahgunrah*."

"*Kantai* Liaz," Dina said, "surely there's no need for you to wait with us? We could be here for hours."

"We've already been here for hours," Juzao said before the advocate could answer. He threw himself into a chair and began to tap rhythmically on the table top with his claws.

"Perhaps I should go now," Shukanao said, getting to her feet. "There's not much I could do to help you at this point."

Before she could move, the door opened, and the staff member who had provided them access to the room stepped through the doorway. "They're ready to call for the vote now, *kentai*," she said to Juzao.

The former Administrator jumped out of his chair and started for the door. "Thank you, *kantai*. I appreciate your help."

The woman stepped back hastily to get out of his way. Kuaron waited for Dina before following his father, and it was left to the advocate to exit the room last.

The central chamber seemed more crowded than it had before. The spectators' row was packed with people, and the four of them had to stand at the back of the room with a great many others. Dina noted that in spite of the crush, no one crowded her.

Prokien Diow stood on the podium looking rather like a *qatraharai*. She waited silently, her arms at her sides, for the room to grow quiet. Dina wasn't certain, but it seemed to her that the Arbiter was scanning the crowd, perhaps looking for a Terran face. When her eyes met Dina's she stopped and held up her arms.

Instantly, the noise died down. Everyone waited expectantly.

"This Legislature is now ready to vote," she said. "Let each Legislator cast his vote, yes or no, on this question: shall we exempt the Terran woman known as *Kantai* Dina Bellaire from our latest edict, based only on her appeal?"

One by one each Legislator rose as his or her name was called and answered yes or no. It was very clear early on that the negative votes were ahead. Dina knew that she needed one hundred and thirty-one votes to win—and conversely, if the same number of votes were cast against her, she would lose. Dina was torn between watching the ballot counter on the opposite wall and watching the Legislators as they voted. When the vote was almost three quarters of the way around the circle, a short, dark-furred Wakanrean man stood up and cast the one hundred and thirty-first no vote.

Dina sighed. "That's it, then."

Kuaron gripped her hand so tightly it hurt, and then immediately loosened his grasp.

Dina knew he was upset. She was holding her own disappointment in check as much as she could in order to minimize his distress.

Very quickly, the Arbiter finished the roll call.

"Let it be recorded," she said in a loud clear voice, "that the vote
was one hundred eighty-seven against, and seventy-three for the
proposal."

"Let's go," Dina whispered to Kuaron.

He put an arm around her and turned up to go, but he stopped
when the Arbiter raised her arms again.

"And now," she called out, "I call for a vote on the second proposal.
Please answer yes or no on this question: Should the Legislature
award Wakanrean citizenship to the Terran woman known as *Kantai* Dina Bellaire?"

"What?" Dina said, forgetting to lower her voice. "What did she
say?"

Kuaron turned back toward his father and Shukanao Liaz, pulling Dina with him.

"Does it matter?" he demanded of the advocate. "Will it make a
difference if Dina is a Wakanrean citizen?"

Shukanao didn't answer for a few seconds, and then she nodded once, in the emphatic Wakanrean manner. "I believe it will,"
she said in an urgent whisper. "The edict requires all non-Wakan-
reans of Terran descent with permanent resident status to get the
vaccine annually. It says nothing about Wakanrean citizens. No
Terran holds citizenship."

Dina and Kuaron stood side by side and arm in arm, watching.
The voting went just as swiftly this time, but the numbers were
far closer. For every 'no' there seemed to be an answering 'yes.' For
a brief time the no votes gained, and then the yes votes caught
up and even passed them. Finally, at one hundred and thirty yes
votes, and one hundred twenty-nine no votes, it came down to the
last Legislator.

She was a middle-aged woman, very light furred, almost like
Kuaron, but with a darker headcrest. She stood up and answered
her name, and then said quite clearly, "No."

Dina bit her lip. Beside her she could feel Kuaron radiating
worry.

"It's a tie!" she hissed at him.

"The Arbiter decides," he whispered back. He tightened his grip
on her hand.

Dina couldn't take her eyes off of Prokien Diow. The Arbiter stood still for one long moment, and then she took a step forward.

"The Arbiter votes yes. The proposal becomes law."

Dina could feel her own heart beating. Kuaron grabbed her and squeezed her so tightly she could barely breathe. For once he was too excited to notice her distress.

"It passed!" he almost shouted.

No one noticed because the room had erupted into a noisy debate.

"Kuaron," Dina said.

Instantly, he let go of her, but almost immediately he folded her into a warm but gentle embrace.

"We won," Dina said into his ear. "We won."

Juzao was slapping Kuaron on the back and patting Dina's shoulder. Dina could hear Shukanao congratulating her. Everything else in the room seemed to fade into a blur as Dina looked up at Kuaron.

"Let's go home," she said.

THEY celebrated with Kuaron's family that night, but the very next day Kuaron and Dina packed the twins into Kuaron's flyter, and flew to the park around the Duanlana for a picnic with just the four of them.

They found a secluded spot at one end of the pool, where they could unroll their picnic carpet and still have a view of the waterfalls. Dina put the twins in their day beds while Kuaron set up serving trays and prepared plates for them both.

"Wakanreans seem to go to a lot of trouble for a picnic," Dina said as she took the plate Kuaron passed to her. "On Fantar we usually just threw a blanket into the skimmer, grabbed some bread and fruit and cold meat, and headed for the beach."

"We don't like to skimp on food just because we're eating outside," Kuaron said, pouring watered wine into two glasses.

"I can see that," Dina said, surveying the array of delicacies Kuaron had put on her plate. "And I'm not complaining. This is lovely. Sometimes the Wakanrean way is better."

"I think perhaps I need to learn to do some things the Terran way."

Dina looked up at him in surprise. "What things?"

"I think we should get married."

Dina almost dropped her plate. "What?"

Kuaron looked very solemn, and Dina knew he was perfectly serious. "I think we should get married."

Dina put her plate down and stretched out her hands to him. "That's sweet of you, but I don't need to be married. I'm happy as your *shahgunrahai*, and I don't feel any need to be a wife, too."

"But I need it," Kuaron said, taking her hands. "Choice is very important to you, and I need for you to choose to be with me."

"But, Kuaron, dearest one, I did choose you," Dina said, smiling at him. She could feel his love for her and his concern. "Unlike any other *shahgunrahai* in the history of Wakanreo, I chose *shahgunrah*—if not at first, then later. If I had wanted out of it, I would have asked ThreeCon for help. But I didn't, because I wanted to spend my life with you."

Kuaron gripped her hands, and Dina sensed the warmth of his feelings grow. She smiled at him. "The vaccine should wear off in about a year. That gives us something to look forward to, Kuaron."

"Yes," he said, gripping her hands. He pulled her close and kissed her mouth, then nuzzled her neck. Dina could feel the faintest tinge of worry coming from him.

"Kuaron!" she said, laughing. "You stop that this minute! I will not have you making me anxious for a solid year! It will come back! The doctors told me all the vaccine does is to stop me from making pheromones. Once that's worn off, my body chemistry will be back to normal, and our *shahgunrah* will be just as it was."

"I know it," Kuaron said. "But I can't let myself truly believe in it. If I do, it might not happen."

Dina tisked at him. "You and your *midanai!*"

Before Kuaron could answer, Yulayan let out a wail that could have served to open a *qatrah*. Dina laughed and let go of Kuaron's hands to pick up her daughter. The baby stopped fussing quickly, and looked at her; her irises were smaller, like Dina's, but their color was a mix of gray, green, and amber, showing both sides of her heritage.

"She's a beautiful child," Dina said. "Are all Wakanrean babies as beautiful as ours are?"

Kuaron smiled as he picked up Kifarao. "No, of course not."

Dina rocked Yulayan in her arms, and the baby cooed at her. "I wonder what their lives will be like. Do you think they can be happy as half Wakanrean and half Terran?"

"I don't know for certain," Kuaron said, looking down at Kifarao. "But they have a chance. That's all anyone has."

"Yes," Dina said. "They have a chance. All we can do is love them and hope for the best."

Kuaron blinked in the bright sunlight. "That's what every parent does. We're no different in that way, and neither are our children."

"Maybe not in that way," Dina said. "But in other ways they are." She looked over at her son and saw the Terran lines to his face. "We'll do our best for them, and whatever happens, we'll face it as a family."

"Whatever happens," Kuaron repeated.

# *Epilogue*

Marochh shu Sstad leaned back in his chair and mentally gave thanks that it accommodated his Shuratanian form so well.

"A long day?" asked his visitor.

"No more than usual," Marochh said, wishing he could prop his feet on his desk without appearing rude. But a Planetary Commander had more cause to worry about giving offense than an ordinary citizen. And besides, the Wakanrean in front of him would go home soon, and then he could relax as much as he liked. "Before I forget my manners, congratulations on your new job."

Juzao Sadoc bowed gracefully in his considerably larger chair. "Thank you."

"Did you ever think of asking the Legislature for your old job back?"

Juzao reflected on the question. "Certainly, I considered the possibility. But it seemed to me that if they were likely to give it to me, they would have done so without my asking."

Marochh concurred, although he didn't say so. "You don't think it's ironic that you gave up being Administrator rather than order the vaccination program to continue, and yet now you're in direct charge of that same program?"

Juzao pondered. Having learned to read Wakanrean facial expressions over several years, Marochh concluded he was amused.

"It's not ironic to a Wakanrean," the former Administrator said. "I resigned rather than endorse the vaccination program when it endangered my son's *shahgunrah*. Now that I have the Legislature's assurance that Dina won't be subject to future vaccination, I fully support the program. I think it's a good thing."

"And how is the vaccination effort going?"

"It's completed in Wisuta. Once we track down the more adventurous Terrans who've settled in other cities, we'll be done."

"Except that you have to keep up with new immigrants," Marochh pointed out.

"True, but that's an easy task by comparison, especially as your people have taken responsibility for incoming tourists and business travelers."

Marochh smiled. "Indeed, we have. We expect great things from this vaccine. And we have every reason to believe its effects will wear off with time. Your little daughter-in-law should be fine."

Juzao let out a gruff bark of laughter. "She's a dainty thing, but she's a good deal taller than you, Commander."

"To a Shuratanian, the concept of large versus small has as much to do with age as with physical proportions," Marochh said, turning to open the cupboard behind his desk. "I understand from Jared Harlingen that you sometimes partake of Terran brandy. Can I interest you in a glass?"

Juzao looked surprised. "I thought Shuratanians drank ale?"

"We're known for our ale, certainly," Marochh said, putting a bottle and two glasses on the desk. "But Jared persuaded me to try Terran brandy, and I confess I've acquired a taste for it."

"It's not bad stuff," Juzao admitted. "I would enjoy a glass. Thank you."

"It's I who should thank you," Marochh said as he poured a generous drink for his guest. "I appreciate your hint about Jared and his feelings for your daughter-in-law."

"I was happy you acted so swiftly."

Marochh was pleased with himself and let it show in his smile. "There was no point in waiting. As it happened, the opportunity on Xuxan was perfect for Jared—just what his career needed. I was fortunate, indeed that you called me when you did, or I might have missed it."

"I felt a little foolish. I never knew many Terrans, so I wasn't sure I was seeing things correctly, but he worried me."

"Ah!" Marochh said, sipping his brandy. "Never doubt your instincts. You were quite right."

"Yes. I almost wish I hadn't been. I know Kuaron misses his *glynunshahai*."

The Commander shook his head. "An interesting custom, *glynunshah*." He pronounced the word carefully, wishing there was a good translation for it. Learning new languages wasn't a skill that came easily to him. "My people have nothing like it." He set his glass down on the desk and sighed. "I also miss Jared. He had a wonderful ear for language."

"He did speak Wisutan very well," Juzao said, as one making a concession.

"The Terrans have a custom called toasting," Marochh said, refilling both glasses. "Do you know it?"

The Administrator looked blank. "I don't think so. What does it involve?"

"Drinking, mostly," Marochh said, recapping the brandy bottle. "It's basically just dedicating a particular drink to something or someone in particular."

"Ah! Like our remembrance circle?"

"In a way, except the person being toasted doesn't have to be dead. In fact, he may even be present during the toast—in which case he abstains from drinking until everyone else has done so."

"It seems strange to honor someone by making him refrain from a pleasure everyone else is enjoying," Juzao said, picking up his glass.

"Many Terran customs are strange," Marochh agreed. He lifted his glass. "To Jared Harlingen. May he prosper on Xuxan."

Juzao's eyes gleamed in appreciation as he lifted his glass. "I can certainly join in that toasting."

They drank with due solemnity. Juzao looked almost benevolent as he put down the glass, and Marochh decided to take advantage of his good mood. "Do you think the vaccination program will make it possible to do away with the no-touching law?"

Juzao's expression went from benevolent to bland. "It's possible—if it works."

"It will work," Marochh said with confidence. "Little Dina's experience proves it very well." He assumed an expression as guileless as the Wakanrean's. "Don't you think the no-touching rule has outlived its usefulness? Think what it could mean for your son's family if it stays in effect."

"Dina is officially a Wakanrean now."

"Yes, but what about your grandchildren?"

Juzao didn't look worried. "If both parents are Wakanrean citizens, then the children are Wakanrean citizens."

"True, but maybe they're something else, too?"

Juzao opened his golden eyes wide in bewilderment. "What?"

"Something neither Terran nor Wakanrean," Marochh said. "A new species altogether."

The former Administrator sat very still, as if he were assessing this statement to determine its implications. "You sound as if you're sure the twins will be able to reproduce," he said at last.

"We're virtually certain."

Juzao couldn't hide his satisfaction at this news, but he shook his head. "You need more than two individuals to make a species. And it's not as if they'll ever be *shahgunrahai* together. Kuaron will see to that. They'll find Wakanrean *shahgunrahai*, and their Terran blood will be diluted in their children, and even more in their children's children."

"Are you so sure of that?"

Juzao stirred in his chair as if this suggestion made him uneasy. "Why would it be otherwise?"

Marochh smiled a serene and tranquil smile. "Most of my people don't believe in a god in the same sense the Terrans do, or even your people. However, we do espouse the philosophy of *gru'ach achta*. I suppose you could translate it as a belief in fate or predestination, but to us it means more than that. It suggests there is a purpose for every circumstance; that there are, in fact, no accidents."

"So Kuaron and Dina met and became *shahgunrahai* to serve a mysterious purpose?"

"Why not?" Marochh asked, pouring another splash of brandy into his now-empty glass.

"Why?" Juzao countered, pushing his own empty glass forward.

"Perhaps because the galaxy can use another sentient species," Marochh said, pouring him an equal amount of brandy. "Or perhaps because Wakanreans and Terrans need help in learning more about each other. Or perhaps there's another reason that won't appear until you and I are long dead."

"And perhaps there's nothing to this philosophy of yours, and Kuaron and Dina are only two people who were lucky enough to find each other."

"Perhaps." Marochh lifted his glass. "To Yulayan and Kifarao Bellaire. May they grow up happy."

Juzao also lifted his glass. "To my grandchildren. May they grow up healthy, fertile—and Wakanrean."

Marochh couldn't resist having the last word. "I'll settle for either wish," he said, and then he downed his brandy in one gulp.

Juzao didn't pursue the point. Instead he sipped contentedly from his glass. "Terrans can be annoying," he said, "but they do make good brandy."

## Glossary of Wakanrean words

| | |
|---|---|
| acubai | Little one, often used as an endearment |
| aifshahgundah | Murder and suicide by an unhappy *shahgunrahai* |
| ayzanai | Father |
| bwaion | A type of brick, or metaphorically, a blockhead |
| cair | A verse of a qatrah |
| chundin | Cat-like predator |
| cirac | Sharp point of a specific plant leaf that can drop off and lodge in a hiker's shoe; metaphorically, an annoyance |
| culahin | A mid-sized Wakanrean predator |
| duiko, | A mixture of grain, fruits, and vegetables cooked with spice and wine |
| eirouth | A length of a brittle plant stem broken in half to make a random decision |
| fareesh | A repulsive animal that eats other animals droppings |
| fijazhai | A stranger or an alien |
| gaichufa | A choreographed meeting of many unmated Wakanreans who hope to find a shahgunrahai |
| glashunrah | False, one-sided *shargunrah* |
| glynunshah | A rite of blood brotherhood undertaken by two individuals |
| glynunshahai | The relationship between two individu- |

als who have gone through the *glynun-shah* ritual of friendship, or the people themselves

| | |
|---|---|
| guarga | A dragon-like creature of Wakanrean mythology |
| guidros | A small, hollow figurine used tas a container for giving money |
| guisha | A small house pet; also an endearment |
| haictor | The sense of knowing your *shahgunra-hai's* location when he or she is nearby |
| heicha | A piece of jewelry worn pinned to the chest fur |
| huishfanai | A Wakanrean who has suffered *glashun-rah* |
| ishgua | A small, very tasty sea creature |
| jashugai | Someone whose *shahgunrahai* has died |
| jiewa | An overwhelming need to protect oneself or one's loved ones that causes Wakanreans to attack |
| jioshai | The director of a club that sponsors performances of the *qatrahs* |
| juija | A small herbivore popular as a food source |
| juoin | A dry bread, often sliced thin and served toasted |
| kantai | Respectful form of address to a woman |
| kapuhai | Elf-like creatures of Wakanrean mythology |

| | |
|---|---|
| kentai | Respectful form of address to a man |
| klunar | Empathy induced by *shahgunrah*, that works only between the *shahgunrahai* |
| kualua | Dirty or foul |
| midanai | Small gods who punish foolish mortals |
| muuin | A grain crop similar to corn |
| naishagundah | Mutual suicide by two mismatched and unhappy shahgunrahai |
| nyesh | Someone who fawns excessively; a flatterer |
| oishah | A Wakanrean religion that considers the natural world sacred |
| Paruian | A Wakanrean woman who led a pacifist movement, considered divine by many Wakanreans |
| parundai | A descendent of Paruian |
| pliquin | A gathering in memory of the dead, similar to a wake, but attended only by family |
| puoulgaio | Animal excrement, used as a metaphor for nonsensical or untruthful speech |
| puousta | Artwork that combines calligraphy and drawings; usually etched on metal |
| puoustahai | One who creates puostas |
| qatraharai | One who sings *qatrahs* |
| qatrahoinai | An aficionado of the *qatrahs* |
| qatrahs | Ancient Wakanrean songs sung in a dead language |

| | |
|---|---|
| quascha | A hot beverage, drunk at all times of the day |
| quayzanai | One's *shahgunrahai's* father |
| quyarunai | Foster parent (or parents) who takes in an adolescent (usually a relative) so that that person doesn't become *shahgunrahai* with his or her siblings |
| schubao | A small rodent-like creature known for wiggling out of tight places; as a verb, to wiggle out of something, literally or figuratively |
| shahglynai | One's *shahgunrahai's* relatives; effectively, in-laws |
| shahgunrah | A biological mating process that occurs when compatible, sexually mature but unmated Wakanreans meet |
| shahgunrahai | The two (or rarely more than two) persons who are mated to each other by the process of *shahgunrah* |
| shainai taul | A fairy tale or fable |
| shakuun | The period of approximately 10 or 12 days after *shahgunrah* starts during which the new *shahunrahai* cannot bear to be apart and are left alone by everyone else |
| shuishfa | Meat and vegetables cooked together and pureed to a pudding-like consistency |
| taal | Overwhelming passion caused by *shahgunrah* |
| toshugai | Not yet mated Wakanreans; the condition of being unmated |

| | |
|---|---|
| tuzouwai | A contaminant |
| Twerpaith | The third day of the Wakanrean week |
| Unpaith | The sixth day of the Wakanrean week |
| weichard | A cow-like herbivore; metaphorically, an unsophisticated person |
| xuschi | A wrap-around skirt worn as a bathrobe |
| yarunai | An adolescent Wakanrean sent to live as a foster child so that he or she doesn't become *shahgurahai* with a siblings |
| zagathuan | An outdoor room, fully furnished but not walled or roofed |

93507488R00214

Made in the USA
Middletown, DE
14 October 2018